PRAISE FOR

THE FREE PEOPLE'S VILLAGE

USA TODAY Bestseller
Indie Next Selection

"Sim Kern's masterpiece burns with righteous fury. This book doesn't pull punches — instead of hopelessness, it sliced straight through frustration, fatalism, and ennui and made me want to fight back."
— **Shana Hausman, All She Wrote Books**

"Incisive and insightful."
— *Texas Monthly*

"A full-throated ode to resistance and the found family that fuels it."
— **Megan Bell,** *Southern Bookseller Review*

"One of solarpunk's most ambitious and insightful voices."
— *Strange Horizons*

"A timely tale that feels like it could be ripped from the headlines… a thought-provoking and unflinching story of revolution."
— *Polygon*

"A powerful story of justice denied and the legacy of activism as well as a personal journey of growth. For those who wish to learn bravery, solidarity, and community."
— *Booklist*

THE FREE PEOPLE'S VILLAGE

SIM KERN

Lantern
Paperbacks

This is a Lantern Paperback
Published by Levine Querido

www.levinequerido.com · info@levinequerido.com
Levine Querido is distributed by Chronicle Books, LLC

Library of Congress Control Number: 2023932256
ISBN 978-1-64614-465-5
Printed and bound in Malaysia

First Lantern Paperback Edition:
September 2024
First Printing

For Jami and Diego. Love you forever.

I.
THE LAB

1

I know you want to hear about the Free People's Village and that literal, fateful-fucking-step at the reflecting pool, but to explain why I did what I did, I have to start the story months earlier, before the tents and tear gas and stirrings of revolution, with the night of the last great party at the Lab—the night Red destroyed the Fun Machine.

I got to the house just before sundown. Even though I taught in the Eighth Ward, just a few blocks away, I always went home to change before a show. My friends would have roasted me alive for showing up to the Lab in one of my linen work suits. So after the last bell, I'd bike two miles to the G train—the only maglev station in Eighth Ward. I'd wait one or twenty minutes, depending on luck, watching the grackles argue in the live oaks around the station, feeling nervous, if I'm honest, as I was usually the only white person on the platform.

Then the G train zipped me to Midtown. After a few minutes, the old, brick cottages and shingle roofs of the Ward gave way to shiny Community towers—their tops angled and glittering black with solar panels. The landscape morphed from yards choked with invasive vines or flat-topped squares of Bermuda grass into swaying prairies, interrupted by the neatly maintained orchards surrounding each Community. Here and there, the prairie humped up in wildways passing over the maglev lines that spiderwebbed across this part of the city, with a stop for each Community and fast connections to Downtown, the Medical Center, and the Galleria. At each stop as we headed west, more Black people got off, and more white people got on.

Disembarking at my Community, I dashed from the station up to my apartment on the seventh floor. Threw off my stale work clothes. Threw on thrifted cotton shirt, denim shorts, and some alligator-leather cowboy boots I'd found at an estate sale. I threw on a thick coat of eyeliner, clipped a take-cup to my belt, and then it was back to the train, back through the prairie and over the bayou, past herons spearing fish along the rocky banks, and finally back through the time warp. To a neighborhood that hadn't changed a bit in the last twenty years of the "War on Climate Change," except that its potholes were wider now.

Navigating those craggy streets on my pop-out bike as the sun set was no easy feat. At least I didn't have to worry about cars running me off the road, like they would've in the olden days. By 2020, the only cars left in the Ward were wheelless hulks in backyards, colonized by bees and weeds, too rusted to be sold for scrap. Only suburban people or rich folks had cars anymore—and those were all shiny, hyperway-compatible electrical vehicles. The carbon taxes on old-school gas guzzlers were so exorbitant that only the richest of the rich could afford to drive them, and all the gas stations in the city had been converted to rapid battery-charging stations.

Despite the treacherous pavement, I pedaled as fast as I could—acutely aware that I was a tiny white girl in a skimpy outfit. I was afraid of the clumps of old men who stood together, chatting on street corners, sipping from take-cups. Sometimes they hollered something as I sped by—nasty or nice, it felt threatening either way. I don't know what made me pump my legs harder though—that vague, unspeakable fear, or the deep-down knowing that I didn't belong there. That I was an invader.

I breathed easier rounding the turn onto Calcott, spotting the Lab up ahead, silhouetted by the last of the sun's rays. Light and loud music spilled from the old red-brick warehouse's windows and doors, every hole in that lovely, ugly face thrown open, filled with people of every race, gender, style, and subculture you could imagine, all of us so young—young enough to have no idea what kids we all were. Barely-adults like me, plus some teens who could be my students, though they never were. Except for Gestas, people actually *from* the Eighth Ward never came to shows at the Lab. They had their own places. The Black kids who came to our parties had white collar parents and lived out in the suburbs or university dorms. Crossing the Ward, they probably biked about as hard as I did to get to the Lab.

Cruising to a stop in the weedy front yard, I was finally home. The throbbing bass line spilling from the front doors enveloped me like a protective force field. I breathed in the haze of weed smoke and chemicals flaring off the refineries in the distance. The sun hadn't set, which meant that the AC wouldn't be on. Most of the early arrivers were standing around the yard in clumps, drinking keg beer from their take-cups, throwing back their heads in laughter, flashing their jugulars at the sky.

I collapsed my bike, stored it in my bag, and shouldered my way inside, past some blondes young enough to be in my English class. It must've been over a hundred degrees inside, and I sweat through my clothes in seconds. The front of the warehouse had once been offices that Fish had converted—rather terribly—into apartments. I popped my head inside Red and Gestas's place, but they weren't there. The guitarist from Okonomiyaki Riot was lying on Red's bed though, strumming "Blackbird" on Red's acoustic guitar while some groupies looked on adoringly. I felt a wild surge of possessiveness. Who the hell was *he* to be on Red's bed, touching *xir* guitar? I shoved the feeling down, reminding myself for the thousandth time that Red was not mine to claim. I was sick of these waves of intense, nonsensical jealousy.

I wove through the crowd in the hallway between the apartments and passed through the door to the main warehouse space in the back. It was cooler in here, as the sliding back cargo doors were thrown open to the dusk air. Still, it was probably 90 degrees, and the few dozen people inside were slumped against the walls or on the curb-scrounged, greasy couches that interrupted the room. Vida was painting an armadillo wizard over a hundred scrawled tags on the back wall, and the bassist from Okonomiyaki Riot was skateboarding down the strip of empty space in the middle of the warehouse.

In the corner that was the unofficial "stage," Fish was plugging in our amps and Red was setting up xir mic stand. I was still Fish's girlfriend, but I'd been wondering for a long time how to extricate myself from that relationship without destroying the band. It was Red—tall and laconic, sweat-slicked black hair falling across xir eyes—the sight of Red made my heart fly off in wild, syncopated rhythms, like Gestas tearing into the drum solo at the end of "Don't Think About Death." It's how I'd felt every time I'd seen Red over the past year, ever since I'd first laid eyes on xim—that cicada-filled afternoon, when xe stood in the doorway to xir apartment, twirling a red patent leather shoe by its heel.

2

When my co-teacher first introduced me to Fish, he'd seemed so exciting. Or maybe that was the bar. I was newly divorced, and I'd never been in a place as seedy as Poison Girl, where a thick coating of grime caked the sticky tables, and taxidermied animals, and velvet paintings of topless women decorated the walls from floor to ceiling. The "good Catholic" voice in the back of my head shrieked that this was a den of sin and sodomy, but I'd made a decision to stop listening to that crusty old fart. In fact, I was making a habit of doing the opposite of whatever she said. Above the shelves of whiskey bottles were four especially mesmerizing paintings. The artists had used just a few brushstrokes to highlight the full breasts and long stomachs of gorgeous girls on soft, black fabric, and I couldn't tear my eyes away from them long enough to catch the bartender's eye. The nun in my head yelled, "Lesbian! Queer! Whore!"

I let myself revel in the thrill. Maybe I am, I thought. So what?

My co-teacher dragged me outside in that heady state, to a gravel backyard strung with party lights, where cockroaches occasionally flew down from the trees into shrieking girls' hair. At a table next to a giant papier-mâché Kool-Aid Man weathered by the elements to a dull pink, she introduced me to a guy named Fish.

It's painful now for me to remember being attracted to Fish, but I was that night. Maybe my feelings for the girls in the paintings got transferred onto him. Maybe the realization that I might

7

be queer had, in fact, freaked me out, and I was grasping for proof of my heterosexuality. Or maybe it was because Fish was the polar opposite of my ex-husband, Colton.

Colton and I had split after four years of marriage when I was the ripe old age of twenty-two. Where Colton had been all compact, hard muscle from marathon training, Fish was a soft, six-foot-two giant. Instead of clean-shaven and buttoned-up, Fish had a wild red beard, mad-scientist hair, and wore torn band T-shirts and jeans. And after being married to a man who'd made me kneel in prayer with him before and after every sexual encounter, the "Hail Satan" tattoo sprawled down Fish's forearm held a magnetic fascination for me. I wanted to lick it.

At the bar that night, Fish was so animated and charming—I didn't realize that he was just in his buzzed sweet spot, somewhere between three and ten drinks. He paid for all my beers and told me about the great bands he hung out with in Houston, how he was about to close on a property in the Eighth Ward—right near my school—which he was going to turn into an anarcho-communist creative space. He had all these big dreams for throwing shows and art installations, and having a farmer's market and makerspace there. The way he talked about all the things he was planning for the Lab, I expected it to be ten times the size it was. I asked him how he'd gotten the money to buy such a place, and he told me about his app.

Of course I used CarbonSwap. Everyone did. Back then, it was the only way to transfer small amounts of carbon credits using your phone. Me and the other teachers had used it that very night to come up with the carbon tax for the pepperoni pizzas we'd split. At first I didn't believe Fish was really its creator, but he pulled up an article to show me. There he was, the twenty-three-year-old wunderkind who'd dropped out of college and created a multimillion-dollar app. Of course, none of those puff pieces explained that Fish had only been able to drop out because he had a cushy trust fund to live off of, which he'd used to criminally underpay the guy who did the actual *coding* for CarbonSwap. But I'd learn about that months later.

I bought Fish's story of being a self-made millionaire tech genius. None of the teachers I worked with had dreams any bigger than going on a solar cruise to Cancún for spring break. Meanwhile, Fish wanted to engineer a new society, starting with this "Lab." And the nun in my head hated him, so that was an endorsement. He was my ticket to the secular, hedonistic world of rock 'n' roll and bad choices, and after surviving the last few years of my miserable marriage, I wanted in.

So I went home with him that night.

He closed on the Lab the next day. A week later, I'd overhear him joking to the dudes in Venus Gashtrap that if bragging about the Lab hadn't gotten him "such good pussy," he might not have signed on it.

What a charmer.

A few weeks later, he took me to see the Lab for the first time. My footsteps echoed in the big, empty warehouse, and the sun streamed through high windows onto a clean, cement floor and walls that were still painted stark white. Fish gestured around the space, showing me where he was going to have the zero-waste food shop and the community 3D printer. Even then, I could tell there wasn't enough room in the space for even half his big dreams, but it was still fun to hear him go on about them. I believed he'd at least make a few of them come true, and I suppose he did. We had plenty of art installations and countless shows at the Lab, but we never did get the bike shop set up or the fibers studio.

Fish must've stepped outside to take a phone call or something, because I found myself alone in the cavernous space. I heard voices coming from the cracked door to the front offices. Fish had moved into the second-floor-turned-loft-apartment a few days ago, and he'd told me that a local band had already claimed one of the ground-floor apartments. He was giving them a steal on the rent because he loved their music so much. Bunny Bloodlust, a guitar-and-drums duo. He hadn't shut up about what geniuses they both were.

Curious to meet his new tenants, I stepped into the hallway to the apartments. The left-side door was wide open, and someone was picking guitar inside. Now that I was in the hallway, I didn't know what to do. Embarrassed for snooping, I made a beeline for the front door, but as I passed the open apartment, someone called out, "Hey, is this your shoe?"

I turned, and that was the first time I saw Red, leaning against the doorframe, twirling that shiny red pump by its heel. Right away, my heart started skipping every other beat, but at the time I figured I was just nervous about meeting someone who—according to Fish—was a local music god. I didn't know that, up to that point, Bunny Bloodlust had only recorded a three-track EP. They'd never even played a real show, thanks to Gestas's legal status.

"It's not mine," I said about the patent leather shoe. "That's not really my style."

"Huh," Red said, scanning my "style" up and down. I cringed, realizing I was still wearing my dorky, linen work clothes. "Some girls were over here last night. I figured you might've been one of them." Red stepped back inside the apartment and chucked the shoe in a corner, but the door was still wide open. I couldn't tell if I'd been dismissed or invited in.

"You want a beer or something?"

Heart in my throat, I stepped inside, where Red was filling a take-cup from a keg in a corner. There were clusters of empty malt liquor and whiskey bottles around the room, and the whole place had that stale-beer-and-weed stink of the day after a party.

"I'm Red, by the way. Xe/xim. That's Gestas, he/him." Red nodded at the dark-skinned Black guy on the futon, fingerpicking a melancholy bluegrass tune on an acoustic guitar.

If I'm being honest, which I never was back then, I was scrambling to "figure out" Red's gender. I'd never hung out with a trans person before. I'd grown up in this queer-hating, strict Catholic world. My brain still wanted to lump people in one of two categories, but I couldn't figure out which Red was. And I couldn't figure out xir ethnicity on sight either. Xir skin was light brown or dark olive. Sharp-cornered, brown eyes and black hair, buzzed short on the sides, and long enough on top to crest on xir forehead. Eventually, of course, I learned what gender Red had been assigned at birth, and which of xir ancestors had colonized which others. But Red *lived* for the squeamishness of white, cishet people not being able to figure out just "what" xe was.

Gestas's gender presentation also made my head reel. He went by he/him, so okay, I thought, he's a guy. But he was wearing this torn, macho-looking, heavy-metal T-shirt with a baby-pink, pleated, A-line skirt. He had a scraggly, curly beard, but sparkly gold eye shadow from the night before was smudged all around his dark-brown eyelids. I'd never met someone so masculine *and* so feminine at the same time. Colton would've spat out his coffee at the sight of Gestas, and that was enough for me to like him on the spot.

I clocked, then quickly glanced away from the glowing, green light embedded just beneath the skin of Gestas's right shoulder. Fish had told me about this—that one of the new tenants was an AHICA inmate, confined to the property through the At-Home Incarcerated Criminals Act. I'd never met an AHICA inmate before, even though I knew there were tens of thousands of them all throughout the city, stuck inside their homes.

I must have introduced myself, and I hope I remembered to share my pronouns. I took the offered beer but felt too nervous to drink much. There was another guitar sitting on the futon beside Gestas, and I picked it up, at first thinking to just move it out of the way. But it found its way into my lap instead. I wanted to impress them, wanted to show them both that I wasn't just some red-heeled groupie they could party with one night and forget the next morning.

I put my ear right up against the fingerboard and barely grazed the strings to check that it was in tune. I listened to Gestas for a few bars, watched his fingers, figuring out the chords. He cocked an eyebrow at me curiously. He settled into a pattern. I strummed a harmony. He moved through a key change. I followed. He sped up, changed the time signature, and I chased him, rounding out his melody. Then he settled into a predictable chord progression, and it was my turn to take the lead. I locked eyes with Red, who was watching us with an unnerving, crooked grin. This was—what? An audition now? A sudden, nervous sweat broke out all over my body. I tried to chart a melody, but I hated the way it was coming out. Too happy, too much C and D major—nothing like Gestas's haunting tune had been. I was gripped with this wild, irrational fear that they were laughing at me, that they could tell all my music was hopelessly infected with Christianity and youth-group aesthetics. I blanked on how to resolve the line. The notes came out jarring and dissonant. "Sorry," I muttered, staring down at the guitar, gut roiling in shame. Expecting them to—what? Laugh at me? Chase me out of their apartment?

"Don't apologize," Red said. "That was just getting interesting."

"You're pretty good," Gestas said, and I must have blushed the color of the orphaned high heel in the corner.

Red reached for the guitar in Gestas's hands, and he offered it up, plus his seat, settling again behind a banged-up, glittery pink drum kit in the corner. He started playing a 4/4 beat, softly, inviting in our guitars. Red took the lead, and for the first time I got to watch xim coax a narrative from the strings. Xe improvised an aching melody, twisted it with tension, then resolved it with a glimpse of a peaceful pasture, before plunging the line into anger and despair. Xe made it seem effortless. I fucked up following some of the chords, but for the most part, I was able to add fullness to xir sound. I don't know how long we played—it could have been ten minutes or an hour. Through the music, we were telling each other a little of what we knew about pain and loneliness and the beauty that springs up in the ugliest places. I started to feel like we'd all known each other for ages, even though we'd still only exchanged a handful of words.

Red resolved a line and stilled xir strings. Gestas faded the drums out with a shimmering brush on the snare.

"Do you play bass too?" Red asked. "We've been talking about getting a bassist."

I was shaking my head no when a voice boomed "I do!" from behind me. Fish had been listening in at the doorway for god-knows-how-long. He strode into the room and placed a hand on my shoulder. That was the first time I ever flinched at his touch.

"I'm not as good as you guys, but if you can write down the chords for me, I can keep up. I've actually got a vintage Ibanez five-string upstairs, real beauty, that'll work great with your sound. And have you thought about upgrading your amps and mics? Because I can totally hook you up with that—and any pedals you need. I wanna invest in y'all! You don't have to let me perform with you or anything, to pay me back, but it'd be hella cool to jam together sometimes. I mean we all live here now, right? Band house!" He pumped a fist in the air. "So cool!"

"You're with him?" Red asked, cocking an eyebrow at the heavy hand resting on my shoulder, an unmistakable note of derision in xir voice.

"Maddie's the one who convinced me to sign on this place!" Fish boomed. I squirmed uncomfortably, knowing that he meant that I'd slept with him after he'd bragged about the Lab. I already regretted my entanglement with him. But Fish owned the building. Soon he'd own all the band's sound equipment. And I would put up with him touching me, way longer than I had any desire to, because I thought that if I ditched him for Red, he'd kick xim out of the house, destroy the band, and use his ever-growing connections in the music scene to make sure Bunny Bloodlust never played another show in town. So I let him buy me dinner, and a new amplifier, and a season pass to my body.

Playing with Bunny Bloodlust was the only thing that had seemed to *matter* since I'd gotten divorced, and lost my faith, and the world turned flat and dull. Even with Fish dragging the rhythm on the floor behind us, playing with our band was the first time in my adult life I'd felt excited about being alive.

3

A year later, on the night Red destroyed the Fun Machine, I was still sleeping in Fish's bed, although we hadn't had sex in over a month. It was a moot point most nights, because he was rarely still conscious by ten o'clock.

The warehouse had totally transformed from the first time I'd seen it. The walls were covered in overlapping layers of graffiti, painted murals, and tags scrawled in Sharpie. Looking at them made my head swim. There was only a narrow strip of clear floor, where the bassist from Okonomiyaki Riot was currently trying and failing to perform a kickflip. The rest of the space was cluttered with the furniture of Fish's half-realized dreams. He'd brought home a drill press one day, hoping to start a machine shop, but I'd never seen him use it. He'd bought a home brewery kit, and this giant tub for like—a fish hatchery, I think? There was a dead bonsai tree, and bolts of fabric, broken TVs, and one of those old-timey popcorn machines for film screenings he never organized. All the clutter was making it harder and harder for us to do the one thing the Lab *was* good for—throwing shows.

As Fish was wiring up the amps that night, his hip smashed into the one big object in the Lab that wasn't his—the Fun Machine. It was nearly dusk, so he'd certainly had a few drinks by then. Rounding the side of the old organ with an aux cable, he crashed into its sharp wooden corner.

"Jesus, fuck!" he cried, turning on Red. "You need to fix this piece of shit, or get it out of here."

Red just blinked at him, real slow, distilling all the hatred xe felt for him in that one look. Could he even feel it? I could never tell.

"Piece of shit?" Red said in a tight voice. "You're calling the Fun Machine a piece of shit?"

"Half the keys don't work. It takes up a ton of space. It's a fucking fire hazard," he yelled, clutching his hip dramatically.

"The *Fun Machine* is what's taking up tons of space?" Red said. Xe leapt over a couch. "Not this fucking thing?" Xe slapped the cracked, sun-faded Ronald McDonald statue Fish had brought home one day. "Or this," Red skirted around a pile of chicken wire and aluminum siding that Fish had meant to do god-knows-what with. "And my Fun Machine is a piece of shit, but this?" Xe hopped up onto an antique cabinet with a built-in record player that was missing a tone arm. "This is a useful, reasonable thing to have in here? Where we're trying to throw a fucking *show*?"

"That piece is mid-century modern!" Fish yelled.

"Red's right," I said, glaring at Fish. My heart was in my throat. Taking Red's side like this felt dangerous. "People can't even dance in here anymore. The Fun Machine isn't the problem—at least it's an instrument."

"Oh sure, gang up against me. Gang up against the cis guy. That's always how it is, huh? May I remind you, this is my fucking building? And I'll put whatever I want in it!" He was roaring in the way that made my brain stem shut down, and all I wanted to do was curl up in a ball and hide.

Fish grabbed his machete from where it leaned against the wall, and the dozen teens hanging around, watching the argument, visibly tensed. When he leapt down from the loading dock into the backyard, they looked around at each other, heaved sighs of relief, and giggled. I felt embarrassed for exposing our underage fans to one of our charming family squabbles.

Out in the backyard, Fish hacked furiously at the cane, the ten-foot-tall elephant grass growing along the old train tracks. Exhausting himself against the invasive plant was his go-to therapy, for any kind of emotion. As his machete blade bit through the thick stalks, I wondered if it was my body, or Red's, that he pictured in the reeds crumpling before him.

4

Red found the Fun Machine a month after Fish and I officially joined Bunny Bloodlust. It was this perfect Sunday
morning, because Red and I woke up early, while everyone else
was still too hungover to move. We went to get breakfast tacos,
just the two of us. The mornings were starting to cool off, so it was
a perfect temperature as we biked to the taco truck in the parking lot of Village Thrift. The taco truck at Al's Stop-n-Go was a lot
closer, but this one was owned by a couple from Zacatecas, where
some of Red's people were from. Their salsa had a smoky-sweet
flavor, and Red was loyal to it.

I didn't feel nervous biking through the Ward when I was with
Red—xe was at home everywhere and nowhere. We biked lazily,
barely touching our handlebars, Red occasionally popping wheel
tricks. I loved being seen with xim in public like that, just the two
of us, because passers-by might assume we were a couple.

We sprang for greasy huevo con chorizo tacos, worth every carbon credit, and ice-cold Mexican Cokes. I wanted to pay, since I
made so much more as a teacher than xe did as a barback, but Red
waved me off, insisting we split. We sat on the curb to eat, in the
shade of a live oak tree. I used CarbonSwap to send Red my half of
the credits—an unwanted reminder of the app's owner. Fish was
my boyfriend, and this little adventure with Red could be nothing
more than platonic. The Lab had become the coolest venue/speak-
easy/art space in Houston by then, and Fish had bought himself

a music blog and a booking company. He'd weaseled his way into becoming a top music promoter. If I broke things off with him, my future as a musician—and Bunny Bloodlust's promise as a hot, up-and-coming band—would be finished. The thought of losing the Lab, of not being able to spend all my free time lounging on its couches, smoking weed and playing music, was unbearable. My personal life would shrink back down to awkward staff happy hours at franchise restaurants. I couldn't risk all that.

Besides, I didn't even know if Red saw me as anything more than a decent rhythm guitar player. For all I knew, the heat I felt under xir gaze could be wishful thinking.

Mulling on my mess of a life, I snuck furtive glances at Red as we biked home to the Lab, sometimes catching xim doing the same.

"What?"

"What? Nothing."

Red smiled dangerously, then xe screeched to a stop in front of a pile of moldy-looking, broken-down furniture on the curb. "Holy shit, is that what I think it is?" Xe was staring at what I thought, at first, was a large wooden cabinet. I swung my bike around the other side of it and hopped onto the curb. Red had already dismounted and was circling it reverently. "Do you know what this is?"

"Some kind of piano?"

"Not a piano—an organ, Maddie!" Red clucked xir tongue at me, grinning wryly. I blushed, noting the stacked keyboards and many pedals. "And not just any organ. This is a Baldwin 1974 Fun Machine." Xe pressed some keys, but no sound came out.

"Do you think it works?"

"If it doesn't, I'll make it work." Red's eyes were lit up, looking at that organ in a way that made me half-jealous. "I can't believe someone put this baby on the curb, like it's trash."

"Can you even play keyboard?"

"I'll learn," Red said, stroking the wood frame gently.

"And how are we supposed to get it home on our bikes?"

Xe bit a thumbnail in thought, then snapped xir fingers. "Lorenzo! The guy that runs sound at Fitzroy's? He does electrical stuff at the refineries; he's got a van from his work."

I didn't think any of our friends would pick up a call that early in the morning, but I guess when people see Red's name, they don't let it go to voicemail. A half hour later, Lorenzo showed up in his big, windowless van. Red and I had waited for him on the curb, guarding the Fun Machine, while Red told me all about the history of synth organs. About Wendy Carlos, who'd popularized the Moog synthesizer—how Wendy was a trans icon, and therefore analog synth organs were iconically trans instruments.

When Lorenzo got there, he was clearly hungover, but he perked right up at the sight of the Fun Machine. "Holy shit! What did you find?" He laughed at the sight of it—that big, booming laugh which could cut through a party of two hundred people. Lorenzo had toned biker's legs and a fat belly, long black hair that fell to the middle of his back, and a thick, dad-like mustache. He popped open the top of the organ and peered inside, said some of the tubes looked shot, but they could be replaced.

The three of us loaded the heavy-as-hell organ into his van. He offered us a ride, so we chucked our bikes in the back with it. There were only two bucket seats up front. Red took the passenger seat, and I wasn't quite sure what to do until xe grinned at me and patted xir lap. I tried to hide how excited I was to climb up there.

I reached for the seat belt and tried to stretch it over both of us, but it auto-locked.

"It's okay, girl, I got you," Red said, wrapping xir arms around my waist. I'd never seen Red lift a weight other than an amplifier, or work out other than beating on xir guitar, but that was enough for xir arms to be cut with lean muscles. I insisted on buckling the seat belt anyways, pressing my back to xir firm, flat chest. Xe smelled like sun and sweat and smoke. My heart was beating about a mile a minute the whole ride home.

Then we were pulling into the weeds in front of the Lab. The Fun Machine was so heavy we had to set it down to rest a few times as we maneuvered it around the back of the warehouse, up the ramp of the loading dock, and through the cargo doors. There were still a few people passed out on the couches from our show the night before.

Red plugged the Fun Machine into the wall. Almost all of the keys worked back then. Lorenzo played some chords, Red fiddled with the switches and sliders, and the sounds shimmered and swelled like an old sci-fi soundtrack. They pulled the back off the Fun Machine and peered inside, talking incomprehensibly about its dusty, wired innards. I slumped on a couch, checking my phone.

The Lab wasn't so cluttered back then. There were three curb-scrounged couches and just a few of Fish's pipe dreams in the corners. The walls were in a good place too. There were all these funny little doodles Red and Gestas had done along the south wall. Vida had painted the mural of the octopus goddess and her cuttlefish minions, and it hadn't been marred by a hundred crappy tags yet. And surrounding the back cargo doors were the rainbow handprints we'd smeared that magical afternoon I took mushrooms with Red and Gestas. The warehouse was still mostly open space, still full of possibilities. So there was plenty of room to dance when Lorenzo synced his phone to the sound system and started playing Wendy Carlos.

They were classical pieces—Bach and Beethoven, waltzes and minuets—but played on a Moog, they sounded like the music played at cyborg Mr. Darcy's annual android ball. Red and I improvised a fancy-schmancy Regency-era dance, with lots of bowing and curtseying, and the thing where you spin in a circle, holding your palms together.

Then Lorenzo put on a country synth album, and Red grabbed my hand and pulled my waist in close. Then xe was leading me in a fast Texas two-step, tracing a large, shuffling circle around the floor of the Lab. My head reeled from the sensation of my old life crashing into the present moment. As a good, Christian country girl, I'd spent half the Saturdays of my teens at the Lone Star Dance Hall for underage night, consenting to get spun dizzy by pale-haired boys whose cheeks were as shiny as their belt buckles. The guys were mostly jerks or creeps, but I'd always loved the fast, intricate dancing. Now it was Red leading me, and Red couldn't be more different than those good ol' boys. Xe swung me out and into a sweetheart move and a few spins, nothing tricky. Then, with an eyebrow cocked, Red looped xir arm over my head, and I ducked under, following xim into a pretzel move, keeping my eyes locked on xirs. Xe grinned huge at that, and I beamed back. What a thrill, to find a competent dance partner here, of all places. I was glad I was wearing my smooth-soled boots, slick along the floor. I couldn't believe Red was managing so well in xir grungy, hole-riddled Vans.

Xe was bold now and started spinning me silly. When I felt xir hands tighten under my armpits, muscle memory knew to lean backwards in a trust fall, sweeping my legs forward. When xe spun me around another way and into a dip, I tipped onto my heels and slid one-legged through xir legs. The song was climbing towards its cowboys-and-alien-invasion climax, and I knew we'd only have time for one or two more moves before it ended. Then Red had me around the waist, and with surprising strength, xe flipped me around xir back and dipped me down, low, *low*, so my ponytail brushed the floorboards. We were panting, our lips inches apart. The song ended, and a slow waltz started up, but for a few long, heartbeats, xe held me in the dip. Our eyes locked, and I got lost in xirs—short eyelashes, like a perfect trace of eyeliner, gold flecks in swirls of brown irises, and the mirror-black of xir pupils. I was screwing up the courage to kiss xim, when applause echoed around the room.

Right, we had an audience.

Red pulled me back up abruptly, and we broke apart. All the kids who'd been passed out on the couches had woken up and were clapping. Lorenzo let out an ear-splitting grito, "Huh-hoyyyy!" Blushing, I turned away to fix my ponytail and spotted Fish glowering at us from the doorway to the apartments. It gave me a sick rush of vertigo, realizing I'd been *that* close to walking our lives at the Lab off the edge of a cliff.

"Cute couple," he said, crossing the room with a clearly forced smile. "Mind if I cut in?" He shouldered Red aside and reached for my hand. "I don't know all those fancy moves, but I can lead my girl in a two-step."

Red had already turned away to head out the back doors, whacking a pack of cigarettes against xir palm. "Let me catch my breath," I said, shrugging off Fish and plopping down on a couch. He brought it up a few more times that night, but I never did dance with him. I didn't want anything to sour the memory of my perfect dance with Red. And I knew in an hour or two, he'd be too drunk to stand straight, let alone dance without crushing my toes.

Later, out on the loading dock beneath a bruise-colored sky, I sat down next to Red and asked how xe'd learned to two-step.

"Why, you think a queermo like me shouldn't be able to?" xe asked teasingly.

"It's not that!" I said, flustered. "Just—it's a Texas thing. Aren't you from Hawaii?"

"I was *born* there, but we were only stationed there until I was three. I don't even remember it."

"Oh right, sorry," I said. I was still getting to know Red, still piecing together the long list of army bases that had marked the chapters of xir early life.

"When I was like nine or ten, my dad had to do this training thing at Fort Huachuca, so me and Angel had to go live with my Cajun family—my *white* family—in this hick town outside Baton Rouge. They two-step to zydeco there, and my grandpa taught me the basics."

"Okay but that was more than the basics," I said, remembering our charged, whirlwind dance. "No one's grandpa teaches them to dance like *that*."

"I guess not," Red laughed. "Okay, in high school, I was living with my mom in La Porte, and I started sneaking into Blazing Saddles with a fake ID," xe said. Blazing Saddles was Houston's queer dance hall. "I learned that getting good at leading a two-step was the best way to pick up the cutest, femme-est girls, like—" Red cocked xir head at me but didn't finish the sentence.

I hoped my blush wasn't neon pink. "In high school . . ." I repeated, marveling. "Honestly, I'm jealous."

"Jealous?" Xe knitted xir brows at me and grinned. "Of those other girls?"

"No!" I cried—a little too loudly, protesting a little too much. "Just, that you were so brave and—and free! I mean, in high school I never snuck out, wouldn't have even known where to get a fake ID. I was such a youth group goody-goody."

"Well, some of that *free-ness* was because Dad was in jail by then and Mom worked the night shift at a gas station," Red said matter-of-factly. "So I just never saw her. It wasn't that I was free. More like, *on my own*. Which wasn't always a good thing when I needed, you know, food and . . . parenting and stuff."

"I'm sorry," I said, feeling incredibly jumbled up by this conversation, and like I just couldn't stop putting my foot in my mouth. "I guess I also meant free like—you knew who you were, even as a teenager. You were this brave, confident—*queermo*," I said, tracing air quotes and throwing xir own word back. "Some of us are in our twenties and still figuring it out."

"What are you trying to say?" Red asked slyly. "Miss Maddie Ryan, are you a ho-mo-sexual?"

"I don't know!" I said, my voice coming out unnaturally high as I shrugged my shoulders to my ears. But there was really no doubt in my mind anymore—that dance with Red, and everything it'd made me feel, had laid to rest the questions I'd started asking myself that night I couldn't look away from the topless paintings at Poison Girl. "I guess, maybe I'm bi or—pan?"

"Does Fish know this?" Red asked, lifting one eyebrow and looking into the Lab, where Fish was holding court with a band of teens hoping for an opening slot on next week's lineup.

"No, I—please don't tell him," I said all in a rush. I was panicking, yet again, that Fish would figure out my feelings for Red and kick me out of his budding music empire.

Red's smile fell. "I would never out someone."

As I reeled from the sudden icy shift in xir tone, Red got up and headed inside. Xe hung out with Gestas, and everyone except me, for the rest of the night. Things were weird between us for days afterwards.

During that time, I ran over the conversation in my mind obsessively, wondering what it all meant. Did Red flirt with me because xe thought I was corny, so it was funny to make me squirm? Or did xe actually like me? Did xe get upset at the end because I'd violated some code of queerness, or because I'd brought up Fish? Late at night, trying to fall asleep, I'd replay our dance together step-by-step. I tried to will myself back there in a dream, where at least my subconscious could finish that interrupted kiss—Fish be damned.

As for the Fun Machine, Red did check out a book from the library on fixing it—*A Beginner's Guide to Tube Amplifier Repair*. But xe only ever read the first chapter, then stuck in a scratch-off ticket as a bookmark and left it on top of the overturned milk crate xe used as a nightstand. There it sat, collecting dust and weed ash and overdue library notices for months. And then one night, our party got crashed by those vintage-motorcycle-gang assholes, Loco Motor, and one of them spilled a full take-cup of beer all over the organ. After that, less than half the keys worked. Red occasionally mentioned wanting to go to Electronic Parts Outlet to get stuff to fix it up, but xe was always waiting for xir next paycheck. And so the Fun Machine became just another piece of junk cluttering up the Lab.

5

By the next August, the warehouse was so full of Fish's junk, you could barely walk through it, let alone go two-stepping. A green-haired girl lounging on the pink silk chaise with the blood stain on it shouted that it was a minute until astronomical dusk. We all sprung into action, shutting doors and windows. The bassist from Okonomiyaki Riot skateboarded to the back cargo doors and slammed them shut, blocking out the sight of Fish's shoulders heaving with the blows of his machete against the tall grass. Red headed for xir apartment and Gestas dashed into Vida's, slamming shut all the windows. I took the stairs two at a time up to Fish's place, where I struggled to close the paint-choked windows on the second floor. I slammed the last window down just as the thirty-second countdown started up.

I shouldered my way back down the stairwell and through the partygoers now streaming in from outside. Lorenzo was working the door, phone out, collecting the five-carbon-credit door price from everyone lined up outside. Fish had tacked up a sign—"Pay using CarbonSwap ONLY!!!"—so that each of those swiped credits would make him $0.05 richer. I squeezed back into the Lab just as the countdown reached "Ten, nine, eight . . ." A hundred people were already packed inside, standing shoulder-to-shoulder, or perched on Fish's hoard of garbage furniture and broken machines. Everyone roared the last few seconds of the countdown. I looked around and didn't see Red—xe must've been outside at the breaker

box. ". . . three, two, one!" Then everyone was cheering and screaming over the *ka-chunk* of the industrial condenser turning on as
cold air blasted from the ducts above. Even with the sun down, it'd
take hours for the AC to make the Lab feel fit for humans, but just
knowing that cold air was finally blowing was enough to give everyone energy. People got up off the couches and danced to the music
blasting on the speaker system. The opening band, Monster Talk,
started tuning their instruments, and soon they were shredding
the power chords of their first song. A gaggle of girlfriends danced
solo at the front of the crowd, until the beats became infectious,
and everyone joined in.

"Big crowd!" Vida called in my ear. "I'm sure we'll collect way
more credits than we need for the AC. Maybe we can even run it
tomorrow while the sun's up." She proffered a joint between paint-
stained fingers. I waved it away.

"Thanks, but not till after our set," I said. The truth was my
asthma had gotten so bad lately that I couldn't smoke. And I wasn't
even sure I liked getting high anymore. It always got me lost in my
own head, depressed about Fish and paranoid that everyone could
tell that I loved Red instead.

Vida shrugged and turned back to the girl she was flirting with.
Vida lived across the hall from Red and Gestas with her husband
Peter, but their marriage was open. She was larger-than-life in
every sense of the word—fat and gorgeous, with thick, loose curls
and full lips, bronze skin, a brilliant painter, and one of the funni-
est people I'd ever met. Meanwhile, Peter was this scrawny, short,
white guy with a graying man bun, twelve years older than her,
with a personality like wet plaster. He was a photographer, mostly
using all his fancy camera equipment to take pics of Vida that he
posted and tagged to her Instagram. He seemed perfectly content
to pay her bills and sleep on the couch while she hooked up with
all the bi-curious girls in town. When I'd first met them, I didn't

get their marriage, but now it seemed like a perfect setup—at least for Vida—and I was envious as hell.

The Lab was filling up fast. The fixie bike kids rolled in, wearing their casquette caps indoors. Rich girls from the Heights pulled the hems of designer dresses tight against their legs to keep from brushing up against crust punks in their filth-stiffened denim vests. Graffiti artists pulled Sharpie pens from their pockets to add more doodles to the overlapping chaos on the walls. Old Jim stood in a corner, clutching a notebook, watching all us kids with a bemused smile. Old Jim wrote the music blog for the *Chronicle*. He was probably only, like, forty, but he didn't seem to mind the nickname.

A lot of the crowd were also musicians—Crawl City and Slim Chuckle and the guys from Los Burros Gordos were there. Third Host was headlining, but I hadn't expected them to show up in time for our set. When I spotted them posted up on the row of vintage movie-theater seats, I was glad I hadn't taken that hit off Vida—not if I was going to play for Houston musical royalty. Third Host had played *The Late Show* once and had a recording contract, and you could stream their songs on all the corporate apps. Red thought they were a bunch of sellouts, but I was starstruck. Gestas reached through the crowd and tapped me on the shoulder. He'd changed into a pale pink, spaghetti-strap dress and combat boots, with pink glitter on his eyelids and butterfly clips in his beard. "Find your man," he shouted over the din. "We're up next."

I winced at the "your man," and Gestas shrugged as if to say, Don't like it? Then do something about it.

I shouldered through the crowd—clambering over a fainting couch, ducking under a carousel horse—to get to the back doors. The sliding cargo doors were all shut now that the AC was on, but on the far-left side, a regular door was propped open to the night air. Outside, smokers dangled their legs off the loading dock or leaned against the wall all along the ramp that led down to the small backyard carved out of the tall stands of cane.

The plant we called cane was this ten-foot-tall grass that grew over the old steel train tracks in back of the Lab. When Fish first bought the Lab, he'd read up on how to get rid of cane, because letting invasive species grow on your property could cost a hefty carbon tax. But it turns out cane spreads rhizomatically through the roots—so he would've had to dig up every bit of grass with a bulldozer or something to really get rid of it. And at this point, the cane stretched for god-knows-how-many miles along the rusting train tracks. So instead, he fought a never-ending war against the unrelenting, advancing army of cane. One man with one machete, trying to keep the giant grass from the property line.

I didn't spot Fish among the crowd standing in the recently cleared backyard. Secretly, I loved the cane, its tassels swaying like the waves on a river that stretched from north to south along the eerily straight lines of the train tracks. A half mile to the south, the hyperway overpass arced through the sky, and its rushing cars sounded a bit like the ocean. Ten years ago, all the interstates in Houston had been converted to hyperways, using maglev tech to zip rich commuters' cars in and out of the city at lightning speeds. The hyperway's shadow traced a dark line across the cane-covered tracks, the retention pond, and the abandoned railyard, towards the massive beast that hunched on the horizon—a monster of tangled pipes, breathing fire and steam: the Valiant Chemical Refinery. Because the ugly truth was that fossil fuels still powered half the city—sending electricity to the maglev trains, hospitals, and the "eco-friendly" hyperways.

I know it sounds weird, but standing on the back loading dock, I found it beautiful—tongues of flame flaring off the smokestacks against the light-polluted, purple-orange sky. Not like I loved fossil fuels or anything. But that view was *real* in the way the manicured prairieways and carbon-sequestering orchards of the rich neighborhoods were a lie. Oil was, still, what powered most everything, underneath the greenwashed fantasy of the US in 2020. Most people outside the Ward wanted to forget places like this existed, but you couldn't ignore the petrochemical industry when it was literally in your backyard.

Monster Talk was thanking everybody for showing up and announcing one last song, so I had to find Fish fast. I stuck my head into the Lab, scanned the room—no sign of him. Back outside, I jumped down from the loading dock and ran to the edge of the cleared cane, where I found a narrow path of chopped stalks leading further in. After ten feet or so, the path ended, without a trace of Fish. I cupped my hands to my mouth and called his name, listened, but couldn't hear anything except the roar of the band and the crowd from inside. I thought about striking out into the tall grass, but it was easy to get turned around in there. And a surge of resentment was rising in my chest. Why the fuck was I Fish's keeper? He was supposed to be a grown man. If he couldn't be bothered to show up when it was time for our set, then fuck him. His laggy bass lines only slowed us down anyways.

But who could cover his part? At the drop of a hat? I scanned the crowd in the backyard, then beelined to Mike Algebra. Mike played practically every instrument, was getting a PhD in composition at Rice, and understood music theory on a math-like level that got him his stage name.

"Hey, Fish is missing. Can you fill in for him?"

Mike Algebra's eyebrows went up to his thinning hairline, and he stammered a bit. "I-I can try? I know the songs pretty well, but . . . You got the chord changes written down somewhere?"

"There's a notebook in Red's room. Just round out the bass a bit. Follow our lead. Don't worry about copying his lines exactly—they're not that good anyways."

Mike let out a high-pitched, snorting giggle at that. "You're a real supportive girlfriend, huh?" he said jokingly, as we hurried up the ramp to the loading dock.

I hated the reminder of my "role" in Fish's life. Fish might be a shit bassist, but he was the promoter that made these giant parties happen; he owned the Lab, he owned all of us, and so that was my epithet—Fish's girlfriend.

"At least I show up to our shows," I snarled. "And I can play on the fucking beat."

6

I hate to admit it, but there *were* times I genuinely enjoyed being Fish's girlfriend. When we were around Red and Gestas, I couldn't help seeing him through their eyes—a blustering, entitled clown who bought all his friends and couldn't play a syncopated rhythm to save his life. But when we were alone together, at least for those first few months, we had a lot of fun.

It was a genuine relief to be with such a laid-back guy after being married to Mr. Crucifix-up-his-ass. Fish was down with eating fast food every night and didn't care if I didn't shave my legs—in fact, he preferred that I didn't shave anything. He projected kung fu movies on the ceiling above the bed, so we could watch them lying down, stoned out of our gourds, eating pizza rolls off a Tupperware lid balanced on his chest.

I even enjoyed having sex with him, at least at first, because of how he seemed to worship my body. Colton had made me feel bad for being short, saying it was a shame I could never pull off an evening gown. Fish called me "snack-sized" and picked me up and spun me around. Colton had used filters and Photoshop to edit my freckles out of every picture of us, but Fish said they looked like stars in the night sky, and traced constellations on my cheeks. Colton had called my hair mousy and too thin to hold an updo. But Fish thought my bob looked "very riot grrrl," and said the color was pretty, like milk tea. But if I didn't like it, he said, I could always dye it purple or platinum. So I did.

Colton had made me feel like a defective woman, like a shirt you'd only grudgingly buy at an outlet store because you couldn't afford something better. But in Fish's eyes, I was irresistible! I was a young, hot thing on the scene!

And so, since he was only the second person I'd ever slept with, I wasn't bothered by the fact that Fish never went down on me, that foreplay was at best a few minutes of sloppy kisses, and the sex never lasted anywhere near long enough for me to come. Just the fact that Fish enjoyed it and could get hard and stay hard at the drop of a hat—that made it far and away the best sex I'd ever had.

And I can't lie—at first it was fun having a guy spend piles of money on me. When my bike broke down, he bought me a brand new one, twice as nice. He got me a vintage starburst Les Paul and Marshall amps and a dozen pedals to mess around with. He took me to fancy restaurants and paid the bill *and* all the carbon credits for the meat and dairy. If we were ever out, and I mentioned I liked something in a shop, it was mine. He even had a car, and he gave me rides back to my place or school if I was running late, or it was raining, or I was just too tired to bike.

And so the day he asked me to be his girlfriend, I said yes, even though there was that voice in the back of my mind saying, But you're in love with someone else, you know? But that seemed like a trivial problem at first. Fish was a hell of a lot nicer to me than Colton had ever been, and being with Fish was convenient. It meant the band would stay together, and I could keep the Lab as a second home, and that was what mattered.

After we became official, Fish wanted to take me to meet his dad and stepmom, who lived out in Katy. He drove us along the westbound hyperway, one hand resting on the steering wheel as powerful electromagnets zipped us to the suburbs. "I gotta warn you, my stepmom's a monster."

"What are we talking?" I asked, as the cluster of skyscrapers that marked Downtown zipped past. "Fangs? Claws?"

"Oh yeah, fire-breathing too." He chuckled, shooting me a startled glance. He always seemed surprised when I cracked a joke. "No, for real, she's just . . ." He massaged the useless steering wheel. "Well, okay, when I was growing up, we had this big magnolia tree out front, right? First tree I ever climbed. Flowers as big as your head." He took both hands off the steering wheel to gesture. "But when Cheryl moved in with Dad, first thing she did was have it cut down."

"What? Why?"

"You get a better carbon tax credit from having a whole bunch of little fruit saplings planted in your yard than you do for a single, mature magnolia."

"That's fucked up," I said, genuinely shocked. "There's got to be environmental value in a big, old tree like that—worth more than a couple of saplings?"

Fish grunted. "Take it up with the BCR."

I stared out the window as the Galleria Tower flashed by. Growing up in Deer Park, a conservative suburb surrounded by oil refineries, I'd heard folks curse the Bureau of Carbon Regulation all my life. Created by President Gore after he declared the "War on Climate Change," the BCR was the reason poor folks couldn't afford to drive cars anymore and had to ration meat. My dad had said the BCR was an evil agency run by "elites who hated freedom." But after I got married, when I started to realize that everything I'd been taught growing up was bullshit, I figured the BCR was just literally trying to save the planet. If that meant more train rides and fewer burgers, so be it.

So it was weird, hearing a self-proclaimed communist like Fish spitting the name of the BCR, just the way my dad used to. But by the end of that god-awful evening, I'd understand what he meant.

After we exited the hyperway, Fish steered us through a labyrinth of identical giant homes, each surrounded by tall, waving prairies interspersed with short saplings planted at regular ten-foot intervals. Each roof glittered black with solar panels and sprouted multiple windmills, which turned lazily against a cloudless sky. Fish didn't use GPS to navigate, and I couldn't figure how he'd ever learned the way through the gently curving maze of streets, all named similarly insipid things like Sunset Cliff and Sunset Ridge.

Finally, he pulled to a stop in front of a McPalace, with fifteen windows facing the street, a turret, a three-car garage, and faux-brick veneers dividing up the beige walls seemingly at random. There was no trace of the magnolia tree from Fish's childhood out front, just the same tall prairie grasses and stubby saplings that surrounded every home in the neighborhood—except the house next door.

"I bet your folks hate those guys, huh?" I asked, gesturing to the old-timey house, with its stubbornly asphalt roof, close-cut lawn, and single sprawling live oak shading the property.

Fish burst out laughing. "You have no idea. Russell—the old guy that lives there—him and Cheryl are sworn nemeses."

"Don't get me wrong, I'm glad he kept the big tree, but would it kill him to grow out his lawn into a prairie?" I asked.

Fish shrugged. "That's how he likes it. And I think half the reason he does it is to torment my stepmother."

As we walked up to the house, I pulled the hem of my skirt down an inch, wishing I'd worn something a bit more conservative. The McMansion loomed over us, shading out the sun. Fish rang the doorbell, and I could hear it echoing around a cavernous interior, past the imposing brass-and-glass door.

A woman with crispy, white-blond curls and ice-chip eyes opened the door and stared at me. I smiled back. She blinked slowly.

"Well, look at your hair!" she said in an East Texas accent. "Isn't that a bright shade of green!"

It was just a streak through my growing-out bangs. Fish laughed. I felt my cheeks turning beet red.

"Cheryl, Maddie—Maddie, Cheryl," he said, still chuckling.

Cheryl seemed to recover her composure at the sound of her name. "Well, come in, dears," she said, all gracious southern hospitality. The bangles on her arms clattered as she waved us inside. She wore a lot of jewelry, and an intricately hand-embroidered linen tunic that looked expensive.

It was chilly as a meat locker inside, and the goosebumps jumped out on my arms. It must've cost a fortune in carbon to keep it so cool, with those twenty-foot ceilings and tall windows all over the open-plan ground floor. This was in May too, late afternoon—the hottest part of the day!

"I am so sorry for the clutter," Cheryl said, waving at a large refrigerator that was standing against the wall in the chandeliered entryway. "The fellas who came this morning to install the new fridge couldn't fit this one in their truck. I guess it's a little bigger than the new one? They said they'd send another truck for it, but I'm not sure anyone's coming. *Their English wasn't too good*," she added in a conspiratorial whisper. "I'll call the store tomorrow and raise hell."

"What's wrong with this one?" Fish asked, opening and shutting the door to the disconnected fridge. It was sparkling clean inside, but I assumed that wasn't by Cheryl's hand. People who lived in houses like this didn't clean them.

"Nothing's wrong with it, but our tax write-off for buying the new, higher-efficiency model is worth more than the cost of replacing it. So you're a fool if you don't swap 'em out. Why, we've got 2021 models of all our major appliances already. Honestly, I don't know why more people don't take advantage of the system."

"Not everyone has thousands of dollars lying around to replace their appliances every year," Fish mumbled so only I could hear, then asked loudly, "Can I have this? We could use it at the Lab."

"Sorry, honey, but we need the carbon credit for recycling the old fridge. Besides, you've got plenty of money from that little app, don't you, Fisher?" She squeezed his arm playfully. He flinched a bit—I don't know if it was from her touch or the sound of his given name.

"Fisher!" echoed a deeper voice as we entered the kitchen. A trimmer, grey-haired, smartly dressed version of Fish brandished a bottle of French wine. He took an appraising look at me and shot Fish a half wink. "So nice to meet you, Maddie, call me Roger." he said, pulling wine glasses down from a high cupboard. "Been a while since Fisher brought a girl home."

There were framed pictures of "Fisher" all over the house— as a fat, bald baby; a tow-headed boy; and a clean-shaven, flat-topped teenager. There were even more pictures of his sister's family—looking like Barbie and Ken with their three blonde kids, always in coordinating outfits. Looking at them soured my stomach. Underneath the wild, red beard and heavy-metal tattoos, Fish looked a hell of a lot like all the boys I'd grown up with. I nearly spit out my wine when I saw the one of him kneeling in a red-and-white football uniform.

It made me feel even more unnerved, watching Fish fall into the rhythms of this palace-like house with ease. He pulled a stool up to the peninsula of a marble kitchen counter, reached for a charcuterie board Cheryl had just set out, and started gobbling down the expensive hard cheeses and meats, talking to his dad between mouthfuls. Cheryl insisted on taking me on a tour of the house. I glanced to Fish for support, but he just called out, amused, "Be sure to point out the therma-lock crown moldings!"

After ten minutes, I was getting a headache from forcing myself to smile and nod. The bedsheets in the *four* bedrooms were organic eucalyptus. The chandelier's crystals were a composite pressed from recycled water bottles fished from the ocean. Even the paint on the wall was plant-based and compostable. Everything was carbon-tax-deductible or came with a carbon credit rebate. Every single object in the house was green and eco-friendly, but it seemed like Cheryl's green-shopping addiction meant that none of them stuck around for very long—and that couldn't be very green, could it?

Finally, as we were admiring a micro-flow toilet from Japan, I had to bring it up. "Okay, but why did this give you carbon credits if you had to ship it here from the other side of the world? Don't most shipping boats still run on oil?"

Cheryl flashed her teeth, but it wasn't a smile. "Oh, honey, the BCR takes all that into account when they do their math. I'm sure it must be better for the planet in the long run for us to have this toilet than if we'd kept our old water-guzzler."

After Cheryl's tour, though, and hearing all the ways she was gaming the BCR's system, I wasn't so sure about their "math" anymore. I was starting to get a sense of where Fish's resentment of the BCR had come from.

As we headed downstairs, I ventured another question. "You buy all this eco-stuff, so I can tell you care a lot about your carbon footprint. But then I can't figure why you're running your AC all summer during the hottest part of the day? Your electric must cost a fortune!"

"Oh sweetie," Cheryl laughed as we returned to the menfolk in the kitchen. "If you're a green shopper, like me, you can run your AC all summer and still have a big ol' carbon surplus at the end of every month!"

"And plenty for steaks too," Roger said, clapping his hands and rubbing them together. "Speaking of, how we doing on dinner?"

"Y'all hungry already?" Cheryl asked, heading for the shiny new fridge, which looked identical to the one cluttering up the entryway.

A half hour later, Cheryl set a thick slab of meat in front of me at the dinner table, and she and Roger watched me with a weird intensity. They probably expected any green-haired girlfriend of Fish's to be a vegan. But my dad had kept up a tradition of

Saturday-night steaks, whenever he wasn't out of work. So I tucked into that T-bone a little guiltily, but mostly grateful for the free meat.

After swallowing my first mouthful, I scanned the room for something to say to break the awkward silence. "I like the painting," I said, nodding to a canvas of the Eiffel Tower at sunset.

"Thank you," Roger smiled. "I took that shot last time we were in Paris, and Cheryl had it printed on canvas for my birthday."

"Wow," I said. "Looks like it could be in a store." Fish snickered, but I hadn't meant it to be an insult. Roger didn't seem to take it that way.

"Those are the cherry blossoms in Tokyo—that was 2018. And of course you recognize the canals—that's Venice from a few years before. And the Big Ben behind you—that's from our honeymoon, back when Fish was still in high school."

"Wow, you guys travel a lot!" I said. "Internationally."

"We try to get away a couple times a year," Cheryl said, sipping her wine. "What's that quote you always say? The Mark Twain one?"

"Travel is fatal to prejudice, bigotry, and narrow-mindedness," Roger pronounced, holding up his wine and swirling it grandiosely.

"Wait," I said, truly just thinking out loud, not intending to start a fight. "So y'all have enough carbon credits to cool this house all summer, *and* eat like cavemen, *and* take international flights 'a couple times a year'? And all because you, like, buy a new dishwasher every year? How does that work out?"

"It's a racket, don't you get it?" Fish snarled. "They use their cash to buy all this greenwashed crap and do the landscaping and all these tricks that give them carbon credits. Then they invest in carbon sequestration funds buying up the rain forest—only not *really*, because we all know those funds are meaningless—but they return steep interest! So these two can jet set around the world, eating all the mammals they like, and they still wind up with a bigger carbon portfolio than when they started." Fish wiped his mouth with the bamboo-cloth napkin, looking disgusted.

"That isn't true about the rain forest." Cheryl's voice was thin and trembling. "Our money does a lot of good down in Ecuador, protecting those trees."

Fish snorted and shook his head.

Roger sighed loudly, tossing his napkin on the table. "Don't disrespect your stepmother, Fisher. And climb down off that high horse, would you? It takes money to make money—you know that. You didn't start your little app from scratch."

I glanced at Fish in surprise. Red blotches bloomed along his cheeks and neck.

"Let me guess—he told you that he dropped out of college and coded it himself, a self-made man? He didn't tell you about the trust fund he used to hire that Indian kid?"

"He's Pakistani, actually, and that's not the—" Fish turned towards me. "It was still *my* idea, okay? No one else had an app that made it quick and easy to transfer small amounts of carbon credits to your friends. Mizhir just helped a bit with the coding."

"Sure," I said. In that moment, I didn't really care who'd coded the app, or how Cheryl's carbon portfolio worked, I just wanted to finish my steak and get the hell out of there.

Roger went on, "So you invested in CarbonSwap, made a return on that investment, and bought this flophouse of yours."

I knew I shouldn't wade in, but Roger had insulted my home. "The Lab isn't a 'flophouse,'" I said. "It's this amazing venue—community, actually."

"Ugh, but that neighborhood it's in. Nothing but short lawns and asphalt roofs." Cheryl shuddered—actually *shuddered*. "Full of carbon criminals, if you ask me."

"That's the neighborhood I teach in," I said, heat burning up my chest. "Not everyone can afford to solarize their roofs or hire gardeners to do restorative permaculture."

"And I worry about the air you're breathing," she cooed to Fish, ignoring me. "You're near all those nasty power plants and refineries."

"Those are the power plants that run your AC," Fish growled.

"What? No, that can't be right. We have the solar panels, and the windmills—"

"No, he's right, dear," Roger interrupted. "Sustainables only make up thirty percent of our electric."

"Thirty percent? That can't be right," Cheryl muttered under her breath.

"Look, this thing with your *Lab*—it's a sound business plan." Roger leaned towards me and started talking like he was explaining something to a child. "You attract arts and culture to an area with low property taxes. Then you can flip houses in the area—for all the young people who want to live near a hot music scene. The 'hipper' the area gets, the higher you can jack up rents. Pretty soon the property taxes skyrocket, and you can sell at a huge profit." Roger leaned back with a satisfied smile. "I never had the stomach for real estate speculation, myself, but there's good money to be made."

"That's not what I'm doing!" Fish roared, way too loudly. His dad only looked more pleased. "The Lab isn't some—some gentrification thing!"

"It's not?" Roger stuck out his bottom lip. "Then what do *you* call it when a rich kid from Katy buys property in the Eighth Ward?"

"You know what? You don't understand anything about me," Fish kicked back his chair as he stood up. It was cringey— something a teenager would do. "You don't understand Maddie, and you definitely don't understand the Lab. Come on," he said to me, heading for the front door.

"Thanks for the meal. Everything was really good," I whispered, tucking my napkin next to my plate. I stared at the last third of the steak wistfully, but things had gotten way too awkward to ask for a Pyrex to take home.

"Oh come on—Fisher!" Roger yelled from his chair. "I'm just yanking your chain, my boy. This is how the world works!"

Fish aimed a kick at the fridge in the entryway, but his foot glanced off a corner pathetically.

I was silent for most of the ride home, as Fish ranted about what a hypocrite his dad was, how he didn't understand anything about what the Lab represented. I nodded along with him. It was the first time I'd seen him lose his temper.

All the admiration I'd felt for Fish—as this self-made tech king, this radical-lefty arts-community builder—it was falling away fast. I'd seen him through his father's eyes, as *Fisher*, just another rich kid who had the audacity to bite the capitalist hand that fed him. An ex-high-school linebacker with tattoos, a drinking problem, and a few memorized quotes from Marx. Once I saw him like that, I couldn't unsee it.

Was Roger right about the Lab? Were we just a pack of gentrifiers who, in time, would destroy the neighborhood we claimed to be a part of? When we got back to the Lab, I started to feel a bit better. A dozen people were hanging out on the couches, and we looked like the damn United Nations. White, Black, Latine, Asian, and most folks were multiracial, representing myriad genders and a rainbow of sexualities. At any given moment, you saw more different types of people at the Lab than you did at any other place in the city.

But still, the idea nagged at me. I went to sit next to Gestas, who was smoking a Swisher Sweet in the old Tilt-A-Whirl car. Gestas grew up in Eighth Ward. He was our only real local. "Is Fish a gentrifier?"

He snorted a laugh, then choked on smoke for a while. When he finally recovered, he said, "Fuck yeah, he's a gentrifier."

"And is this whole place—the Lab—is it gentrifying?"

"Uh-huhhhh," he said again, stretching out the word. "Didn't you hear—those dudes from Anklebiters moved into a house a few blocks away, on Crayton? And those synth guys—what's-their-names—" He snapped his fingers.

"Cody and Brad?"

"Yeah, Brody and Cad, they got a place on Lewis and Tenth. And you know, white people moving into Black neighborhoods are like roaches. By the time you notice a few of them, there's already an infestation." He let out a long, thin stream of smoke. "There goes the Ward. Before you know it, folks actually *from* here will be getting priced out, and they'll be tearing down all these houses to build those big, shiny Community towers. Like the one you live in!" he said, gesturing at me with the miniature cigar and an ironically cheery grin.

The smoke made me cough for a moment, before I could continue. "If it's bad, then—the Lab—why do you live here?"

Gestas leveled one of those deeply disappointed looks at me.

"Because your man Fish charges us half what the rent's worth, because he's so desperate for some friends 'of color,'" he said, making air quotes. "And if I want to play music, I got to be able to perform where I live. In case you hadn't noticed, I have limited options." He scratched his left shoulder, right at the spot where the faint, green light glowed just beneath the surface of his skin.

7

I pushed Mike Algebra in front of me, using his height to make a path through the crowd. By the time I grabbed the coffee-stained notebook full of our songs from Red's room, Red was already tuned up, with the set list written in Sharpie at xir feet. Lorenzo was running the sound check. Instead of the standard "Test, test," Red always spat, "Death, death," into xir mic. It was cheesy, but the teens in the crowd ate it up.

Gestas was adjusting his seat, fiddling with drum keys. I grabbed my guitar from the corner and slung it around my shoulders. Mike Algebra put the notebook of penciled lyrics and chords at his feet and started plunking out lines, leaving Fish's bass unplugged. Red shot me a questioning look with a raised eyebrow.

"No Fish?" xe asked, glancing around at me and Gestas. I shrugged. Xe smiled, and so did Gestas, and so did I. When Lorenzo gave us the double-thumbs, signaling the sound was good to go, I leaned over to Mike Algebra. "You ready?" He bobbed his head with a big, eager grin.

There was that hush before the first note, when we all glanced around at each other—in on the big secret we were holding back from the crowd. I always got nervous, then, heart hammering, palms slick with sweat, and a voice in my head yelling, "Imposter! Go back to your little youth group! You don't belong here!" But one glance at Red, and a flash of xir grin—the one xe kept only for me—and the voice shut the hell up.

45

Then Gestas crashed into the opening riff of "Cotton Candy Mountain," and for the first time in history, all the members of Bunny Bloodlust came in together, a wall of sound tearing from our amplifiers, blowing back the crowd that was thrashing to our beats like cane in the wind. I couldn't look at them though, not yet. I was way high up on the musical plane—seeing and hearing our lines dancing with and around each other, anticipating my entrances, feeling the strings slick under my fingers—just intensely in-the-moment and alive in the way I only ever was when playing music with my friends.

Mike Algebra did great, his bass lines rising to meet each of my chords effortlessly, like a bridge being built under my feet. I was drunk on the fun of playing without the fear that Fish would miss his entrances—and the cringe when he inevitably did. Gestas felt it too, pushing our tempos faster than we'd ever practiced, drumming so fast his arms blurred, but his face was serene, lips parted in a half smile. Red met his challenge, slamming xir fist into the strings, spinning solos I'd never heard out of thin air—wild-caught melodies, fleeting as shooting stars. I tried my best to keep up, just happy to be swimming along in the stream of their sound.

As we got into the middle of our set, and the songs were older, more familiar, I was able to come down out of my head a bit and look around. The crowd was drinking us in. The teens in the front who never missed a Lab party—our "fans"—were singing along and dancing. Over by the sound board, Lorenzo's long hair thrashed like a headbanging octopus, and his right pointer finger jabbed the air to the beat of the drums. The goth queens from Count Choke-ula never, ever danced, but even they nodded to the beat with their arms folded. The folks from Third Host were super into it, throwing up fists and yelling approval at the end of every song. I could stare at all of them with impunity, because no one was looking at me.

No, every one of the three-hundred-or-so people crammed into the Lab, jumping on the dance floor, or swaying atop precarious perches of stacked shipping pallets—they were all watching Red. And I loved to watch them watch xim. Disarmed by the music, emotion flitted undisguised across their features—hunger and lust, envy and rage, and, most of all, love. Impossible, one-sided, unrequited love. Because how could a bonfire like Red ever love you back? Each of them was a mirror, reflecting my own heart back at me—but they were out there, while I was the one who stood just beside Red and a bit to the left, rounding out Red's harmonies with my chords, adding my soprano to the *oo-ee-oos*. I was *in* the band. I was special to Red in that way, and there was nowhere on earth I'd rather be.

As we were revving up our cover song, T.Rex's "Metal Guru," my eyes snagged on someone new—someone who'd snuck in late, and very obviously *wasn't* looking at Red. Angel caught my eye and held up his fingers in a low wave. I bobbed my head in greeting as I sang the "yeah, yeah, yeahs."

Red's twin brother, Angel, had almost the same face, but where Red was sly and wolf-like, Angel was a barrel-chested lion. He stood out in the crowd, not just for his height, but for his ramrod posture and that chin held high. It was easy to spot the lone soldier amid all us hipsters.

He must have driven down from Fort Hood after work—probably speeding all two hundred miles of hyperway on that motorcycle of his, just to catch a bit of his sibling's set. Suddenly I remembered what Red had said—how this was the last weekend we'd have with Angel before he deployed.

The realness of his going to war hit me hard then, but he'd looked away, so he didn't see my eyes blur with tears. When I blinked them back, I noticed who he was staring at, just as the song drifted towards its end in a riot of feedback and reverb and Red's guttural panting.

So that's how it is, I thought. Everyone in the room was watching his sibling, but Angel only had eyes for Gestas.

8

first met Angel when he came home on leave for Christmas. He'd just been restationed to Fort Hood from somewhere out in Arizona. We were at Rudyard's—a grungy pub in Montrose. We being the band, Vida and Peter, the pop-punk synth trio Tricky Pink, Lorenzo, and Maura Screams, the performance artist.

Red kept checking xir phone, chuckling at a text thread xe had going with Angel. Usually, Red wasn't the type of person to be looking at xir phone all the time.

"So what's he like?" I asked.

"Angel? He's the best dude you'll ever meet," xe said. "Real golden boy—everything our parents—and step-parents—ever could've wanted. The son of a bitch." Xe grinned, and there was no bitterness in xir voice. "But I was born ten minutes earlier, so I'll always have that."

Around midnight, I was outside standing with the smokers, and a guy with the build of Captain America, wearing all neon-green-and-black motorcycle leathers that matched his Kawasaki bike, roared up to a parking spot outside the patio. Normally, I would've sneered at a dude who looked like that, assuming him to be some frat-boy douchebag. But Red vaulted over the iron fence around the patio to greet him. Angel pulled off his helmet, revealing Red's face—only with a fuller jaw and a thicker neck, and a shorter, pomade-slicked haircut.

"Baby brother!" Red said, jumping into his arms, crossing xir legs theatrically like a damsel in distress. Angel spun xim around faster and faster until their heads blurred and he staggered sideways, slamming into the patio fence, both of them collapsing into laughter. When Red introduced me, Angel said, "Of course, you're Maddie! Hey, if you're in the band, that makes us family!" And he lifted me off my feet into a bear hug that made me feel incredibly happy.

Angel ordered shots of Fireball with a hard lemonade backer for everybody, which was about the corniest, uncoolest of all possible drink orders, but no one turned it down. That was the start of a wild night of barhopping, shouting in each other's faces, laughing on crowded patios, singing on the maglev trains, and winding up at the Greenlight Speakeasy for absinthe shots at two a.m. Those fucking vintage-motorcycle assholes were there, Loco Motor, scowling miserably at everyone from the porch. Vida's tiny husband Peter puked into the mounds of kudzu climbing up the side of the house-turned-bar and stumbled back to our group, but on the way, he staggered, briefly laying a hand on one of those souped-up dirt bikes for support.

All of a sudden, the half-dozen Loco Motor guys charged off the porch, and the bike's owner grabbed Peter by the shirtfront. Red tried to get between them. Then our group was shouting at those grimy-vest-wearing, Loco Motor shits. People started shoving. I remember Angel kind of towering over all of them, the only person calling for peace. I was on the sidelines, pleading, "Let's just go," worried about getting caught up in a bar fight at an illegal speakeasy and getting arrested. I could lose my teaching license.

Then a long, loud hocking sound rang out. For a moment everyone stilled, and time slowed, as a giant wad of spit arced from Red's mouth, traced a line through the air, and splattered on the front fender of the motorcycle in question. The guy who'd first accosted Peter reared back and threw a punch, catching Red just under the eye.

Then Angel roared, and it was like seeing the Hulk transform. I mean, he just tore through those Loco Motor guys, throwing one against the fence boards, suplexing another into the mud. Me and Lorenzo and the others who'd stayed out of the mess just laughed nervously, watching him toss them around like rag dolls, hoping no one would call the cops.

Then Toothy Gus, the owner, ran out brandishing a shotgun, and I nearly pissed my pants. "Get the fuck out of here, and don't let me catch any of y'all's faces here ever again," he yelled. We ran practically all the way to the K train. At one point, the Loco Motor guys thundered past us on their bikes, yelling curses. Angel dropped his pants and flashed his bare ass at them, slapping both cheeks. Red howled with laughter.

By the time we got back to the Lab, I fancied myself half in love with Angel. After all, he had Red's face, but he was a *soldier*, a man's man. I could conceivably bring him home to my parents someday, and they'd be delighted. Fish was nearly as in love with him as I was. He wouldn't shut up about how awesome Angel's moves had been in the fight, and he watched the big alpha male with puppy-dog eyes. I was wondering if Fish worshipped Angel enough to forgive me for sleeping with the guy.

Because I was, let's be honest, sloppy drunk at this point and flirting with Angel pretty shamelessly. It's cringey, but I remember doing that cheesy, *CosmoGirl* move of putting both hands around his bicep, marveling that my fingers didn't even touch. Angel, enjoying all the attention, flipped me into the air and started bench-pressing my whole body as I giggled, and everybody watching laughed. I was sure Angel liked me then, but when I sat back on the couch next to Red, xe whispered in my ear.

"He's not for you, Mads."

I blushed all the way up to my ears, realizing how transparent I'd been. I must've looked panicked, because Red clarified, "What I mean is, he acts straight, 'cause we grew up on post, and army brats aren't exactly the most tolerant kids. But trust me, Angel only likes boys."

"Ohhhh," I said, a few of the non sequiturs of the night clicking into place. "But hey, you grew up those places too, right? And you don't act straight."

"No, I do not." Red barked a laugh. "And I also didn't join the fucking military."

That was the most Red ever acknowledged xir brother's career choice. I noticed that any time Angel was down for the weekend and mentioned something that had happened that week on post, or anything that even touched on the army, Red would get silent and stare off into the middle distance. Maybe xe thought that if xe ignored the fact that the military owned Angel's life, the problem would just disappear. Even the weekend he told us about his deployment, Red simply got up and went outside for a smoke, didn't say a word. I was the one who went over and pulled Angel into a big hug. I apologized for Red, and he said, "I know. I know how xe is about this stuff."

The only thing we were supposed to be "at war" with in the twenty-first century was climate change. But now Angel was going off to real-life war—people shooting and blowing up and actively-trying-to-*kill*-each-other-all-the-time—*war*. It was something that was only supposed to happen in old-timey movies. Not to our big, lovable Angel. And Red wouldn't even acknowledge the fact that he was leaving.

After getting those orders, Angel came down to visit just about every weekend. He would wake up before any of the rest of us and start working on the Lab while we were still hungover and useless. He did all this free labor—replacing Red's busted toilet, the light switch that electrocuted you a little every time you flicked it, Fish's bathtub that was leaking into the wall and rotting out Red's ceiling. One weekend, he cleaned out Red and Gestas's entire filthy fucking refrigerator with a toothbrush and a can of Ajax. No one asked him to do these projects, and no one, besides Fish, helped him. I don't know why he did all that for us. Maybe out of pity for our uselessness. Maybe out of love for Red. And maybe it was because he felt he had to earn his keep, because for some reason, deep down, he felt insecure next to us noodle-armed slackers. But he had it twisted. Angel might not've been *cool*, but he was worth all of us combined.

He even cooked for us, making Spam musubi or fancy ramen with eggs and sliced jalapeños, food that made Red and him wax nostalgic. Those recipes were how their mom cooked during their best times—when they'd had enough carbon credits for canned meat and dairy.

I was still piecing together the full story of their childhood from glimpses they'd let slip of a life hopping between army bases and put-upon relatives. I knew their dad had always been cruel and mentally unstable, that he was jailed for DV shortly after being discharged from the army, around the time Red and Angel started high school. But I didn't really grasp how horrific their early lives had been until one time, when we were sharing a blunt up on the roof of the Lab. Angel didn't partake, of course, on account of the army's drug testing. It was a mild, spring night, with only a couple stars shining through the permaglow of Houston's light pollution. Vida and Peter were there, and a couple others, and we were sitting on half-broken camp chairs and milk crates. Someone brought up childhood pets, and Angel and Red started listing off all the pets they'd had as kids. At first we were laughing with them, but as they kept talking, the rest of us fell silent with horror.

"You had that guinea pig!" Angel said. "When we lived at Fort Lewis. What was its name?"

"Donut," Red said.

"That's right. What'd Dad do to it?"

"Drowned him in the bathtub."

"I wasn't there for that one," he said, laughing perversely.

"I sure as shit was," Red said, giggling. "And then there was your lizard."

I looked around in shock at the others—none of us could understand what was so funny.

"Rex," Angel said. "It bit Dad one day, and he just wrang its fucking neck."

"Fuck, that's right," Red said, laughing harder.

"Wrang? Wrung?" Angel repeated. "How do you say it? Had wrongen?" Red was wiping away tears of laughter.

Vida looked like she was going to cry. I felt a tightness in my chest too. "Wait, what are you saying?" she asked. "Your dad killed all your pets?"

"Yeah," Angel said. "Usually in front of us."

He and Red took in our stricken faces, and their smiles faltered. They both swallowed and looked at the ground. But then Angel glanced back at Red, stifling a smile. "Remember your rooster?"

"At least we got to eat him!" Red cried, and they both busted out laughing again.

"Damn, he was good too," Angel wiped his eyes. "I think we'd only had lentils for like a month before that."

"Okay, and wait, am I crazy?" Red asked. "Or didn't you used to have a cat?"

At that, Angel's face finally fell. He nodded, still smiling, but looking genuinely pained. Red's energy came down too, and they stared at each other for a long time.

"It's funny, 'cause we have *never* talked about this until right now," Red said. "Not once. So like . . . it almost seemed normal to me?"

"Yeah," Angel agreed. "I just figured everyone's dad killed their pets in front of them once in a while." He looked around at all of us. "But I guess that's . . . not the case."

"No-o-o," Vida breathed.

"I mean, shitty dads are a dime a dozen," I said. "But that . . . no, not like that."

Later, the mosquitoes chased us back inside, and we were hanging out in the Lab. Vida was painting another mural, perched up on a stepladder, using a Hall & Oates LP for a palette. I was playing pretty, slow songs on Red's acoustic guitar. "Hey Jude" and "Blackbird" and hymns from my church days too. Angel flicked on the Fun Machine and the organ hummed to life. This was before it got beer spilled on it, so most of the keys still worked. He fiddled with the sliders a bit, and then started playing chords to round out my melodies. We looked at each other and smiled. I'd had no idea he was musical at all—let alone brilliant.

I set the guitar down then, backing off, inviting him to take over, and Angel launched into a flawless concerto, somehow skipping over the keys that didn't work, so you didn't even notice the holes in the melody. Later, Red told me how Angel had been this child prodigy. How, all through high school, he'd stayed in the practice rooms until the custodians locked up the building, because of course they didn't have a piano at home, just a cheap keyboard. He'd been angling for a music scholarship to college, and the summer before his senior year, their mom scraped together enough money to send him to an elite music camp in Michigan. The other students were all rich snobs—kids who had baby grand pianos at home, took two-hundred-dollar master classes, and had encyclopedic knowledge of piano repertoire. Angel got it in his head that he could never compete with the likes of them. At all his college auditions the next year, he choked, making tons of mistakes he'd never made in practice. After that, the army became his only route to college.

That night, as Angel filled the Lab with dreamy, synth-baroque hymns to a robot god, Red lay down next to me on the couch, resting xir head in my lap. I glanced around, confirming Fish wasn't watching us from a doorway. Cautiously, I stroked Red's hair. Xe closed xir eyes and smiled, listening to xir brother play piano, like xe must've done a million times throughout their childhood. Hearing him play every day must've been one of the few consistent, beautiful things in xir life. I'd never seen Red look that peaceful.

9

Half a year later, on the last weekend before Angel went to war, on the night Red destroyed the Fun Machine, Bunny Bloodlust finished our first-ever set with Mike Algebra on bass, and the crowd thundered approval. We unplugged and headed to Red's apartment to lock up our instruments.

Third Host took the stage as we reached Red's bedroom, the sousaphone and snare drummer's warm-ups vibrating the panes of the French doors to Red's room.

"That was so great, you guys, just awesome!" Mike Algebra said, grinning ear to ear. "I hope I filled in okay? I know I didn't play Fish's lines exactly, but I couldn't help improvising a bit. I love your songs, Red. They're so simple, but also so *epic*, you know? Any time you want me to fill in—"

"You're in the band," Red said, flopping on xir bed, cradling a hand behind xir head. "I can't play with Fish anymore. If that fucking ogre kicks us out of the Lab—" xe broke off, looking around the room. Ivy grew through the cracks in the windows and trailed along the ceiling. There was the brown streak of water damage, speckled with black mold, from when Fish's tub upstairs had leaked into the wall. A half-dozen, dead, thumb-length Texas cockroaches lay belly-up in the drifts of filth lining the corners of the room. Red shrugged. "—so fucking be it."

I was zipping up my guitar in the soft case, and my heart started slamming out of my chest with panic. No, no—Red couldn't kick

Fish out of the band, because then Fish might evict Red and Gestas, and our whole lives here, and the band, and everything I cared about would unravel.

Mike Algebra bowed out, closing the door behind him, and then Red and I were alone. Xe pulled a bottle of bourbon from the crack between xir mattress and the wall and swirled it in the air playfully, slowly crossing the room.

"Stay and have a drink?" Xe leaned against the wall beside me.

My heart hammered and my blood caught fire. This was it. Red had never made xir interest so blatant. I couldn't lie to myself anymore—couldn't tell myself I was just overthinking things. Not when Red was staring down at me like that, with a crooked, hungry grin.

My head dipped forward until my forehead was pressed against xirs, pulled there by a force stronger than gravity. I braced a hand square in the middle of Red's chest and felt the muscles there and the heat coming off xir heart. This was really going to finally, at long last, happen—

And then the officious, middle manager who ran my brain started screaming. If I slept with Red, then Fish would for *sure* kick xim out of the Lab. Then the band would be over, and I'd just be another notch in Red's bedpost.

With all the willpower I could muster, I wrenched myself back a step. "I should really go find Fish," I muttered. "He disappeared hacking cane. He might be in trouble or something."

Red scowled and took a long swig from the bottle. "If only."

"You didn't really mean it—about kicking him out of the band?"

"Fuck yeah I did."

"Let me go find him," I pleaded. "He needs to apologize for missing our set. Oh, and hey, I saw Angel in the crowd. You should hang out with him. It's his last night in town, before—"

"I get it," Red cut me off. "I fucking get it, okay? I don't need *you* to tell me who to hang out with. Go fuck your ogre boyfriend."

Xe had never looked at me like that before—like I was scum on the bottom of xir shoe. I turned and bolted from the room, before xe could see the red in my eyes.

Outside xir apartment, I pressed my hands to my eyes. "What the fuck is wrong with you," I moaned to myself. Red had offered me what I'd been dreaming of all year, and I'd panicked and ran, and now xe hated me.

Back in the Lab, Third Host had everybody jumping up and down to their drumline-meets-noise-rap sound, and the whole warehouse was shuddering. Rather than trying to push through the crowd, I headed out the front door and around the back to look for Fish, the tall weeds of the side yard tickling my calves. My only move was to give Fish a stern talking-to. Make him grovel for Red's forgiveness. Then maybe xe would let him stay in the band, and we could keep going on like nothing had happened. Red and I wouldn't be *together*, but we'd still get to hang around all the time, and play music, and that was the best I could hope for. The thought of just . . . not being in Red's life at all anymore? That was death.

In the backyard, the only person I knew among the smokers was Vida's husband, Peter. When I told him Fish had gone off into the cane and missed our set, he looked genuinely concerned. Of everyone in the house, I think Peter was the only person who had any real affection for Fish. Maybe because they were the only two white guys, and boy do they stick together.

Peter and I followed the trail of hacked grass to where it ended, calling Fish's name. Hunting around with our phone lights on, it didn't take long to spot some bent stalks where a big guy had crashed through the tall grass. We tracked the signs of a blundering drunk guy to the other side of the train tracks and off to the north, where the cane abruptly ended at the edge of an asphalt-covered lot. Fish's body lay splayed out on the cracked concrete.

"Shit, is he—" I began, unable to say the awful word.

Peter nudged Fish's shoulder with the toe of his shoe. Fish snorted and rubbed a hand across his face, but didn't regain consciousness. I sagged with relief. No dead boyfriend to deal with, just a drunk one. The machete and an empty bottle of MD 20/20 lay by his side. His bare torso was slick with a sheen of sweat, with bits of grass fibers stuck all over. His right hand still clutched a paper bag, and I pulled it free—knowing already what I'd find. Inside, there was a canister of butane. Huffing butane was something Fish had picked up just in the last month, because the dudes in the graffiti warehouse on Canal were into it, and he was desperate to get cool with them. I'd yelled at him when I'd first caught him huffing in the backyard.

Sure, we all drank too much, and smoked a ton of weed, and tripped shrooms once in a while. And I knew Fish did coke too, even though I hated the stuff—it gave me killer migraines. So it's not like I was anti-drugs or anything. But huffing was different. It was something desperate teenagers did because they couldn't get their hands on better methods of oblivion. And Fish—shit, wasn't he rich? Couldn't he get any drugs he wanted? Yet here he was, passed out on gas station wine coolers and lighter fluid. There was something so fucking phony about it.

And suddenly I was furious. For a year, I'd stayed with Fish, trying to see the best in him, sticking up for him when he wasn't in the room, only to watch him do his damndest to destroy himself. I'd just fucked things up with Red—the only person my heart really wanted—and for what? For Fisher-fucking-Wellman?

I could see it clearly now—the Lab, the band, the wild and reckless life we'd had here—it was all on its last legs. Fish was never going to turn the Lab into the anarchist art collective of his dreams. He would just keep hoarding furniture, while everyone who lived here developed more and more serious substance addictions. Nothing would get better, just more rotten, termite-ridden, and mold-infested, until the whole damn building was condemned and torn down.

I decided then and there that I wasn't ever going to sacrifice *anything* for Fish ever again. I turned and left him there to sleep off the holes he'd just put in his brain. I headed back to the Lab. I was going to find Red and kiss xim, consequences be damned.

10

2005–2018

Growing up, I thought everyone's dad slept in a recliner in front of the TV, a tallboy of Coors Light still loosely held in his hand, an empty, plastic six-pack ring discarded on the carpet beside him, which I would snatch in the morning and dutifully cut up into tiny pieces, having learned in school about the sea turtles that get stuck in them.

My dad was a mean drunk, but only to the people on TV. Every night, as soon as he got home from work—when he had work—he'd park himself in that recliner. If there wasn't a Texans game on, it was Fox News whipping him into a frenzy. Doing homework in the evening was punctuated only by the occasional shout across the house, "Those sons of bitches!" "The bastards are ruining America!" or "Oh, *fuuuuck* you!" His target would be the president, or whichever congressional Democrat or BCR rep was getting lambasted onscreen. Before the "War on Climate Change," before the BCR shut down half the fossil fuel production in central Texas, Dad laid electric for new refineries and oil wells all around Texas and Oklahoma. He had a union, the IBEW Local 520. He had a salary and benefits and a sense of dignity that never recovered when the BCR went after Valiant Oil, and he lost his job.

Mom was always nagging him to get a job in green energy—laying solar panels on people's roofs, and didn't they need electricians at windmills? Dad made it seem like he refused to get those types of jobs on purpose, but then he worked setting up a solar farm for a few months before getting laid off. Later, I'd learn that there just weren't nearly as many jobs to go around in green energy as there had been in oil and gas, and they tended to be temporary and non-union.

So, Dad took random electrical jobs around the city. Wiring up someone's garage or rerouting lines for a ceiling lighting fixture. Stuff like that. Stuff he considered beneath him. And when those jobs were too scanty, he'd work for a while at a big-box store to keep our own power running. He was so bitter about the BCR that he didn't make all the updates to our house that would've earned us carbon credits, so when the carbon appraiser came around each year, our carbon tax went up instead of down.

Though he was an angry drunk to the people on TV, he was always sweet to me when I was little. I liked him a hell of a lot better than Mom, since occasionally we could get him to run around the backyard with us, chasing us like a monster, or spinning us on his shoulders. Mom never drank, but she was always in a poison mood. She was the hitter—smacking me across my face for talking back, or spilling a glass of milk, or getting my new jeans muddy. It's only now, looking back, that I see she was worn to the bone doing everything for us kids—working the only steady job as a receptionist at the high school to keep the mortgage paid, doing all the shopping, cooking, cleaning, and driving us around to doctors and such. The only thing Dad ever did around the house was yard work, and only after my mom had nagged him ragged, and they'd shouted at each other for days, in a way that made me hide in my room, with the volume on my CD player cranked all the way up.

So as a little kid, I was a daddy's girl. But by high school, I'd realized that if Dad had ever lifted a *finger* to help her, maybe Mom would've been less of a miserable bitch. So I hated both of them pretty much equally. And then, on accident, I figured out the teenage rebellion that would freak them out the most.

I got super into Jesus.

We were Catholic—the low-key, Mass-at-Christmas-and-Easter, cross-yourself-near-the-cemetery, go-ahead-and-have-premarital-sex-as-long-as-you-don't-get-pregnant kind of Catholic. But Carly, a girl down the street, was into this charismatic youth-group thing and asked me to go with her the summer before ninth grade. When I told my parents I was going to church on my own, I noticed how they widened their eyes at each other. And then when I came home, and told them how I'd been filled with the Holy Spirit, they squirmed in their seats and picked at crust on the kitchen table. My newfound religious fervor made them super uncomfortable, but they were still *just* superstitious enough that they couldn't discourage me from it.

I got sucked in very deep, very fast. I carried my teen study Bible around in my backpack and doodled hearts next to the passages I liked. I picked up the lingo quickly. Instead of saying I'd think about something, I said I'd pray on it. Nothing was ever attributed to chance or my own work. If me and Carly got smoothies after school, it was because "God put this Jamba Juice in our path." I thanked God for my straight As, and for leading me to attend youth group, that night in the annex behind St. Hyacinth church, with its drop tile ceilings and beanbag chairs and jugs of Hi-C, when Colton—a junior, two years older than me, who didn't go to my high school—showed up with a guitar. With a shiny black pompadour and sideburns like Elvis, Colton laid his hands on my head and prayed over me, and I was sure I felt God's presence lighting up my blood. Of course, I was just hormonal as hell. It was horniness I was feeling, not the Holy Ghost. But after that, I was a true believer.

Colton taught me to play guitar. His late 1950s–early 60s aesthetic extended to his clothes—cardigans and khakis, even in Houston's summers. In his room, he had a neatly organized vinyl record collection of the Beach Boys, Elvis, and Buddy Holly. That first night we met, he told me I looked like Natalie Wood. A few days later, I showed a picture of her to my mom's hairdresser and got my hair cut in the same flippy bob. Colton asked me out soon after that. From then on, we were inseparable. Always dashing after school to church events, weekend retreats, or going on period-appropriate "dates" to the drive-in or the bowling alley, where we'd spend half the time trying to snap the perfect, seemingly spontaneous picture for Colton's carefully curated Instagram.

On those dates, Colton never tried anything more than a quick peck on the lips. I burned for him, though. I had dreams where he tried to gain carnal knowledge of me, and I didn't want to wake up. He was so handsome, tall—with a jaw that could cut glass and a velvety-smooth baritone voice. He ran cross-country and track, so he had these long, lean calf muscles. I figured we were both so close to God that it'd be alright in Jesus's eyes if we were to wind our legs together and see what happened. But Colton was ever the gentleman.

He bought me A-line dresses and sweater sets, and he was a lot more attentive to me when I wore them. If I showed up for a date in a church camp T-shirt and jeans, he'd be grumpy the whole time. So I learned not to do that. At school, I wore what I wanted, but as soon as I got home, I slipped on the petticoats that eventually started to feel like a uniform.

By my senior year, Colton started to get cruel. One time I bought an actual poodle skirt—you know, pink with the poodle on it, and he snarled that I looked ridiculous, that it was polyester Party City trash. So even though it'd cost me fifty bucks saved up from bagging groceries at the co-op, he made me get changed. From then on, the skirt lived at the back of my closet, mocking my bad taste every time I opened the door. Colton started nitpicking everything about me—I had foolish opinions, wasn't funny, ate too fast, and laughed too loud. I told myself that once we got married, we'd be able to have sex, and that would fix everything. I really thought that not being able to fuck was the only thing wrong in our relationship.

Red asked me about my marriage once. We were at a noise show at the Silo, this big, caved-in factory being devoured by kudzu and cane. The party was fun, but the music was just electrical feedback and screeching. Red claimed to love it, but xe can't have loved it that much, because when I shouted that I needed to get further away from the stage because I was getting a migraine, xe followed. We took refuge behind a crumbling wall and climbed up on some colossal, rusted machine jutting out of the weeds.

I was checking my legs for ticks when Red asked me, out of the blue, how Colton had proposed.

"First, he took me to the vintage car museum."

"You're kidding." Red snorted.

"It gets worse—we basically just went to take selfies, like a pre-engagement photo shoot. He spent half the next day editing the pictures and uploading them to Instagram."

Red busted out laughing.

"Then he took me to Olive Garden."

"No!" Red screamed.

"Yes." I grinned.

"Oh, Mads," Red clasped xir hands to xir mouth dramatically. "That's horrible. That's so disgustingly normcore. Oh my god, I've lost so much respect for you."

I laughed. "Also . . . he'd arranged for a waiter to bring over a dozen roses, and the ring box was like—tucked inside."

Red howled with laughter.

"I was eighteen! I thought it was the most romantic of all possible proposals. I thought I was the luckiest girl in Houston. Are you kidding? Such a handsome, well-dressed, *godly* fiancé?"

"So you were happy?" Red asked, more serious.

"Oh my god no. I was in so much pain, all the time. He was so mean."

"Jackass," Red scowled. "Hey, if we ever run into him, you'll point him out, yeah? I've got some words for him." Xe cracked xir knuckles, and I laughed.

"I wish I'd been two-stepping with you at Blazing Saddles, instead," I said, a little breathless from how close this was to an outright admission of my feelings.

"Me too," xe said. I smiled hugely but couldn't think of what to say next, so I just kicked my legs awkwardly, skimming the tops of the weeds with my boot soles. "So, did you have a wedding?" Red asked, breaking the silence. "White dress and all that?"

"No, my parents thought we were too young, so they wouldn't give us a dime. Colton's family was super religious, so they might've approved *if* I'd been rich like them. But we weren't, so they thought I was after their money. They even told Colton that, and they had this big blowup fight. The day after I graduated high school, we had a courthouse wedding—just the two of us. And we moved into this apartment that was full of bugs. Like, all of them."

"All the bugs?"

"Roaches, millipedes, ants." I ticked off on my fingers, "Even swarms of termites that would burst out of the walls at random."

"Sounds like the Lab."

"Well, yeah. But not nearly as fun."

"Because Colton was mean?"

"That, and . . ." I hesitated, embarrassed by some bone-deep modesty that still made it hard to talk about these things. "We had a *lot* of trouble in the bedroom. Colton had so much religious shame around sex— I mean, I'm not hideous, right?"

"No, Maddie. You are not," Red said softly.

"Well, on our wedding night, he couldn't stay hard. A few nights later we tried again and like . . . technically, we accomplished sex."

"What does that mean? He came?"

"Yeah, I sure as shit didn't though." Red shook xir head. "Afterwards I just felt like, So this is it? This is what I've been waiting for? And then he was always crueler than normal the day after we'd had sex—especially if he had failed to, uh, *perform*."

Sex was rarely an issue anyways that first year, as we were mostly too tired to do anything but pass out at the end of the day. I'd gotten a decent scholarship to University of Houston, but I had to work every spare minute in a coffee shop to make ends meet. Colton wasn't working, but he was taking a super-heavy course load so he could graduate early.

Red wanted to know how it ended.

"That's a long story. But I guess when Colton started to drink, that was the beginning of the end. The whole time we'd dated he'd never touched alcohol. I'd figured it was a religious thing. But then one day—he didn't make an announcement or anything—he just started buying boxes of cheap red wine at the grocery store and having a glass with dinner every night. I asked him if drinking was Christian, and he quoted Ecclesiastes 9:7 to me: 'Go, eat your bread with joy, and drink your wine with a merry heart, for God has already approved what you do.'"

"I gotta remember that one," Red mumbled.

"Right? So I started drinking with him. And you know, a glass of wine made him a hell of a lot nicer. We both had a sweet spot in our buzz, about a drink and a half in, where he'd get horny, and we could have sex without overthinking it. Sometimes it was even kind of *okay*."

"It should be criminal, being married to a girl like you and being so goddamn awful in bed," Red said.

"My sophomore year, things got easier, because Colton had graduated, and he got this good-paying, exec-track job at A&G Plastics. We moved into a bigger apartment near the Galleria, bug-free, and I didn't have to work after school. But we didn't have any time together. Colton was always busy and stressed. When he wasn't at the office, he was training for these ultramarathons he ran with his new work friends—Dean and Trevor."

"I knew it!" Red said, xir face lighting up.

"What?"

"Dude. Your man was totally gay."

"Nooo," I said, feeling like I'd got the wind knocked out of me. "You think?"

"I *strongly* suspected when you told me about the whole rockabilly-selfie-life thing. And also he couldn't get it up? With *you*?" I tried not to blush. "And then, I'm sorry, but this 'training-for-marathons' thing," Red said, tracing air quotes. "He was probably sleeping with Dean and/or Trevor. Or at least fantasizing about it."

"I don't know," I said. "He was so hung up on god stuff when it came to sex. Then again, maybe he was just like that with me?" I shook my head. "But like—we didn't even *know* any gay people."

"Wait, was I the first queer you ever met?" Red asked giddily.

"No, no—actually, that sophomore year I was in this Shakespeare seminar? And there were these two girls. Even *I* could tell they were lesbians. And they always called me Martha Stewart."

Red laughed through xir nose.

"They kind of bullied me, asking if I got my clothes from a time machine. If my ring was a real blood diamond. If I always hurried out of class so quick so I could be sure to get a pot roast on the table for my husband."

Red snickered into xir hand. "I mean . . . fair."

"It was! I Googled 'blood diamonds' and got disgusted by the rock on my finger. I did have to hurry home to figure out dinner. Not like I can cook. I'd just plate take-out or ready-made stuff from the grocery store because any time I tried to make something more complicated than Mac n Cheese, Colton would mock my cooking ruthlessly. And my clothes *were* all from vintage stores. I was honestly getting really fed up at that point with all the ironing, and the scratchy tulle petticoats, and wearing nylons in the middle of summer."

"He made you wear nylons?!" Red cried. "That monster."

"He thought it was trashy for women to show bare legs," I said, bowing my head with embarrassment. How'd I ever let myself get so pushed around? Something about telling it all to Red made me realize how fucking awful it was—all that shit Colton put me through.

"Forget waiting around to run into him. I'm gonna need an address for this clown," Red said, punching xir fist into xir hand. That made me smile, though I wasn't about to let Red catch an assault charge for Colton's sake.

"So anyways, once Colton got rich, he signed up for this sub-scription wine service from the *Wall Street Journal*."

"Ooh, fancy."

"Towards the bottom of his nightly bottle, Colton would get mean, then pass out, usually with a glass in his hand. He just criticized me all the time. The cooking, the cleaning. 'Stains all over the fucking counter.' He was moving away from his 1950s aesthetic, had shaved off his sideburns and wore Brooks Brothers suits to work. When I told him about the girls at school calling me Martha Stewart, he'd say the same thing. Said I was still dress-ing like a corny high schooler. But I didn't have any nice clothes besides the ones I'd bought to impress him. And he didn't give me any money to buy new ones. So I went back to wearing jeans and old church-retreat T-shirts."

"Like where everybody signs their name in Sharpie?" Red asked.

"Exactly." I laughed. "So then when Colton was *in his cups*, he'd call me a slob, and ask me why I couldn't *make an effort*, and no wonder he didn't want to have sex with me. And if I ever talked back, or asked for money to buy something new, he'd call me a bitch, or a nag, or a harpy. So I'd just shut up and take it. Most nights I hid out in the bedroom watching stand-up on my laptop until he passed out on the couch with a drink in his hand."

"Just like your dad used to do," Red said.

"Exactly. Except with Colton, it was a stemless wine glass instead of a Coors Light."

"I can't listen to this anymore." Red jumped down from the machine we'd been sitting on, landing in the weeds. "Or I'm gonna murder a bitch named Colton."

11

That's why, as I looked down at Fish's insensible hulk, passed out on wine coolers and industrial solvents, I just felt completely fucking haunted by drunk cis men. I did not want to make space for them in my life, ever again. Whatever contract had still existed between me and Fish was rendered null and void. Now, I was going to get what I wanted.

I charged back through the stand of cane, fully intending to find Red, push xim up against a wall, and plant a mind-altering, destiny-shattering, the-gods-look-on-and-weep type of kiss on xir lips.

Third Host had finished their set, and by the time I vaulted back up on the loading dock, a lot of the crowd had already cleared out. Inside, there were only fifty-or-so people left in the Lab. I spotted Red across the room, standing with Angel and Gestas. Xe saw me. I smiled hugely, heading right for xim. Red scowled, then bent and grabbed something off a table. Xe started towards me, stumbling a bit, drunk. I kept on, even though the look on xir face was unnerving. Red was still glaring at me angrily, like in xir bedroom earlier. Like xe hated me. But I was going to make it right. I'd take xim by the hand, pull xim somewhere private, and show xim just how I'd felt all this long, aching year.

But then Red grinned at me, and there was something off about it, like how a villain in an anime smiles. Xe must've been really drunk. Xe raised xir hand, and I saw what xe was holding—a hammer. It glinted overhead, suspended for a moment, and then Red brought it crashing down, with all xir strength, onto the keyboard of the Fun Machine.

Everyone whipped their heads towards the crash. Red hadn't touched me, but I *felt* that blow in my bones. "Dude, what the fuck?" Gestas said. I was looking at the damage, thinking just a few keys were busted—maybe we could still fix the Fun Machine, *really* fix it this time. Then Angel could play that beautiful concerto again, and Red and I would two-step around the Lab, and everything would be alright.

But before I could move to stop xim, Red cackled, gripped the hammer with both hands and started bringing it down over and over, smashing the keys to pieces. Splinters of wood flew as xe started in on the rest of the organ. One shard skittered to a stop at my feet. Lorenzo roared, "That is rock and roll as *fuck*," and started laughing his ass off. When Red stepped back, panting, still shooting me a death glare, the sousaphone player from Third Host grabbed the hammer out of xir hand. Red made a gesture like, "By all means," and after that, a bunch of people started taking turns obliterating the Fun Machine. My eyes were full of tears for some reason.

Gestas shouldered past me. "Fucking asshole," he muttered under his breath. Angel was following him.

"Remember the time you played that concerto?" I asked Angel.

"Yeah." He shrugged, looking back at Red. "RIP Fun Machine."

Red was taking another turn with the hammer, and it felt like watching xim slaughter a helpless animal. I couldn't take it anymore and followed Gestas outside.

Angel proffered a pack of cigarettes at me, which I waved away, but Gestas took one and sat down in his usual spot, dangling his boots over the edge of the loading dock—the edge of his prison. His sparkly eye shadow glittered in the flares rising off the Valiant Refinery. Angel and Gestas tried to blow their smoke away from me. I still inhaled enough to trigger a tickle of asthma in my lungs, but I appreciated the gesture.

"You ever find out what happened to Fish?" Gestas asked.

"He's over yonder," I said, gesturing in the direction of the empty lot across the tracks. "Passed out on lighter fluid."

Gestas huffed. "Figures."

"Red says he's out of the band for this," I said.

"Red says a lot of shit when xe's drunk. But we all know that our dear landlord could make our lives very difficult if we don't keep him happy," Gestas said. "So, Red's throwing a temper tantrum about it."

"I thought that was about me," Angel said. "You know xe hasn't said a word to me about deploying? Not 'good luck.' 'Come home safe.' Nothing."

"It doesn't mean xe doesn't care," I said. "You know Red. Can't talk about xir feelings, so xe smashes an organ at you." I thought of the way Red had stared me down as xe brought the hammer crashing into the Fun Machine's keys. "I think Red's working through a lot of stuff right now."

I turned back to Angel, my eyes stinging. "Well, I'll say it: Good luck, buddy. Come home safe. I mean it." Angel smiled and pulled me into one of his big bear hugs. "Going off to war. It's so fucking unreal," I said when he let me go. "How do you feel—are you scared?"

He carefully stubbed out his cigarette and slipped the butt back into the pack, in between the cellophane and the cardboard. "I'd be lying if I said I wasn't. Of course I'm scared. But I'm excited too, you know? This is what I've been training for, for five years. I'm ready to do some good in the world. *Literally* fight the 'War on Climate Change.'"

Gestas burst into a fit of coughing laughter, sending smoke shooting out his mouth and nostrils. When he recovered, he choked out, "Wait, you actually believe that bullshit?"

Angel knitted his eyebrows at Gestas, like he was genuinely confused by the man's reaction. "Of course I do. We're going to stop the burning of the Amazon."

Gestas's eyes widened comically. "So you think that the US Army is invading Brazil out of the goodness of their hearts?" He clutched both hands to his chest. "And that—again, the *US Army*—is running this mission purely for the good of the rainforest?"

"I don't think you know how the *US Army* operates," Angel said, exaggerating the words the way Gestas had. "And it's not just the US. It's the whole United Nations Climate Security Force. We have thirteen partner nations."

"Yeah, hmmmm . . . what do all those countries have in common. Could it be . . ." Gestas drummed his fingers on his chin. "White Supremacist Imperialism?"

Angel made a noise in the back of his throat, then stammered, "We have South American partners too."

"Newsflash, South American countries can still be white supremacist if they're run by US-backed fascists," Gestas said.

"What does that—" Again Angel knit his brows in frustration, like he couldn't believe what he was hearing. "Look, someone has to step in and stop the burning of the Amazon. Literally all life on earth is at stake." I held my breath, cringing internally but also glued to the spectacle of the high-speed train wreck that was about to happen here. I wouldn't be able to explain it all as well as Gestas could, but I knew that what Angel believed—that the war was this good-hearted conservation mission—was dead wrong.

Gestas sighed, staring at Angel. "So pretty—" He shook his head, clucking his tongue. "—and so ignorant." Angel's skin started to turn puce. But before he could protest, Gestas was off, launching into one of his fast-paced tirades that left you in pieces, shaking and humbled by his fire hose of analysis. "Why have people been burning the Amazon—for decades, might I add?"

Angel opened his mouth to answer, but Gestas cut him off. "Because they were poor, right? Poor as shit. And raising cattle on forested lands was their only way to make a living. So they burned the forest to raise cows. But Brazil was one of the wealthiest countries in the world. So why were so many of its people so poor in the first place?"

Angel stammered and looked to me for help. Gestas kept going. "Racial capitalism, my guy. Racial capitalism. The poor Black and Indigenous people who live in and around the Amazon have been kept as the permanent underclass that props up the white ruling power structure in Rio. And no one in our government had a problem with this, for decades on end, as thousands of square miles of rain forest burned each year."

"That's not true," Angel managed to get in. "*I* had a problem with it. People are always talking about—"

"Oh, our leaders have cried crocodile tears over the burning of the Amazon, all while profiting obscenely off the corporations running carbon-kickback rackets for 'protecting' acres of rain forest from being burned. And these transactions, by the way, are rarely more than meaningless digital scribbles. The more the Amazon burned, the more profitable carbon credits for acres of the Amazon became, and the more the politicians and the net-zero corps and the green lobbyists made bank." Gestas rubbed his fingers together in the gesture for cash. "There was no talk of war, no talk of invasion, until the poor Black and Indigenous people of Brazil organized, and elected Delgado, who has nationalized the forest and returned its stewardship to the people who actually live *within* it. He declared all the contracts that gave away pieces of the Amazon to carbon-offset corps null and void." Gestas stabbed his cigarette towards Angel's chest. "*That* is why you are going to war, Angel. Because the *property* of corporations is threatened. If Delgado's plan was allowed to proceed, you'd see the burning stop very quickly. Because all this wealth pouring into 'Save the Amazon' efforts would actually go to the people who *live* there. They wouldn't need to burn the forest to eke out a living as cattle ranchers. They could just kick back and rake in the funds from all us guilty, carbon-guzzling colonizer nations. As well they should!"

Angel frowned. "Just *give* them money? Just because they live in the rain forest?"

"Why not?" I added, shrugging, when Angel looked to me for support.

"That would end the burning, wouldn't it?" Gestas said. "But it would cut off all the banks profiting from net-zero schemes. So instead, *you're* being sent in there to murder these people—who, honestly, you probably share some ancestors with on your dad's side. You're going there to kick out the Indigenous people who've lived there for thousands of years, all so that white colonizers can have sole control over one of the world's greatest terrestrial carbon-storage systems, which grows on top of a mountain of gold, by the way, and has one of the largest fresh water sources in the world running through it. You are an invader, Angel. A colonizer, a killer. *Fuck.*" Gestas had gone on so long his cigarette went out. He pulled out a pack of matches to relight it.

"No, no," Angel shook his head vigorously. "You're wrong about all that. You—you're twisting it up to sound terrible."

Gestas shrugged, puffing on the glowing butt. "Sure, pal. Okay. What do you want me to say? Uhhhh, good luck? Was that it? Good luck genociding the Native peoples of the Amazon?"

Angel looked to me for help.

"I mean, I'm definitely not as up on politics and stuff as Gestas is," I shrugged. "But . . . yeah. From what I understand, I think the war is pretty . . . fucked?"

Angel rubbed his hands over his face. "I don't understand this—this reaction. President Donnelly is a Democrat. Aren't y'all Democrats? Aren't y'all liberals?"

"Hoo boy, here we go," I said.

Gestas spat—whether from the stale cigarette or disgust, I wasn't sure. "No, I am definitely-fucking-not a *liberal.*"

12

DECEMBER 2019

The lab was usually full of people, so a few months had passed before I got the chance to talk to Gestas one-on-one, even though we hung out in groups all the time. I'd come by on a weeknight after work. By then, I didn't even text before coming over, just showed up to see who was around. The front door was never locked, and there were always people to hang out with. That evening, though, even Red and Fish had gone somewhere. I looked all over, stunned to find the Lab empty, and finally found just one person. Gestas was in his apartment, cooking a pot of ramen on the stove.

"Hey," I said from the open doorway.

"Oh, hey." He glanced up. It was awkward. We'd played in a band together for months, but we'd only ever hung out in groups. A long silence hung in the air while I stood in the doorway, wondering if I should split. I didn't want to intrude on Gestas's alone time—something that was probably pretty rare living at the Lab. Plus, I got the vibe that Gestas didn't really like me—which I understood. When he looked at me, I saw myself as this cheesy, naïve white girl, trespassing in his neighborhood, whom he only barely tolerated because I could read music and play decent rhythm guitar.

But he dropped a couple frozen dumplings in his ramen and asked, "How was school?" I took that as an invitation and stepped inside.

"Fine," I said, staring at the show posters taped to the walls. "No fights today, so that was good."

"That *is* good, for Washburn," he said. Gestas had gone to the high school I taught at for the first six months of his freshman year, before his mom left his dad. After that, she took Gestas with her to Spring Branch, where there were more white people and the schools were better funded.

"Nobody's reading the book," I said. "Well, I've got a couple kids who have an idea what's going on—but otherwise it's just me talking to myself. And they tolerate that for a while, until they don't."

"What book?" Gestas asked, flicking off the burner. He carried the pot to the table and set it on a T-shirt for a coaster. He gestured at it like, "You hungry?" but I waved him away. I *had* shown up hoping to find someone to go get food with me, and the ramen smelled amazing, but I didn't want to take any of his soup.

"*To Kill a Mockingbird*," I said.

He snorted. "No wonder they're not fucking reading it."

"Wait, why though?" I asked, sitting down across the table from him. "Because I thought they'd find it more relevant than our first unit? At least it's about Civil Rights. Our last book was *Animal Farm*, and I thought, what do they care about a bunch of pigs? But maybe more of them read that because it was short."

Gestas shook his head at me, while he slurped up a column of ramen. When he finally swallowed, he spoke. "Damn, you really underestimate their intelligence, don't you?"

I sputtered a response, but he cut me off. "*To Kill A Mockingbird* is a book by a white lady about good white people saving Black people from Jim Crow. The whole narrative's designed to make *y'all* feel good about *y'allselves*. What message does it send to your students? That they should feel grateful for all the *good white people* like Atticus Finch—" He clutched his fist to his heart dramatically. "—for saving them from segregation? Never mind that white people *created* Jim Crow. You think there's a single book by a Black author about the Jim Crow South where the hero is a white man? Hell the fuck no. And y'all aren't teaching Richard Wright or Zora Neale Hurston or Toni Morrison, are you?"

I shook my head, really hoping he wouldn't ask me if I'd even read those authors, because the awful truth was I hadn't.

Gestas went on. "No. Your one 'Civil Rights' book is by a white lady, because why? It's the best? It's such brilliant literature?" He laughed, slurping up another column of noodles. "The implied message to your students is that *you're* their Atticus right? They're supposed to feel gratitude to good white teachers like Ms. Maddie. Is that it? Is that how you expected it to go?"

I must've looked like a fish, with my mouth hanging open in the air. The truth of what he'd said knocked the wind out of me, and I couldn't find a single lie to argue with. How had I never seen it like that? How had no one in our district—not the other teachers, or the district administrators who told us what to teach—how had none of them ever brought this up?

"Your students see right through that shit, don't they?"

Suddenly all the rolled-eyes, the teeth sucked in my direction when I asked them about the passage we'd just read—they started to make sense.

"Now *Animal Farm*, I'm not surprised that some of your kids latched onto that. But please, god, tell me you didn't teach it as a book about 'a bunch of pigs'?"

"No I—I got into how Orwell was writing about the Russian Revolution, how it's anti-communism and everything."

Gestas put his head in his hands, like he couldn't even bear to look at me. "It's not anti-communist, it's anti-*authoritarian*." Gestas chopped the air with one hand for emphasis. "Orwell was a self-identified socialist, who spent his whole career writing for the working classes. Napoleon the pig is Stalin. *Stalin* is the villain—because he betrayed Marxism and the hopes of the working classes. But Jesus, you're really teaching it as McCarthyist propaganda, huh?"

"Look, I don't pick the books. I don't even write the lesson plans!" I said defensively. "We get everything handed to us from the district offices, and it's like, 'Teach this.' If we go off script even a little while the assistant principal's in the room, we get in trouble."

"Cool, cool, I see the assembly line has finally completed its takeover of public education. That tracks." He sat back, arms folded, and stared past my head, unseeing.

"How do you know all this stuff?"

He focused on me with a wry smile. "You sound so surprised. Why, 'cause I'm Black? 'Cause I never graduated? Or 'cause I'm a prisoner? Which one of those things makes you think I don't know shit about books?"

"It's not like that, Gestas. I just meant—hell, you seem to have a better analysis than even these so-called 'curriculum experts' who write our lesson plans."

"It's *because* I'm Black and a dropout and a prisoner. That's why I have a 'better analysis,' and that's something you can't buy, not like a college degree. Plus, I read a fuck-ton. What else am I gonna do when everyone else goes out at night? Have you seen my room?"

I shook my head—I hadn't, actually. Gestas kept his door locked when he wasn't in there, and I'd never been invited in. He led me there now and swung the door open. A mattress was pushed up against the back corner. His Harris County Corrections-issued laptop sat open on a cheap, secondhand IKEA desk, where he did his white-collar penal work eight hours a day. And besides that, there were about a thousand books. A few mismatched bookcases stood against the walls, stuffed full, with books stacked sideways on top of the vertical rows. More books lined the rustic shelves Gestas had nailed up all the way to the ceiling. And even more books lived in piles taking up almost all the floor space in the room. Most of the books had yellowed pages and cracked spines, and the stack nearest to the bed wore cellophane covers—library books. The room smelled of dusty, old paper, like a used-book shop.

"Wow, your collection is amazing!" I said, peering inside. "Can I—can I look around?"

He gestured at the open doorway to say, "by all means." I stepped through and started inspecting all the spines. Gestas came in and sat on the bed. "Would it be alright—could I borrow something?" I asked.

"What do you want?" he asked.

"I don't know, you tell me. What do you think I should read?"

He started to rifle through a nearby stack. "You realize this is unpaid intellectual labor I am doing for you?" He quirked an eyebrow at me, but he was grinning. Book people can't help it—we *love* recommending books. He paused at a dusty, red cover. "Now are you sure you can handle this? It's gonna fuck you up." He handed me a well-worn copy of Paulo Freire's *Pedagogy of the Oppressed*. Taking it in my hands felt like holding a bomb. But I was ready for it to blow up whatever walls it was coming for. I worked so hard to be a good teacher, but no matter what I did, every class felt like a battle, every day a miserable slog through failure. If communists knew why my students loathed me, I was willing to hear what they had to say.

"I'll start it tonight," I said. I kept scanning his shelves, curious to see what else he had. Most of his collection was nonfiction—leftist theory and scholarship and history. But there was a whole bookshelf of fiction, mostly by Black and Indigenous authors. Novels I'd heard of, and knew I *should've* read, but hadn't. There was a section of manga and graphic novels, and a pile of Modernist poetry near the bed. I found a shelf of atheist theory, side by side with every religious text I'd heard of.

"So you *are* interested in religion," I said, almost to myself.

"I am. Why?"

"Your name."

"Oh?" He smiled, putting his hands behind his head. "So you know the story of Gestas? That's a deep cut."

"Well, I used to be in pretty deep. Even dabbled in the apocryphal texts."

"This was when you were married?"

"Before," I said, my face falling at the mention of my ex-husband. I changed the subject away from me. "Now, Gestas . . . Was he crucified to the left or right of Jesus?"

"The left, of course. The *sinister* side," Gestas waggled his left hand in the air, and for the first time, I realized he was left-handed.

"What was the other thief's name?"

"Dismas," Gestas supplied.

"That's right. Gestas and Dismas were crucified with Jesus. They were both thieves, right? And Dismas was the good one. He repented and said he believed, so Christ saved him. But Gestas . . ."

"Oh, that Gestas." Gestas shook his head and clucked his tongue like a disapproving priest.

"Gestas was *not* sorry for having stolen. What was the word . . . not impertinent—"

"Impenitent."

I snapped my fingers. "That's it. Gestas, the impenitent thief."

"That's the one."

"That's who you're named after?" He nodded. "Are you—I mean—is that why?" I couldn't think of a polite way to phrase my question, but me staring at his faintly glowing shoulder gave it away.

"You're wondering if that was my crime? Stealing?"

I nodded.

"Technically, I was selling fake carbon credits," he said. "But the BCR considers that stealing from the government."

"I see," I said. Ever since I'd met Gestas, I'd been dying to know why he was incarcerated, but it'd seemed rude to ask—him or anyone else.

"And you're impenitent?" I said, putting the pieces together. "So that's why you chose the name."

"Why're you assuming I chose it?" he asked in faux outrage.

"Oh come on, no one names their kid *Gestas*."

"Hey, people name their kids Adolf. And Andrew and Christopher, and all kinds of names held by famous genociders. An impenitent thief is a hell of a lot better of a role model than most boys' namesakes."

"But come on, you picked that name!" I cried, getting tired of him messing with me.

He laughed. "Okay, yeah I did."

"I remember learning about Dismas and Gestas in youth group. And I just couldn't understand Gestas at all. Like there he was, crucified next to God himself, and he can't just say he's sorry. Jesus was *right there*, trying to save him, and he got himself damned to hell for all eternity—because he couldn't see past his pride. It scared the hell out of me. Back when I believed in hell, I mean."

"Me too," Gestas said. "That was before I realized just how precious pride is. How dangerous it is to the people in power, and that's why they want to take it away from you. That's why they scare little kids with stories of burning for eternity just for having a backbone."

"Okay, but also—I mean, it wasn't just pride. Gestas *did* sin, right? He did steal."

"What did he steal? Why did he steal it? What if he needed it to survive, or for his family? What were the material conditions that led to the theft? And why is stealing a crime anyways? What is property? What is ownership? Why is it valued more than a man's life?"

"Whoa, whoa," I said, holding up the Freire book. "Give me a chance to read this first."

He laughed at that.

"If I can ask—and you don't have to tell me, of course," I said, feeling bold. "What were the material conditions that led to your, uh, theft, or fake-carbon-credit-selling thing?"

"I needed money to pay for T," Gestas said, matter-of-factly. "Red and I had our first apartment together. I had a job as a barista, but I wasn't making enough for rent and food *and* my meds. I knew a guy who did coding, and he knew how to reload carbon stamp cards with fake credits."

"I see," I said, though the words felt inadequate.

"Joke's on them, though," Gestas said, clapping his hands and rubbing them together. "Because now the Feds pay for my hormones! And all I have to do is, you know, some Excel-based slave labor."

We both glanced at the thick, decade-old, workhorse of a laptop on the desk. "What do you actually *do* on that thing anyways?" I asked.

"Different contracts. Right now, I'm taking tens of thousands of files for an insurance company, updating them from an old file format to a new one, and then entering the data line by line into an Excel spreadsheet. It'll take me a couple months. I try to move as slowly as possible, because fuck them, you know? But the laptop has built-in inaction timers and retinal scanners that will dock my time if I'm not entering the data quickly enough or looking away from the screen too often."

"Ugh, I'm sorry, that sounds like a nightmare," I said, feeling the words were inadequate. I started picking through a nearby pile of books, wondering how to keep the conversation going. Gestas was opening up to me, and he'd invited me into his room, where no one but Red ever got to go. I'd made him laugh, which was kind of a rare thing. I was feeling cooler, maybe, than I ever had in my life, even at our shows. And then, in the next moment, I stepped into a giant metaphorical pile of shit.

I said, "Your room is so cool. I'm jealous."

It was just a throwaway thing to say. Making conversation. I didn't think about what it meant.

"You're jealous?" He blinked at me slowly. "Of my prison cell? You realize that's what this is, right?" He launched himself off the bed and stormed out into the main room, spreading his arms wide. "You realize I can't ever leave this *fucking* building?"

And for some ass-backwards reason, rather than just apologizing and shutting up, I tried to make a joke, to lighten what I'd said. "As far as prisons go, though, it's not so bad, right?" I followed him to the doorway. "We throw some killer parties. And compared to how prisons used to be—"

"Oh I'm supposed to feel gratitude?" Gestas raked his fingers through his beard. "Should I feel *grateful* the state decided it was too expensive to actually feed and house prisoners, when they could just stick a chip in our arms and lock everybody in their own homes instead? Should I feel *grateful* that my slavery only takes the form of typing data eight hours a day, rather than working in a plantation prison or breaking rocks for a railroad? Grateful that rather than making nothing, I get paid five bucks a day for my labor? Grateful that I can't sleep at night because there's always a bunch of nineteen-year-old assholes drinking and smashing beer bottles off the roof here, and I can't even get fucked up with them, because this thing in my arm monitors my blood alcohol content?" He rubbed his shoulder, where the green light always glowed. "And if I slip up, there's still plenty of brick-and-mortar prisons they can lock me up in as punishment. Is *gratitude* how you think I should feel about all that?"

I really didn't know how to stop rolling in the shit I'd stepped in. "But that's what I mean," I said. "You admit—it *is* better here than in an old-school prison, right? You get to live with your friends and play music! Aren't you glad they passed AHICA?"

"*Glad, gratitude,*" he said. "You really know best, huh? You know a bunch of alliterative fucking bullshit words for how I'm supposed to feel? *Glad* and *gratitude* are not anywhere near how I feel about my oppressors. The Democrats didn't pass AHICA out of the goodness of their hearts! They did it because it increases corporate margins on locking up and enslaving Black people. It's for profit." He spat the last word. "Because that's what it's about—what this country has *always* been about. How many times you rip off the BCR, huh, white girl? You ever hop on a train without paying the fare?"

"Well . . . not since college," I mumbled.

"Exactly. You ever buy some meat tamales from the ladies who sell them in the bars at night, and pay cash—no carbon tax?" I nodded guiltily. "Or leave your AC running when you're not at home? Or stand around an unregistered campfire? You ever buy and consume illegal drugs, for which there is no regulated carbon tax? Of course you *fucking* do, every damn weekend. I've seen you. But you're in no danger of getting picked up on carbon violations. Why?" He raised his voice. "It's not a rhetorical question, Maddie. Why? Why won't you get arrested for that?"

I knew the answer, and desperately didn't want to say it, but he stared at me long enough that I finally did just to break the silence. "Because I'm white?"

"Well, at least you know that much." Gestas shook his head. "Do you know there's been a two-hundred-percent increase in prisoner deaths since AHICA started? Because how the fuck are we supposed to live on five bucks a day? People are starving to death in their own homes. We gotta rely on the kindness of strangers, or family, to feed us and house us—and so do you know how much that opens us up to abuse? Not everyone's got someone like Red looking out for them. If there's a single thing I'm grateful for, it's Red." He made a sound of disgust. *"Glad, grateful.* You know what? Get out." He pointed to the door. "I mean it, get the fuck out of here with that bootlicking bullshit."

I felt horrible, lower than dirt—like some nasty, pale grub that squirms *under* the dirt. I headed out quickly, so Gestas wouldn't see me cry. At least I wouldn't subject him to my white-lady tears. But I couldn't help them, thinking this was probably it for me and Bunny Bloodlust. Gestas would tell Red what an asshole I'd been, and neither of them would want anything to do with me anymore.

Just as I stepped out the door, I realized I still had *Pedagogy of the Oppressed* in my hand. I turned and held it back out to him, assuming he wouldn't want to lend me the book anymore. He held my gaze, started forward—but then something in him unspooled, and he waved a disinterested hand.

"Just read it," he said. "And give it back when you're done."

I started chapter one on the train ride home. And he was right. Freire blew my mind. And after reading that, it was really only a matter of time before I got fired from teaching public school.

13

Over the next six months, I read half a dozen of Gestas's books. After *Pedagogy of the Oppressed*, he gave me *Assata: An Autobiography* by Assata Shakur and Angela Davis's *Are Prisons Obsolete?* and Marcus Osaka's post-AHICA follow up, *Is AHICA Obsolete?* He'd most recently given me Marx's *Communist Manifesto*, but only as a precursor to the book he *really* wanted me to read—Cedric J. Robinson's *Black Marxism*. I started identifying as an abolitionist, and I wasn't sure the word *Democrat* really described my politics anymore. I still hadn't put any of that theory to good use though, not in my classroom or in life. But I told myself I was still in a "learning" phase, and I'd get to activism, and living my new, radical values later on, when I had a better idea what they were.

I knew enough now, though, to understand that Angel had stepped in some shit when he called Gestas a *liberal*.

Gestas launched into it, how no, he was an anarchist, not a fucking liberal. And how Democrats were shills and disaster capitalists and greenwashing fossil-fuel bitches and war profiteers. And finally, Angel interrupted him.

"But you're going to vote for Donnelly, right? In the election?"

Gestas let out a huff of exasperation. "Why should I vote for a party that wants to lock me up and steal my labor and start wars all around the globe just because poor people are organizing to feed themselves, while the rich glut themselves on carbon and—"

"So you're gonna vote Republican?"

"No, I'm not voting for Horneck! He's a full-on fucking fascist."

"You know, if it weren't for the Democrats, you wouldn't be able to vote at all. Being, you know . . ." He gestured at Gestas's arm. "Democrats passed the AHICA Votes Act a few years ago. I mean, aren't you glad—"

"Oh fuck," I said. "Not the G-word."

Gestas caught my eye and barked a laugh, then laid into Angel—same schpiel he'd given me earlier that year about *glad* and *gratitude* to the Democratic party. Even as Gestas was tearing into him, Angel wore this adoring look on his face, like he just couldn't take his eyes off the man in the pink dress. I got up and stretched, couldn't watch, couldn't take the secondhand embarrassment anymore. There was a rustling at the edge of the cane, and Peter and Mike Algebra emerged, each carrying one of Fish's heavy legs. A moment later two folks from the YumYums appeared, carrying Fish by the arms. It was good they'd brought him back—at least Fish wouldn't be murdered or eaten by a coyote or something. I didn't feel even a flicker of guilt for not helping them out. I just felt tired.

Inside the Lab, the Fun Machine lay mutilated in a million shards littering the last of the open floor space. Red sat on a couch with xir arm around the piccolo player from Third Host, the cute one with the heart-shaped face and long, pink hair. Red spotted me, pulled the girl in closer, and they started making out. Suddenly, everything in the Lab looked like garbage. The overlapping graffiti on the walls made me want to puke. Even the people—everyone who'd earlier seemed so cool and exciting and charming—now, in the buzzing overhead lights, they all looked cheap and sallow and sloppy-drunk. Even Red.

14

The party we threw to ring in the new decade had been a true rager. When I crawled out of bed midafternoon the next day, it was just me, Gestas, and Red who were up—my favorite configuration. We were out on the "porch," really just a slab of poured concrete in the front of the Lab, because the cold felt weirdly helpful for our hangovers. I was perched cross-legged in the broken rocking chair, a blanket around my shoulders, holding a stack of vocabulary quizzes I couldn't quite bring myself to grade. Like me, Gestas was bundled under hat-gloves-puffy-coat-and-blanket, but Red was wearing only a tattered, old Blondie T-shirt and plaid boxers, drinking a hair-of-the-dog Natty Light.

"How are you not freezing?" Gestas demanded.

"Feels good," Red said, spreading xir arms wide, like xe was embracing the stone-gray, overcast sky and the weedy lawn, still trashed with burned-out sparklers and abandoned cans of beer. "I'm gonna remember this feeling next August."

"You'll catch your death of cold," I said in a jokey, schoolmarm voice.

"Can't wait," xe said.

Red joked like that all the time—little comments about expecting or wanting to die young. I never knew how to respond. I hated when xe said that stuff.

Gestas caught my eye. "Xe doesn't mean it, you know? It's just xe can't help being a tragically emo Zinkr-Queer."

"Zinkr-Queer?" I repeated, at the same time as Red yelled, "How dare you?!" in faux outrage. I knew Zinkr was a social media blogging site that had been popular five or six years ago, but I'd never used it much.

"When Red was in high school," Gestas leaned forward eagerly, "Xe had this Zinkr blog that was all black and pink, with a border of twirling skulls, and xe'd post up the cheesiest screamo song lyrics."

Red was pinching xir lips into a line and staring hard at the floor of the porch. "If I remember correctly," xe said, "you must've thought my Zinkr was pretty cool, because *you* were the one who followed *me*, and you commented uwu emoticons on all those song lyrics."

"Hang on," I said. "You guys met online?" I racked my memories. "I don't think I knew that."

"We did indeed meet on Zinkr, maybe like—junior year of high school, I think?" Gestas settled back onto the patio couch and pulled the quilt closer around his shoulders.

"Were you sneaking out to Blazing Saddles with xim?" I asked, remembering Red's stories about picking up older lesbians at the queer dance hall.

"Hell no, I was *good* in high school. Straight As and debate team," Gestas said.

"This was when you were living in Spring Branch?" I asked. That was a northern suburb, and Red had gone to La Porte High School, way to the south. "So you two were like an hour-and-a-half drive apart. How'd you go from Zinkr mutuals to living together?"

"Well, first, Red started dating my cousin," Gestas said.

Red's face darkened. "Natalie." Xe scowled. "I *did* pick her up at Blazing Saddles."

"She was a piece of work," Gestas concurred. "We don't talk anymore, not since we all lived together."

"You *all* lived together? Like, you, Natalie, and Red?" I was trying not to show it, but I was reeling from the intel that Red had once had a serious girlfriend—one xe *lived* with, even. I'd never seen Red spend more than a week involved with anyone.

"They took me in when my mom kicked me out," Gestas said. "I was pretty psyched to be living with DeathOctave666 all of a sudden," he added, bobbing his head towards Red.

"Your mom kicked you out?" I repeated. "That's so awful. Was it—because . . ." I trailed off, suddenly unsure if it was too invasive to ask the reason why.

"Because of all this?" Gestas said, stroking his beard dramatically, like a cartoon villain. "Yeah. But what's wild is, two years earlier, she'd left my dad when we all thought I was just a lesbian. He was shitty about it, in the way you'd kinda expect from a Baptist preacher. Mom stuck up for me. But then a few years later, when I figured out that actually I *like* boys, and that gender and sexuality are different things—"

"Thanks, in large part, to Zinkr forums," Red added, gesturing towards Gestas with an unlit cigarette.

"Facts," Gestas said, holding up both hands. "I never said I wasn't a tragic Zinkr-Queer too. Anyways, when I came out to Mom as trans, she couldn't handle it. Said she was fine if I wanted to be gay, but transitioning was 'defying God's plan' for me and 'mutilating His creation.'"

I searched Gestas's face for signs of lingering pain, but his tone was mocking, and if he still felt hurt by his mother's rejection of him, he'd buried it deep down.

"That's awful. I'm so sorry."

He shrugged. "Anyways, Natalie and Red had just moved in together—"

"After like a *month* of dating," Red mumbled, shaking xir head in frustration with xir former self.

"Me and Natalie were close because we were the only queer cousins in the family. So she and Red took me in," Gestas said, beaming at Red. "I slept on their couch for two years."

"You were with this girl for *two years?*" I asked—way too intensely. I hadn't meant to reveal that I was dying to hear every detail of this relationship.

"A year and a half. The last six months, we'd already broken up, but we had to ride out the lease," Red grumbled.

"Oof," I said.

"You have no idea," Gestas said meaningfully.

Red was hugging xirself and shivered, whether from the memory or the cold, I didn't care. "This is ridiculous," I said. "Would you please put on a coat? My teacher brain is exploding. It's like thirty-three degrees out."

"Fine," Red said, rolling xir eyes dramatically, and xe squeezed next to Gestas on the patio couch and tried to steal his blanket. Gestas protested sharing, and they squabbled over the quilt like siblings until Gestas finally relented and let Red huddle up with him.

"You were saying—" I said, trying to seem only casually interested, "That Natalie was a piece of work."

"She was passive-aggressive and a pathological liar. Lied about the most random little stuff, like she'd be all, 'I did the dishes yesterday,' to us, and we were like, 'Uhhh . . . we were here. No, you did not. There's your mac-and-cheese bowl in the sink.'"

"She lied about big stuff too," Red said, finishing xir beer with one last, long swig.

"Right, that too. She cheated on xim," Gestas said. "With our coworker."

"Two, actually," Red said, waggling a couple fingers.

"And she turned out to be a shitty transphobe."

"What, really?" I said. "But she let you move in when your mom kicked you out for being trans?"

"She was okay with *Gestas* being trans," Red explained.

"But then I infected you with my transness!" Gestas said and lunged for Red, tickling xir armpits. Red arched xir back and giggled in a register I'd *never* heard come out of xim.

"Stop! Stop!" xe cried, and Gestas immediately relented.

"Is that what she said?" I asked, horrified.

"Those were her exact words. *Infected*," Red said. "But she only brought it up after I caught her cheating. She blamed it on my transition. She said being nonbinary was a trend, and she wasn't going to indulge my 'delusions' by calling me 'made-up' pronouns," Red said, tracing air quotes.

"All pronouns were made up at some time or other!" Gestas cried, splaying both hands, which caused the blanket to slip. Red made a noise of protest and gathered the quilt higher on xir shoulders. A cold drizzle had started falling beyond the overhang covering the porch.

"That's so weird to me. Both your mom and Natalie were cool with you being gay, but not the gender stuff?" I said.

"You know that's like . . . *super* common, right?" Red said. I shook my head in ignorance. "Well, it is. It's a whole thing."

"The gender binary is an essential prop to white supremacist capitalism, so challenging that is more threatening to people who have not divested their sense of self from kyriarchy," Gestas said, like his point was so obvious, it barely warranted being explained. I knitted my eyebrows and nodded as though I understood.

"So wait," I said quietly, "*after* Natalie said all that awful stuff, and cheated on you, you had to keep living with her for six months?"

"Well, she only stuck around for two months, before she moved in with Todd-fucking-Morgansen," Red scowled. "After that she stopped paying rent, and I was on the hook, because my mom had actually cosigned the lease with me. Natalie wasn't on it at all because she had debt."

"And we didn't want to ask your mom for the money because it would've gotten her in trouble with your jackass stepdad," Gestas added.

"Yup," Red agreed.

I gasped. "Oh my gosh—is that when you started selling the fake carbon credits?"

Gestas nodded. "That's when I decided to get a side hustle to cover Natalie's share of the rent."

"He insisted," Red said. "*I* wanted to sell weed to make up the extra scratch, but noooo. Gestas thought it'd be safer to do the carbon-credit selling thing." Red shook xir head bitterly. "I'm so sorry, dude."

"I've told you not to say that," Gestas said testily. "I offered to sell the fake credits because I didn't want your mom to get screwed. Because she made us hot pot whenever we were sick."

"Sorry, I know—fuck! Sorry for saying sorry for saying sorry!"

Gestas shoved Red to the side with his shoulder. "You don't owe me *or* need to apologize. Our relationship is not transactional."

I got the sense that he really meant it. That this was all well-trodden ground, and Gestas held no bitterness towards Red for his arrest. But Red's face looked pained, like xe was roiling with guilt. Only much later would I learn just how much Red was suffering in secret to pay Gestas back for what he'd done.

"Wow," I breathed out. "*Fuck* Natalie."

"Fuck Natalie, indeed!" Red cried.

"Well," Gestas's head listed to one side. "Fuck landlords, and city officials who oppose low-income housing, and a capitalist society that requires you to labor for shelter in the first place—"

Red was glaring at him in exasperation, and Gestas caught the look.

"Okay, and also, fuck Natalie."

I counted back the timeline in my head. "So y'all broke up— what? A year and a half ago?"

"Two years ago," Red said. "And some change."

"And have you dated anyone since? Like, seriously?" I asked.

Red shook xir head, "Nope. I'm done with all that. Love is a trap. It's all about power and possession and control."

"'Love is a trap'?" I said. "Okay, now you *do* sound like an emo Zinkr-Queer."

Gestas busted out laughing, which always made me feel amazing.

"It is a trap!" Red protested. "Romantic love as it was defined by the fucking Victorians, anyways. You're always telling us to *decolonize our minds*," Red said to Gestas. "And my way of doing that is being an enormous slut."

"So you're polyamorous," I said, clinging to hope, suddenly asking myself, for the first time, if I could handle being in love with someone who had other partners. Jealousy flared in my chest.

"Uch, no. I said I was a slut, not poly." Red shook xir head. "Poly people have *multiple* serious relationships, just this tangled web of drama and endless conversations about feelings." Red made a face. "That's, like, exponentially worse."

"So, what?" I said, all my unspoken hopes balled up like a knot in my throat. "You're never going to be in a serious relationship again? You'll never fall in love? Because of this *Natalie*?"

"Never," Red said conclusively.

My heart cracked a little, but Gestas snorted in disbelief. "Never say never," he said. "After all, sometimes it even snows in Houston."

Gestas stared into the yard wistfully, and suddenly I realized there *was* something funny about the drizzle. It was falling too slowly or something, and it was more glittery than usual. It took my brain a few seconds to realize what was happening, because I hadn't seen the stuff since the last freak snowfall, when I was ten years old.

"No way," Red breathed, sloughing off the blanket and getting up. I shoved the stack of quizzes I'd totally forgotten to grade back in my school bag and followed. Red and I jumped down off the porch into the yard. Delicate, tiny crystals landed in Red's hair, glittering for an instant before melting.

Then, like the sad, Southern, snow-deprived kids we were, we started running around the yard, giggling excitedly. Red scooped up pathetic snowballs from the tiny drifts accumulating on the windshield of Fish's car and threw one at me. I dropped to the ground and tried to make a snow angel in the barely frosted grass, managing to completely soak my backside in ice water. When I got up, I opened my mouth to call Gestas to join us, before remembering a half second later that he couldn't. Gestas sat with just one leg dangling off the edge of the porch, one hand outstretched past the overhang, catching a few glittering flakes on his palm. Even though I hadn't said anything aloud, I cringed with guilt for forgetting that he couldn't leave the porch to enjoy the twice-in-a-lifetime snowfall.

I turned back to Red, who was trying to catch snowflakes on xir tongue. Xir lips were blue. I used my best teacher voice to bully xim back inside, where Gestas made us all a pot of tea. It took nearly an hour for Red's teeth to stop chattering, even after we'd piled half the blankets in the apartment on top of xim. By the time the snow stopped and night fell, Red was running a low fever. School had been cancelled across the city, so I decided to stay another night at the Lab. Peter and Vida had finally woken up, and Peter projected a movie on a bare patch of wall. We piled on couches, under lots of mildew-and-cigarette smelling blankets, to watch it. Red snuggled up against my side, claiming xe needed my body heat to stay warm. Xe refused to get up even when Fish finally appeared from upstairs and tried to squeeze between us. I told Fish to let it go and get his own spot because Red was sick.

I don't remember what the movie was—some old, cheesy sci-fi thing—because I couldn't possibly pay attention to it with Red pressed against my side. I kept running through the conversation we'd had earlier over and over in my mind, the pieces of Red's backstory finally coming into focus.

It wasn't that Red couldn't love, xe was just traumatized by a toxic ex. I didn't buy that xe *really* believed "love is a trap." Maybe it was residual magical thinking from my Bible-beating days, but

I believed Red had said that for my benefit. To see how I'd react. To dare me to prove xim wrong.

Red had fallen asleep in the crook of my arm halfway through the movie, xir body radiating unnatural heat. The physical contact was dizzying, and I desperately wanted to fall asleep there. When we woke up the next morning, in each other's arms, Red would be in love with me. People would gossip about the two of us—about how we'd "slept together." They'd speculate, and the rumors would freak out Fish, and maybe I wanted that.

But no, the timing wasn't right. Fish was still our landlord and promoter. And maybe he was just a convenient excuse to keep me from proving the as-yet abstract concept of my queerness. I was trying to unlearn compulsive heteronormativity and internalized homophobia and all that, but only in an intellectual way. I treasured my fantasies of kissing Red and falling into bed with xim, but the idea of actually *doing* those things still scared the hell out of me. I had this hunch that if I ever gave into those desires, everything about my life and even my sense of self would get blasted away. And what if I was wrong about Red's feelings for me? What if I wound up being just another one-night stand to xim? What, if anything, would be left of me in Red's wake?

So even though it was the polar opposite of what my heart and my body wanted, when the movie's credits rolled, I extricated my arm from underneath Red's head, eased up off the couch, and headed back upstairs to fall asleep in Fish's bed.

15

As they sucked each other's tonsils, Red braced one hand on the other side of the pink-haired groupie, and she hooked a leg around xir hip, pulling xim prone on top of her on the couch cushions. I didn't even feel the familiar stabs of jealousy, just a bone-deep tiredness. I was thinking that the next time Red ran into a snowstorm in a T-shirt, I would let xim freeze to death, like xe wanted.

I trudged upstairs to Fish's apartment and kicked out some guys smoking weed on the couch and a couple who were dry humping on his bed. After they left, I locked the front door, for once. As I peed, it hit me how disgusting the bathroom was. Thick cobwebs crowded the ceiling. Paint peeled and molded around the tub that had leaked for months before Angel fixed it. Four dead cockroaches lay belly-up around the corners, one of them still pitifully cycling its serrated legs in the air. Nastiest of all, the toilet bowl was stained a collage of browns from thousands of drunk shits. It had never been cleaned, not once in this long, exhausting year.

In Fish's bedroom, I glanced out the window and saw Gestas and Angel making out on the back loading dock. The two of them together didn't make any fucking sense to me, but I was glad they'd found a little comfort in each other. Someone should kiss a soldier the night before they go off to war. I'd never seen either Gestas or Angel hook up with anybody before. Both of them were very selective about who they spent time with. Not like Red. Why the hell had my heart stuck itself on xim?

I couldn't face sleep yet, so I just wandered around, examining all the damage we'd done in the past year with fresh eyes. The hardwood floors were torn up from skateboarding inside and lazily dragged-around furniture. There were holes in the walls where angry men had punched through plaster. Every surface in the kitchen was filthy and crusty and broke-down *nasty*, despite the fact that I'd never seen Fish cook an actual meal. Nothing ever got cleaned here. Everything just got more degraded. Part of me wanted to hop a maglev home to my apartment in my shiny Community tower and never come back. Except no, I didn't. Community towers all felt like soul-sucking voids. And besides, the trains had stopped running an hour back.

And that's how I was feeling—that everything was doomed and over and empty—when I saw the red envelope lying on top of the pile of mail in the corner of the kitchen counter. "URGENT: THIRD NOTICE" was stamped on the front in block letters. It was addressed to Fisher Wellman, and it was from the Texas Department of Transportation. I got a deep-down bad feeling looking at that letter from TxDOT. And I was pissed enough at Fish to slide a finger under the flap and read his mail.

I had a hard time understanding the letter, partly because I was still buzzed, partly because it was written in bureaucratic legalese. But by the end, its point was horribly clear. TxDOT had decided to expand the eastbound hyperway that ran just south of the Lab, and that meant the Lab must go. Notice of eminent domain. Immediate eviction. The period of public commentary had already passed. Demolition crews would arrive August 21. I checked the date on my phone. That was in a week. The Lab, this community, our world—all of it would fall beneath bulldozers and wrecking balls in one fucking week.

II.
THE FREE PEOPLE'S VILLAGE

16

I lay awake for hours that night, feeling like my heart was rotting away in my chest. Eventually I gave up trying to sleep and started researching the hyperway expansion on my phone. I never looked at Houston's local news. It made me panicky to read about all those road-rage shootings and angry dads murdering their families. So I'd missed the story of the hyperway expansion, even though it had been making headlines for months. There was a coalition of non-profits fighting it, headed by a group called Save the Eighth, and some property owners were suing TxDOT. By dawn, I'd hatched a plan to join the fight, and it gave me enough peace to doze for a few hours.

I woke up again around eleven o'clock—still early for the morning after a big show. Coming down the stairwell, I caught that pink-haired girl sneaking out of Red's apartment. She flashed me a conspiratorial grin, which I did not return. It was all I could do not to yell "fuck off" to her. But I knew she didn't deserve that.

Someone—probably Peter—had remembered to cut the AC off before dawn. Through the open back cargo doors, fluffy heads of cane glowed gold in the late-morning sun. Up in the rafters, paper wasps dragged their long legs through the air, hunting for spiders. It was already getting uncomfortably hot. Lorenzo was curled up in the bumper car, Mike Algebra snored on a filthy divan, and a dozen more kids sprawled across all the couches, sleeping off hangovers. The shards of the Fun Machine crunched under my boots.

I found Fish lying slumped against the back wall. Someone had drawn a Juggalo clown design on his face in Sharpie.

"Hey," I said, fanning the envelope from TxDOT in front of his face. "Wake up." He groaned and rubbed an arm over his nose without opening his eyes. I started nudging his feet with my boots. "I mean it, get up."

"What?" he snarled, cracking an eyelid. It took a second for him to register where he was—and *when* he was. "Fuck. What time is it?"

"After our set. *Way* after, if that's what you're wondering."

He groaned and slumped forward, putting his head into his hands.

"Mike Algebra filled in for you. It was our best show ever, actually."

"Fuck you," he groaned.

"Real nice," I said. "That's how you talk to your girlfriend?"

"What girlfriend?" he moaned, rolling to one side and slumping down further so he could lie flat on the floor. "It's not like we do anything anymore."

"Fish," I sighed. For an instant I was tempted to take the bait, just end it all there. But if I dumped him today, how would I get him to go along with my plan? How could I save the Lab, if the guy who owned it wasn't my boyfriend anymore? So instead I said, "Listen, you owe us for last night. And for *this*. You recognize this?" I held the letter up in front of his face.

He snatched it out of my hand and rolled up to a seat—clutched his head in pain for a few moments—then started to read.

"Fuck," he said when he reached the bottom.

"Did you know about this? It says *third* notice. Did you get the other two?"

"Maddie, come on, you know I'm not awesome at staying on top of the mail."

"Fish, what the hell? People live here! They're counting on you! You have to tell them what's happening!"

From across the room, someone yelled, "Keep it down!" But Lorenzo was sitting up and squinting at me, combing back his long hair with his fingers.

Fish staggered to his feet. "Can't this wait until after coffee?" He headed towards the apartments. After getting halfway across the Lab, he looked down at his feet. "What the hell—" He crunched on the pieces of the Fun Machine. "What is all this shit?" he said, raising his voice.

"Red smashed the Fun Machine," I said. My voice caught in my throat. I know it sounds silly, but I felt real grief for the organ, almost like it'd been a friend.

"What the fuck—why?" Fish yelled.

"Because of you!" I snapped back. "You were hounding xim about getting rid of it before the show, remember? And then you disappeared, and, I don't know . . . Red got pissed off. About lots of things."

"Well, xe didn't have to leave such a big fucking mess," Fish grumbled, kicking away a keyboard key. "I'm not cleaning this shit up."

I followed him through the door to the apartments. "You're just going to go back to sleep, aren't you?" I asked, as he headed upstairs.

"Look, I feel like shit. I just got some fucked up news. I need a little sleep before I can deal with any of this."

"No, Fish. There are things you have to do *today*. Starting with telling your tenants that the Lab is getting knocked down in a week!"

"What's this now?"

Back from a run, Angel stood in the front doorway in only shorts and sneakers, his muscled, waxed torso slick with sweat, like a golden-skinned god.

"They're expanding the hyperway," I said, flapping the red envelope in Angel's direction. "According to this, we have a week to vacate the property."

"What the—? Do Red and Gestas know about this?" Angel asked.

"Oh my god, can it wait a few hours?" Fish started back up the steps.

"Can what wait?" Vida stood in the door to her and Peter's apartment.

Angel rushed inside Red and Gestas's place to wake them up.

"We need to have a house meeting," I said. Fish rubbed his hand over his face and groaned.

17

Ten minutes later, all the tenants of the Lab gathered in Red and Gestas's living room. Our other friends were either headed back to their own places or smoking out on the back cargo deck. Lorenzo had biked off with the leftover carbon credits from the party to buy a mess of breakfast tacos for everyone.

As everyone took their seats, the mood was one of restrained giddiness. Fish still hadn't noticed the clown drawing on his face, and no one had cared to inform him. But as he began to explain what was going on, the vibe grew deathly somber. "So, apparently the state is buying out the property, and I don't get a say in it. I'm sorry, everyone, okay? Is that what you want to hear? I'm really fucking sorry I didn't find out sooner. But it's not like there's anything I could've done."

"Actually, there is," I said. "I spent all night researching. People are fighting this hyperway! Fish, you need to talk to your lawyer and see if you can join the lawsuit against TxDOT."

"I don't have a lawyer."

"Then you need to get one."

"I don't know, Maddie," Fish whined. "All that seems really expensive."

"Aren't you a millionaire?" Vida asked.

"Well, technically, yeah, but not like—liquid assets. Look, CarbonSwap has a lot of competitors now. The new patch isn't ready. And the Lab is a carbon pit! Do y'all have any idea what the carbon taxes are on this place each month?"

"So, what are you saying? You'll be glad to be rid of it?" Gestas asked, staring Fish down, his mouth pressed into a thin line.

"What? No . . . But I just don't know if I can fight the government on this right now!"

"What the fuck, Fish? You know if I can't get on a lease, I get transferred to a brick-and-mortar prison!" Gestas shouted.

"That's not going to happen," Angel said, glaring at Fish. "Right?"

"Right, right," Fish said, glancing away from his alpha-male hero. "If the Lab gets knocked down, we'll—we'll find someplace else to live. I promise."

Gestas snorted. I didn't believe Fish either. If the Lab got knocked down, I could see *Fisher Wellman* running back to his daddy's house out in Katy and never looking back at us.

"It's not very big, but worst case, you can always stay with me at my apartment," I offered. Gestas shot me a half smile, and I made up my mind.

"Look, it doesn't take any money just to *talk* to a lawyer, right?" I told Fish in my sweetest voice, my *girlfriend* voice. I laid a hand on his arm. It was the most I'd touched him in weeks. "Just talk to somebody today, okay? Find out your options. You own the property. You have legal rights to fight this."

Fish held my gaze, and I wondered if he could see right through me. Finally he said, "Yeah, okay. I guess I can talk to someone."

I felt gross and phony, returning his smile. But I reminded myself that I wasn't putting on this act for Fish. It was for Gestas, and the Lab, and all our lives here.

"Before you talk to a lawyer, Fish, you might wanna"—Vida made a swirling motion in front of his face—"look in the mirror."

"Wha—" Fish headed into the bathroom, then roared a moment later, seeing the Juggalo mask. "Which one of you assholes—"

"It wasn't any of us," I called. At least, I didn't think it was. Even Red wasn't *that* immature, although xe was snickering pretty hard.

"Better get scrubbing," Red called. The faucet in the bathroom whooshed on.

"We can fight this too," I said. "Even though we're not owners—"

"You're not even a renter." Red scowled. "You're just the land-lord's girlfriend. I don't know why this even involves you."

Vida mouthed "ouch" at me.

So Red was still pissed about last night. I shook my head, bit back the hurt, and kept going. "There's this group, Save the Eighth, meeting at the South Davis Baptist Church tonight at six. They're fighting to stop the hyperway, so let's all go together!"

I looked around hopefully, but no one met my eyes. Peter sucked air through his teeth. "Sorry, I've got work," he said. Peter bartended downtown most nights.

"I really, truly, wish I could," Angel said. "But I have to get going in the next hour. You know"—he swung his arm cheesily—"off to war." No one laughed. Gestas looked like he was going to throw up. Red stared blankly at the ceiling. Tears sprung to my eyes again, but I blinked them away.

"Right, of course," I said.

"I also cannot attend. Obviously." Gestas swept a Vanna White gesture beneath the glowing AHICA tracker in his shoulder.

I looked to Red, who shook xir head. "I'm not going to that shit. It's pointless. If the government is coming for this place, there's nothing we can do. It's over. Felt it coming, anyways." Xe headed for the door, pulling a pack of cigarettes from xir back pocket.

"You can't be serious," I said, heat rising up the back of my neck. "You're just gonna give up? Before doing literally anything?"

"You. Don't. Even. Live. Here," Red said, whacking the pack against xir wrist with each word. Xir eyes flicked up and down my body, dismissively. "And we don't need *you* to save us." With that, xe disappeared through the door. I slumped back down on the couch. What did xe mean by that? Was it a crack about me being white? Was I doing a white-savior complex here?

Vida was the only one who hadn't spoken. She opened her mouth, hesitated, then sighed. "I have a meeting for the RadArt Collective at four, but I should be able to come to your thing after. Might be a little late."

I smiled back gratefully.

Fish blasted through the door of the bathroom, now wearing a gray and melted-looking clown face. "This shit isn't coming off."

"Try rubbing alcohol," Gestas said.

"Right," Fish snapped, disappearing behind the door.

Gestas turned to me. "So you're gonna go to a Save the Eighth meeting? At a Baptist church?" He was biting back a smile. I didn't see what was so funny.

"Yeah . . . so?"

"No, it's just . . ." He could barely contain his giggles. "I wish I could go with you. Be a fly on the wall. I really do." I didn't get what he thought was so funny. Maybe because this would be my first time inside a church since I'd lost my faith?

"Oh shit, is that your Dad's church?" I asked, remembering Gestas's dad was a Baptist preacher.

"No," he said, shaking his head gleefully. "Never mind."

I couldn't puzzle over Gestas's meaning for long, though, because Angel announced it was past time for him to head back to Fort Hood. Then everyone was tearing up again, and we all took turns hugging him tight. Red tried to give him only a half wave in the hallway, but Angel picked xim up and held xim in a long, one-sided hug, Red's arms squished flat at xir sides.

Angel and Gestas stayed talking in the open front doorway for a long time after that, heads close together. The rest of us headed into the Lab to give them some privacy, and then Angel was gone. I tried not to wonder whether I'd ever see him again.

18

After Lorenzo got back, and we devoured the breakfast tacos, I went home to my Community to rest up before the Save the Eighth meeting. I swiped my card to pass through the high wrought-iron gate that surrounded our Community's gardens. In the citrus orchard, the tangerines looked ripe, so I picked a few to stuff into my bag, feeling guilty that I'd skipped my last two gardening shifts. In the lobby of the tower, some of my neighbors were milling around, schmoozing before their yoga class started. They shot dirty looks my way—I wasn't sure if it was because of my obvious hangover or because I never attended these Community meet-ups. I only knew the names of my nearest neighbors on the seventh floor.

Inside my apartment, dirty dishes from microwaved meals were stacked up in the sink. A pile of essays glared at me from the counter. I had planned to spend the day grading, but that would have to wait. It wasn't like my students were punctual about turning in their homework. Why should I be punctual about grading them?

Suddenly my brain made the connection—that the hyperway was cutting through the entire Eighth Ward, where I taught. I wondered if any of my students were facing eviction, and what their families were planning to do about it. Surely going to the Save the Eighth meeting was a better way to fight for them than grading their half-assed, barely coherent paragraphs on "the significance of the character Boo Radley in *To Kill a Mockingbird*."

I felt so grimy that I allowed myself a long, fifteen-minute shower, figuring I could splurge on the carbon, just this once. My hangover still pounded in my skull, so I decided to nap until the meeting. I set an alarm on the window-dimmer, and the glass turned black. I passed out as soon as my head hit the pillow. When I awoke to a blaze of light, the sun was already low on the horizon, glinting off of other Communities and gilding the prairies of Midtown in rose gold.

Back in the Ward, my GPS led me to an old movie theater rather than the church I was expecting. I hopped my bike onto the sidewalk and double-checked the address on my phone. Finally I realized the marquis didn't list movie titles—it said "Jesus Saves!" in black plastic letters. This *was* the Baptist church. I folded my bike into my shoulder bag and headed in.

As soon as my eyes adjusted to the darkness inside the old, one-screen theater, I knew why Gestas had snickered at the idea of me coming here. There were maybe three dozen people inside, chatting in the front rows of seats or schmoozing up on the stage. Every one of them was at least ten years older than me, and every one of them was Black. I don't know why it hadn't occurred to me that there wouldn't be any other white people at this meeting—but it hadn't. I looked around for Vida but didn't spot her.

My heart started pounding with shyness, plus that other feeling—that monstrous, I'm-an-invader-here feeling. For a moment, I thought about turning around, bolting back to the Lab, and forgetting this ever happened. But a bunch of people had turned their heads when I'd entered, and now they were squinting at me curiously. How would it look if I just fucking *fled*? So I forced myself to walk down the center aisle. One of the younger-looking people—and by that I mean mid thirties—jumped off the stage and approached me. She had light brown skin and freckles, and twists that reached her mid-back, black at the roots and gold at the tips.

"Hey," she said. "What, um . . ." Her eyebrows scrunched up at me. "I'm sorry—What are you doing here?"

"I'm here for the Save the Eighth meeting?"

"Oh, okay!" she said, sounding confused but cheerful. "Cool. Well. I'm Shayna, she/her. I'm one of the organizers with Save the Eighth."

"Maddie. She/her also."

"What, uh . . . what brought you out here today?"

"Yeah, so I live at—well, actually my boyfriend and all my bandmates—live at this place at the end of Calcott Street. It's—we call it 'the Lab,' um—4121 Calcott?"

"Ohhhh, yeah. That makes sense. Yeah, I'm aware of that place."

"Oh, okay! It's great, right? We throw shows, and art installations, and we're trying to get a community garden going. It's like a cool, art-hub thing."

"I'm sure it is—a cool, art-hub thing," she said, waving a hand vaguely. "What *I* know about it is y'all play loud-as-hell music until four a.m. on *school* nights, keeping up kids and people who've got to work, and y'all leave empty beer bottles lying around your front yard. Is that the place?"

My face must've turned beet red. My stomach roiled with shame.

"Well, anyways," she said, "I guess it's cool you showed up to this, since you *do* live in the Ward. Or—what was it—your boyfriend lives here?"

At the word *boyfriend,* I wanted to cease to exist. But I just nodded, and thankfully, Shayna turned and headed back to the stage to call the meeting to order.

I tried to disappear into a seat behind all the other organizers, but to my horror, Shayna called everyone onstage for an opening meditation. She told us to form a circle and hold hands. My hands were cold and sweaty from anxiety, so I felt bad for the

115

middle-aged woman and the gray-haired guy on either side of me who had to hold them. Then Shayna had us close our eyes and instructed us to center ourselves. I followed along, taking long, steady breaths. Maybe me being here was fine. After all, I *was* trying to help our community, help keep Gestas—who was actually from the Ward—from being evicted. But another part of my brain hissed, "Gentrifier!" It knew that me being here was 99 percent selfish, that I just wanted to keep crashing at a party house, playing shows to giant crowds, so I could feel like a rock star. I didn't give a shit about the Eighth Ward, not like these people did.

Lost in these thoughts, I missed half of Shayna's instructions for the next activity. Something about naming powerful, Black leaders who inspired us maybe? To invoke their spirits, she'd said? We were still holding hands, and people were saying names, as they felt moved to. "Harriet Tubman," the man to my right boomed out. Across the circle someone called, "Nina Simone!" Someone else named "Fred Hampton," who I knew about from that Assata Shakur autobiography that Gestas had loaned me. Then it was "Barbara Jordan," whose name sounded kind of familiar, but I couldn't place it. I peeked around, but everyone's head was bowed. Were we *all* supposed to say someone? Was it rude of me *not* to participate?

That autobiography of Assata Shakur had really blown my mind. She'd been a member of the Black Panther Party in the 1960s, and she'd watched the FBI and police murder her friends one by one for doing "dangerous, anti-American" stuff like making sure the kids in their neighborhoods got breakfast. After being falsely accused of crimes six times, on such flimsy evidence that the cases were all dismissed or acquitted, Assata was charged with the murder of a police officer in a shootout instigated by law enforcement, despite clear evidence that she hadn't used the gun in question. She detailed her time in prison—where she was forced to give birth in shackles—and her eventual escape to Cuba. I'd torn through the memoir, feeling like I understood for the first time why people said ACAB—All Cops Are Bastards.

During that Save the Eighth meditation, I figured I'd name Assata Shakur, who was radical as hell. Maybe if I named her, Shayna would know that I was not just some miserable, white gentrifier party kid. I was a miserable, white, gentrifier party kid *who had read Assata Shakur's autobiography.* So when the names started dwindling down, and I was about the only person who hadn't spoken, I summoned up my most confident voice and said, "Assata Shakur."

There was a heartbeat of silence, and then everyone's heads whipped in my direction. Shayna scrunched her face up at me, and I knew I'd somehow fucked up terribly. And then someone across the circle said, "Assata Shakur is *alive.*"

"Yes," Shayna said, not even looking at me, like she couldn't stand the sight of such clownery. "We are naming *ancestors.* Sister Assata is still very much alive in Cuba, and doing good works in the world, and we are so grateful for her."

Fuck. So that's what everyone they'd been naming had in common. Now I remembered Shayna saying something about "invoking ancestors" when she was explaining the exercise, and I was only half listening. Ancestors meant *already dead.* Why the hell couldn't I have paid attention? Or just kept my damn mouth shut?

After what felt like an eternity, we were finally allowed to drop our hands and go back to our seats. Every fiber in my body wanted to run the fuck out of that theater and get blackout drunk and forget any of this had happened. But the shame of running away like that might've actually killed me.

It took Shayna a good five minutes to quiet down the crowd once they were back in their seats. Everyone seemed to know everyone else, except me, and folks leaned across aisles to catch up. Despite the seriousness of what we were all here for, the mood was party-like. A clump of women in their seventies, in matching "Save the Eighth!" T-shirts were particularly rowdy, howling with laughter at each other's jokes until Shayna pulled out a megaphone and blasted a siren two times.

Shayna handed the meeting over to her co-organizer, Toussaint, a tall, dark-skinned guy wearing a dashiki and frayed jeans. He was on the younger side of the crowd too, maybe late thirties, but his dreadlocks were already graying at the roots. He gave an overview of the status of the hyperway expansion. What the state legislature had said, and how City Council had responded, and who on TxDOT had been bought out by which contractors, and which groups were working on what to try and prevent the expansion. I tried to pay attention, although all the bureaucratic details were mind-numbing, and every time Toussaint looked my way, perceiving me, my brain went, *Assata Shakur is alive!*

What I did manage to gather was that this fight over the hyperway expansion had been going on for years, that Toussaint and Shayna and the other people in this room had worked very hard for a long time, exploring every possible option for stopping the construction, and every one of their efforts, to date, had failed. Many of the people in the room lived in houses that were slated to be torn down. And these weren't band houses they'd crashed at for a year, but *homes* their families had lived in for decades, even generations.

I also learned that the expanded hyperway wasn't just adding a few lanes to the existing one. It was going to be a massive transportation clusterfuck out to the suburbs—with commuter trains, expanded hyperway lanes, express lanes, and, running beneath it all, fiber-optic cable, electrical lines, and the dirty secret at the heart of all that "green" infrastructure—an oil pipeline.

When the original hyperway was first built in 2005, TxDOT had torn down just a few homes for the pylons that supported it. But the real damage to the neighborhood had come from how it routed traffic right over the Ward. No one stopped for gas or a bite to eat in the Eighth anymore, restaurants and grocery stores closed down, and it became a food desert. Now this new expansion promised to deal a killing blow to the already struggling neighborhood, cutting the Eighth in half and tearing down hundreds of homes.

Shayna took over the meeting again, showing us how to log on to an app that would call a series of lawmakers for us. Then she had us spread out around the theater so our voices wouldn't overlap. I took a seat in the very back, close as I could get to the doors. I was barely coherent on my first call to the Texas Railroad Commission as I tried to remember the talking points from Toussaint's presentation. Shayna had stressed we should speak from the heart, share our "personal reasons" for opposing the hyperway. But mine—that my band would break up and my friends would have to move out—seemed way too petty to mention.

While the phone was ringing for the second call, the doors swung open and Vida stepped through. She didn't see me right away, as I was off to her side, but she marched right down the middle aisle and hugged Shayna. Vida looked around the room, waving excitedly at Toussaint and a couple other people who she clearly knew. Just as the Houston City Council Member's voicemail picked up, Vida spotted me. She told Shayna, "I'm gonna go say hi to my friend!" Shayna made a funny face when she saw I was the friend Vida was talking about.

I left a quick message for the council member before hanging up and hugging Vida like a drowning person hugs a life raft.

"Sorry I'm late!" she said.

"It's fine!" I said, meaning it. I was glad she hadn't seen me make an ass of myself during the meditation. "It seems like you know everyone here! Have you been to these meetings?"

"No, but Shayna is the girlfriend of this chick who worked on Artcrawl Bike Experiment. And Toussaint and Keila and Nichelle are just like . . . I don't know, they're just in the *scene*, you know? So anyways, what are we doing? Catch me up!"

I showed her how to access the app, and we made calls together for the next half hour. Vida's booming voice, full of righteous passion, often cut across the entire theater. She was so good at her messaging, and I tried copying some of her phrases while I stammered through my phone calls.

By the time the meeting ended, I was feeling total social-anxiety overload. As people filtered out of the hall, Vida lingered, apologizing to Shayna and Toussaint for coming late. Standing around with them, I felt acutely aware of myself as an ignorant, white, gentrifying clown, and all I wanted was to turn into slime and ooze away into the cracks in the floorboards.

But the fact that Vida was friends with me must've meant something to Shayna, because before we left, she asked me my name again.

"Maddie," I said.

"Maddie, right. Well, thanks for showing up to the fight. You're in it now. So we'll see you at the next meeting?"

My heart dropped into my stomach. I had just been focusing on getting through this one. I hadn't considered that there'd be indefinite future meetings, and therefore that the Assata Shakur moment would haunt me forever. But I said, "Of course." Because of course I'd come to the next one. If I didn't, I'd prove all of Shayna's worst assumptions about me.

19

meant to go home after the meeting to write lesson plans. But Vida convinced me to go back to Calcott with her for a drink and a bowl of some vegan frijoles a la charra Peter was cooking. Everybody was hanging out in the Lab, except Red, who was at xir barbacking job. Fish was wearing a suit I didn't even know he owned, with the jacket thrown over the back of the couch and a tie loosened around his neck. He'd spent all day with lawyers, filing to join the lawsuit against TxDOT. From what he'd gathered, there wasn't much hope of saving the property. Best-case scenario, the property owners might win a bigger settlement from the government.

"Maybe even millions," Fish said excitedly. "And if that happens, I can buy another building. We'll just start the Lab somewhere else!" He was rosy cheeked and on his third beer.

"How'd the Save the Eighth meeting go?" Gestas asked, eyes twinkling with amusement, right as I was taking a spoonful of bean soup. I froze, midslurp.

"That bad, huh?" He laughed.

Vida explained about the calls we'd made, and all the political stuff we'd learned at the meeting. "So they're still trying, but even Shayna and Toussaint seem to think stopping the hyperway is pretty hopeless at this point."

I looked around the Lab, picturing all of it crushed into rubble. Vida's beautiful murals, all the curb-scrounged furniture and equipment, a million splinters of Fun Machine, still scattered across the floor, countless beer bottles, cigarette packs, and roaches—insect- and weed-related—in every nook and cranny. Part of me wanted to sob, and part of me was relieved at the thought of a fresh start.

"I guess we'd better start packing," I said.

Everyone groaned dramatically.

"Let's smoke this bowl first," Peter said, brandishing a large glass pipe full of sticky weed. That was my cue to leave. I was trying to smoke less for my asthma, plus I hadn't done any work for class on Monday. Even if I rushed home, I'd probably only catch five hours of sleep.

As I was heading out, Gestas caught me in the front hallway.

"What made you look like a ghost when I asked about the Save the Eighth meeting?"

I hadn't wanted him to find out about this, but then again, I loved making Gestas laugh. So I told him the whole humiliating story. What Shayna had said about the Lab, and how I'd called out "Assata Shakur" during the ancestor invocation.

Gestas was doubled over laughing by the time I finished. Even though I knew he was laughing *at* me, not with me, I had to join in. He slumped against the wall, wiping the tears streaming from his eyes.

"Oh my god," he panted. "I needed that."

"Are you crying?" I asked, realizing my own eyes were wet too.

"I think so," he said. "Fuck." Then he hunched forward, and his shoulders were shaking, and I could see he was crying-crying, not just laugh-crying.

"Shit, Gestas," I said. "What is it?"

"What isn't it?" He sniffled. "I'm about to lose my house. Probably won't be able to play music wherever we end up. And plus . . ." He leaned with his head against the wall, staring up at the cellar spiders crowding the ceiling. "I think I might be in love with a fucking *soldier*."

"Uh-oh," I said.

"Yeah." He looked at me. "Uh-oh. Angel asked if he could write to me this morning. Paper letters! Like he's going off to the trenches, and I'm—what? His little wifey back home?" Gestas shook his head.

"What'd you say?"

"I said yes, of course! Have you seen how beautiful that boy is?"

He wiped his eyes one more time and snorted some snot up his nose. "Well, thanks anyways for sharing your shame, Maddie. I needed the laugh. Please keep going to those Save the Eighth meetings. If nothing else, do it for my entertainment."

I laughed and said I would.

As I biked down Calcott, I took a long last look back at the Lab. I knew it might be a few days until I came back, and by then, everything might be different. I assumed that, like normal people threatened with bulldozers, my friends would spend the next week packing and cleaning and finding new places to live.

I should've known better.

20

Because I hadn't worked at all over the weekend, the second week of school knocked me on my ass. I didn't make it back to the Lab. I had to stay at school late every night playing catch-up, making it home long after dark, barely able to feed myself before passing out.

Thursday night, I headed straight from work to an emergency Save the Eighth protest outside the County Judge's office. There was some last-ditch possibility that the judge could step in and stop the hyperway temporarily.

Shayna seemed pleasantly surprised to see me. There were fewer people here than at the meeting, maybe because folks were working, or maybe because they were starting to give up hope. It certainly felt hopeless—two dozen people standing in the shadow of towering skyscrapers, chanting "Save the Eighth!" in halfhearted voices. Shayna shouted anti-hyperway talking points into the megaphone, which just made her voice tinny and harder to hear, seeing as all of us were standing six feet away. No press came. The judge didn't show his face. After barely an hour, Toussaint gave a speech about how this fight over the hyperway was part of a longer war. Even if we weren't victorious now, the work we had put in mattered, sowed seeds for the future. The words felt empty to me, and I was trying not to cry, bidding farewell to the Lab in my heart.

On Friday afternoon, the judge in Fish's case was going to rule on whether or not to halt construction on the hyperway, so I headed straight to the Lab after school to hear the news.

As soon as I steered my bike down Calcott, I saw the brick face of the Lab had been utterly transformed. The porch had been cleared of furniture, and its corrugated-plastic overhang had been torn down, so that the front of the building was now an uninterrupted surface—painted in a blaze of color. Giant, rainbow-colored bubble letters proclaimed "SAVE THE EIGHTH," the words surrounded by twenty-foot-tall Texas wildflowers and insects.

Vida was hanging out of one of the windows of Fish's apartment, a large, dripping paintbrush in hand, adding shading to a giant bluebonnet. A couple dudes from the graffiti house on Canal were there helping, block-coloring the bottom half of the mural with spray paint.

"Vida, it's gorgeous!" I yelled up.

She and her helpers turned to me and smiled.

I'd felt a bit salty that Vida hadn't shown up for the Save the Eighth rally outside the County Judge's office, but that feeling instantly melted away. Clearly, she'd been busy protesting in her own way.

I expected to find the inside of the Lab similarly transformed—with piles of boxes and at least some of the junk cleared out. But as I wound through the ground floor, poking my head in the open doors to the apartments, I saw nothing had changed. Not a single box had been packed, not even a cigarette butt picked up off the floor.

Gestas, Red, Peter, and Lorenzo were lounging on the couches in the Lab. As I reached them, Red got up, mumbled something about working out a song, and headed for xir apartment. The snub was for my sake, I was sure of it, and it gave me a hollowed-out feeling that I shoved to the back of my mind.

"Got a lot of packing done, huh?" I said, plopping down next to Lorenzo.

"We were going to start on Monday," Peter began. "But then Bleak Kingdom wanted to shoot a music video here—to like, record everything the way it was. So that took a few days."

"And then . . . Wednesday was it? We all got really into watching these old wrestling videos. So we stayed up real late watching WWF matches from the 90s," Gestas added.

"And then it was Thursday, and Red was like, 'Might as well wait to find out what the judge says on Friday, 'cause what if we do all that packing for nothing?'" Lorenzo finished.

"Besides, it'll take me two hours to pack, max," Gestas said. "This is Fish's problem." He waved around the Lab. "And if he thinks I'm helping him move a single goddamn piece of furniture, he's got another thing coming. That fool's rich enough to hire movers."

"Or one of those hoarder-house cleaners," Peter said, and Gestas snorted a laugh.

"Speak of the devil—any news from your man?"

"I'll try texting him again," I said, and added another "Any news?" to the string of one-sided texts I'd sent over the course of the day. The judge's verdict should've come in already—it was nearing five o'clock. I thought the others were in denial about the likelihood of the judge ruling in the landlords' favor. From what I'd learned at Save the Eighth, there was less than a million-to-one chance of the judge ruling against TxDOT.

Gestas sent me the link to Bleak Kingdom's music video. It made me tear up, watching them dance around the Lab to a heart-sick rock ballad, knowing this place was not long for the world.

Then the graffiti guys and Vida came in, speckled with a zillion flecks of neon paint. I had a beer, which made the feeling of creeping doom recede a bit. The graffiti guys offered that everyone could come stay at their warehouse on Canal if we lost the case. I wasn't thrilled at that idea—they were the ones who'd gotten Fish into huffing butane. They were a couple of white guys in their late twenties who were always creeping on too-young girls at our shows, and they didn't seem to have much personality besides painting and supplying people with drugs. One of them went by the name Slime, and the other, I shit you not, was called Filthy Ed. I guess they'd decided to go all-in on the whole scumbag, gutter-punk aesthetic.

Finally, after another hour or so, we heard the front door open, and Fish appeared in the doorway. He had a man with him. A fortysomething, blond-and-gray-haired, former-frat-boy-looking man's man. This golf bro seemed familiar to me, but I couldn't quite place him. Maybe he was one of those lawyers who put up billboards of himself around the city? He looked around the chaos of the Lab with amusement, pulling off his suit jacket in the heat.

Fish's face was sunken. "We lost," he said.

The doomed feeling roared back into my stomach. Lorenzo and Peter yelled "Fuck!" simultaneously. Vida looked like she was going to cry. Red had come in behind Fish and shook xir head, muttering, "I knew it."

"*But* we're going to appeal," Fish said. "And—" He looked to the aging Ken doll.

"—We'd like some of you to consider launching your own suit against TxDOT," the man finished.

"Y'all, this is my lawyer, Chad McMannis. He's also my brother-in-law."

Now I knew where I'd seen him—in picture frames at Fish's dad's house.

Chad looked around at us. "Who here is—" and he said a girl's name I'd never heard around here before. I felt rather than saw Gestas recoil next to me, like his skin had iced over.

"It's *Gestas*," Gestas said softly. The lawyer had just dropped Gestas's deadname in a room full of people. I felt horrible for having learned it that way.

Chad took in Gestas's look—braids and sparkly beads in his beard, baby-blue maxi dress and a sleeveless denim vest covered in patches of metal bands. Chad's eyebrows shot up, but he just said, "Right, Gestas. Well, for the legal documentation, of course we'll have to use the other name. But I'm sure you're used to that, what with your, uh, legal experiences." Chad stepped over a crate of LPs to get to the couch across from Gestas.

"We're thinking that you have a particularly strong case. We can sue TxDOT for failure to provide adequate notification directly *to you* about the building demolition. Since you're enrolled in AHICA, you obviously have a lot at stake in maintaining a stable residence." Chad brushed weed crumbs off the couch and sat down.

"I don't have any money for a lawyer," Gestas said.

"Oh no worries," Chad said, rolling up his shirtsleeves. "The hyperway is a multi-billion-dollar infrastructure project that the state of Texas is *very* motivated to complete. That means they'll shell out whatever it takes to get us to shut up and go away." Chad flashed a bleach-white set of perfect teeth. "I'll accept a one-dollar retainer from you, and then if you don't make money, I won't make money. But trust me"—he leaned forward with his hands in a prayer posture—"we stand to make a *lot* of money if we win."

Chad snapped open his briefcase and pulled out an iPad. "I've got the contract and the filing paperwork drawn up already—just need a bit more information from you that Fish couldn't provide. An added bonus is that if I file this in court on Monday, you can all legally continue living at the Lab until the case is resolved. Gives you a bit more time to, uh"—he looked around pointedly—"pack."

Gestas just sat there, eyebrows knit together.

"That sounds like a pretty good deal, right?" I prompted him.

Gestas shot me that glare of his, that how-can-you-still-be-so-naïve-after-all-the-books-I've-given-you glare.

"Here's what it sounds like to me," Gestas said. "If I agree to do this thing, then you stand to make a whole bunch of money if we win. But if we lose—you've lost nothing but a little of your time, right? But for me . . . well, I'm going up against the state of

Texas here, aren't I? And they'd already prefer I stop existing, being a Black trans man, locked up in AHICA. Why should I provoke them? If I'm standing in the way of their hyperway, they'll get rid of me. Shit, all they got to do is send in a cop to shoot me. They'll plant a gun and say it was self-defense. Way I see it, I'm risking *everything* to help you make a pile of money, *Chad*."

Chad bobbed his head vigorously. "I understand your concern, I do," he said. Gestas sucked his teeth, unconvinced. "You're incarcerated for—what? Carbon credit fraud?"

Gestas nodded slowly.

"Now that's not my area of expertise, but in my firm, we have some *fantastic* lawyers who specialize in carbon credit fraud defense. These guys regularly get clients off the hook for hundreds of thousands. I'm going to take a wild guess that your case didn't involve nearly such a big sum?"

"Your guess would be correct," Gestas said, frowning.

"My guys can get you out of AHICA, even get your record expunged, piece of cake. So what I'm going to do—I'm going to put it in our contract, that as soon as this property case is resolved, one of them will represent you in an appeal of your criminal case." Chad started typing so fast on the iPad that his fingers blurred. "Win or lose, they'll represent you."

Gestas shot a look at Red, who shrugged. It was a "fuck it, why not?" kind of shrug.

Gestas rubbed a hand over his face. "Fine, okay, yeah, if you'll represent me for my criminal case, then I guess . . . and this is all free, right? I'm not going to pay a dime for *either* case?"

"Well, there's that one-dollar retainer," Chad said, grinning. "And if you win, we'll take a portion of what the state pays for the property suit. But the criminal case will be pro bono, Scout's honor." He actually held up three fingers in the Boy Scout salute, which was about the corniest thing I'd ever seen.

Gestas let out a long sigh. "Okay, I'll do it."

Chad clapped his hands and resumed typing on the iPad. Everyone else sagged with relief. With Gestas filing this suit, we'd all get to stay in the Lab a little longer.

Chad encouraged everyone else on the lease to sign on to the lawsuit, but explained that because they weren't AHICA prisoners, their suits were less likely to succeed. "The exciting thing about Gestas's case, is that the law is really murky where AHICA rules, tenant's rights, and eminent-domain seizures converge. I'm pretty sure a case like this is unprecedented, which could mean a massive settlement for him."

"So this is all just about money?" I asked. "You're not actually trying to save the Lab?"

"Look, the state of Texas is *going* to build this hyperway. The only question is—are y'all going to be properly compensated for your displacement?" Chad flashed a sympathetic smile. "Now the more high-profile we can make this case, the better. I saw that mural out front. Love it. Post it to your socials. You're creative people—do whatever you can to draw the media's attention to this case. If we can get the public on our side, we're more likely to win."

Chad's voice turned more serious. "It's important, though, that you don't give the police any ammunition to shut you down early. They may show up to try to intimidate you. If that happens, you lock the doors and ask for a warrant and *call me* ASAP. Finally, I'm going to need you to clear this house of any kind of drug paraphernalia. Even these little crumbs," he kicked at the weed bits he'd swiped off the couch earlier. "If police do come inside and find that, your friend Gestas could be in trouble for violating his AHICA agreement. So we can't mess around."

I looked around the Lab, scanning for the billions of weed bits that must be hiding in its nooks and crannies. How the hell were we going to clean it all up?

21

AUGUST 22, 2020

I got up early Saturday morning and started cleaning, mostly by myself. Red said scrubbing the Lab was pointless, because if cops wanted to bust us for weed, they would just plant some. Happened all the time, xe said. Gestas didn't want to help clean up a mess he had no part in making. He had never let anyone smoke in his apartment, anyways. Fish grudgingly agreed to drive a box of his weed paraphernalia over to his dad's house in Katy. He loaded up the car with other things too—his nicer clothes, LPs, and his video game consoles and TV. I asked him if he was jumping ship on us, but he just said that if we all had to get out of the Lab in a hurry, he wanted his valuable things to be safe. He said he'd come back and help me clean, but he never did make it back from his dad's.

Vida and Peter scrubbed their own apartment, but that left just me to clean Fish's apartment, the front hallway, the stairwell, and the entire Lab. I vacuumed and dusted and mopped all day. I couldn't help thinking that if Angel were here, *he* would've helped me. Then I got to wondering about him—where was he? Traipsing through the jungle? Was he in danger? Had he fired his gun? Did he still believe in the war? Had he killed someone? Thinking about all that, I couldn't complain too much about cleaning.

I got sucked into such a perfectionist frenzy that I didn't pay much attention to what everyone else was up to. It was Red's idea to throw one last show. Peter suggested doing it out front, with Vida's new mural as the backdrop. I didn't realize until I was done cleaning how many acts Red and Lorenzo had booked, or that Lorenzo had gotten a dude he knew at City Hall to issue a sound permit, or that Jaciel's Hideout had lent us their badass sound system.

Late afternoon, I finally finished up and took a long, glorious shower. When I cut off the water, I could hear the roar of a crowd downstairs. I peeked out the bathroom window and saw what looked like a music festival in the front yard. It was early—just 5:00, but already the lawn was packed with two hundred of our friends and regulars. Slip Drip was opening with their folk-emo sound, all pretty banjo music and whiny screaming. They weren't very good, but that was okay, because no one was listening—everyone was sipping from take-cups, talking loud and laughing. I swiped on some eyeliner and headed downstairs.

Since the front of the building was the stage, I had to go through the back doors to get outside. The warehouse was packed, with long lines of people waiting to fill take-cups from a few kegs. I wove through them, jumped off the back ledge, and headed around to the front.

Slip Drip was playing their last song. I recognized just about everyone in the crowd—practically the whole local music and street art scenes were there. The air smelled amazing from the taco cart and Korean street-food truck that had pulled up. I saw Old Jim, and this time he'd brought a photographer with him.

Red stood at the edge of the crowd, nursing xir take-cup in long fingers tipped with chipped black nail polish. Xe hadn't made eye contact with me since the night xe destroyed the Fun Machine. But xe hadn't actually told me to leave xim alone. Something needed to end this weird stalemate between us, or I was going to lose my mind. So I screwed up my courage, braced for rejection, and walked right up to xim.

"Good turnout for a show you threw together in a couple hours," I said.

Red still didn't look at me, but nodded.

"So, uh . . . are we in the lineup?"

"Third," Red said curtly. "After Slip Drip, it's Okonomiyaki Riot, then us."

"Good to know, good to know," I repeated.

"I asked Mike Algebra to play with us," Red said, shooting me a look. It was a test. Would I stick up for Fish again?

"It's the right move musically, of course." I sighed. "But I just worry about keeping Fish happy, especially right now. Especially now that his brother-in-law is y'all's lawyer."

Red shook xir head in disgust and looked away. "For some of us, there's limits on what we're willing to do to keep Fish happy. Besides"—xe spun around, arms out dramatically—"yet again, Fish is not even here."

I scanned the crowd for Fish, but he hadn't come back from his dad's place yet—probably still hiding there so he could get out of cleaning. He probably didn't even know about the show. For half a second, I considered texting him to come—but then I realized it'd be very convenient if he missed another set entirely.

Peter bounded up to us, more animated than I'd ever seen his sleepy self.

"The algorithm has blessed us! Twitter gods be praised!" He smiled so big we could see his dead canine tooth, which he usually kept carefully hidden. "Check it out—1K likes already, and it's only been twenty minutes since I posted!" He shoved his phone under our noses. The tweet featured a shot of the lead singer of Slip Drip doing a midair splits while playing the mandolin, framed perfectly by Vida's mural. You couldn't tell from the shot that the music was bad or that the people in the crowd weren't into it. And Peter had applied some filters to make the pic look timeless and magical. The text said, "RT AND BOOST! TxDOT & OIL COMPANIES want to destroy EIGHTH WARD, a historically Black & brown neighborhood!! Come out to 4121 CALCOTT tonight in solidarity!!"

"This tweet's doing numbers!" Peter said. "This party's about to blow up!"

"In that case, we're going to need more alcohol," I said. "The kegs are going fast."

"I'll go on a beer run," Peter offered.

"No," Red said. "Remember what Chad McBrosef said? We gotta get lots of social media attention. You keep taking pictures and tweeting and all that. I'll see if Lorenzo can pick up some more kegs in his van."

Okonomiyaki Riot took the stage then, and the crowd instantly perked up. Janey, the lead singer, was Japanese American, wore pigtails and six-inch platform sneakers onstage, and she sang like a lovelorn demon with this deep, soulful growl that seemed impossible coming from her four-foot-eleven frame. Eiko, the bassist, was Japanese, like born in Japan, and he had an 80s punk rock aesthetic, with a bright red streak down his spiked hair. I didn't know the drummer or guitarist, a couple of white guys with beards and manbuns, but they could play. Together, they had this roaring, vintage, pop-punk tornado of sound that had everybody in the crowd jumping, and a mosh pit broke out near the porch.

Vida appeared at my side and grabbed my hand. "Isn't this your favorite song? Come on!"

"I have to play next!" I protested.

"*One* song," Vida pleaded.

"Fine," I said, grinning, and I let her drag me into the crowd, away from Red, still sulking into xir take-cup.

Fuck xim anyways, I thought to myself, as Vida found us a pocket of crowd to dance in. I started jumping to the gatling-gun beat of "I Was a Teenage Banshee," whipping my hair around and trying to pretend my stomach wasn't in knots over Red.

After the song ended, I headed back inside, despite Vida's pouting. The crowd had swelled, and I had to shove my way through the press of bodies in the Lab. Finally, I made it to the door to Red and Gestas's apartment, which—for maybe the first time ever—was closed. Without thinking twice, I plowed inside, shut the door behind me, and then froze.

The room was packed, but I barely recognized anyone. Gestas was sitting on the couch, next to Shayna from Save the Eighth—which was weird, seeing her here. Toussaint was leaning against a wall, and there were a couple other folks from Save the Eighth. There was a big guy on the futon I vaguely recognized but couldn't place. He was wearing a flat cap and a matching black-and-green tracksuit, and you could tell by how it draped that it was expensive. He had a bunch of almost-as-well-dressed friends around him, some sitting on the floor, some leaning against the wall. All of them wore pristine sneakers, which was such a contrast to the filthy, hole-ridden, knock-off Converse most of my friends wore. I was staring at everybody like a deer in the headlights because, once again, I was the only white person in this—meeting? And I could tell by the way everyone was looking at me that I wasn't exactly welcome.

"Can we help you?" one guy asked with a raised eyebrow.

I opened my mouth, but before I could say anything, Gestas jumped in. "That's Maddie. It's cool. She's in the band."

I grinned at him gratefully.

"She just barges in like that?" Shayna asked Gestas. "Without knocking?"

He shrugged. "Everyone does it." Shayna pursed her lips at me, and for half a second, I wanted to explain that all the apartments had an open-door policy, that people were always just dropping in, that I wasn't the white, entitled monster she seemed to think I was. But then it occurred to me that maybe Gestas actually wasn't cool with all the comings and goings. I'd never asked.

"Hey Shayna, Toussaint," I said, and I waved vaguely at the other Save the Eighth folks whose names I didn't know. I was surprised to see Shayna here, considering how much she'd seemed to hate the Lab. "What are y'all doi—I mean, uh . . ." Maybe it was rude to ask why they were here, so I pivoted. "Thanks? For coming out to the show?"

"Don't get me wrong—I still think this place is a monument to gentrification," Shayna said. "I'd rather Save the Eighth boost one of the grandparents who've lived in this neighborhood for decades." She held up her phone and wiggled it. "But y'all's little party is blowing up on social media, and Vida's mural is awesome. Gotta use the optics you can get. So we're going to do a speech out in front."

"Right after our set," Gestas added. "And then Chem C is gonna perform."

I sucked in air, and my eyes darted to the rich-looking dude. So *that's* who he was. I wasn't too familiar with his music, but I knew Chem C was a Houston rap legend, and that he'd been nationally famous in the early 2000s.

"*If* this thing doesn't get shut down by the cops first," Toussaint said.

"Oh we don't usually have trouble with cops," I said. "I guess because we're at the end of the street? And there's nothing but tracks behind us?" It was what everybody said about our uncanny ability to throw shows and never get shut down for sound violations.

"*That's* why you think cops don't shut you down?" Shayna shook her head at me.

"Cops are always hassling *our* shows in the Eighth," said one of Chem C's entourage.

"They leave you alone because you're a bunch of white kids," Shayna explained.

I wanted to point out that *actually* we tended to attract very racially diverse crowds, but then I realized she was right. There were probably a ton more white kids at our shows than at a typical Eighth Ward party.

"Well, I think Lorenzo got a sound permit, so maybe that'll help?" I offered.

"Maybe," Toussaint said, and there was a long, skeptical silence.

"Well, I gotta tune, so . . ." I trailed off, pointing towards Red's bedroom, where my guitar was stashed. The room was so packed, I had to squeeze past people and step over their legs to get there. Once inside, I shut the French doors and tuned up as quietly as possible. I ran through all our songs and my solos. Knowing that Chem C, and the Houston Police Department, and Shayna—especially Shayna—would be watching me play made my nerves even more shot than usual.

22

I was not prepared for the size of the crowd that roared in greeting as we stepped out the front door. Nearly a thousand people filled the lot, spilling across the road and into the yards across the street. Stripped of its furniture and overhang, there was more room out on the porch, but it was still just a concrete slab, five feet high, and eight feet wide, with steps and ramps going down to street level. It was so narrow that instead of playing in a clump, we had to stretch out in a line—Gestas's drum kit, then me, then Red, and finally Mike Algebra. All our friends and regulars from the music scene were bunched close to the stage, their heads at the level of our shins. But around them was a sea of faces I didn't recognize—folks actually from the neighborhood. I didn't know if they'd seen Peter's tweet, or if they were here with Save the Eighth, or if they'd come for Chem C. Whatever had drawn them, the crowd was now about two-thirds Black folks, a lot of them way older than us, and I had no idea what they'd think of our post-punk, glam-metal music.

My hands were slick with sweat as Gestas counted off. Red belted a primordial scream, and then we were off, tearing into the opening of "Maiden Head Shop." I was so nervous I missed the strings on the third chord, slicing my knuckles across them. I glanced at the crowd, half expecting them to start booing, but no one had noticed. Our friends were thrashing to the beat as usual, and the folks from the Ward—well, they were talking amongst themselves. They weren't paying us any attention, but it didn't matter. The party was a bona fide rager.

A family had shown up to sell tamales, and a paletero hocked ice cream and chicharrones, both without charging carbon taxes. The steampunk circus folks were warming up at the edge of the crowd, spinning unignited poi balls and finding their sea legs on stilts. Everyone was having a great time, and I got this righteous, good feeling. This was history happening here, a cause gathering momentum, and I was in the middle of it. Plus, with Mike Algebra on bass, we sounded seriously tight. That put Red in such a good mood, xe actually caught my eye and grinned. Only for a second, but it was enough to fill my heart with hope. My nervousness vanished, and I let myself enjoy playing to the biggest crowd of my life.

Then I spotted the first drone.

It was one of those undercover, gray-and-white ones with four propellers. Even though I couldn't make out the HPD logo, I recognized the shape of it. Cops were the only folks who had drones that nice in this part of town. It was hovering over the rooftop of the house across the street, just out of view of most of the crowd, but with a clear shot of the stage.

During our next song break, I nudged Red and gestured with my head at the drone. Xe shrugged as if to say, "Whaddya gonna do?" and launched into "Whore Moan Therapy." I tried to catch Gestas's eye, but as usual, he was too lost in playing, turquoise-painted lips parted in ecstasy, gold-dusted eyelids closed as his limbs blurred with speed. No one in the crowd seemed to have noticed the drone either, but I couldn't stop glancing at it, wondering who was watching us, and what they had planned. As we finished up our T. Rex cover, two more drones appeared above the rooftops across the street.

At the end of our set, Red always said, "That's it," matter-of-factly, instead of, "Thank you." Our friends up front chanted, "One more song," but since we could see the rest of the crowd wasn't into us, Red ignored them and unplugged xir amp. We were

139

supposed to bring in our instruments after the set, because the stage was so narrow, and Chem C and his crew would need space to spread out. I dashed inside to stow my guitar, then came back out to haul more stuff. Gestas was still breaking down his drum kit, and he headed inside with the toms and bass drum. I tried to follow with his stool and high-hat, but something tugged me back. One of the zillion cords draping the stage had gotten threaded through the high-hat's pedal. I followed the cord to the lead singer's monitor and found myself staring up at Shayna, who'd just grabbed the mic off the stand. The stage was now packed with Save the Eighth organizers. I backed away from the mic while the crowd screamed as Chem C and his entourage emerged from inside the Lab. I was squatted down in front of all of them, holding a tangled-up high-hat.

Shayna started to speak, so there was no way I could unplug the monitor now. Panicking, I abandoned the high-hat on its side and snuck to the back of the group of organizers. But they were packed together on the narrow stage—there was no way I could push through to the door of the Lab. I looked for a way to hop down to the ground, but the crowd near the stage was packed so tight, I would've had to crowd-surf out. No, I was stuck up there with rap royalty and the Save the Eighth veterans. Feeling extremely white and imposter-y, I hid behind a tall organizer, pressed my back to the wall, and willed myself to camouflage chameleon-style into Vida's mural.

Shayna had finally managed to quiet down the crowd and introduce herself. "We are here to protect our community. We are here to say *enough is enough*!" At the ends of her phrases, some folks would echo back her words or shout encouragement. "Our government has *always* waged war on Black communities. First it was slavery, then Jim Crow, then the War on Drugs, and what is it now?"

She let the question hang there, and a few folks in the crowd hazarded a guess. "The hyperway!" "Gentrification!" And then someone shouted, "Carbon fraud!" Shayna pointed in the direction of the answer.

"Ever since its founding," she said, pacing the front of the stage. "The Bureau of Carbon Regulation has put the burden of solving climate change onto poor communities. Onto Black and brown communities like this one." Claps and hollers of affirmation. "Millions of Black people have become literal prisoners in their own homes for minor carbon fraud offenses. Meanwhile, white people and corporations keep polluting to their hearts' content—as long as they pay a pittance to 'offset' their carbon footprints."

Shayna flicked the mic cord out of her way. "Rich white folks remain the greatest polluters on earth! But they're not the ones getting locked in their homes with AHICA implants, are they?"

Someone yelled, "Preach!" and people pumped their fists in the air. Our friends, now pressed into a semicircle up against the stage, looked around uncomfortably, and there was a stark divide between their varied, lighter skin tones, and the crowd of darker-skinned Eighth Wardians surrounding them. A glint of light overhead caught my attention—more cop drones. There were half a dozen of them now, hovering over the street. We were surrounded.

I was glad Gestas, at least, was inside, where Chad the lawyer had promised he would be safe. And I was glad to see Peter near the front of the stage, streaming everything from his phone, and Old Jim and his camera guy snapping pics of Shayna. Surely the cops wouldn't do anything too terrible with the media here.

"Every time they want to build a new hyperway, we're told how clean electromagnetic roads are, how they reduce gas consumption by thus-and-such. But what *powers* the electromagnets of the hyperway, huh? What's running through the pipeline they want to bury underneath it?" She gestured behind the Lab. Though our view was blocked from stage, I knew the folks towards the back of the crowd would be able to see the Valiant Refinery in the distance, belching steam and flaring gas. "The big, dirty secret that still powers our lives. However many prairies Houston plants and maglev lines it builds, the fact of the matter is—this city, this country, this *world* still runs on oil. So how about the BCR knocks down that refinery back there, instead of our homes?"

Roars of approval. A flash of movement down the street caught my eye. Police cars—driven by actual human police—crept around the corner of Calcott and Dunmer. They kept their distance, but I had a horrible feeling as more and more eased around the corner, including three big, black paddy wagons.

"How about instead of another energy-guzzling hyperway, this city takes those billions and invests in *our* community for once? We only have one maglev line in the Eighth. That's a travesty. We don't have any grocery stores or orchards or community gardens, besides the ones we make for ourselves. We get no help from the government to greenify our homes, and we're continually punished for it."

"That's right!" called several voices at once, and others clapped with their hands held high in the air.

"So we're here to say *enough is enough*." Shayna pointed the mic at the crowd, and a hundred voices echoed back the phrase. "We're taking a stand. We've got people here being displaced from homes they've lived in for generations. We've got an AHICA inmate living at this very address"—Shayna pounded a fist on Vida's mural—"who was only given a few days notice before eviction!"

The sun was setting now, the sky lit up all fiery fuchsia and magenta, with gold-glazed clouds. Shayna glanced at Toussaint. He nodded, and she turned back to the crowd. "And that is why Save the Eighth will be occupying this building!"

The crowd cheered. My mind reeled—*occupying*? So Shayna was moving in? Is that what they'd been talking about with Gestas?

"We're taking a stand *here* to protest the eviction of hundreds of families in this community. If you believe that Black neighborhoods matter, join us. If you believe we should invest in our existing communities, rather than building new hyperways out to developments in the suburbs, join us! If you want the government to stop blaming climate change on our most vulnerable people, join us! And together, we can save the Eighth!"

The crowd roared almost as loud as the beats that started blaring out of the amp stacks. Shayna passed the mic to Chem C, who took center stage. He started rapping the lyrics of a song I recognized from the radio, but he only got through a few lines before a horrible shrieking rent the air. I pressed my hands to my ears, but it did little to block the siren. A robotic voice boomed out from all the dozen drones hovering overhead.

"This is an unlawful assembly. You are ordered to disperse."

I was furious—how could they just declare the assembly unlawful? Didn't we have a sound permit?

Time moved in slow motion. A few people at the edge of the crowd took off running, jumping over the fences of houses across the street. Most people just looked above in confusion, noticing the drones for the first time. At the soundboard, Lorenzo brandished a piece of paper in the air, shouting, "We have a permit!" The other Save the Eighth organizers on the porch crammed into the Lab, and Shayna was holding the door open, waving people from the front of the crowd to come onstage and get inside. A line of cops, looking more cyborg than human, rounded the corner and marched towards the crowd with riot shields, helmets, and body armor.

I felt frozen, pinned against the colorful bricks behind me. The drones above had faces—two camera lenses of different sizes formed the eyes, and an aperture beneath made a round mouth. Now the jagged teeth of those mouths swirled open and clouds of pink spilled out onto our friends below. As I caught the first whiff, my eyes stung like I was cutting onions, and I understood what was happening. Again, my first instinct was outrage. They'd ordered us to disperse mere seconds before—so how could they be gassing us already? We hadn't had a *chance* to disperse!

Then everyone was screaming, but I couldn't see them. My eyes were on fire; I could barely see for my tears, and I was choking. I groped my way across the stage, stumbled over something metal that clanged—the fucking high-hat. I left it behind and joined the press of people shoving their way inside the Lab. A huge black-clad form mounted the porch, raised its arm, and brought down a club on someone directly to my right. I heard a scream of pain just as I squeezed through the door, and someone slammed it shut behind me.

The bolt slid into the lock. I leaned against the wall beside the doorjamb, blinking furiously, trying to suck in air, but it was getting harder and harder to breathe. A fist hammered at the door, and I heard Red's voice shouting back, "Where's your warrant? I won't open this door without a fucking warrant!"

I sunk to the floor and curled into myself, sure that bullets would come ripping through the door any second. But the hammering stopped. I guess the cops had enough people outside to terrorize without bothering us.

Gestas appeared in front of me with a take-cup full of water and had me tip my head back. He poured it over my face, and I blinked furiously and snorted some up my nose. My vision cleared a little, but the pain was still overwhelming.

Squinting now, I could make out blurred forms around me—Peter crouched on the stairs with his phone out, streaming everything. Friends and Save the Eighth organizers slumped along the hall, leaking tears from bloodshot eyes. I'd seen protestors tear-gassed on live streams before, but I'd never imagined it hurt like this. And as my airway swelled shut, I had to fight against panic and the certainty that I was dying.

I pawed my pocket desperately, but my inhaler wasn't there. I grabbed the arm of the person closest to me—it was Red. "My inhaler," I pushed out in a thin whisper. "It's in my bag—in your room." Red took off, and a few terrifying, strained breaths later, I felt xim push the plastic inhaler into my palm. I took two big sucks of the steroid, holding each one in as long as I could stand to. Air started coming a bit easier after that, and my vision started to clear.

Someone slid down the wall to sit next to me.

"You okay?"

I wasn't sure anymore if I was crying because of the tear gas, or because Red had finally said a kind word to me. I let my head fall onto xir shoulder, and then xe was pulling me into xir chest, wrapping both arms around me. "I'm sorry, I'm so sorry," xe whispered into my hair, and I didn't know what for, and I didn't care. In the cave of xir arms, the air was sweet, and my breath came a little easier.

"Can I tell you something, Mads?" Red whispered. My heart stuck in my throat, and I looked up, hoping for a declaration of love, at long last. But instead xe said, "You have, like, an amazing amount of snot on your face."

I burst out laughing. And then xe held out the bottom of xir Ghost T-shirt for me to use as a handkerchief. As far as I was concerned, it was the most romantic thing anyone had ever done for me.

23

I slept with Red that night. Just slept. After I'd taken my turn with the shower and rinsed the chemical agents from my hair, xe offered me a clean T-shirt and boxers. We were talking on xir bed, and I started crying because of the *everything* of the day, and Red rubbed my back, and then I was on xir pillow, and we were curled towards each other, whispering about how wild and awful it all was, or scrolling through our phones side by side, watching videos of our show and the mass arrest. It was horrible seeing it all again, seeing friends of ours attacked by cops with clubs and getting dragged away.

But it was also thrilling to rewatch the clips of Shayna's speech, retweeted tens of thousands of times now, with more comments loading every second. Most people were supportive—critical of the hyperway and outraged at how the police had behaved. But racist trolls had also found Peter's thread, and they were calling Shayna and the Save the Eighth organizers racial slurs. Right wingers blamed "those people" for climate change and said "inefficient" neighborhoods like the Eighth should be burned to the ground. On the videos of our set, some people left trans-hating comments about Red and Gestas, and some straight up insulted our music. One comment was, "That white girl plays like a weak bitch." I showed it to Red, and we both laughed. But later, even though so many more important and terrible things had happened, I couldn't stop wondering what the commenter meant, and whether they'd perceived a deep, inscrutable truth about me.

Around midnight, Red got a call from Lorenzo, who was at the Downtown jail with a bunch of our friends. Red had a spare key to Lorenzo's van, so xe left to pick up our people. Soon after I fell asleep.

When I woke in the morning, I didn't know where I was for a few seconds. I couldn't understand why there was ivy growing through the cracks of the window into the room, or why the arm around me felt so light. Then I looked down, and saw Red's smooth, golden skin, rather than Fish's pale, hairy arm, and my heart swelled with a joy so intense—better than the body high from a line of cocaine or a hit of weed. It was a feeling I remembered from way back in childhood, when I was very small. Like the world was a wondrous place, full of surprises, and for the first time in a long while, I felt excited to be here.

24

The living room of Red and Gestas's apartment was crammed with the sleeping bodies of our friends and Save the Eighth organizers. All the couches were claimed, and more people had curled up on the floor, using sweatshirts or their arms for pillows. I tiptoed between them to the kitchen, hoping to make a pot of coffee.

I found Lorenzo dropping a pile of chopped onions into a giant stew pot. There was a deep purple-and-yellow bruise around his left eye.

"Hey man, you okay? Didn't you get arrested?"

"Nah, they just took a bunch of us to the jail and held us there for a few hours. It was fucked up. I want to talk to Fish's lawyer-guy to see if I can sue them for this." He pointed to his eye with the tip of a chef's knife. "I was just trying to show the pigs our permit."

"I'm so sorry. I hope you can sue," I said. "Shouldn't you be resting though? Why are you cooking this early?"

"All the couches were taken, and I can't sleep on the floor. I figured I might as well get some red beans and rice going. Folks are going to wake up soon and be hungry."

That was Lorenzo—he loved cooking for people. His ability to make huge quantities of delicious food for our dirtbag friends was like a magic power. Most of us could barely make a box of mac and cheese.

All I wanted at that moment was to snatch some caffeine and climb back under the covers with Red. But now I felt guilty, because I'd had a bed to sleep in while so many were on the floor, and because I hadn't gotten arrested or beat up by cops. So I offered to help Lorenzo cook.

Cooking was a very unusual activity for me in those days. I lived off takeout and raw produce from my Community's orchard. Lorenzo asked me to chop the bell peppers, so I started turning one around, no idea where to start. "Really? You don't know how to cut a pepper?" He laughed. I shrugged. He showed me how to bisect it, pop out the seeds, and cut it into thin strips. It took me half an hour to chop four of the things. In the meantime, Lorenzo cut up a head of garlic, a mess of tomatoes, and a package of vegan sausage, and added a whole bunch of spices to the pot without measuring. We also made cornbread and rice to pad out the meal. I'm not sure I was much help, as Lorenzo had to explain every step to me like I was a child. But I think he appreciated the company.

The living room opened onto the narrow hallway of a kitchen, so I caught snatches of the conversation out there over the sounds of sizzling onions and chopping veggies. As folks woke up, a meeting started up organically between the Save the Eighth organizers and the residents of the Lab. Shayna's announcement about an occupation had caught everyone but Gestas by surprise, but no one seemed upset by it—more curious as to how this was going to work.

Shayna and Toussaint shared some history of sit-ins and protest occupations. We'd gained the public's attention on Twitter last night. Now the plan was to keep that attention by holding events every day to draw large crowds and media to the neighborhood—concerts, performances, protests. Meanwhile, we'd try to gather a large encampment of protestors around the Lab, to deter a forced eviction.

"The cops didn't give two shits about attacking a big crowd last night," Peter pointed out.

"But trust they're facing backlash for that now," Toussaint said. "The video of that sergeant clubbing that white girl was all over KHOU this morning."

"Of course, the only clip that got played on TV was of that white girl," Shayna said, shaking her head. "Nothing from my speech. No clips of the people who actually live here being attacked by the cops."

"Her parents must be campaign donors, or some shit, because the mayor came out and said he 'regrets' the use of force last night," Toussaint added. "So for the moment we have the media's sympathy, if not their understanding. But if we're going to pull this off, we need to get organized."

An intense philosophical argument broke out with Shayna on one side, and Gestas and Toussaint on the other, where they were throwing around so much leftist terminology I could hardly follow. I was making cornbread batter, carefully checking each step from the recipe on my phone three times, so I was only half listening. Red got up and caught my eye from across the living room. Xe raised a curious eyebrow, which I took to mean, "You? Cooking?" and I shrugged. Xe grinned, and my blood bloomed with heat.

Red didn't say much but listened intently to the debate. Shayna wanted to make sure Save the Eighth stayed in charge of the occupation. Otherwise, she argued, the movement would inevitably get co-opted by a bunch of outsiders who didn't really care about the Ward. Toussaint and Gestas, though, were arguing that the movement had to be leaderless, or it was doomed to replicate authoritarianism. Shayna countered that only by centering Black folks as leaders could they avoid replicating white supremacy within the occupation.

I felt bad for Shayna. I thought she was making good points, but Toussaint and Gestas were both against her—and there was an edge of condescension to how they talked to her, cutting her off, mansplaining. I wondered if things might've gone differently if Shayna had been a man. I was wishing I'd read more of Gestas's books already, so I could support her. But as it was, me wading in seemed like a real bad idea—not just because I was still ignorant when it came to leftist praxis. But also—as a white person, it seemed wrong to enter a debate between Black organizers.

When Toussaint asked the room to vote—on whether we'd move forward with a vertical organizing structure as Shayna had proposed, or a horizontal one as Gestas and Toussaint were advocating for—the votes went with the boys. Only Vida and two other women from Save the Eighth sided with Shayna. Red sided with Gestas, which wasn't surprising. Lorenzo and I didn't vote, as we weren't residents or organizers.

Right around then, the food was ready. Most people hadn't brought a take-bowl to the show, but everyone had at least a take-cup on them, so we filled those with the red beans and rice and plopped a slice of cornbread on top. There weren't enough forks to go around either, but luckily, the food was slurpable. It felt good—doling out the meal we'd made to the crowd of hungry, exhausted organizers. For the first time, I understood why Lorenzo loved cooking. Everyone was so grateful. Even Shayna gave me a big smile and said, "Thanks so much, y'all. It smells amazing."

Lorenzo and I started in on the dishes, but a couple Save the Eighth organizers insisted on taking over, so I finally escaped the kitchen. It was nearly noon by then and hot as hell, so I was sweating through Red's borrowed T-shirt.

Despite the heat, the Lab was a bustle of activity. There were dozens of people around—friends of ours and Save the Eighth organizers, and they were clearing Fish's junk furniture out of the Lab and into the back yard. There, five burly folks were hacking back the cane with machetes. Already, they'd expanded the yard by nearly double.

My gut clenched as I worried how Fish would react at the sight of his precious garbage strewn about the yard. I checked my phone and saw that I had ten texts from him, which I'd missed, because I always kept his notifications on mute.

4:37 P.M.

Think I'm gonna stay at dad's tonight. Accidentally got high as fuck. Whoops. 4-2000000. How r u?

6:13 P.M.

What the fuck, you guys threw a show? And didn't even tell me? Why am I hearing about it on Twitter and not from my girlfriend? Or my bandmates?

Oh you're just gonna keep me on read, huh?

6:42 P.M.

Are you even my fucking girlfriend anymore?

Y'all are ASSHOLES. I am the bassist of Bunny Bloodlust, in case you forgot, and you couldn't even tell me you had a show?

8:04 P.M.

ANSWR ME!!1!

8:53 P.M.

Bittch.

11:01 A.M.

OMG, just woke up and saw the videos of the riot. R U OK?!?!!?

11:05 A.M.

Coming over!!

Fuck. If he'd left at eleven, that meant he'd be here any minute.

I walked around the side of the Lab to the front, where a dozen people I didn't recognize were pitching tents, and painting protest signs and staking them into the yard. "No More Hyperways" and "People Not Pipelines" and "Protect Black Communities." The groups out here were clearly organized, but they weren't from Save the Eighth.

"Who are y'all with?" I asked a white woman in her fifties, wearing a visor over her long, grey braid.

"Oh we're not all together. Them over there"—she pointed at some thirtysomethings painting signs—"they're the Socialist Democrats." She pointed to another group of folks cleaning up trash from last night. "And they're the Socialist Alliance."

"My group here," she pointed to a few other baby boomers in Teva sandals, "we're the Revolutionary Communists."

"Oh, badass," I said. I hadn't imagined Houston even *had* a Revolutionary Communist Party. I certainly didn't expect them to be a couple of boomers in fishing hats.

"Can I give you some literature on the writings of Bob Avakian?" she asked, shoving a pamphlet into my hand. Her shirt had a long quote on it, also attributed to Bob Avakian.

"In BAsics 1:3, Avakian says that the U.S. is not actually a democracy, but capitalism-imperialism."

"Yeah, right on," I said. I knew that much from reading Gestas's books.

"And in here, Bob Avakian says . . ." and the lady just kept talking about this guy, Bob. I agreed with what she was saying, but it creeped me out the way she mentioned that guy's name over and over. It reminded me of how I'd talked about Jesus in my high-school days. She was proselytizing!

"I'll be sure to read this later," I said, holding up the pamphlet. But she grabbed my arm.

"Now you'll really want to pay attention to this section—"

I was wondering how the hell to get away from her politely, when a sleek, black truck pulled up to the front of the warehouse.

Suddenly, I pretended to be engrossed in the pamphlet, ready to convert to the cult of Bob Avakian if it meant I didn't have to deal with—

"What the actual fuck, Maddie?" Fish roared as he jumped down from the truck, and I froze. He had never yelled at me like that. Everyone in the yard turned and watched him storm up the front walk.

"I thought you were dead, or arrested! You can't answer a fucking text?"

"Oh did you . . . text me ?" I mumbled, ears ringing with panic. I made a half-assed show of pulling out my phone. "Must've had it on silent."

"Why the hell did no one tell me that you were throwing a show, on my property, with my band?"

"Not your band," said an icy voice behind me. Red and Gestas were standing in the doorway. Red stepped out onto the porch, where Gestas's high-hat was still lying on its side where I'd abandoned it last night. "It's our band, actually, me and Gestas started it, and after missing our last two shows, you are no longer a member."

"That's fucking bullshit," Fish roared. The cane-hacking folks out back, bare chests slick with sweat, came around the side of the building to see what was going on. They were still carrying machetes. "I want all my equipment back. Every fucking amp and pedal I bought for you guys."

Red just shrugged. "Sure."

The onlookers scowled. I heard people whispering, "Who the fuck is this guy?" and "What an asshole."

I caught Red's eye, and xir expression was ice cold. I had a horrible feeling that this was my very last chance. If, after last night, I went back to being Fish's girlfriend, xe would never forgive me. But if I broke up with Fish, would he turn against us? Would he kick us out of the Lab? Betray us to TxDOT? My gaze flicked to Gestas, who was counting on this house to keep him out of brick-and-mortar jail. He needed Fish's lawyer to appeal his carbon fraud case. I couldn't understand why Red was deliberately provoking Fish in the face of all that.

Shayna stepped out of the house next to Gestas.

"And you!" Fish rounded on her. "Who the fuck are you, and where do you get off inviting the whole world to 'occupy' my warehouse??"

Angry mutters rippled through the crowd of onlookers. Shayna stood for a moment with her eyebrows clear up to her hairline. In that moment of silence, Fish's eyes scanned the crowd, and he blanched sickly white, realizing that thirty strangers were scowling at him.

"Who the fuck are *you*?" Shayna said, in a voice so much quieter than Fish's. I was glad I wasn't in Fish's shoes.

"I own this building, actually. I live here."

"Oh I see," she said, drawing out the words. "So *you're* the landlord. The gentrifier."

She'd struck his Achilles' heel, the same sore spot his dad had ripped open at that catastrophic family dinner months before.

"Wha—no. It's not like that. I'm not really a landlord. I mean, we're all friends here. This place is like an anarcho-communist community space—"

"Then I don't see what the problem is," Shayna interrupted. "Look we got your communists right here," she gestured to the Bob Avakian stans pitching their tents.

"And we just voted to run this place on horizontal organizing principles. No leaders. Very anarchist," Toussaint added in his calm baritone. Fish's face betrayed battling emotions, and I could read each one like a book. When he looked at Toussaint, he desperately wanted to impress this new, extremely cool Black guy. But when he glanced between Red and Shayna, his skin flushed with rage. He shot hurt looks to Vida, Peter, Lorenzo. And when he spotted the machete-wielding strangers, he looked straight-up scared.

Fish let out a long breath and ran his hand through his hair.

"This is what you always wanted this space to be, right?" Gestas said, with a look of incredible satisfaction. "This is revolutionary shit. This was your dream."

Fish nodded reluctantly. I fought the urge to bust out laughing. They'd backed his white male rage into a corner using his number-one weakness—wanting nonwhite people to think he was cool.

"But it's just killing you not to be in charge, isn't it?" Shayna added. Gestas cut her a look like, "Enough."

"Why don't you come inside, man? Join us," Toussaint said with this warm grin, and I couldn't tell if he actually meant it or was just an amazing actor.

But Fish looked around again, then shook his head. "Nah, my uh—my lawyer said that I should keep some distance from the property while we're in court. It's not good for my suit if I get caught up in this occupation thing."

I wondered whether that was true, or if Shayna was right, and he just couldn't bear to be here if he wasn't the boss of everyone. Either way, my heart beat wildly with giddiness. Was he really going to move out? It seemed too good to be true.

"Man, fuck this," Fish said, kicking the dirt. "Here I am helping you guys. I bought this place. I got y'all a lawyer to fight for y'all. And this is how you thank me? I've lost my house. I've lost my band . . ."

Shayna opened her mouth to say something, but Toussaint shot her a death glare that said, "Leave it." She bit her lip and just rolled her eyes.

"So you want us to load that gear into your truck now or what?" Red said, xir voice like ice. I got a weird feeling that there was something between Red and Fish that I had never fully understood. Some reason that xe hated him that ran deeper than—well, the obvious.

"What?" Fish said, confused. "Oh right, the amps and stuff? Um." He glanced around at the crowd again. Everyone was looking at him like he was dog barf on the bottom their shoe. "Fuck it. Whatever. Keep them. I don't care."

He started walking back towards his truck, and I sagged with relief. But then he froze and turned and glared right at me. "And what about you? You coming with me? Or are you with them?"

The heat of everyone's gaze burned my face, and my blood pounded so hard my ears were ringing. This was it. My chance to get free, if I would only take it.

"Um," I cleared my throat and met his eyes. I imagined getting in his truck, riding next to his silent rage all the way back to Roger's house out in Katy.

I'd rather go to literal hell.

And fuck, hadn't I'd already broken up with a husband—and even a god? I could break Fisher Wellman's heart too. My eyes cut to Red's. Xe was trying and failing to look aloof. I smiled reassuringly.

"Them," I said. "I'm staying with them."

25

Watching Fish's truck speed off down Calcott, I felt giddy, like my blood was full of bubbles. It was how I'd felt the day I'd left Colton, and the day I'd filed the paperwork for divorce. I was free.

How the hell had I let myself get trapped with a man I loathed—*again*?

It had seemed so impossible to extricate myself from him . . . until suddenly it wasn't. All it took was a crowd of onlookers to see through his shit. All it took was Shayna, who'd taken over his building and stolen his power. I almost felt she was a wizard who'd defeated an evil dragon. I must've been staring at her worshipfully, because she caught my gaze and gave me a weird look.

And then my eyes met Red's, and xe gave me a small smile. I wanted to rush right up and kiss xim, there in front of everyone. But instead, I just smiled back. An understanding passed between us—an inevitability. We could be together now, we would be, soon. And I felt no need to rush. I wanted to savor every second of anticipation—wait until the moment was perfect, and a bit more private.

I had a hunch Red felt the same way.

The rest of the day was hectic, as our groups came together and transformed the Lab into a home for dozens of people. I didn't mind the work. Every inch of me felt electric, making mundane tasks joyful. Red joined up with the buff folks who were moving furniture and rotting statues and machine equipment out of the Lab and onto the curb. I doubted the city would be coming to pick it up, but maybe some locals would find treasure in all that crap, like the day Red found the Fun Machine. More likely the pile of junk would get rained on and rot. That would infuriate Fish, but I wasn't afraid of him anymore.

A couple Save the Eighth folks who had trucks were ferrying organizers to their apartments and bringing back mattresses for them to sleep on. Peter was live streaming and tweeting everything, documenting it all, and he and Vida huddled over a laptop for a few hours and made a very slick-looking website for Occupy the Eighth with links for people to donate and a calendar of events. Gestas meanwhile, was sweeping and mopping the floor of the Lab as it gradually cleared of Fish's hoard. Later, I found him in the living room, huddled over a notebook, scribbling furiously.

"Writing a song?" I asked, surprised. Usually Red wrote our lyrics.

"A letter," he said.

"Ooo-oo-oooh," I singsonged. "Is it for Angel?"

"Maybe," he said, bringing his knees up to his chest to hide what he was writing. But he couldn't hide the huge grin on his face.

"Gestas loves a soldierrrrr," I sang.

"Shut up!" he cried, throwing the pen at me. I ducked, and it skidded across the living room. "For your information, I'm critiquing the logical fallacies and historical inaccuracies he used in his last letter to me, where he had the gall to continue to defend his participation in this evil-fucking-imperial war."

"He sent you a letter already?"

"Mailed it before his plane took off."

"Ahhh!" I squealed. "Angel lo-oves Gestas." Gestas started up off the couch after me, and I ran for the kitchen.

"Save me, Lorenzo!" I grabbed his shoulders and hid behind his broad back. Lorenzo turned, chef's knife in hand, to face Gestas.

"To be honest, I'd let you at her, if I didn't need the help," Lorenzo said. I scoffed in fake outrage.

Gestas pointed at his eyes with two fingers, then shot them towards me. "Watch your back, little lady," he said, sneaking out of the kitchen.

I stuck out my tongue at him.

"Y'all are both acting like a pair of lovesick fools," Lorenzo mumbled, sounding slightly bitter. He was always crushing on girls who only saw him as a friend. It might've been his dad energy, what with the mustache and always cooking for everybody.

"Get those greens out of the fridge and rinse them in the big bowl, would ya?" he said.

Midafternoon, a guy named Damian approached Lorenzo and me and offered to help out in the kitchen. He was a fiftysomething, dark-skinned dude, shaved bald, with one gold canine and faded, illegible tattoos down his arms. We had a little informal meeting to plan out meals for the next few days, groceries we'd have to get, and how we could utilize the three apartment kitchens to feed the occupation that had grown to nearly fifty people over the course of the first day. Damian revealed he'd worked in kitchens most of his life, and it was clear he knew way more about how to feed everyone than we did. I worried Lorenzo might feel upset about Damian basically taking over. But the two of them hit it off right away, and Lorenzo seemed happy to learn from a more experienced cook.

For dinner that night, Lorenzo and I stewed a big pot of collard greens in Red and Gestas's kitchen, and we baked twenty-five sweet potatoes, so everyone could have a half. In Vida's kitchen, Damian fried cauliflower bites and made a giant pot of vegan mac and cheese.

Someone had hit up all the thrift stores in the area and brought back a bunch of used take-plates and forks—so everyone had a meal kit now. We served the food in the cleared-out Lab, sitting down around the big, empty, wooden floor to eat and have our first meeting as an occupation. This nightly ritual came to be known as the People's Muster.

I tried to love the People's Musters, I really did. Intellectually, I understood that they were a vital part of horizontally organizing a large group of people. Still, they usually made me want to tear my fucking hair out. They reminded me of staff meetings on campus—the part where the principal would open the floor to questions, and your least favorite people would ask about things that only pertained to them, or were ridiculously unlikely, or made tedious, semantic points that wasted everyone's time.

That first night, though, there was some magic in the air. The AC had just kicked on, so the room was starting to cool off. Moths fluttered around the lights in the rafters. Shayna, Gestas, and Toussaint all opened the meeting together, explaining how things would work—how anyone could add to the agenda or make a comment, how we'd use hand signals to get quick temperature checks of the crowd, how we'd try to make every decision through consensus. This was real, radical democracy in action! I tried to pay attention, but it was hard when I was sitting next to Red, and xir thigh was pressed against my thigh, which made my whole body light up with fireworks.

That night, we formed the committees that would structure our lives over the next few months. Kitchen was up first—Lorenzo and Damian did the talking. They asked for five more recruits from the crowd to help us with the cooking and cleaning, and funds to buy groceries for the next few days. Everyone's face illuminated blue as they swiped cash and carbon credits from their phones to Lorenzo's. A sanitation group was also organized to keep the Lab clean. Red volunteered for that one, which surprised me. Red had never seemed like much of a joiner, and had never been big on cleaning either.

Shayna asked for recruits to join her working group—actions—which would plan future events and protests. And Peter asked for people to help out with social media and comms. Vida wanted to start a group of artists to make works that would support the mission and beautify our space, and all the street artists in the crowd signed up with her. Finally, Toussaint asked for people to work with him on operations—basically, organizing and leadership. More hands went up for ops than any other call for volunteers. A lot of the folks volunteering were newcomers—the RevCom boomers and the younger socialists. Pretty much every white man in the room had his hand up to join ops. That didn't sit right with me, and from the look on Toussaint's face, it worried him also.

Gestas then led us into the morass of defining our mission and beginning to draft the guiding principles of the occupation. That was where I started to lose my mind with impatience. After forty-five minutes of arguing in circles, the discussion was finally tabled—with no consensus reached. Finally, to my astonishment, Lawyer Chad appeared from a corner of the Lab. Surprisingly, I hadn't noticed him come in, even though he stood out in a crisp, pink polo shirt and khaki shorts.

"Gestas asked me here to offer some legal advice," Chad said, rubbing his hands together. "Two nights ago, when I told y'all to get the public's attention, I didn't expect all this!" He laughed and looked around the crowd amusedly. "Tomorrow morning is the date stipulated by the original eviction order. Now, since we're still tied up in court, the legality of anyone forcing you off this property is dicey. Keep trying to gain media attention—I think Peter's set up some interviews for tomorrow. Get your message across, and try to be sympathetic. I'd shy away from saying anything too, uh, controversial." He cut his eyes towards Shayna. "And don't allow any illegal behavior here. The cops are going to be looking for reasons to storm this place." A bunch of heads nodded. He reminded us again that if cops showed up, to get inside, lock the doors, and refuse to let them in unless they could produce a warrant.

As Chad was leaving, Shayna stood up. "If the owner won't be living here anymore, what's the deal with his apartment upstairs? Can we use it for an office space?"

"I'm not sure," Chad said. "I did advise Fisher not to reside here for the duration of his suit. Better if he appears to be a more traditional landlord."

"So if he's not coming back, can we have the key to his place?" Shayna asked.

"You'll have to check with him on that," Chad said.

"Um . . ." Fifty heads whipped towards me as I tentatively raised my hand. "I have a key to his place? He moved all his stuff out already, so it's probably fine for y'all to use it."

"Don't *you* live there?" Shayna asked, squinting at me.

"Not really, not formally, uh . . ." I was blushing bright red under everybody's eyes. I didn't want to be associated with Fish anymore. I didn't want to sleep in his damn bed ever again. "Not anymore."

"Cool. I'll grab that key from you then," Shayna said.

The meeting adjourned, and people started stretching, milling, and talking. Shayna came over and I gave her the key. Red nudged me with xir elbow. "So if you're not staying at Fish's anymore, where you gonna stay?"

"Oh I don't know," I said, blushing all the way up to my forehead. "Maybe some kind soul will take me in."

"With the way you snore?" Red scoffed.

I shoved xir shoulder. "I do *not* snore."

"Oh you most certainly did last night. Sounded like a damn table saw."

"Fish never had a problem with it." I instantly regretted the words. At the mention of his name, Red's joking grin melted and xir eyes turned cold.

But it was only for a second, then xe smiled. "You wanna get out of here? Maybe go up on the roof? All these people are starting to make me feel claustrophobic."

"Yeah, sure," I said.

Red grabbed my hand, and my insides melted. I hadn't felt all turned-to-goo like that since my youth group days, when Colton stole a kiss after choir practice. I let Red lead me through the crowd, up the stairwell, past the door to Fish's apartment and up the ladder to the roof. I was glowing with pride. *Look who's holding my hand!* I wanted to shout to everyone we passed. *Look who I'm with!*

Then it was just the two of us on the roof, looking out over the tossing cane to the refinery lights beyond, the sky a hazy purple that only the brightest stars could penetrate.

"Don't get me wrong," Red said, bouncing on the tar roof. "I think the occupation is badass and this cool anarchist thing and all. But it's like . . . a lot."

"Yesss," I said, letting out a hiss of air. "Everything changed so fast."

"Yeah, shit, like the cops fucking gassed you last night! And now there's fifty people living here, and who knows how many more tomorrow? I'm down for the struggle, but I can't shake the feeling this is all gonna end in tragedy."

"I know what you mean. Hell, I still don't even know where I'm sleeping tonight," I said, cutting a glance at Red.

"Aren't you going back to your shiny Community? It's a school night."

"Fuck," I said, clasping a hand to my face. "I totally forgot it was Sunday. Oh my god—how can I go to work tomorrow, though? It's the first real day of the occupation!"

"So call in sick." Red's eyes twinkled with mischief.

"I can't do that. My kids have an exam on Thursday. I—" Two visions flashed before my eyes—me hurrying out of here so I could pass out in my sterile, lonely apartment, wake up at five a.m. to teach a hundred thirty kids who could barely conceal their loathing of me . . .

Or I could stay. And see where things were headed with Red.

"I guess I do still feel congested from the tear gas. I mean . . . maybe I need a day to recover from that shit? If I said I had a cold it wouldn't technically be lying."

"There you go."

I shot off an email to my principal and smiled at Red, feeling like a kid playing hooky.

"But the problem stands that we still"—xe sucked air through xir teeth—"don't know where you're gonna stay tonight."

"Oh come on," I said. "You're really gonna make me ask?"

"Ask what?" Red said, quirking up a sharp, black eyebrow.

I was nearly biting my lip off in frustration. "Fine," I said, blushing all the way up to my hairline. "Red, can I please stay at your place?"

"At my place? Sure, there's still some room on the floor of the living room. I'm sure you can find a spot to squeeze a sleeping bag."

Xe was tormenting me, watching me squirm on purpose. I gave xim a tiny shove in the chest, and xe staggered dramatically, clutching xir heart.

"Shoving me on a rooftop? Where's those police drones?" Xe scanned the skies. "Help! Someone help! There's a violent Christian girl trying to push me off the roof!"

"Oh my god," I said, turning for the fire exit in exasperation.

"Wait, wait," Red said, jogging up to me. "Are you trying to say—would you like to sleep *in my bed* again?" xe asked, with mock astonishment.

I sighed and looked up at xim, and xe was grinning, and even though xe was being absolutely maddening, I couldn't help grinning back. "That would be . . . ideal."

Xir face fell, suddenly serious. "And you and Fish? Is that really over?"

"It's been over for a long time. And I know—I know I should've officially ended it sooner, but I was just scared."

Red fell quiet and pulled a hip flask from xir pocket. Xe took a long swig before responding. I had a wild urge to grab the flask and chuck it off the roof, before Red could destroy ximself with alcohol like everyone else I'd ever been with.

"See that's what I don't get," Red said, twisting the cap shut one-handed. "Me and Gestas had to tiptoe around his fucking ego because he could literally throw us out in the street if we didn't. But what did he have on you? I could tell you hated his guts from way back. Why'd you let him—if you didn't—how could you . . ." xe trailed off, shaking xir head in disgust.

I sighed and looked off at the flaring smokestacks, "I was worried that if I broke up with him, I wouldn't be welcome at the Lab anymore. And I'd lose you two, and the band . . . and that felt like death."

"What?" Red cried, outraged. "We would've kept you in the band if you'd broken up with him! Hell, we would've hung out with you more. Sure, at first, I let him play with us 'cause of all the gear he bought us." Red chuckled. "But once I got real fed up with his shit, I only let him keep playing because I was worried you'd quit if I kicked him out."

"Fuck, really?"

"Hell yeah, Mads." Red barked a laugh. "You could've been sleeping in my bed this whole time."

And then xe bit xir lip. Stepped close to me. I wrapped my arms around xir neck, and my heart was beating so hard it hurt. Everything in me ached for xim, so it felt like I might die if xe didn't kiss me soon.

And maybe I haven't done Red justice, haven't found words yet to explain that not only was xe unnervingly gorgeous, and achingly cool, and brilliant at songwriting, and envied by everyone—xe was so fucking funny too, and sweet when xe wanted to be, and xe was brave, and didn't give a fuck what anyone else thought—rock-and-roll personified—and xe saw me, better than anyone ever had. Xe got my whole deal and still wanted me for it.

And every bit of attraction and pleasure I'd felt in my life, every kiss with Colton or Fish was like a flickering candle compared to the nuclear fusion at the heart of the sun, which is what it felt like—kissing Red.

That's all I'm going to say about that night. Red would've hated me writing even that much, and I owe xim some amount of privacy, at least. It's enough for me that the world knows that I was with Red, from the first day of the Free People's Village. I was xir person, and xe was mine, there at the dawning of a new world.

26

THE FIRST WEEK OF THE OCCUPATION

I called in sick on Tuesday too, my breath still coming short, throat still scratchy from the tear gas. On Wednesday I felt almost normal, but I called in sick again. If I had the sick days to burn, why not use them? As for Thursday and Friday, I figured, might as well round out the week. The truth was, I couldn't seem to tear myself away from the bustle of activity around the Lab, which people had started to call the Free People's Village. Every moment felt pregnant with history, every conversation momentous, as if all of it was being documented for posterity—and a lot of it was, with Peter and his team's cameras omnipresent. I couldn't bear to miss a second.

Most of all, though, I couldn't tear myself away from Red.

No cops showed up on Monday or Tuesday. On Wednesday some came sniffing around, but we did what Chad had said—shut the doors, asked to see a warrant. They didn't have one, so after poking around the yard, finding some discarded take-cups, and writing up a carbon fine for littering and invasive weeds, they left.

During the week, most people had to go to work, so the occupation shrunk to a few dozen folks. Red was barbacking in the evenings, so after I helped in the kitchen cooking breakfast, we'd have the afternoons together. We spent a lot of time alone in xir room, in our own little world. We watched movies, wrote songs together, read books in silence, lying next to each other on the bed. Xe would leave a hand resting on my calf—just because we couldn't bear to be without that contact. I felt a little guilty that we had that safe haven. Most people in the Free People's Village counted themselves lucky to have a mattress on the floor or a tent, while we had a whole room to ourselves. Sure, it was the size of a rich person's closet, with vines growing through the windows and moldy walls that riled up my asthma—still, it felt like a kingdom to the two of us.

When Red left for work in the evenings, I forced myself to go to the People's Muster, even though the snail's pace of defining our mission made me want to chew through my own wrist. Sometimes a moth would get caught in one of the spider webs in the rafters, and there'd be that whole drama to distract me from the arguing. The RevComs and anarchists thought the socialists were sellouts. The socialists thought the RevComs and anarchists were do-nothing idealists. The anarchists thought the communists were fascists, and the communists thought the anarchists were naïve. I didn't know who was right, but I often felt like their arguments had more to do with ego than ideology.

Save the Eighth organizers sometimes voiced their frustrations that the specific racial oppression that had sparked the occupation was getting lost in all the class-centric whitewashing. White occupiers would nod vigorously when Toussaint or Shayna voiced these concerns, but then they'd go on making their same old Marxist talking points. And while there were a few women who participated, 80 or 90 percent of the time on any given night, a cis man was talking at the center of the People's Muster.

Despite all the infighting, though, a lot of shit got accomplished, and life at the Lab was unrecognizable by the end of that first week. There was a kitchen staff of ten now, spread across all three apartments' kitchens, working together to make huge amounts of food for breakfast and dinner each day. Vida and her arts working group had painted white primer over all the chaotic graffiti inside the warehouse, starting on a mural celebrating the Eighth Ward that wrapped around the Lab—with portraits of famous civil rights leaders, artists, and rappers, against a skyline of iconic buildings threatened by the hyperway.

The gorgeous backdrop was helpful for Peter and his team, who were always live streaming. Most of his videos got likes in the 1–5K range. Clearly, we had a solid cohort of fans who were following the occupation closely. But Peter was frustrated we hadn't had a post go viral since the night of the tear gas attack.

His website had raised over ten thousand dollars, so a finance working group had been formed. For their first big purchase, they bought a couple of port-a-potties and set them way out by the tracks, since our current bathroom situation was proving woefully inadequate. Enterprising Villagers with machetes had cleared the cane all the way to the property line, though the ground was studded with sharp, severed stalks sunk in clay. A gardening working group was painstakingly removing the roots and preparing a large area on the west side of the Lab for planting.

I figured we had a few weeks max before the police shut us down—barely enough time to see sprouts come up. But it was a sweet idea to plant a garden, even if the seeds were doomed to lie trapped under a new hyperway.

27

AUGUST 31, 2020

Normally, I would've dreaded my first day back at school after missing a whole week, knowing that piles of emails and ungraded work would be waiting. Plus, there was a decent chance my students had said and done horrible things to each other while under the dubious supervision of subs, so there would be fresh, simmering drama to contend with.

But that morning, as I headed to Washburn High, I'd never been more excited to get to school. Ever since I'd read that first book Gestas lent me—Freire's *Pedagogy of the Oppressed*—I'd felt constrained, frustrated, and ashamed of parroting back the lessons handed down to me from the district offices. My day-to-day work wasn't *teaching*—Freire would call it *prescription, dehumanization,* and *conditioning the students to their oppression.* But the night before, I'd stayed up until three a.m. planning, lit with the fire of pedagogical inspiration. Today would be different.

I waited until the teacher's lounge was empty to make copies, then carried the warm paper clutched to my chest, feeling like a kid sneaking booze into school.

"Ms. Ryan! Where you been?" Princess asked as I walked into first period. "You get a new man? Too busy for us kids?"

I hoped she didn't catch my blush. Princess had an uncanny ability to see right through people.

I was surprisingly glad to see my first period students. I'd only known them a few weeks, and they'd given me a real hard time over those district-planned lessons. This year, the curriculum directors had us teaching To Kill A Mockingbird for our very first unit, and it wasn't making for a great impression.

Most of the class was already inside. Jazmin and Jaylen were seated at the front with *To Kill a Mockingbird* already set out on their desks. Trey and D'Unte were sitting in the back row, eyes bloodshot, giggling together as they shared a pack of M&M'S. Princess was sitting on the desk behind Naiya, fixing the ends of her friend's braids. Shanelle was sitting in Rishad's lap, which was fine—I was relieved if I could get through a lesson without them making out or breaking into a couple's fight. LaMarcus and Owen, two football players, were sharing earbuds, watching something on Owen's phone. Antoine had his head on his desk, hoodie pulled over his head—probably asleep. I'd decided I would only ever fuss at him about sleeping if an assistant principal came into the room. Antoine was living on an aunt's couch, where he said he couldn't get much sleep. Awake, he had a quick, unpredictable temper, so maybe it was best if he just napped through first period. I was going to let Kenya alone too, unless an AP walked in the room. Kenya had seemingly loathed me from the moment I first stepped in the classroom, but at least she was always reading. Never what I assigned, but still! Reading! Today's book was *If Beale Street Could Talk.*

"Haven't read that one, but I love Baldwin," I told Kenya, earning me a quick, devastating glare. Maybe she'd believe me if I actually taught Baldwin. Now that I was all fired up on the energy of the Free People's Village, maybe I would.

The first bell rang, and I let the kids keep talking through the principal's droned announcements and the Pledge of Allegiance to the national and Texas state flags. I'd have to choose my battles carefully today. Finally I said, "Alright, let's take your seats," and waited a good three minutes before everyone wrapped up their conversations, and Shanelle unwound herself from Rishad and sat in the desk beside him.

"I forgot my book," Naiya said. "The subs just showed movies, so I didn't think I'd need it."

"Yeah, we thought you were dead," Princess added.

"That's fine, we're actually going to take a break from *To Kill a Mockingbird* today and do something else."

"For real?" Shanelle asked. Only Jazmin looked put out, as she and Jaylen slipped their books into their backpacks. Everyone else perked up—even Kenya glanced up from *Beale Street.*

"Today we're going to read about something that's happening in this community right now," I said. "Have any of y'all heard about the hyperway expansion?"

A few kids raised their hands. To my surprise, Antoine was one of them, although his head was still resting on his desk, covered by his hood. I called on him first.

He made a big show of slowly rolling up to rest his cheek on his hand. "That's that road they're building. My aunt's gotta move, 'cause they're knocking down her building."

"They're tearing down my granny's house too," Naiya said. "My mom was born there. She's real fucked up about it."

I let the curse word slide. Freire says that "the act of rebellion . . . is grounded in the desire to pursue the right to be human." All my friends cussed like sailors, didn't they? Why would I try to dominate and suppress my students for doing the same?

Other kids chimed in, sharing folks they knew who were facing eviction. As they talked, I passed out copies of the latest *Chronicle* article about the hyperway expansion.

I sat down in an empty seat at one edge of the semicircle of desks. I'd rearranged them in a purposeful attempt to break down the teacher/student hierarchy. I also invited anyone who liked to start reading aloud—an opt-in thing, never assigned. Jazmin, as usual, took the lead.

After two sentences, I heard the click of the door open behind me, and my heart sank to my gut with dread. Nora, my AP,

173

tiptoed into the room, laptop half-cocked, and shot me a saccharine grin. I tried not to panic as she checked the lesson attached to the clipboard by the door. We were supposed to print out the lesson plans from the district every day and post them there "for accountability." I always forgot to do it, because it was a pointless redundancy—everything was already posted online. I cringed, guessing the plan she was looking at was a few weeks old.

Nora started walking around the room, peering over all my students' shoulders, making them nervous. Watching the kids, though, I took heart. All of them—I mean *all,* were following along with the reading. Nora was always knocking points off my evaluations for the kids sleeping, texting, or carrying on a whole-ass separate conversation while I was trying to teach. They'd *never* all looked so engrossed in something we were reading. Surely that would matter more than the fact that I wasn't teaching the district-approved lesson.

Nora took a seat at the back of the room and started typing fast, the clatter of keys becoming white noise. I took a deep breath and figured that I was in it now, no way to pivot back to the district lesson plan, so I might as well commit. I'd show Nora what I could do when teaching my own kind of lesson.

"Thank you, Jazmin," I said, as she reached the end of the first paragraph. "Alright, what do you notice so far?" My question was purposefully vague, another tip from Freire. I wanted to start an open-ended conversation, not run a *Jeopardy*-style Q&A where I held all the answers.

"The title is kinda fucked up," an unfamiliar voice said. When I saw who had spoken, my heart skipped a beat. Kenya, for the first time ever, was participating in my class! It occurred to me I should probably address that *fuck*, what with Nora typing up every word, but I didn't want to risk alienating Kenya at this sign of interest.

"And what do you mean by 'f'd up'?" I said, arching an eyebrow in an attempt to communicate, "Please stop cussing in front of my boss."

"It's like . . . the news is supposed to be objective, right? But by saying 'clean commute,' it's like they're already on the side of the hyperway."

Rhetorical analysis, and with the AP in the room! Surely that made up for the cussing. My heart was fit to bursting when Princess jumped in.

"Yeah, and look at that little author picture—she looks like a white lady. Deborah Tillsen. Shit, Deborah don't know our neighborhood. She don't care about us. She's . . . what's that word?"—Princess waved her hand in tiny circles—"Social studies teacher always going on about it—"

"Biased?" Kenya offered.

"Yeah, she biased!"

I could've jumped for joy. Identifying bias in nonfiction writing was a major state standard. I hoped Nora had written that down, and not just the cuss words.

I decided to wade in—get more kids talking. "Princess has pointed out that even the news is written by *someone*, yeah? And it's always good to interrogate their motives. But Princess also made an assumption—that Deborah doesn't care what happens to the Eighth Ward. What do y'all think. Is that assumption fair?"

"I don't know," Owen began—to my absolute delight. The JV quarterback was usually almost as reluctant to speak as Kenya. "Just 'cause she's white, you can't say she don't care. Isn't that, like, reverse racism?"

"Reverse racism isn't real. Keep up," Kenya said, snapping her fingers in Owen's direction.

"*You* keep up," Owen muttered. "'Least I don't got a dimpled-potato-looking-ass nose and—"

"Hey, hey!" I jumped in. "We are *not* doing that today, alright? Y'all are doing a great job thinking critically about this article. Let's keep it civil." I shot a pleading look at both of them. "Now we have a disagreement about the author. Kenya thinks she's biased against the Eighth Ward. Owen says we can't assume that yet. How can we gather more evidence?"

Oh, the conversation that unfurled was a work of art. Everyone got into it. Shanelle thought we shouldn't make assumptions about a journalist based only on their identity. That we could only trust the words on the page. Rishad actually disagreed with his girlfriend, saying the author's identity did matter. Antoine backed him up, saying the world would be a better place if only Black folks were allowed to speak on Black neighborhoods. After a healthy debate, I suggested we keep reading and see if we could find any other evidence of bias in the text. I hadn't expected this discussion to pop up—I thought we'd just be going through the points of the article summary-style, making sure everyone understood what was happening with the hyperway and the Free People's Village. My students' critical analysis had taken me pleasantly by surprise, and I was glad to go down that rabbit hole with them.

I'd never led a class through such a close rhetorical analysis— Shakespeare, Harper Lee, and Hemingway had never inspired such assiduous reading. But the kids were set on teasing out Deborah Tillsen's bias. They caught that Tillsen glossed over the environmental impacts of the hyperway construction, while singing the praises of a "clean commute to the suburbs." They caught the use of passive voice and bureaucratic euphemisms to discuss the impacts on Eighth Ward residents. And while the Free People's Village protest was briefly described, the last word was given to the police chief, who characterized the occupation as a "dangerous and misguided disruption."

No fights broke out, no one fell asleep, everyone was reading along and participating—this was what teaching high-school English was supposed to be like. Ten minutes before the bell, Nora picked up her laptop and snuck out of the room. I shot her a big smile at the door, but her heavily made-up face was inscrutable as ever.

I wasn't surprised when I got an email notification during the next passing period that she wanted to conference with me during third. That'd take up my whole planning period, but I wasn't even mad about it. I actually felt *excited* to talk to her about my plans for a new unit on "literature of resistance."

Nora Wagner was hard to read because she always smiled, even when she was giving you terrible news, and she used this slick, professional voice and all the latest corporate jargon. She wore stiletto heels and false eyelashes to school every day, which seemed an absurd getup for prowling around a high school, but it did make her terrifying in a Disney-villain kind of way that seemed to work on the students. I was a bit terrified of her too, but I also knew she was extremely intelligent, and had total power over my career. She'd never seemed to like me much, and I was desperate to earn her approval.

As I sat down across the desk from her, I was certain I had.

"That was incredible, right? I can't believe how engaged everyone was!"

One sharply gelled eyebrow shot up. "Engagement *was* higher than average," she said. "I think you should take a few moments to go over your scores before we discuss the observation." She punched a key on her laptop. "They should be in your inbox."

Even before I opened the attachment, my gut churned at the tone in her voice. I bit down hard on my lip as the document loaded, fighting back the absurd tears that were stinging the back of my eyes. Every time we were observed, we got graded on thirty-two metrics, on a scale of one to four. Fours meant excellent teaching—and if your average for the year was over a three, you got a raise. Ones meant "unsatisfactory," and too many of them meant you got fired.

There were a hell of a lot of ones on today's rubric.

I cleared my throat to keep the tears out of it. "I-I don't understand . . ."

"What exactly is confusing you?"

"Well, like—okay, you gave me a one for rigor. But the kids were doing a rhetorical analysis! On their own! Those standards are some of the most rigorous in the curriculum."

"I don't think making assumptions about an author's bias based on their race counts as rhetorical analysis," Nora said.

"They were picking apart Tillsen's diction!" I said. "And they were debating the *validity* of making assumptions about an author's bias based on their race. That's Socratic debate! That's examining their own biases! Isn't that exactly what this kind of textual discussion is supposed to sound like?"

Nora tented her fingers and pressed her lips to them. "It's a moot point, Maddie. You got a score of one for rigor—and a one for all the instructional design metrics, because I didn't see anything in that classroom that matched your lesson plan. In fact, I couldn't tell what the lesson plan was! Was it the assigned district lesson plan for today? Or the one attached to the clipboard by your door, which you should've taught a week ago?"

"I decided to do something different today, okay? And it worked! Just—can't you look at the big picture here? The article actually connected to these kids' lives! They've never been so engaged in a reading!"

"It's your job as the teacher to get kids to connect to the district-approved text. Which in this case is *To Kill a Mockingbird*. And speaking of rigor—I don't think that an eight-hundred-word *Chronicle* article really compares to the rigor of one of the greatest works of American literature, do you?"

"*To Kill a Mockingbird* is a white savior story that white teachers like because it's all 'good white people saved Black people from Jim Crow.' It's supposed to make our students grateful to us or something," I said, trying to parrot Gestas's points from our conversation months before.

"I see. And you, a second-year teacher, understand *To Kill a Mockingbird* better than the district content leadership team? Which I'll remind you, is very diverse, including a number of Black women. All of whom have master's degrees in education. But you know better than them? You understand your students' needs better? Who's the white savior here?"

It wasn't *my* analysis; it was Gestas's. But I didn't think explaining that I was taking teaching tips from my incarcerated bandmate would help. So I just muttered, "It's ass-backwards that the *one text* we teach from the civil rights movement is written by a white woman."

"You may tolerate obscene language in your classroom," Nora said sternly, coral-painted lips pressed in a furious line. "But I do not."

I scoffed in frustration then, and I could hear how much I sounded like one of my students. I saw how easy it was for her to dismiss me and everything I was trying to do as childish. To her, I was a surly kid, and she felt obligated to crush my spirit.

"While we're on the topic of unprofessional behavior . . ." She picked up her phone and swiped it unlocked. "This came through my Twitter feed a few days ago." My stomach was already in knots, but now they twisted harder. What had she seen? So much of what I did at the Lab had been captured this week. So much of what went on there was unprofessional, fire-able, even illegal. She held up her phone. I sagged with relief—it was just the viral video of our show— the set right before Shayna's speech and the tear gas and the cop riot. "Would this little activity have to do with why you called in sick all of last week?"

"Little activity?" I repeated. "Look, what I do in my free time is my business. And that *little activity* was part of a protest that's trying to save this neighborhood! Did you even pay attention to the article we read in class today? Do you know that many of our students and their families are facing eviction and displacement?"

"Save the neighborhood. Interesting you're using that word again, since you're the one who mentioned white saviors."

"Oh come on, that's not what I mean—"

"As a Latina woman of color—" she began, pressing a hand to her chest.

I'm sure it was true that Nora Wagner had a grandpa from Argentina, as she liked to mention, but she was at least white-passing, with her blue eyes and skin as pale as mine. Still, she often referred to herself as BIPOC, especially during Diversity & Inclusion seminars on professional development days. Teachers might shoot each other raised-eyebrow looks when she did that, but no one ever challenged her on it.

"—I believe the best thing you can do for your students is show up for them. And do your job."

I was furious, but I couldn't think of a comeback to that. I had skipped out on my kids for a whole week. Mostly so I could make out with my new person. Who the hell was I to claim some moral high ground here? "I was sick," I muttered, sure she could hear the lie.

"And to answer your question," Nora continued. "Yes, I do know what's going on in the neighborhood, and I'd warn you to be very careful in your involvement with this occupation. As you should know, the state of Texas does not suffer criminals to be teachers." She swiped down a few tweets, to the video of the cops' attack, the clip of a pig's arm bringing a club crashing down onto that poor girl's skull. "If you get arrested on a felony charge, you'll lose your license, and there will be nothing I can do to help you."

She met my eyes then, and I could see the barely suppressed smile there. She was loving every minute of this. "But let me stress that it will not take a felony for me to remove you from the class-room. You're on thin ice, Maddie. If you take another sick day, I'm going to need a doctor's note. And I better see a district-approved lesson plan—on your clipboard, and being taught—every time I pop into your classroom for the rest of the year."

She wagged her phone in the air. "And when it comes to social media, I expect you to conduct yourself in a manner that represents our school's values. I'll be watching."

28

THE SECOND WEEK OF OCCUPATION

"She sounds like a fucking bitch," Lorenzo said.

I had come straight to the Lab after work to help him cook dinner. I shouldn't have. I should've gone back to my Community, read through the district-assigned lesson plans for the week, and gotten caught up on grading. But I just couldn't bring myself to do it. As much as I felt a responsibility to my students, I also felt a responsibility to the Village now.

More than that, I couldn't resist seeing Red. Xe was already at work and wouldn't return until long after I fell asleep. But there would be that half-awake moment at three a.m., when xe'd slide into bed next to me, reeking of the bar, waking me only long enough for me to scoot backwards into xir arms. And in the morning, I could catch a few groggy kisses before I left for work.

So I was back in Red and Gestas's kitchen, venting to Lorenzo while we chopped vegetables for a giant pot of chili.

"What are you going to do?" he asked. "You gonna teach what they want?"

"I guess I have to, if I want to keep my job," I said. But the thought of it made me feel like I was dying inside.

"Do you *want* to keep your job?"

"Shit," I said, never having really thought about it. I'd worked so hard for my degree. I'd been so in love with the idea of teaching. But in truth, my job was exhausting and miserable, and it made me hate myself—because I knew school made kids feel the same way. I felt like a cog in a brutal, soul-crushing machine. Abuse trickled down from the superintendent, through the principals, to the teachers, and finally to the students. Now that I'd gotten a taste of what teaching could be like, if only I could free myself from the "Pedagogy of the Oppressor," I didn't think I could keep toeing the line like the district wanted.

"I don't know anymore," I said honestly. "But I have student loans, and a lease, so . . ."

"Yeah, I get that," Lorenzo said. He hated working for an oil refinery, but he was doing it so he could become a certified electrician. He wanted to retire his parents someday.

All that week, I kept spending nights at the Lab, even though I was getting more and more exhausted. Most of the folks camping outside were college students, and they partied even on weekdays until well after midnight. I could only fall asleep after they quieted down, and then I had to wake up at six a.m. to shower.

The occupation was growing steadily. At the People's Muster on Wednesday, I counted a hundred and twenty-three of us. Between working and being in the kitchen, I hadn't had time to meet many of the new members. But Lorenzo filled me in that the Brown Bloc had joined our cause, and the Coalition of Young Palestinians and Jews Against Apartheid had shown up in solidarity, as well as organizers from other historically Black neighborhoods—Third Ward Strong and the Coalition for Urban Justice. The Urban Gardeners and Food Not Bombs folks were donating produce and groceries. And there was a rumor that the Gulf Coast Indigenous Alliance was coming—with two vans of Indigenous activists from Brownsville and Corpus Christi.

29

Red, Gestas, and I were holed up in Red's room, working out some songs when Vida came in with the news that the Gulf Coast Indigenous Alliance van from down south had arrived. "The GCIA is about to do some kind of ceremony or blessing or something, at the edge of the encampment. Let's check it out!"

I started up off the bed, but Gestas and Red stayed put. It took Vida a half second to realize her mistake. Her brows crinkled up. "Oh Gestas, I'm so sorry. I didn't think—"

Of course. Gestas couldn't go to an event if it was more than a few feet from the Lab.

"It's fine," he said, seeming more annoyed at the earnestness of her apology than the oversight.

"Maybe we can see it from the roof?" I suggested.

"Yeah, okay," Gestas said, setting his drumsticks on top of the tom.

Red threw up xir arms in exasperation. "So much for band practice, I guess." But xe followed us out of the room.

As we made our way to the roof, I realized that even though I'd lived in the United States—in Houston—my entire life, I'd never met a Native person. Suddenly that struck me as bizarre and sad.

A big group was gathered at the south end of the property, the side that faced the hyperway. The crowd formed a semicircle around the group of a dozen newcomers.

"That's them?" I asked.

Surprise must have crept into my voice, because Gestas said, "Don't tell me you were expecting buckskin and headdresses."

"No!" I said, blowing air through my lips. But Gestas had seen right through me. The folks from down south seemed like any other middle-aged Latine people, and that had surprised me. The guy who beating a large drum with a fat stick was wearing a polo shirt, had a mustache and a crew cut, and looked like he could be Lorenzo's dad. Heck, Lorenzo, with his hair to the middle of his back, looked more stereotypically Indigenous than most of the other men.

A woman in her forties in a long, patterned skirt, wearing a beaded necklace and earrings, looked the most like what I'd been expecting. She was holding a bowl that was smoldering—the smoke rising and entwining around her graying braids. As the hand drummers behind her picked up momentum, she and a few others began chanting along to the rhythm.

"What's that they're burning?" I asked to the group, not sure who would answer.

"Smudging," Vida corrected. "Don't know. Could be sage or cedar, maybe tobacco." Her eyes were glued to the ceremony. Vida was interested in anything spiritual—she collected crystals, read tarot cards, talked about Buddhism and chakras and her sun and moon rising, and had a tattoo of the Sefirot on her left forearm.

"Hey look," Red said, cupping xir hands around the burning end of xir cigarette. "I can bless the land too. Hell, with all the drumming you do, Gestas, and all the cigarettes we smoke, we've been blessing the shit out of this place and didn't even know it!"

"Stop. Show some respect," Gestas said, and it was the harshest tone I'd ever heard him use towards Red.

"What?" Red protested. "You two rag on religion all the time," xe said, pointing between me and Gestas. "But this is sacred?"

"Yes. This is fucking sacred," Gestas said, looking back to the ceremony. We were all silent for a while, listening to the heartbeat of the drumming and the mesmerizing chants. I think we were waiting for Gestas to clarify, but he was just watching intently.

"You know, Red, you *do* kind of have a point," Vida said tentatively. I looked at her with wide eyes, not expecting her to side with Red on disrespecting anything spiritual. "You *could* do a blessing. Not as a joke. I'm saying—this is your spiritual tradition too. Not these tribes, exactly, maybe. But—well, aren't you part Indigenous?"

"What?" Red said, scrunching xir forehead at her.

"Aren't some of your dad's people from Zacatecas?"

"Yeah. My dad's mom's family. But they're all Catholic."

"Have you seriously never thought about this?" Vida said, eyes going wide. "Catholicism came from Europe. Do all your family on that side look one-hundred-percent European?"

"No, they're not white," Red said.

"So where do you think the brown came from?" Vida said, stretching out each word in a kind of patronizing way.

Red shook xir head and exhaled a long stream of smoke. I coughed a little, my bronchia tightening with asthma. I kept hoping Red would quit smoking of xir own accord, now that we were together, knowing how much the smoke bothered my lungs, more than ever since the tear gas exposure. But xe hadn't.

"At some point, way back, sure," Red said. "Some of my great-great-grandparents had to be Indigenous. But the Catholic missionaries came and did what they did, and now that side of the family, they've been Catholic so long, they don't remember anything else. I think my great-grandma did some brujería, but that died with her."

The drumming ended and we all fell silent as the woman who'd been smudging handed off the bowl to someone else, took up a mic hooked to a small PA system, and started to speak. First she spoke in a language I'd never heard before, then in Spanish, then in English. When she got to the English part, I learned she'd been welcoming everyone, introducing her fellow members of the Gulf Coast Indigenous Alliance, and finally introducing herself. Her name was Rio Hernandez, and she was Karankawa Kadla.

"Whaaaaat?!" I whispered, as she switched languages again. The Karankawa were the Native people who had lived right here—in Houston—before colonization. "But they told us all the Karankawa were extinct!" I hissed, certain I was remembering correctly from my seventh-grade Texas history class.

"That's a convenient lie for genociders to tell, isn't it?" Gestas said. "One way to erase people is to kill them. And Stephen F. Austin, namesake of our great capital city here in Texas, he did—he killed a hell of a lot of Karankawa. But if you can't kill every last person in a civilization, you can just lie and say you did. That's another kind of erasure. You can't give justice or owe reparations to a people who no longer exist. At least, officially." Gestas raised an eyebrow at me. "Did you believe everything else they taught us about the Karankawa?"

I gasped and put a hand to my mouth, remembering the only other fact about the tribe that was stuck way back in my memory. How had I ever believed it? All over Texas, every year, every seventh grader in the state was taught the same thing. "They told us the Karankawa were cannibals. That's another lie, isn't it?"

"Ding, ding, ding," Gestas said.

"Cannibals?" Red cried. "I must've been living out of state for that part of the curriculum. Holy shit, they really taught y'all that?"

I nodded. "I even remember what the textbook page looked like. There was this illustration of Native folks with fishing gear in some grasslands. It looked all peaceful. Maybe that's why I remember it so vividly, because it was so shocking when the book was like, Oh yeah, and they ate people. And now they're extinct."

"Extinct," Gestas shook his head. "Like they're animals."

"And we definitely did not learn that it was Stephen F. Austin who did the genociding," I said. "Oh my god, everything here is named after that dude!"

Gestas raised his eyebrows and nodded, but then we fell silent, because Rio had switched to English again. She started describing what this land—her people's land—had looked like before colonization. "Coastal prairie stretched from the piney woods north of the city all the way to the Gulf. These wetlands were a home for thousands of species of our nonhuman relatives. This was a resting place for birds migrating from North to South America, a nursery for all the sea life of the Gulf. The bayous weren't bordered with cement retaining walls and channeled into straight lines." Her voice turned derisive. "They rambled. They trickled at some times and flooded after rains, because that's what they were meant to do, and they were full of life! Fish that weren't sick with chemicals swam here, along with alligators and otters."

My eyes went wide at the thought of otters splashing in and out of our bayous. She went on. "Where that refinery is"—she pointed at the steaming Valiant refinery on the horizon—"herds of deer grazed for millions and millions of years. Coyotes, wolves, ocelots, and jaguars hunted here. And have you ever wondered why it's called Buffalo Bayou?" she asked and waited a beat. And I felt the crowd collectively exhale in understanding. "Buffalo used to live here! They would come down to the coast to escape the harsh winters on the Great Plains to the north."

Again, I felt stricken by my own ignorance of the history of the land I had always lived on. Everything around here—streets, restaurants, bayous, bars—got named after buffalo, but I'd never really thought about how once, there must have been herds right where we stood.

"And my *people* have lived here," Rio said, her voice thick with emotion. "For tens of thousands of years. But when white colonizers showed up, they brought so much death with them." She waved a hand to gesture at the surroundings—the hyperway arcing through the sky to the south, roaring with passing cars, the Valiant refinery, and the polluted retention pond.

She pulled out a piece of paper from a pocket in her skirt and started reading a prepared statement. "The Gulf Coast Indigenous Alliance stands in solidarity with the residents of the Eighth Ward who are fighting to defend their homes from yet another oil pipeline, disguised as a 'green' hyperway. Many of the residents of this neighborhood are descended from Indigenous African ancestors who were brought here against their will, who have fought to make a home for themselves. We also affirm that many Karankawa, Atakapa Ishak, Coahuiltecan, Caddo, and other Native people of this land were enslaved alongside African people, and we aided one another in surviving, in resisting our oppressors, and often in building lives and families together. Today we embrace you as brothers and sisters in the fight against the ongoing white-supremacist violence threatening our land, our homes, our culture, and our peoples."

Rio looked up from the paper at Shayna, who had a hand pressed to her chest. Rio spread her arms in offer of a hug. Shayna hurried forward, and the audience cheered as the two women held each other for long moments. Peter, kneeling at the front of the crowd, caught the whole thing on his DSLR, and I knew already the clip would go viral.

"Now, we would like to offer up a prayer," Rio said. "Creator, we give thanks—"

"Okay! How is this any different?" Red hissed. Vida and Gestas shushed xim but xe kept on. "*God, Creator*—y'all are always rolling your eyes when Maryanne tries to get a prayer group going after the Musters. But this is so serious?"

"Christianity is ours to make fun of," I whispered, trying to shut xim up. "We have trauma!"

"It's more fundamental than that," Gestas growled—regretfully, as if he really wanted to listen to Rio's prayer but couldn't bear not to make his point. "Christianity claims to hold the only path to salvation from eternal punishment." He pushed against the half wall circling the roof like he wanted to crack the bricks. "It creates a pathological fear of that punishment in adherents—a hell complex. It teaches subservience to your oppressors and provides a moral justification for ethnic cleansing, colonization, and genocide. It is a trillion-dollar pyramid scheme selling afterlife insurance! It is the opiate of the masses! It is the carceral-fucking-surveillance state of religions!" he hissed, only stopping because he'd run out of breath.

"Tell us how you really feel," Vida joked.

"Okay, to be fair, yes. Christianity is mostly like that," I said, feeling weirdly defensive. "But just saying, Jesus made some solid points." Even though I agreed with Gestas, some part of me had to defend whatever was good in the ideology that had ruled my early life.

"Sure, yeah, Jesus was a radical, brown communist, but no Christian actually lives by what he said. Camel, eye of needle, et cetera, et cetera," Gestas said, waving a hand dismissively.

"Maybe Christianity's particularly bad, but it's all magical thinking, isn't it?" Red said, gesturing with xir cigarette to the crowd beyond the tents, now starting to disperse. "It's all talking to some Creator—Spirit—whatever that doesn't exist?"

"No, Indigenous religions are fundamentally different," Gestas said. "And maybe you would've learned that if you hadn't talked through the whole damn ceremony."

"But why?" Red asked, with a big, trolling smile, even though Gestas was getting seriously pissed.

"Because Christianity is in service to white supremacy, and these spiritual traditions resist it! Why do you think colonizers forced their religion on Indigenous people? Because a culture and spirituality that's rooted in the land is powerful! People aren't going to give that up!"

"But they mostly did," Red said. "My grandparents are, like, a case in point. Vida, yours too, right? They Catholic?"

"Okay, but these folks didn't!" Gestas said, gesturing to the now-empty side yard. Shayna had led the GCIA folks into the Lab already. "They held fast to their culture, despite an onslaught of colonial violence. And what was irretrievably lost, they've been working for generations to reconstruct. And that's fucking badass! And you should show some respect."

"Just imagine," Vida said, looking across the roofs of Eighth Ward towards the far-off Downtown skyline. "Imagine if the millions of us here who have Indigenous heritage—imagine if we all still knew our stories, and medicine, and history. If we still spoke our ancestors' languages, and knew where they were buried, imagine how powerful we'd be." She shook her head bitterly.

"Yeah, I don't know," Red said, crushing xir cigarette onto the asphalt roof. "I got ancestors on three continents. That seems like a lot to keep up with."

"Maybe, but it might be really powerful to learn about any of them—or all of them," Vida said.

"Ehhhh." Red grabbed one wrist and bent at the waist to stretch. "I think I'd rather get high and play video games. Peter got the new *Zelda*!"

I hesitated to weigh in. I suppose far enough back, my Irish ancestors had been colonized, and their culture, language, and spiritual traditions had been violently stomped out. I had never really spent much time thinking about them. I was white, and whiteness erased ancestors, like Gestas had said. Maybe that was why I'd screwed up so bad in that first Save the Eighth meeting, when Shayna had asked us to name ancestors. I hadn't really understood the concept. Now, I was swept up in the beauty of Vida's vision. Imagining what the world would be like if all of us suddenly knew the stolen secrets of our ancestry.

Red headed for the door that led to the access ladder.

"Red's hopeless," Gestas said.

"Red's only religion is *rock 'n' roll!*" I teased, in my best Axl Rose imitation, throwing up devil horns and sticking my tongue out at the end. Gestas laughed, and Red shot me a middle finger without turning around.

Then xe jumped out of the way of the door, which suddenly swung open. Shayna emerged, with the entire GCIA in tow, before Red slipped behind them and disappeared downstairs.

"And this is the roof, where the smokers like to hang out." Shayna cast a disapproving gaze at our group. I gave her a "not me" signal. "Actually, y'all should meet," Shayna told the GCIA folks, waving them over. "Gestas here is one of the original tenants. He's part of the suit against TxDOT."

Gestas gave a small acknowledging wave as Shayna named off each of the GCIA folks, including Rio, who'd spoken below. They were mostly at least ten years older than us, and they were all polite and smiled, but they didn't entirely manage to mask their surprise as they took in Gestas's look. Today, he was wearing combat boots, Hello Kitty knee-high socks, a neon-yellow plaid miniskirt, a sleeveless Rammstein shirt, and braids in his beard.

"Nice to meet you," Rio said politely.

Shayna started to lead the delegation back downstairs, but one person hung back. He was one of the guys who'd been playing a hand drum during the ceremony. He was taller and younger than anyone else from GCIA. His black hair hung to the middle of his neck in a bob that flipped out at the ends.

"Could I bum a smoke from anyone?" he asked with a fluid wave of his wrist. "That bus ride was lo-hong."

Gestas pulled a bag of loose tobacco from his back pocket and started rolling up a cigarette for the newcomer. "I'm sorry, Shayna rattled off everyone's name so fast, and I didn't catch yours," he said.

"Gerónimo. But it's Nimo," Nimo clarified. "He/him." He looked at me and Vida expectantly, so we introduced ourselves, gave our pronouns.

"I think your tour group is leaving," I said, as the last of the GCIA folks disappeared through the access door.

"I'll catch up to them later," Nimo said, shifting his weight to one hip and cupping one elbow with his opposite hand. "They are all so wonderful, and very open-minded, you know. Juan Pablo is a macho dude, but, like, such a sweetheart."

"I feel like there's an *and yet* coming," Gestas said, licking the rolling paper to seal it.

Nimo laughed—a single, dramatic *ha!,* head flung back—"And yet, after four hours on a bus with him trying to talk to me about sports the whole way, let's just say—it's nice to find some queer folks a little closer to my age."

Gestas stretched out a hand to offer the freshly rolled cigarette. "So what's your deal, Nimo?"

Gestas always asked that when meeting new people, where many people said, "What do you do?" That question, he said, *reinforces the false capitalist construct that we are defined by the labor we do to generate profit for our corporate overlords.* "What's your deal?" elicited more interesting answers, anyways.

"Goodness, my deal, what *is* my deal . . . can I borrow a light?" Nimo took a lighter from Vida and puffed as he considered the question.

"I'm twenty-six, so, a bit older than y'all?" He arched an eyebrow in question. Vida nodded confirmation. "Also, I'm a Leo. So, you know. Watch out." He pawed the air like a vicious kitten. "Grew up in Galveston, but now I'm in Corpus. According to family tradition on my mom's mom's side, we are Ishak. Who are like, original to *here.*" He pointed down, through the tar-strip roof and two floors of brick, to the earth trapped beneath the slab foundation of the

Lab. I remembered learning in school that the Atakapa Ishak were also extinct, *also* had been cannibals, and now struck those facts from my memories. "Although my family all became Christian and tried to be white as possible. Exvangelical," he said, pointing to himself and cringing.

"Oh my gosh, welcome!" I blurted out. I pressed a hand to my chest. "Ex-Catholic!"

Gestas pointed to himself. "Ex-Baptist."

"You're in good heathen company," Vida said. "This is so random—ooh, or maybe *not* random—but we were just talking about belief and religion, and the difference between Christianity and Indigenous traditions."

"Our friend who was leaving as y'all came up is one of those obnoxious, edgelord, Richard-Dawkins-type atheists," Gestas explained.

"Mmmm, gotcha," Nimo said, exhaling smoke. I took a step back from the circle.

"So you're like, um, just reconnecting to your Indigeneity, as an adult then?" Vida asked, trying to seem casual, but I knew her too well. She was bursting with excitement at the possibility that she could do something similar.

"Yeah, the GCIA folks have been really cool about welcoming me in and teaching me stuff. There's no other Ishak organizing with them, but they're gonna try to, like, help me connect with some elders they know of? Maybe?"

"That's so cool," Vida breathed, letting a rush of air out from between her full, scarlet-painted lips. "I'd give anything just to know the name of the tribes my ancestors came from."

Nimo twisted his lips in a sympathetic frown. Vida watched him a moment, as if she was hoping he'd say something. When he didn't, she went on. "I'm a spiritual person, you know, but I've never felt I could explore, like . . . my actual ancestry. Because I don't wanna be appropriative. Not saying you are!" She said the last in a flurry.

"There's a way to go about reconnecting respectfully," Nimo said. "At least I think so. There's a guy in the McAllen GCIA chapter who just identifies as Chicano, because he doesn't know what tribe his ancestors belonged to. He's showing up to organize with us, but he's not claiming to be from some specific tribe and stealing their traditions, you know? You could talk to Rio about it. I can introduce y'all."

"Oh my gosh, that would be amazing," Vida said.

"To be honest, there's people who think I have no business claiming to be Indigenous also, because I was raised Christian, or because the Atakapa-Ishak aren't federally recognized, or because I wasn't born on a rez," Nimo said, tucking his hair behind one ear. "I've only been going to the GCIA meetings for a few months, so this is all kind of new to me too. The amount I know about Christianity compared to my Ishak side is like—" He held one hand above his head, and one down by his ankles. Vida laughed and nodded. "Maybe they're right. But then—giving up on my ancestry because white people forced my grandparents to assimilate doesn't seem right either."

Nimo turned to me and Gestas. "So what made y'all leave y'all's respective church families?" He said the last two words sarcastically. "I hate to assume, but was it, you know, all the *gay*?" Gestas was visibly queer, but maybe Nimo was trying to suss what me and Vida's deal was.

Gestas laughed and answered first. "It was a gradual thing for me. My dad was a Baptist preacher and such a fucking hypocrite." He punched his fist into his hand with the last two words. "Preaching on Sundays about how people needed to dig deep in their hearts and pockets to give to the church. Then all week he's driving around in the air-conditioned Escalade they bought him, and he can't spare a dollar for an unhoused pregnant girl standing at the stoplight. In a hundred-degree heat. In August!"

"That doesn't sound gradual, that sounds like a very specific moment," Vida said.

"There were a million moments like that. Where what he said and how he acted just didn't add up. Sometime around age ten or eleven, I was just like, Fuck this guy and his whole deal. I started questioning everything." Gestas leaned on one hip as he rolled another cigarette for himself. "Although it also wasn't *not* all the gay stuff. If he'd ever been kind to me, maybe I'd have bought into his bullshit. But he was emotionally abusive, because I couldn't correctly perform girlhood."

"Oh, I see," Nimo said, eyes going wide, like maybe he'd only just figured out that Gestas was trans.

"What about you?" Vida turned to me. "When did you lose your faith?"

"Huh," I said. No one had ever asked me that before. I had to take a few moments, to carve a narrative out of the curdled, gray blob of memories which marked the worst period of my life, the last few months before I left Colton.

"I had this high school boyfriend who was really into religion. We got married way too young, and it was awful," I told Nimo. "He'd weaponize scripture at me. We'd be arguing, and he'd say, 'Ephesians 5:22.' Like that should just shut me up."

Nimo and Gestas nodded.

"I associated religion with him, so that the more I resented him, the more I started to resent religion. This snarky, inner voice started up in my head, jeering during Mass, making fun of Colton when he said grace before dinner."

"But the final straw—okay, I wish I could say it was reading *Portrait of the Artist as a Young Man*." Vida furrowed her eyebrows at me, so I clarified. "It's this famous James Joyce novel about a Catholic wrestling with his faith. I wanted to read it as a kind of test. See, at first, Stephen Dedalus wants to be a priest, but then he starts realizing that the Christian god is so vengeful and stifling and cruel, and that Christianity enslaves people's minds with the fear of going to hell, so they can't be, like, liberated and shit? Or make good art?

And all that got to me, it really did. But the moment I *actually* lost my faith—" I cut off at the memory and blushed.

"What?" Gestas asked, sniffing out my embarrassment.

"It's awful," I said. "But my a-ha moment was—okay, I was listening to this stand-up comedy special."

"Who was it?" Gestas asked suspiciously.

I shaded my eyes with a hand. "Will Dunker," I said reluctantly.

"The guy who sent dick pics to an underage fan?" Vida said.

"In my defense, that story broke like six months after this!"

"His bits were always pretty racist though," Gestas said.

"I know, I know. But at the time, I was a big fan, okay? I regret it. I'm sorry!" I threw my hands in the air as if exasperated, but my tone was joking. "You want to hear the story or not?"

"Continue," Gestas said, with an accommodating hand gesture.

"Anyways, I was just, watching this special on my laptop, and Will had this throwaway joke where he's talking about praying for something, and then he says, 'But god's not fucking real.'"

Suddenly I was back there, in the bedroom I shared with Colton, the only light the glow of my laptop and the spotlights over the Kroger parking lot next door, filtering onto the bed through cheap plastic blinds. I was lying on my stomach on the slick polyester duvet, chin propped on one hand, stemless white-wine glass in the other. I heard that joke, and then the sound of the audience laughing cut out, because my ears were ringing, and I was suddenly, terrifyingly aware of every inch of my skin—and its beautiful, irrefutable mortality.

"I just—" I mimed a head-exploding motion. "I had this out-of-body experience. And in that moment, I knew two things. God wasn't real. And I had to leave Colton." After a half second, I turned to Nimo to clarify. "Colton was my husba—"

"I gathered," he said.

"Anyways, it took about a year after that to figure out I was gay—pan, actually," I said. Nimo flashed me a big smile—suspicion confirmed. I felt a thrill of pride to be part of this cool-queer club. "What about you?" I asked him.

"It was the gay. I had a friend in high school. We were very close, sang in church choir together. He went to college; I didn't. And when he came home the next summer, we were hanging out, and he was like, 'I'm gay, and I think you are too.' And then he kissed me." Nimo splayed his hands at his sides. "Sure enough, he was right!"

"Did y'all date?" I asked.

"For a while—it didn't work out. My fault. I was still figuring myself out. And of course my new identity was incompatible with my family's religion, so they disowned me, and that was a lot to navigate. I may have used a few too many substances to cope."

"That sucks," Gestas said. I was pretty sure he meant about the family disownment stuff, but Nimo took it differently and got defensive.

"I needed it at the time! LSD is surprisingly helpful for recon-structing your entire worldview and personality from scratch. But then I got way too into pills, and—" Nimo swiped a hand at neck-height. "Not good."

"I meant that sucks about your family rejecting you," Gestas said.

"Oh, yeah. Well, my sister and I are still tight. She left the church with me." Nimo brightened with false cheeriness. "And now I have a therapist—and an excellent sponsor!"

"Finally!" Gestas shouted, startling everyone. He reached for Nimo's hand, yanking him in for an enthusiastic dap. Nimo looked happily confused as Gestas pounded his back.

"What's this for?" Nimo asked.

"You have a sponsor! You're sober!" Gestas cried, still clasping Nimo by the shoulder. "I finally have someone to *not* drink with. Let's go downstairs and celebrate—you like root beer? I got root beer. Real old-school, spicy stuff; it'll clean out your sinuses."

30

Downstairs, folks were already gathering in the Lab for the People's Muster. I popped into Peter and Vida's place and found Red killing skeletons in Hyrule. I tried to get xim to come to the meeting, but xe had "just gotten to the fire temple boss" and waved me off. In the Lab, I squeezed onto a bare patch of floor beside Gestas and Nimo, who were sipping their spicy root beers.

After Shayna quieted us down with a few siren whoops from her megaphone, a sanitation team rep spoke—pleading for people to do a better job cleaning up after themselves. "If you buy beer, please pick up all the cans and bottles. Bring it back to your permanent residence, if you have one, or take it to a recycling dumpster. Our trash cans are like ninety percent beer cans right now, and we can't keep up." Next, Damian asked for more volunteers to join the dishwashing working group. And someone raised a motion—which quickly passed by consensus—for the finance team to either buy more porta-potties, or at least get them emptied more frequently.

Shayna took the mic, and I sat up straighter. Even though we were supposed to be a "leaderless collective," I still saw her opinion as the one that mattered most.

"As we're ending our second week, I just want to say how proud I am of all of us. This occupation, what we're accomplishing here, is truly incredible. And I want to thank y'all who have been working so hard to make it happen. Particularly the logistics people—sanitation and kitchen. Without them we wouldn't be able to live here, folks, let's give it up for them!" Applause broke out, and I couldn't help but grin, glowing with Shayna's appreciation.

"But," she said, and paused. The whole room tensed up, knowing we were about to be fed some medicine. "This occupation is not a camping trip. It's not a party. This is a protest against the state violence that is once again targeting our community. I see a lot of y'all nodding." She looked around, and some people froze in the act. "Then I don't understand why at yesterday evening's action at Buffalo Bayou Park, we had only four people show up. FOUR. Out of all y'all." She swept her hand around the room. "The night before that, seven. The night before that, a dozen. Now I know some of you had to be here because you're on shift, and we need people to hold down the fort. And I know some of y'all work evenings. But this was an action at 5:30, just three miles from here. And when I got back, there were fifty people outside, drinking and smoking weed, and sitting around a damn drum circle. Next time, bring your drums *to* the protest!"

We all looked like kids caught cutting class as Shayna pursed her lips at us.

"Now I'm gonna bring up Juan Pablo, from the Gulf Coast Indigenous Alliance. They drove up here today and led a beautiful land-blessing ceremony. Some of these folks are staying through the weekend, some have to head back tonight, but I hope you'll all make them feel welcome."

I mouthed "Welcome" to Nimo, who rolled his eyes and took a sip of his root beer.

"How long are you staying?" Gestas whispered to him.

Nimo shrugged, then whispered, "Was supposed to head back Monday, but I might stick around longer. Visit my sister in Galveston."

Juan Pablo strode into the cleared space in the center of the Lab—he was the guy I thought looked like Lorenzo's dad, with a mustache and crew cut, cowboy boots, and a Spurs polo shirt, which he kept tucked into his dungarees.

"Buenas tardes, good afternoon!" he called in a booming voice. "We are here to support you in the fight against this oil pipeline they're calling a 'hyperway,'" he said, and folks cheered. "Because, as Shayna said, we need to show up for one another in solidarity. And so I want to let y'all know about *our* fight, about what's going on back in Corpus." He looked around the room, rubbing his hands together. "Some of us have to drive back tonight, because tomorrow we're testifying in court against DCI, this corporation that's trying to open three new concrete batch plants in our city. These batch plants poison the air and water, and they make our kids sick." His brow was furrowed with concern. "We've been fighting these batch plants for years—*years*—and we've never gotten the kind of media attention y'all are."

"What can we do?" a deep voice called from the back of the room. It was Toussaint.

"We have a petition and a legal fund on our website," Juan Pablo said, and he quickly rattled off the URL. "Anyhow, thanks, we appreciate your support," he said, holding up a hand in farewell, and he started to walk out of the circle.

"Hang on!" Shayna called. "I don't see enough phones lighting up. Pull 'em out, folks. I'll wait." She stood there with arms folded, until I, and just about everyone else in the room, had unlocked our phones. "What's that website, Juan Pablo, one more time?"

Juan Pablo repeated the address, and all our faces glowed blue as folks signed the petition against the batch plants and donated to the GCIA fund. I hesitated on the donation form, typed in ten dollars, glanced at Nimo. Felt cheap. Changed it to fifty dollars, but choked before hitting "Confirm." I wound up sending thirty dollars. It was more than I would've donated if Nimo hadn't been sitting right next to me. It was kind of a lot, given my tight budget and measly teacher's salary, enough to feed me for a whole day. And, of course, it was also woefully inadequate—a tiny drop in the ocean of reparations required for me to make up for being a colonizer, and benefitting from white supremacy, and living on stolen land, and gentrifying the Eighth Ward, and—like Shayna had said—treating the occupation like a party for the last two weeks.

"Thank you, Juan Pablo," Shayna said. "Now let me remind y'all what this occupation is about!" She turned to address the entire Muster.

"Four blocks down Calcott, there's a seventy-five-year-old woman named Miriam Johnson who has lived in her house for fifty-three years. She raised her three kids and seven grandkids there. Miriam is refusing to vacate the property, and her family is camping out with her there—don't put your phone away yet!" She'd called out someone specific in the front row. I also froze, halfway to slipping my phone into my back pocket. Gestas snorted a laugh as I guiltily brought my phone back around to rest on my knee.

"Today, bulldozers and heavy machinery started tearing down the abandoned homes on Miriam's block. So we are going to have a *big* action at Miriam's house tomorrow," Shayna said. "Gestas will stay back, obviously, with a skeleton crew, but I expect all the rest of y'all to be there." She pointed around the room, making intense eye contact with random people. "We are going to turn up in solidarity with Miriam—and we're going to turn out our networks too. So take those phones back out . . ."

The room re-illuminated with the blue light of a hundred cell phone screens. Shayna directed us to post the protest flyer to all our social media accounts. As I watched, the number of folks "going" to the protest on Facebook jumped from seven to over a hundred.

I hadn't been to a protest action since the night of the show— the night we got gassed. My throat burned with the memory of it.

I'd had reasons not to go to any of the actions so far—I was at work, or cooking in the kitchen, or just plain exhausted. But I'd run out of excuses. I would go because Shayna wanted us to. And because I felt guilty about only donating thirty dollars to the GCIA.

But I was dreading Friday night. I couldn't stop picturing those cop drones circling overhead, spewing clouds of gas on the heads of all my friends.

31

After work I biked to the protest with Vida and Peter. Red was working, and Nimo had stayed behind with Gestas. As we pulled up to the grassy lot, I was glad I had come. There were already three "mosquitoes" buzzing overhead—that's what folks had started calling the aerial cop drones. But the crowd of around three hundred people gave me courage.

Miriam had white hair set in stiff curls under a big, blue organza hat that matched her floral dress. She sat in a wicker chair on the front porch of her tract house, surrounded by a dozen younger people who were all clearly related to her. Shayna was up on the porch too, megaphone tapping against her leg, as she talked with Miriam, casting occasional glances out at the crowd and checking her phone.

I only recognized sixty-or-so people from the Free People's Village. Half the crowd was made up of older Black folks I didn't recognize—possibly Miriam's neighbors and friends. The rest were young, college-age-looking kids. These must be the folks we'd "turned out" with our social media posts.

I was also cheered to see three professional news crews, with their live broadcast vans parked further down the street. Surely, with this much media coverage, the cops wouldn't gas us again.

That's how my brain worked back then. I thought cops cared about journalistic freedom and the eye of the public. I believed that in the United States of America, freedom of assembly and speech were held sacred. And even though a week prior, I'd been gassed with a chemical weapon, I still clung to the belief that state violence was an aberration, not the rule.

Shayna held her megaphone to Miriam's lips as she thanked us all for being there. She started telling us what her home meant to her, but she barely got two sentences out before she got choked up, waved her hand, and sat back down, her eyes wet with emotion. Shayna took over, launching into a rousing speech against the hyperway, stressing how it wasn't an eco-friendly initiative at all, because a wider hyperway would only drive housing development out in the far suburbs, where white suburbanites lived in McMansions, which, for all their greenwashing, required much larger carbon footprints than century-old tract houses like Miriam's. Shayna rhapsodized about the beauty and resilience of the Eighth Ward, despite a long, racist history of state violence-via-permitting. "A company's planning to poison our air? Let 'em build in Eighth Ward! Need to knock down some homes for a hyperway? Send 'em to Eighth Ward!"

As she spoke, three more mosquito drones joined those buzzing overhead. A few dozen of the four-legged-type drones jumped down from a police vehicle and prowled to spots encircling the crowd. The robotic "dogs" watched us in perfect stillness, with eerie, eyeless, clamp-like heads. My heart beat faster, and I scanned the area for an exit strategy. We were at the edge of the crowd, near a neighbor's chain link fence that was low enough for me to vault over.

"I can't get gassed again," I whispered to Vida. "I forgot my inhaler."

Vida looked around, noticing the growing number of drones.

"You should get out of here then," she said. "No judgment."

"But you're going to stay?" I asked

Vida looked at Peter, and they both nodded grimly.

I chewed my thumbnail nervously. The idea of walking away from the crowd, in the middle of Shayna's speech, was humiliating.

But I was terrified of getting gassed again, especially without my inhaler. I decided to wait a while and see what happened. No human cops had gotten out of their vehicles, so maybe they were just keeping an eye on things, not planning another riot.

Shayna had just called the BCR an "instrument of white-supremacist violence disguised as a climate initiative," when a familiar earsplitting alarm blared out overhead. I bolted, even before a robotic voice declared us "an unlawful assembly." As I ran, I swung my messenger bag around, pulled out my bike, popped it open, and jumped on it. I pedaled hard to the end of the block before turning and looking back.

People fled from Miriam's house in every direction, chased by the drone dogs. When a dog caught someone, its viselike head clamped around their ankle, then in a move that looked more arachnid than canine, it'd wrap its legs around its victim's leg, locking the knee outstretched, rendering them temporarily disabled.

Some of the captured folks were trying to kick the drones off with their free legs, but the things were indestructible. Others tried to drag themselves away with their remaining working limbs. A cloud of gas streamed over Miriam's yard from above, and with a wrench of guilt and horror, I saw Miriam herself had been grabbed by a drone dog. Coughing violently, Shayna and Miriam's family members dragged Miriam inside the house—droned leg and all. Cop cars and tank-like vehicles pulled up to the yard, and then human police stepped out for the first time, safe in their gas masks, to arrest the choking, immobilized protestors.

I scanned the fleeing crowd for Vida and Peter but didn't see them. My throat started to burn from a whiff of gas, and I turned for the Lab. I pedaled as hard as I could, fleeing from the gas, and my fear, and the shame of leaving my comrades behind.

32

I was wheezing by the time I got back to the Lab, my airway the size of a silly straw. The tent city that had sprung up outside felt weirdly empty, since so many had gone to the protest. When Gestas saw me burst into his apartment, he followed me into Red's room. "What happened? Where is everybody?"

I held up a finger until I could get two deep breaths off my inhaler.

"You got gassed again?"

I nodded, shaking the inhaler meaningfully.

"Motherfucking pigs." He scowled. He peered out the window. "Here come some of our people. What happened to Vida and Peter?"

"I don't know," I said, my voice still thin, and I started to cry. "I just ran, dude, as soon as I saw the gas. I knew I didn't have my inhaler, and—"

"Of course you did," he said kindly. But his words only made me feel even more sick with myself.

Because there was this moment—before I'd left for the protest—when I'd seen my inhaler sitting on Red's bedside overturned-milk-crate, and I'd thought, I should take that. Just in case.

But I hadn't. I hadn't grabbed it. Some part of me had thought, If I *don't* have it with me, then I'll have an excuse to run the second the cops show up. Which was exactly what had happened.

People started streaming onto the property, coughing and red eyed. Gestas, Nimo, and I brought them water to flush out their eyes and sinuses. Gestas got a message from Shayna asking him to round up anyone with a car, so we could get our people from the police station. She didn't know if they'd actually arrest people, or just hold them for hours like last time. Nimo drove the GCIA van to the station—some of their group had been kidnapped by the cops along with ours. I wished I had a car to help with transportation, but all I could do was swipe another chunk of my checking account over to the bail fund on the website. It did nothing to assuage my guilt.

I was peeling potatoes for dinner when Red's voice cut through the kitchen. "You okay?"

Xe stood in the doorway, one arm leaning against the frame. Xe was panting a little, a sheen of sweat on xir forehead—must've biked hard to get here. Xe wasn't supposed to be home from xir barback shift for hours yet.

"I'm fine. Why are you back so early?"

"I saw the videos. I was worried about you—with your asthma and all." Red came towards me, snaking xir arms around my waist. Without even thinking about it, I shrugged out of xir hold. I felt irritated, and I didn't know why.

"What is it?" xe asked, looking hurt.

I took a deep breath, forcing my voice to sound pleasant, despite how I felt. "Sorry, we're just slammed right now trying to get dinner ready. All those people that got gassed—I don't want them waiting around for food." I kissed xim quickly on the lips. "Talk after dinner?"

Red held up both hands, backing out of the kitchen smiling.

Red didn't come to the People's Muster that night either. We were a smaller group than usual because so many were being held at the police station. Shayna wasn't there. I sat through half of it, mostly people venting about the cops and wondering what the hell we were going to do if every peaceful action invited police violence. Toussaint announced that we'd be supporting Miriam again tomorrow, sitting in her yard, so the bulldozers couldn't demolish her home. A few people shimmered their fingers in the air—that was the hand gesture for agreement—but the rest of us shifted uneasily. What would be the point? The cops would send their mosquitoes to gas us, their dogs to tackle us, and then they'd just drag us out of the way.

Peter took the floor and shared that the videos from today were exploding on Twitter—particularly one of Miriam being tackled by the drone dog, her organza hat spilling off as robotic limbs curled around her leg. That one already had 20K shares. "This is going to be huge for us," Peter said. The eagerness in his voice juxtaposed with the looping video of Miriam's pained and terror-stricken face made me feel sick.

A white guy from the Socialist Democrats said we should start a political-pressure campaign on City Council. Next in the "stack" was a white guy from Houston Socialist Alternative, who said petitioning City Council was a waste of time, and that what we needed to focus on was mutual aid and fundraising for Miriam's family. Another Socialist Democrat—still white, but a cis woman!—argued that mutual aid was a short-term solution but wouldn't effect long-term change like a political campaign. I was picking at a hole in the cement floor, probably gouged out by a skateboard in the days the Lab had been a party house. When Toussaint read off the next name in the stack, I barely suppressed a groan. One of the more long-winded Revolutionary Communists stood up (also a white guy, but thirty years older than the other two, bald, with liver spots on his scalp), and he said that what we really needed to do was heed the words of Bob Avakian, who said—

I got to my feet, hunched over, and slipped out of the crowd of cross-legged people in search of Red. I searched all the apartments, and out among the tents, but couldn't find xim anywhere. Out in the backyard, though, I heard voices on the roof.

Everyone fell silent as I climbed up the ladder. I got a bad feeling, seeing who all was up there. Red and Gestas were sitting in a huddle with Slime and Filthy Ed, plus some gutter punks who were self-described "tankies"—fans of authoritarian communism and violent revolution—who were always saying we weren't going "far enough" at the People's Musters.

All the irritation I'd felt towards Red earlier got swept away by a wave of fear. Something was going on here—something Red didn't want me knowing about.

"Hey," I said, trying to sound casual as I walked up to the group. Most of them were smoking cigarettes, so I had to keep my distance.

Red stomped xirs out on the roof and came towards me. "Just couldn't take the Entmoot tonight," xe said. Gestas snorted a laugh.

The other guys started stretching, putting out cigarettes, casting me and Red weird, lingering side-eyes as they headed back for the stairs. Red gave each of them a curt head bob in acknowledgment. Gestas was the last to leave the roof.

"So what were y'all talking about?"

Red kissed me, then rested xir forehead against mine. "I was so worried about you when I saw those videos. Fuck, Maddie. I don't think you should go to these protests if they keep gassing people. Let people without asthma go."

"If you're so worried about my asthma, you could quit smoking." There it was again, the irritation. I pulled out of xir embrace. "Black people are statistically more likely to have asthma than white people, because they grow up in neighborhoods like this—near refineries."

"So?" Red said. "Why does that mean you should risk your life getting gassed?"

"I need to do my part for the movement."

"You are! You're in that kitchen cooking for us every damn day—and that's after working a full-time job. You don't have to be a martyr." Red reached for my hips, but I jerked away again, almost involuntarily. "Okay, what's going on for real?" xe asked.

"I'm not a martyr—okay? I'm not what you think. I'm—" My throat closed up with emotion. The scene back at Miriam's house played before my eyes. The old woman tackled by the drone dog, gas streaming down from above, Shayna helping to drag her inside. Where was I? What had I done?

"I'm a fucking coward, okay? I'm chickenshit. As soon as they announced the protest was 'unlawful,' I bolted. I was the first one to run."

"Good! You almost fucking died last time you got gassed."

"No, no, but—I'm not more fragile than Miriam, am I? She's, like, seventy. And they gassed her and a drone dog got her leg."

"But you knew you didn't have your inhaler. It would've been suicide to stick around. What would that accomplish?"

"You don't understand!" I shouted. I hadn't meant to shout. I hated myself in that moment. It was torture to see Red looking at me like I was some kind of hero. I wanted Red to hate me too. So I told xim. I told xim about seeing the inhaler, and thinking about taking it, and making the decision to leave it behind—precisely so I'd have an excuse to run, if the cops started gassing us.

I expected Red to look horrified, disgusted, maybe to throw me off the roof. Instead, xe laughed.

"Is that all?" xe asked, pulling a flask from xir back pocket. Xe held it out for me to take a swig. "That's your big secret?"

I nodded and took the drink, the whiskey scorching my throat and kindling a fire in my belly.

"Well, thank god it turns out you're mortal like the rest of us, Mads."

"Hey!" I cried, shoving Red a little.

"You know your whole 'moral integrity' thing gets kind of exhausting sometimes? Is that a Catholic thing? Next time you give me crap for missing the People's Muster, I'll just say, 'Inhaler,'" xe whispered the last word seductively in my ear.

A laugh snuck out of me, but I immediately felt guilty for it. "I still feel like shit for running away like that. So many people got hurt and arrested."

"What would you have accomplished by sticking around, huh? Getting tackled by a drone dog? Letting the cops drag you down to the station, maybe arrest you—meaning you have to pay bail—meaning giving them more money. Or maybe the gas would've killed you. Would that have helped the movement?"

"I don't know, maybe. Martyrs are pretty powerful."

"Fuck that, Maddie. I don't want to ever hear you talk like that. Look, if you're gonna torture yourself with guilt about this, then—" Red bit xir lip and stared at the access door to the ladder, where the others had disappeared inside. "Ah, I don't know if I should tell you though."

"What?"

"You have to swear, fucking *swear*, like blood-oath-to-Satan swear that you won't tell anyone."

"Is this about what y'all were talking about up here?"

Red's eyes sparkled. I knew it. Those tankies were planning some shady shit.

"Look, Shayna has her way of protesting. And she's all about keeping it peaceful, and staying within the bounds of what is deemed acceptable by the powers that be, and then getting gassed and beat and arrested for her trouble. And that's fine. But there are other ways of fighting the state."

"And Gestas is okay with this?" I asked warily.

"It was Gestas's idea. Of course, he can't come with us."

My stomach roiled with fear, but also a thrill of excitement. After the cops had crushed our protest so brutally today, I desperately wanted there to be a better way to fight them.

"I want in," I said.

"Swear you'll never tell anyone," Red said. "In fact, swear you won't mention it, ever, once we step off this roof, because Gestas figures the Feds probably have the house bugged already."

"Sure, I swear."

"Blood oath to Satan?"

"C'mon, Red. Catholic, remember? I'm an atheist now and all, but that shit runs deep. Can we do a pinky swear instead?"

"Fine," Red hooked a finger around my extended pinky. "You're going to need to borrow some of my black clothes."

33

I needed another swig from Red's flask of whiskey after xe told me the plan. It was reckless, and dangerous, and extremely illegal . . . but if we pulled it off, we would strike a meaningful blow against the state.

I sat near the drum circle out behind the Lab, waiting for my assigned time to disappear into the cane at the edge of the property, watching the video of Miriam's arrest over and over. Every time the page refreshed, the number of views on Twitter had grown by hundreds. The old woman struggling against the drone dog clamped to her leg was going to be our most viral video yet. I was gathering up all the shame and anger it stirred in me, balling up those feelings, and trying to transform them into courage. I felt shaky and hyped and still buzzed from Red's whiskey. At 11:17 p.m, I wandered to the back of the lot, where a group of people were smoking, and slipped behind them into the cane.

Once inside, the cane was disorienting as ever, but tonight I found it comforting to be a small, scared thing hidden in tall grass. Ten feet in, I stopped to listen for the whistle of a grackle, played from a cell phone. I headed in the direction of the bird sounds and found the others from the roof, dressed in black, with balaclavas over their faces. Someone handed an extra one to me, and I pulled it on as Red checked over the contents of a few backpacks—crowbars, bolt cutters, and a bunch of innocent-looking water bottles.

"You sure she's cool?" one of the gutter punks asked, eyeing me warily.

The sight of those crowbars stirred up my fear. What if I wasn't "cool" with all this? Was it too late to back out? Could I run back to the house?

But Red said, "She's cool." And I knew I had to live up to that. We were off to strike a direct, tangible blow against the apparatus of racial capitalism. And I, with all my comfy, white, cis-girl privilege, was going to be a part of it.

We set out south, following the cane-submerged tracks towards the old hyperway arcing across the sky. Red kept checking the GPS on xir phone, and finally xe made an abrupt right turn, leading us to the edge of the river of tall grass.

Before us, the land was gouged and rutted clay. The old hyperway was almost directly overhead now, casting its long shadow over the bulldozers and excavators, hulking giants sleeping after a day of tearing down homes.

Until this moment, I'd been vaguely hoping there'd be an unscalable fence around the machines, or guards on duty—something to stop Red from enacting xir plan. But whoever profited off these machines was so secure in our obedience that they'd left the million-dollar equipment unattended through the night. Now, we were going to fuck them up.

We waited and watched for a few long minutes, scanning the skies for the whine of a drone, squinting at the ruined field for any sign of movement. Finally Red gave a nod, and Slime and Filthy Ed took off squat-running towards the nearest digger. As soon as they reached it, two of the tankies dashed for a bulldozer a little further on. The first team was already using a crowbar to pry open the gas tank of their digger. Then they pulled one of the bottles of salt water from their backpack and dumped it inside. The brine would irreparably damage the machine's engine. Then they were off, running towards a wrecking-ball crane.

Red waved at me, and xe took off running. I followed, trying not to think about what we were doing, or why, or the consequences, or anything at all. Dashing across the torn-up earth, I just clung to the thread of the only thing that seemed to matter—not disappointing Red.

Then my toe caught in the rut of a tire track, and I was tumbling forward. I slammed into the earth, barely catching myself with my hands, bashing my head against the packed clay. The pain of it shocked me into sobriety, and as I picked myself off the ground, reeling, seeing colored balls of light exploding across my vision, a cascade of barely restrained fears flooded over me.

What the fuck were we doing? The state was a vicious, bone-crushing, murdering, neighborhood-destroying, all-powerful monster. We were a couple kids with crowbars and water bottles! This was big-time illegal. This kind of thing could get us serious AHICA time—even brick-and-mortar jail time.

It also hit me that everyone here was white, except for Red, and that suddenly felt very wrong. Shayna wasn't here. And I had a hunch she'd be very fucking pissed off at us for what we were doing. This would bring all kinds of retaliation from cops and the construction companies and the state of Texas down on the heads of the occupation, and the people who would be most targeted and suffer most were Black people, and there were no Black people here, in this moonscape. Sure, the plan had been Gestas's idea, but no one from Save the Eighth had been involved, and I wasn't sure at all that any of this was right anymore.

My heart was slamming in my chest with panic, my airways were squeezing shut with anxiety, my head was ringing—and there was Red, who'd doubled back for me, with a hand on my shoulder.

"You okay?" xe asked.

I opened my mouth to pour out all the fear that had slammed into my mind when I hit the dirt, but I couldn't—I didn't want xim to see how afraid I was.

"Sorry—guess I'm a little drunk off that whiskey," I said. "I've got the spins."

"Lightweight," Red said. "Go back to the cane. I'll hit our rigs on my own."

"But you need a lookout—"

"Go!" Red commanded, and xe turned and took off running for the cement mixer that had been our mark. I turned and jogged back to the cane, and my eyes started leaking tears. When I reached the darkness of the tall grass, I collapsed at the edge, where I was hidden but could still see out between the stalks. There, I broke down into sobs—mostly tears of relief. That I was no longer out in that open field. That I didn't have to pour brine into an excavator's fuel tank—which was probably a felony. I hadn't even checked. A felony would mean my losing my teaching license forever.

Along with relief came the certainty that I was, through and through, a coward. I hadn't stood my ground when the cops descended on the peaceful protest earlier. And I hadn't had the guts to do crimes with Red. I couldn't bring myself to risk everything for a cause the way Shayna and Red had done, even though I was a white girl who had the most privilege to protect me. I had always been a tourist at the Lab, and a tourist in this neighborhood, ready to flee at the first hint of danger. I knew what I was now, and I was no hero. Blood dripped down my head from where I'd slammed into the dust, but I had nothing to staunch it with, so I just let it drip.

I don't know how long they were out there—ten, twenty minutes? It felt like hours. Every muscle in my body tensed for a siren or a shout or the mechanical howl of a drone dog. Red had been drinking whiskey all night, and xe was out there, somewhere in the darkness, risking god-knows-what jail time. It was madness, and why was it taking so long?

Then all seven of them came barreling back into the cane, and we ran north, the grass hissing between our shoulders. Finally, we stopped to pull off our masks and catch our breath, and after a few heaving pants, one of the tankies rounded on me.

"I knew she was a fucking narc!" he hissed. I don't remember his name, but he was a white guy with fat gauges in his ears and a soul patch on his chin. "Why wasn't she out there?"

"Maddie fell and hit her head," Red said. "Look, she's fucking bleeding all over. I sent her back."

"I don't care. She didn't get her hands dirty, so she's a fucking liability."

"And what if she is?" Red asked, pushing aside a swath of cane to come between me and the guy. "What are you going to do about it?"

"I won't narc," I said softly.

"I don't like it," Filthy Ed said, ignoring me. "Why the hell did you bring your girlfriend along?"

"She said she won't narc, so she won't narc," Red hissed between clenched teeth, xir words slightly slurred. Xe was drunk, and ready to fight all six of those men.

"Look, I swear, okay?" I hesitated, reminding myself I believed in no gods. I put a hand on my heart and pushed out the words. "Blood oath to Satan. I'll never mention tonight to another living soul ever again."

Red's eyebrows shot up. "You know you're supposed to actually draw blood to do a blood oath—"

I smeared a hand across my bloody forehead and waved it in xir face.

Red snorted a laugh, turning back to the group of angry men. "Very Catholic upbringing," xe explained, pointing a thumb at me over xir shoulder. "Satisfied now? Maddie's not gonna snitch."

The guys grumbled, but like Red said, what were they going to do about it? For weeks after, they shot me suspicious looks anytime I ran across them. But I kept my word, until now, of course, when all those statutes of limitations are long past.

Even with Red, we only talked about it one time, later that night.

We were lying in bed, and I still couldn't stop shaking, like I had a high fever or something. "You need to talk about it?" Red asked, and I nodded. Red put on the Coathangers and cranked it up loud, for the benefit of any Feds who might be listening in. Then xe pulled the blanket over our heads and whispered, "So what's wrong?"

"What's wrong? What's not fucking wrong?" I hissed. "I'm terrified, dude. You could get in big trouble. I could too. And—and I don't even know, now that I've sobered up, if any of that was worth it? I don't think Shayna would like it."

"Oh my god, here we go again with your guru, Shayna."

"She started this movement, and what if y'all just fucked it up? Like what if, because of what you did, the cops get big-time pissed?"

"They're already big-time pissed, or did you forget that they sicced a drone dog on an old lady today and gassed her whole family?"

"I don't know, Red, I just don't know if that was right . . ."

"So you did chicken out?"

"Yeah, okay? Yeah I did." I lay back, unable to meet xir eyes anymore, staring at the roof of our little blanket fort with tears streaming out of my eyes. "It was just like earlier, at the protest. I got real fucking scared, okay? I'm a coward. You're dating a fucking coward."

"Big deal," Red said.

"It is a big deal. You just went out there—and you did that," I said, and there was real awe in my voice. Cracking open the gas tanks of bulldozers and brining them? That was some real *Anarchist-Cookbook*, Rebel-Alliance, fuck-the-police-state shit. "I could never do that," I whispered. "Obviously."

"So? I don't need you to be like me. I don't need you to be like Shayna. I'm dating you 'cause you're Maddie."

"I'm a piece of shit."

"Once again, welcome to humanity! Have you met us? We're all kind of pieces of shit. You want to know the truth? I didn't do that tonight because of my fucking ideals or whatever—that's Gestas's thing. And I didn't do it for the Free People's Village, because you know it's doomed, right? I did it because . . . I don't know." Xe lay down on the pillow, tenting the blanket with an upheld arm. "Like for the same reason I used to spray-paint stick figures with boobs and dicks out behind Target when I was sixteen. Because it's fun. And because fuck it. And because I've always figured I'll die before thirty, might as well go out with a bang. So don't go turning me into some heroic revolutionary, because I really and truly do not give one fuck about *the movement*." Xe said the last word in a ridiculous British accent. "Please believe me. I wish we could go back to just playing music and smoking weed and not having to listen to that fucking drum circle all the damn time!" Xe shouted this last bit in the general direction of the djembe-jam that was still raging outside.

I didn't believe xim. I still don't. But I didn't say that.

"So I'm a piece of shit too, okay?" Red said.

"We can be pieces of shit together."

"You're about the cutest piece of shit I ever saw," Red said and xe kissed me, and that's all I'm going to tell you about the rest of that night.

34

was a wreck that entire weekend. I expected aerial drones to appear at any second, or cops in riot gear to bash their way inside to arrest me and Red. I made the mistake of researching and learning the name of the crime we did—first-degree felony criminal mischief—and the sentencing laws—a minimum of five years brick-and-mortar jail time and up to ninety-nine years. After reading that, I was pretty much a quivering ball of terror, jumping at loud sounds, or someone saying my name, or simply existing in a place I hadn't noticed them standing.

Any time I caught a glimpse of the graffiti guys or the tankies, I felt a self-loathing so intense I wanted to run away from the Lab and never look back. Shayna had gotten bailed out again, and every time I saw her or Toussaint, my guilt about what we'd done was equally unbearable. The only thing that calmed me down in those moments was the memory of Red's grin underneath the blanket, as xe said I was "the cutest piece of shit" xe ever saw. That became a kind of mantra for me. "I'm a piece of shit. But at least I'm cute shit." And that would calm my heart rate enough for me to exist for another ten minutes.

I was so wrapped up in these anxieties, I only vaguely registered how things were changing around the camp. The video of Miriam getting dog-droned and gassed had gone extremely viral. Now there were national news vans camped at the periphery of the Free People's Village at all hours. Once, someone from CNN

221

tried to stop me as I was headed out to the latrines, asking why I'd decided to join the occupation, but I waved them off. I was the last person who was qualified to speak for the movement.

We were prepping dinner Sunday night when Lorenzo told me the mayor had apologized for the police "overreaction" at Miriam's house on Friday. It turned out the drone dog had broken her leg. I set down the knife I was using to smash garlic and pulled up the news story on my phone. Some judge had ordered a temporary halt on construction of the hyperway, until all the affected residents' court cases were concluded. No more demolition. No one would be climbing up in those excavators and bulldozers and discovering that they'd been sabotaged. The brine in the gas tanks would do its work, and any evidence that might link Red and me to the damaged construction machines would hopefully be washed away by the passage of time.

I started laughing hysterically, and Lorenzo asked me what the hell was so funny. I just gave him a big hug and said I was glad Miriam's house would be okay. I mean, that was also true, but to be honest I was about a zillion times more relieved that it was a lot less likely that me and Red were going to jail. I still wasn't religious, but all the same, I prayed that TxDOT wouldn't turn those bulldozers back on for a long, long time.

That evening, I felt like I was back in the world after forty-eight hours of living a nightmare. As we were serving dinner, I actually noticed the faces of the people coming through the line—many of whom I didn't recognize. And for the first time, we ran out of food before the line ended.

Folks packed into the Lab shoulder to shoulder for the People's Muster that night, with more crowding the hallways and the backyard. After a delayed start, Shayna got up on a couch with her bullhorn and announced that, due to the unprecedented crowd, we'd be holding the People's Muster in the front yard. We all shuffled outside, the crowd spilling across the street. Two mosquito drones hovered at the end of the block, but they kept their distance.

I wound up sitting on the lawn near a girl my age who seemed very stylish and arty—like she should be one of our friends, only I'd never seen her before. I struck up a conversation before the Muster got underway and asked what part of the city she was from. She pointed to a couple guys to her right and said they were from Brooklyn—like, the one in New York. They were part of an anarchist quick-response activism group. They'd seen the video of Miriam's arrest, found out about the Free People's Village, and hopped on a bus to be part of the action. I couldn't believe it. I'd heard of activists from Houston traveling to New York or DC for big protests, but never of folks from northern cities coming down here. That was the first time I realized the Free People's Village was bigger than Houston, was something that might just change the course of history.

This whole movement had been built thanks to Shayna's way of organizing—and she still didn't know about the bulldozers. What would happen when our sabotage was discovered? Would it help the movement or destroy it?

Red wouldn't talk with me about what we'd done. The few times I tried, xe pressed a finger to my lips and said, "Blood oath to Satan, remember?" I needed to talk to the mastermind—Gestas. But the Lab was so crowded now, that it was days before I had a chance to. Finally, I caught him up on the roof, smoking by himself. The din from the massive AC units and the drum circle was enough to provide us with some sonic privacy.

He was reading a handwritten letter as I approached, which he folded up and tucked in the strap of his maxi dress.

"Angel?" I asked, glancing at the letter.

He nodded.

"How's he doing?"

"Hard to tell." Gestas shrugged. "He just talks about the shitty food, and how it's even more humid there than in Houston. Nothing about what he's doing, but I guess that's to be expected. He read the Chomsky book I sent him and says he has thoughts. Wants to talk about it next time we can face-call."

"Aw, I'd love to see his face," I said, resting my arms on the half wall that encircled the roof. Hundreds of tents spread below, past the borders of the property and onto the tracks, now completely cleared of cane. Nimo had a tent pitched somewhere out there. The rest of the GCIA had gone back to Corpus, but Nimo had decided to blow off his barista job and stick around the occupation for a while.

"Have you told Nimo about Angel?" I asked.

"No, I don't think it's come up."

"You might want to . . ." I said.

"Oh." Gestas sagged against the wall. "You think he has a thing for me?" I made a noncommittal noise, but I was remembering the way Nimo had shadowed Gestas's footsteps all weekend. "I mean, I'm not sure me and Angel are exclusive, but Nimo's just not my type," Gestas said.

"Maybe I'm wrong." I shrugged, meaning it. Maybe Nimo had just been as glad to find a queer, sober friend as Gestas was.

"Is that what you came up here to talk about? Or do you want to bum a cigarette?" he held out his pack jokingly. He knew how I hated smoking.

"No," I said firmly. I dropped my voice softer. "Did Red tell you that I, um, went with . . . that night, with the bulldozers—"

"I might've heard something about a head injury and a blood oath to Satan," he said with a faint smile.

"Dude, I need to talk to you about it. It's eating me up inside. I'm freaking out."

Gestas sighed and held out a hand. "Give me your phone."

I was puzzled, but I handed it over. He pulled his own out of his pocket, crossed the roof to the far side, and set our phones down gently on the tar strips, then trekked back.

"I've been reading up on InfoSec. They can bug us through our phones, even when they're turned off. Be really fucking careful who you talk to. It's loud out here, so"—he scanned the sky for drones—"we should be alright. But keep your voice down. And instead of the b-word, just say . . . go-karts. Got it?"

"Right. The night with the go-karts. I'm worried that what we did was, um, like . . . wrong?"

"Wrong? Like *morally* wrong? Swords into plowshares, Maddie, you should know that verse."

Isaiah 2:4, but I wasn't sure why he was bringing it up.

"What is a go-kart but a sword—one that demolishes entire communities—and what were you doing but beating those swords into . . . well not exactly plowshares, but at least not swords anymore—"

He'd misunderstood me. "No, no, I don't think destruction of property is fundamentally wrong or anything. But I'm worried about consequences. What happens when someone discovers that the go-karts were sabotaged?"

"Do you know the origin of that word—sabotage?" Gestas asked.

I shook my head.

Gestas stubbed out his cigarette, and instead of flicking it, he slid the butt back in between the cellophane of the pack and the cardboard—something I'd only seen Angel do.

"Etymologists claim this is an urban legend—but it's a damn good one if it is. Think of it as a Marxist *parable*." Gestas said the word with an ironic grin. It felt cozy when he used religious terminology with me—a special language for us fallen heathens. "There were these French textile workers who wore wooden clogs called *sabots*. Well, when mechanical looms were invented in the nineteenth century, their nice cottage industry got devoured by industrial capitalism. But these laborers didn't take their exploitation in stride. They *sabotaged* the textile factories by chucking their wooden shoes into the machinery, destroying the looms."

"Badass," I said.

"As a result, they won real concessions, and joined in a grand tradition of French labor organizing. Maybe if we'd done more sabotage here in the US, we'd have a fraction of the social services and workers' protections they have in Paris."

"Very cool story, but you admitted it might just be an urban legend."

"Ehhh, there's truth to it," he said, looking to the horizon.

"Okay but look," I gestured towards the sprawling tent city. "Shayna accomplished all this just through peaceful protests."

"Yeah, and cops broke that old lady's leg," Gestas said, folding his arms. "And you almost died of an asthma attack, and who knows how many of us will have fucked-up permanent side effects from getting gassed or beat down?"

"But look how much media attention that got! She's winning people over by taking the high ground!"

Gestas pinched the bridge of his nose. "High ground? Look, Shayna's just playing by the ruling class's rules. She's protesting in exactly the way capitalism loves for us to protest. You take the collective rage and grief of a thousand people, give them a permit to march down the street, then let them shout until they're tired and go home. They let us feel like we've done something—only we've disrupted nothing." He flung his hands out in exasperation. "We've dealt no damage to the economic systems that are burning up the world, or the structural inequalities that keep Black Americans poor and enslaved through AHICA. We've just made wind, going up to space."

Gestas came to stand beside me, leaning out over the tent city. "That's why they're allowing this occupation to continue. They figure—let us camp out here, until everyone's sick of sleeping on the ground and shitting in overflowing porta-johns, and this'll all dwindle away. And they're right! Unless we continue to ramp up the stakes, this movement is doomed." He hocked up a loogie and let it drop, splatting on the cement porch two stories below.

"Maybe, but I feel weird about ramping up the stakes for other people, without their consent. When the cops figure out we fucked up the bulld—er, go-karts—they're gonna unleash hell."

"Maybe," Gestas shrugged.

"Definitely," I said.

"Okay, I got another story for you. About consequences and retaliation. You ever hear of the Ngäbe people?"

I shook my head.

"Okay, so when Columbus got to Panama, he tried to fuck around with this tribe, the Ngäbe. Now, they didn't know any of the horrific shit he'd already done to the Taíno and Arawak people. But their leader, Quibían, recognized that Columbus was a bad dude, and he said the colonizers were not welcome in their territory. Of course Columbus tried to kill him, but Quibían got away and destroyed Columbus's brother's ship when it went up their river. Sabotaged the fuck out of it."

"So what happened to them?"

"I can't say they've been unscathed by colonialism. They lost a lot of territory and a lot of people fighting colonization—fighting to this day. But the Ngäbe are still living autonomously. And they still fuck up machinery when people come and try to cut down their forest. A lot of tribes who didn't fight back . . . they're not around anymore. But the Ngäbe are, because they fucked up Columbus's ship."

"And Columbus's ship? That's like the go-karts?" I asked.

"That's the go-karts."

"Fuck up Columbus's ship," I repeated.

The talk with Gestas gave me a lot to think about, but the battle in my mind kept raging. I still flinched at every cop drone overhead. I still worried that Shayna was right, that peaceful protest *was* the best way to save the Eighth Ward. And I worried that our sabotage was a ticking time bomb, and when it was discovered, it would destroy everything we'd built.

35

At school I was carrying around another big secret, one I hadn't told anyone, not even Red. Some part of me felt like if I explained it out loud, I would lose my nerve.

The day after Nora had told me to stick to the district lesson plans, my first-period kids had groaned when I told them to pull out *To Kill a Mockingbird* again.

"Can't we talk about the protests?" Shanelle had said. "Y'all see the video of that party getting gassed?"

"Yeah, can't we read more about the hyperway stuff?" Jaylen asked.

I was feeling real run-down and brutally honest, so I just sighed and said, "I wish."

"Well, why can't we? Are you the teacher or what?" Naiya asked.

And I just . . . told them the truth. I told them how I'd had big plans for a unit on literature of rebellion. I told them about reading Freire, and how his ideas of a truly democratic classroom had electrified me. And I told them how Nora had threatened my job if I ever veered off the district plans again.

Antoine sucked his teeth. "Always knew that AP was a bitch."

I let the cuss word slide.

"Look, Miss, what if we promise not to tell that crusty ol' clown-face hag what you're up to?" Princess said. "Just don't make us keep reading this book." She smacked the thick paperback against her forehead. "It's *so* boring."

I smiled at the thought, but said, "No, we can't—if I got caught—"

"We'll keep the books out on the table like this, and if she starts coming in the room—whoop!" Naiya stuck yesterday's article inside her binder, real quick.

"I guess it's unlikely she'll come back to this class period . . . at least not for a month or so. She has like thirty other teachers on her caseload . . ." I couldn't believe I was entertaining the thought of illicitly teaching off script, after Nora had warned me that I'd be fired for doing just that.

"What would Guy Fieri do?" Kenya asked softly, looking up from *Beale Street*.

"*Freire*," I corrected, fighting off a rebellious smile. My heart was hammering in my chest. "If we do this, you'll all have the power to get me fired."

"We won't tell anyone, right? Right?" Naiya looked around the room. "Okay, who votes we do Ms. Ryan's *experimental* lesson plans? And you got to promise not to tell."

Everyone's hand went up except my most studious girl, sitting in the very front. But when Kenya yelled, "Get your damn hand up, Jazmin!" she blushed and put it up tentatively.

"See Miss? It's unanimous. I don't give a fuck about that little Scout bitch or her daddy or stinky, ol' Boo Radley. So what you got for us?"

And that's how it began. The kids had all sworn to tell no one, so I didn't either—not even Red or Gestas, who would've found it funny. It was exhilarating walking around campus with that secret. For second through seventh period, I stuck to the district lessons. But first period, I followed only my heart and my students' curiosity.

I guess I'd already accepted that my days at Washburn High School were numbered, so I might as well teach how I wanted while I had the chance. After about a month, Nora did pop in to observe one of my classes—but thank god, it was an afternoon period, and the scores I got were mediocre but satisfactory. I had to bite down on my cheek to keep from giggling during our debrief. I couldn't believe I was getting away with it.

With my first period, we discussed Baldwin, Assata Shakur, Ruth Wilson Gilmore, and Cedric Robinson, and a whole bunch of R&B and hip-hop lyrics that they brought in for my education— Tupac, Marvin Gaye, and Queen Latifah, and local heroes Chem C and Third Host. We analyzed the bureaucratic rhetorical horrors of eviction notices and hyperway development permits, and we read about the history of protest occupations—first-hand accounts, poetry, and news clippings from Alcatraz, Wounded Knee, and Tiananmen Square. We read about the fight against concrete batch plants in Corpus Christi and a GCIA Land Buyback in the RGV.

I started sleeping at my apartment again, a few nights a week, so I'd have a quiet place to work on planning and grading for just that first period. I understood what teaching was supposed to be for the first time, and I was living for it.

36

The Free People's Village was a city unto itself by the one-month anniversary of the occupation. We dominated national, headline news. The encampment had spread well past the borders of our yard. Tents sprawled for half a mile in both directions along the tracks, spilling into nearby abandoned lots.

There were so many kitchen volunteers now that I didn't need to take a daily shift, especially since I wasn't the fastest with a knife. I had a hunch Damian only kept me on the schedule for Tuesday and Saturday dinners because I'd been there since the beginning, and he didn't have the heart to tell me I wasn't needed anymore. The lightened schedule let me spend more nights in my apartment, prepping for my first-period class. And when I was at the Free People's Village, well, I enjoyed myself. There were always people to make music or art with, or the People's Muster to attend, or someone to stay up late with debating art and science and politics and metaphysics. There were these fiber artists who'd started crocheting massive, rainbow-colored nets that stretched between telephone poles and trees, casting shade or serving as megahammocks. They made the whole place look like it was covered in Technicolor spiderwebs. Vida and the art working group had painted new murals on the outsides of all the houses down Calcott—both those where tenants had already vacated, and those where families were still clinging on, counting on the occupation to save them.

Every day was a media circus, and also just a regular ol' circus, ever since the fire spinners and steampunk acrobats had joined our ranks. There were always drumming or acoustic-guitar jam sessions going on from ten in the morning until eight at night, when Shayna would stand right in the middle of the folks pounding their hand drums (mostly cis boys, mostly white, three of whom had blond dreadlocks), shouting through her megaphone that it was now QUIET HOURS. That this was a NEIGHBORHOOD. That kids needed to SLEEP.

Shayna was doing everything she could to keep the media's attention on the movement's original aims—preserving the Eighth Ward and stopping the hyperway expansion. But five thousand other people had shown up, from all over the country, all with their own agendas. At any of Shayna's planned protests, you'd see anti-war, anti-incarceration, anti-capitalist signs, all manner of Pride flags, "Meat Is Murder," "Fuck Wall Street," "End Fossil Fuels"—and there was always a giant blow-up rat and a papier-mâché guillotine for the billionaires.

So despite Shayna's best effort to keep the focus local, the national news media characterized the Village as a chaotic hodgepodge of pie-in-the-sky dreams from lazy, out-of-town leftists with nothing better to do but smoke weed and disrupt the civic order. The media treated us with patronizing bemusement. How adorable that we were a leaderless movement practicing direct democracy! How hilarious that we'd argue for an hour every night over what, exactly, our mission was! How cute that thousands of people were so fed up with society that they'd left their homes to live in a tent on a field of earth that was rapidly becoming saturated with human excrement! There were a lot of bits where a journalist was performatively gagging near the porta-potties.

Sometimes Fish came down to the property to give interviews in front of the Lab, unrecognizable with his fresh haircut and black suit, looking like he and his lawyer-in-law Chad could be old frat brothers. He was playing the role of the benevolent capital-ist—amused by, but not one of, the idealistic hippies camping out on his property. He spoke to the omnipresent camera crews about property owners' rights in the emotionless legalese expected of a white man in a suit.

After recording one such sound bite, he showed up on the roof, where me and Red and some other folks were having beers on a Friday afternoon. He'd loosened his tie, lost the jacket, and rolled up his sleeves, but I still snorted at how square he looked.

"Hey," he said, holding up a hand to our group.

"Hey," I said.

Red got up and headed for the ladder back inside without making eye contact with Fish. Xe looked back at me like, "You coming?" But I shrugged. I was kind of curious to see how things would play out with Fish. I could tell Red was pissed I was staying, probably from misguided jealousy. The last thing Red needed to worry about was me going back to Fish.

"You wear suits now, huh?"

"Yeah, you know, Chad convinced me I can be more useful to the movement like this, so—" He shrugged, looking down at him-self. "Small price to pay. These things are hot as hell though." He bloused the front of his button-up shirt to let air in. There were big rings of sweat around the armpits. "How are you doing anyways?"

I shrugged. It was a hard question to answer lately.

"I heard, uh, you and Red are . . . ?"

"Yeah, we're together."

"Cool, cool," he said, nodding and staring out at the refinery. His cheeks were flushing crimson.

"You still living at your dad's?"

"No, got a place actually. Not too far from your old apartment. The Prairie Sunset Community, off Hermann Park?"

I whistled. "That place is fancy."

He grinned sheepishly. "Yeah, it's not bad."

"Rooftop infinity pool?"

"It's awesome—hey, you and Red should come over sometime, check it out. I promise it won't be weird."

"Maybe we will," I said, grinning at the thought of a minivacation from the struggle of life in the Free People's Village. To spend an afternoon at a luxurious Community, sipping cocktails in a chilled pool, floating over the city of Houston—it sounded nice.

When I brought it up to Red later though, xe scowled. "No, I fucking do not want to go hang the fuck out at Fisher-fucking-Wellman's fucking infinity pool."

"Are you jealous?" I asked, teasingly. "You know you've got nothing to worry—"

"I'm not jealous! It's not *you* I'm worried about! It's—" Red was shouting. Red had never shouted at me like that before, and it had come out of nowhere. Xir eyes instantly softened, "I'm sorry. It's just—can we please not talk about him? And can you please promise me you won't go over there?"

I wanted to point out that Red was, indeed, acting jealous. But there was this panicked, desperate look in xir eyes. We were getting ready to head out to a bike protest Shayna had organized, and I didn't want to be in a fight. So even though I thought it was ridiculous (and very cishet) to not allow me to hang out with my ex, I said, "Sure. I promise."

Red relaxed into a grin, took a shot of bourbon, slipped the bottle in xir backpack, and we headed out to the bike protest. We pedaled off from the Lab in late afternoon, so the sky turned sunset colors as Shayna led our mass of thousands of bikes on a tour of the Eighth Ward. Peter and Lorenzo rode up front, keeping near her and Toussaint, so they could hear as she stopped to explain the historical significance of various sites—a diner where Martin Luther King Jr. had met with organizers over pancakes. An abandoned H&R Block, which had once been a recruiting office for the Buffalo Soldiers.

Red and I tried to keep up, but with my asthma, I couldn't stay at the front of the pack. We ended up falling back among the casual riders, alongside Nimo and Vida, chatting away on their bulky beach cruisers. I never found out if my suspicion about Nimo's feelings for Gestas was correct. But shortly after I'd brought it up with Gestas, Nimo started spending almost all his free time with Vida. The two of them were organizing a GCIA chapter in the Houston/Galveston area, although I think so far their only other member was Nimo's sister. When they talked with each other, they used a fast, slangy, distinctly queer Texan Spanglish that Red and I weren't fluent enough to understand.

So Red and I biked side by side, watching the overgrown lots and neat tract houses slip by beneath the fuchsia-orange clouds. Some folks had decorated their bikes with Christmas lights, or blasted music from Bluetooth speakers. One guy was steering an empty paletero cart, with a Save the Eighth banner clipped up where the chicharrones bags usually hung.

We passed a boarded-up gas-station-turned-nightclub that was bursting with people, the parking lot packed with tricked-out vintage rides with elbow hubcaps. Folks drinking out front called to us as we passed. Some supportive: "Save the Eighth!" Some not: "Go home, whitey!" But most folks just looked confused as to why a thousand people—most of whom were clearly not from the Eighth—were biking past their bar. Their quizzical frowns made me question us too. Was there a point to this bike protest? Or was this what Gestas had said—just a way to vent our anger uselessly into thin air?

Before tonight, I'd thought I knew the Eighth Ward pretty well. But I was starting to realize that beside a few routes I knew by heart—the routes between the train station, my school, and the Lab—I had never seen most of Eighth Ward.

Now Shayna led us down a side street that suddenly felt like plunging into another world. The trees shading the road were so choked with kudzu that they formed a tunnel of greenery overhead. Invasive Koelreuteria trees grew in all the gaps between the close-set houses, adding to the jungle-like feeling. All that plant life muffled the ubiquitous sounds of the city and bathed the street in a cool, green humidity.

The road was weirdly narrow. Back in the days when people living here might've had cars, there wouldn't have been room for two to pass on this street, not with those steep ditches on either side of the road. Our procession slowed to a crawl, as the road was more loose gravel and potholes than smooth asphalt.

Most of the houses in Eighth Ward needed at least a new roof and a paint job. I was used to that. But these homes seemed half rotted away, with caved-in porches and several generations' worth of kids' toys, sun-bleached, and discarded furniture lying in the overgrown yards. Some of them looked like they must be abandoned—but then one by one, people streamed out of the houses to watch our unusual procession go by. Kids and unleashed dogs raced alongside us, jumping back and forth over the ditches. Some of the elders watching us from stoops had the sunken cheeks of those who have no teeth. These folks were another level of poor from those who lived around the Lab.

All the people watching us go by were Black. Those of us riding bikes were mostly not. Shayna had wanted us to see this part of the neighborhood, but I felt bad to be seeing it. Like a voyeur. A tourist. I suddenly understood that though I taught here, and lived here, I did not really know or understand the Eighth Ward. Not at all.

One kid drove up alongside me and Red on an electric ATV, riding barefoot and shirtless, with a chillingly realistic air rifle tied to his back with pantyhose.

"What y'all doing here?" he called to us, specifically.

"Riding bikes," Red answered.

The boy gave xim the most unimpressed scowl I'd ever seen. "Why?"

"Because they're trying to build a hyperway here. It's like a protest?" I said.

"Oh right. Fuck TxDOT!" the kid yelled, pumping his fist in the air, and a bunch of the folks around us cheered and took up the refrain. The boy couldn't have been older than seven or eight, but he knew enough to hate the state transportation department.

"He's like a little Gestas," I said, once we'd turned down a wider, more open street and left the kid and the dense, oppressive greenery of that block behind. "Did Gestas grow up around here?"

"You think Gestas grew up around here?" Red exclaimed. "On *that* street?"

I shrugged, knowing I'd screwed up somehow. "Didn't he grow up in the Ward?"

"Not on a street like that! Ooooh, Maddie, you racist!" xe teased, grinning.

"What? I just asked—"

"You wanna see where Gestas grew up?" I nodded. "Okay, hang on. I'll be back." Red put on a spurt of speed. Standing up in xir seat, xe wove through the bikes ahead to get close to Shayna. I lost sight of xim for a little while, left to wonder why my question had been racist.

A few minutes later, I caught up to Red, resting on the side of the road, waiting for me. "Okay," Red said, pushing into the flow of bikes. "Shayna says we're about to turn on Bayou Drive. So you'll get to see Gestas's old house."

"Will you please explain to me why my question was so ridiculous?"

"Because those people were poor as hell!" Red cried.

"So?" I asked.

"So, do you think everyone in Eighth Ward is poor? Was Gestas's family poor?"

"I don't know."

"You should! Think about it. What did Gestas's dad do?"

"Ohhhh, right," I said, the pieces clicking into place as we turned onto Bayou Drive, a wide, curving, oak-shaded boulevard. "Gestas's dad was a preacher." Our mass of bikes swelled to fill both lanes of the street. To our left, the bank dipped down towards wildflowers and the green waters of the bayou. To the right, the land swelled up towards a row of ostentatious mansions behind wrought-iron gates. "Gestas's dad was rich."

"*Is* rich," Red clarified. "I'm pretty sure he still lives here."

Many of the mansions were falling into disrepair—relics from the years before the original hyperway, perhaps—but some of them still had carefully manicured grounds and fresh paint. Red was peering at them all closely, then pointed excitedly. "That one! With the waterfall!" The white driveway was bisected by an artificial waterfall tumbling down a series of terraced rocks. Behind the wrought-iron gate at the top, several luxury SUVs were parked in a circular driveway, before a pink-and-white, three-story mansion flanked by stone lions.

"Damn," I said.

"That's church money for ya," Red said.

I was cringing at the contrast between this home and the street I'd assumed Gestas might've grown up on, just because he came from the Ward. "Hey. Don't tell Gestas what I—"

"Don't worry, Mads," Red said, with a half wink. "I keep all your secrets."

I rolled my eyes.

We had reached the border of the Eighth Ward, and I figured we were about to head back towards the Lab. But then, perhaps emboldened by how easily we'd dominated the streets, Shayna decided to lead us up onto the hyperway.

We bottlenecked as we reached the feeder road, and Red and I had to stop briefly and wait for our turn to get on the on-ramp. Someone waving nearby caught my eye. It took my brain a second to register who it was, since I hadn't expected to see them in this context. It was Kenya, my student! She shot me this big, real grin, which I'd never seen in school before.

"You're here!" I said, half-questioning, half-excited.

"I follow the Free People's Instagram and saw the post about it."

Kenya scooched her bike closer, and another girl followed. She wasn't one of my students, but I recognized her from school as one of the few Latina girls on campus.

"I didn't know you actually were like *with* the Free People," Kenya said. "I just thought we talk about it in school."

"Yeah, I kind of live at the Village? Part time, at least," I shrugged.

I glanced over at Red, and xe was hanging back, looking a bit terrified at the prospect of meeting one of my students. "By the way, this is Red—xe/xim," I said, grabbing Red's handlebars and scooting xim closer.

"This is Cely, she/her," Kenya said, nodding at the other girl, and they shared a look I thought I recognized. If my suspicion was right, I wanted them to know that they could be open with me. I wanted them to know that I was one of them.

So I went on. "Red is my—" But in that moment, I realized we'd never discussed a name for us. *Girlfriend* or *boyfriend* was unthinkable. *Partner* felt business-y. I settled on, "Person. Red is my person."

Red grinned back at me in happy surprise. Maybe xe'd expected me to try and hide my queerness around the kids.

"Oh cool, uh . . . yeah, Cely is my girlfriend," Kenya said.

"But don't tell anyone!" Cely cut in.

"Ms. Ryan won't, right?" Kenya arched an eyebrow at me.

"Of course not."

"It's just my family's not cool with it. Neither of ours are actually."

"I know how that goes," Red said. "Cool thing is, in a few years years, you'll be eighteen, and you never have to see them again if you don't want to."

"That's the plan," Kenya said. But Cely frowned, looking down at her handlebars.

"Well, you can tell whoever you want about me and Red," I said. "I want all the queer kids to know there's a teacher who's got their back." Red shot me this proud look like, "Look at you, Ms. Queermo. Who would've thought?"

The bikes in front of us started moving again. As we pushed up the ramp to the hyperway, Red said, "Your *person*, huh? I like that. Should I call you my person?"

"You could," I said, a little out of breath from the steep climb. "Or you could say girlfriend." As soon as the word was out of my mouth, I wanted to snatch it back. Hadn't Red once said that love was a trap and sworn xe'd never have a girlfriend again? Was applying a label going to freak Red out and make xim run away?

But Red was smiling.

Just as we crested the feeder up onto the hyperway, Red said, "Okay. Girlfriend."

The first bikes to emerge on the hyperway were the hardcore fixed-gear kids, risking their necks during a break in the cars to ride off the feeder, their bikes instantly tripping the hyperway's crash-sensors. The cars coming up behind them whooshed to a sudden, silent halt, as the maglev rails beneath their chassis reversed polarity. Then the drivers inside were honking and screaming out their windows. But by the time we emerged on the highway, there were thousands of us, and we just laughed at the disgruntled drivers. The low, rounded maglev rails which propelled cars forward had intermittent breaks in them to allow the cars to switch lanes and exit the hyperway. Bikers swerved between these breaks to claim all four outbound lanes of traffic. A few folks with old-school steel bikes wiped out if they got too close to the maglev rails. I was alright on my aluminum frame, but I swore I could feel my hoop earrings defy gravity whenever I got close to one.

Past the guardrails, the whole city spread before us, maglev trains threading through the neighborhoods, the twinkling lights of Community towers, the swaying prairieways, and the dark streets of Eighth Ward directly below us, obscured by the cloud-like crowns of mature trees. My mind was going, *Girlfriend, girlfriend, I'm Red's girlfriend!*

Police drones appeared—mosquitoes buzzing overhead and drone dogs trotting at the edges of our critical mass—but they kept their distance. The cops hadn't attacked us since the PR disaster at Miriam's.

My chest swelled with a soaring feeling of certainty and safety and justice. Free People's Villages were springing up all over the country—New York, Chicago, Portland, Oakland, and Detroit. All the doubt and voyeuristic guilt I'd felt earlier melted away. Shayna must be right about the power of peaceful protests. We weren't just out here to exhaust our energy and go home sated, as Gestas had said, with nothing fundamentally changed. We were reclaiming the streets of our city. We were building momentum and community. Zooming above the city lights, the moon overhead, Red at my side, it was all so fucking *beautiful,* and that had to mean something!

Taking my hands off the handlebars to stretch my shoulders as the city flew past, the word "revolution" entered my mind for the first time. Was that what was starting here? If it was, for that brief, fleeting moment, I felt sure we would win it.

"I wanna try something. Wait for me!" Red called with a grin, and xe headed for the edge of the hyperway, weaving between bikes. I pointed my handlebars in xir direction. The closer xe led us to the guardrails, the more dread spiked in my chest. What was xe up to?

Red vaulted off xir bike and, before I could even scream, xe jumped onto the guardrail and grasped the metal pole of a hyperway exit sign. Xe hugged the pole with both hands, feet braced in front, and started scrambling up like a monkey. It looked impossible, superhuman—where the fuck had xe learned to do that? When Red reached the scaffolding that held up the exit sign, xe scrambled up to the top and stood—fucking *stood*—on the slick metal pole, twenty feet above the hyperway, hundreds of feet above the ground far below. Xe raised a fist in the air, and the folks streaming past all cheered.

I was shouting too, "Come the fuck down! What are you doing?" Red laughed, stuck out a tongue at a cop drone overhead, and flashed it both middle fingers. Then xe lost xir balance, swaying dangerously. My heart froze. Xe dropped to a squat. I held my breath.

And then xe was clambering back down, reverse-hopping down the pole with all four limbs outstretched.

"What the fuck? Why would you do that?" I yelled, pounding xir arm with my fists when xe was safely back on the road.

"Pretty badass, huh?" xe laughed. I sobbed into xir chest.

When we got back to the Lab, I wanted so badly to make love to Red, to feel the length of xir skin, feel xir aliveness, and share together the *everything* of that ride. But when we got off our bikes, xe fumbled for a minute with the catches of xir pop-out bike, then stumbled up to the house. As soon as xe flopped into bed, xe was snoring. In xir bag, I found an empty bottle of bourbon.

I sat at the edge of the bed, dizzy at the thought of how drunk Red must've been, high up on that road sign. How a tiny miscalculation, or a gust of wind, could've taken xim from me forever.

I was angry. At Red, for holding xir life so cheaply, and for spoiling my memories of tonight. I'd never be able to think about that ride again, without remembering that hitch of terror, when xe'd nearly plummeted to xir death. I was angry at myself too. What was wrong with me? Was this some kind of curse? First Colton, then Fish—was I doomed to love drunks?

This time was different though. This time, I was in real trouble. Because this time, I was sickeningly, incurably, in love.

37

I was up before dawn the following Monday, stepping over bodies, showering, making coffee in the dark. I always listened to NPR on my earbuds as I biked to school. That morning, the news made me skid to the side of the road.

The Fifth Circuit court had overturned the stay against construction on the hyperway. TxDOT had planned to resume construction immediately, so in the wee hours of the morning, the job site had opened back up. Workers had returned to their bulldozers only to discover—sabotage.

The estimated cost of the damage was over ten million dollars. Police were asking for anyone with information to come forward.

My ears started ringing, and all my muscles went shaky. I crouched next to my sprawled bike, staring at some fungus growing out of a live oak root that had burst through the sidewalk. I was there a long time, pressing my shirt over my mouth, trying to stop hyperventilating. I felt like there must be drones in the sky, watching me, seeing my freak-out, knowing what I'd done. I needed to get it together. I needed to collect myself and calm down and go teach class like nothing out of the ordinary had happened.

Somehow, that's what I did. I shoved the news into a corner of my brain, way back. I put my phone on silent and forced myself not to check it during my planning period. And that's why I didn't know—I didn't hear what had happened. It wasn't until the end of that interminable school day, when I rounded the corner to the Lab that I instantly knew that everything had changed.

A cordon of cops with assault rifles stretched across Calcott in front of orange-and-white road barricades. Overhead, a dozen drones swarmed through the air. Smashed tents, garbage, tooth-brushes, and blankets littered the ground around the Lab. A few protestors I recognized were picking through the wreckage, but it was eerily quiet—no drum circle thundering away, no one giving a speech on a megaphone. The evidence of violence, the stillness, felt horrific. Like finding the corpse of someone you love.

A news reporter nearby was talking into a camera. "Earlier today, police descended on what protestors call the Free People's Village with a warrant to search for evidence in connection with the attack on construction equipment that was discovered late last night. Hundreds of protestors were detained and are being held for questioning."

I was already texting—Red, Gestas, Vida, Lorenzo—everyone I could think of. No little typing dots appeared, from any of them. I called Red. It went right to voicemail. Goddammit, xe was always letting xir battery get low. I was flying into a panic again. What should I do? Try to get past the line of cops? Head to the nearest jail? Finally, Shayna texted back.

"Strategy meeting at my place. Can you get here?" The address was a few blocks away. I was already pedaling off.

Shayna lived in a row house near the university, and the place was packed with displaced occupiers. I found Peter on the porch with his laptop, uploading videos of the brutal police crackdown. Without looking up from his screen, he told me that Gestas had been scooped up in a paddy wagon along with Lorenzo and the whole kitchen staff. Red hadn't been there—Peter thought xe was at work. I sagged with relief—that's right, Red had gotten an early shift today. But Gestas! My heart clenched for what would happen to him if anyone ratted us out.

Peter said a bunch of folks with cars had already gone to the jail to bail out anyone who got arrested. Though he figured, once again, the cops probably wouldn't charge people. They were just trying to scare someone into coming forward with intel on the bulldozers.

"I bet it was some of those teenagers from Brooklyn," Peter said. "They can afford to get arrested and scurry home to their daddy's trust funds."

My stomach twisted with guilt. Both me and Red, who'd actually done the sabotaging, had escaped the police violence, while hundreds of folks who'd had nothing to do with it had gotten attacked.

And what about the others? Slime and Filthy Ed usually only came by the Village to party on weekends, so they might've escaped the paddy wagons. I scanned the crowd for the other tankies who'd done the brining but didn't see them. If they had been detained, I prayed they'd keep their mouths shut.

Shayna stepped outside with her megaphone in hand. "Mic check!" she called, and the hundred folks scattered around the yard called "Mic check!" in response. This was the way every People's Muster had started for the past month, and I got choked up all of a sudden. Shayna was still here, still fighting. Maybe the movement wasn't dead. Everyone crowded around in a big huddle—maybe two hundred strong. Some TV cameras had found their way to Shayna's house, and she gave them a few moments to set up before continuing.

"Earlier today, we faced an unprovoked attack on our community," Shayna began. She railed against the violation of our constitutional rights, how the cops had no evidence and no justification for instigating their riot and detaining hundreds of peaceful protestors. "Save the Eighth has nothing to do with the sabotage of Ramcorp Construction equipment, and we condemn that act in the strongest possible terms." Her eyes burned through the crowd, seeking out the anonymous culprits. I wanted to dissolve into the dirt. "The leadership of the working groups of the Free People's Village"—she waved a hand behind her at the group of mostly white dudes—"have no knowledge about the sabotage, and they condemn this act in the strongest possible terms." Blond, dreadlocked heads nodded. "Whoever did this acted alone and jeopardized the integrity of this movement, which has been entirely peaceful and nonviolent."

Shayna was furious. It occurred to me that there was nothing violent about attacking a bulldozer, but obviously I wasn't going to interject. I still didn't know who was right. Gestas had talked about the proud history of sabotage. *Fuck up Columbus's ship.* But Shayna had done far more than Gestas to build this movement. I couldn't shake the feeling that I'd betrayed her.

"I've gotten word that our people, who've been so unlawfully detained, have just been released, and they are making their way here. At eight p.m. tonight, we are going to march back to Calcott Street, to take back our home."

"Whose streets?" she called, and everyone replied, "Our streets!"

"I invite everyone out there watching"—Shayna spoke directly to the media cameras now, all her passion and charisma and urgency making the crowd hush so still, you could hear a pin drop—"who believes in free speech and democracy, who believes it's time to get serious about racial justice, and actually fixing the climate, who wants to see an end to police brutality—please join us. We need you."

38

We took back the Lab, and it was glorious.

In the following days, I must've watched the videos of our sea of people flowing around the police cordon a hundred times.

There were always cops around the Village after that—a few dozen human ones, in riot gear with big guns strapped to their chests. Flying drones buzzed incessantly overhead, like so many never-ending leaf blowers. And drone dogs stalked the edges of the crowd with their eerie, loping gaits.

"Look what we've done," I said miserably. That night, me and Gestas and Red were all up on the roof.

"What are you talking about? This is great," Gestas said, gesturing at some mounted pigs nearby. "All these cops here, babysitting us, means they're not out there, terrorizing people trying to live their lives. And now we've got them too." He pointed at the "media area"—now an entire tent city unto itself, in the yard of an abandoned house across the street, where CNN and MSNBC, even the BBC and Al Jazeera had permanently installed their reporters. "We're top news across the globe. Free People's Villages have sprung up in Paris, London, Gaza, and Hong Kong—dozens of places overseas, and new protests are springing up every day."

"Look at you, blushing groom," Red said. "You find out Angel's coming home on leave in a month, and suddenly you're all sunshine and roses."

248

"I am *never* sunshine and roses," Gestas said dangerously.

"Your soldier boy is coming home from war," Red said in a falsetto, clasping xir hands together and fluttering xir eyes.

I laughed and Gestas shoved Red, but he was smiling hugely. "I'm serious. This movement was doomed to die out if someone hadn't come along and provoked a big battle with the state. A battle which we won, I might add, and which has made them"—he nodded towards the cops—"extremely nervous."

It was true. After the bulldozer sabotage was discovered, our story had gone international. The media had certainly tried to make it seem like a terrible, despicable thing we'd done. But we had more supporters than ever now, here in the city and abroad. People got a real kick out of that act of "felony criminal mischief." Sabotaging the bulldozers wasn't just a protest—it was an attack, a *win*. It had cost the state many millions of dollars. And a lot of folks who hadn't believed that we could ever win against the state and its corporate puppeteers—they'd found hope in that win. Polls showed overwhelming sympathy for our movement among Democrats—which must've been why President Donnelly had finally spoken about our protest. At a recent campaign rally, he said he "admired our spirit," and that the Free People's Village was part of "a long, proud tradition of Americans making their voices heard."

"But now we've got *them* to deal with," I said, nodding to a clump of our counter-protestors across the street. Fourteen big, white dudes with AR-15s wore army-surplus camo and bandanas emblazoned with skulls and Celtic runes that I was pretty sure were Nazi symbols. They were standing near the line of cops, chatting away and laughing, like they were all best buds. One of them had a flagpole sticking out of his backpack, and flapping in the wind, in deep navy letters—almost black against a red background—were the words *Horneck 2020*.

Lately, the Republican candidate had centered his campaign around opposition to the Villages. For decades, Republicans had dismissed Al Gore's "War on Climate Change" as Democratic fearmongering. My dad had believed them—believed that the Democrats had lied about climate change in order to destroy the American fossil fuel industry. Out of spite, I guess.

But this election was different. With extreme weather events getting undeniably frequent, Horneck had embraced the "War on Climate Change" as a necessity, one that Democrats were too weak-kneed to wage. He blamed hurricanes in the Gulf on people who "refused to solarize their homes." He said the drought out west was the fault of "inefficiency." His platform stated that old, inefficient neighborhoods like the Eighth Ward should be bulldozed in their entirety and rebuilt from scratch using the latest eco-friendly tech. His adoring fans knew these phrases were dog whistles— "inefficient" had replaced "urban" or "ghetto." "Carbon thieves" meant Black people. Us Villagers? Well, we were filthy, drugged-up carbon guzzlers, standing in the way of an essential, green hyper-way. His crowds cheered the loudest when he said, "Under my administration, every traitor in the War on Climate Change will be tried for treason! And we're not going to put a widdle chip in their arms. We're putting 'em behind bars!"

Gestas turned his back on the Horneck supporters across the street. "They're like spiders—more scared of us than we are of them," he said.

"Yeah, they bring those big guns, but there's thousands of us and a dozen of them," Red said. "The cops have guns too. So what?"

"I don't know," I said, watching a guy with a skull balaclava over his face glaring up at us. "They think *we're* to blame for climate change. So by that logic, killing us would mean saving the world. Doesn't that freak you out?"

"Let 'em try to start some shit," Red said, cracking xir knuckles.

"There you guys are!" said a voice behind us. "I mean, sorry, not guys. I shouldn't say, um . . . There you people are? Oof, that doesn't sound right either." Mike Algebra pinched the bridge of his nose.

"Relax, Mike. 'Folks' works fine," Red said.

"There you folks are," Mike said, trying it out. "Yeah, okay."

"What's up, buddy?" Red asked.

"Well, um, I don't know if you recall that we were in a band?"

"A band . . . a band . . . now why does that sound familiar?" Red joked.

"I remember something vaguely," Gestas said, continuing the goof. "What was it called? Puppy Parade?"

"Kitten Catastrophe?" Red suggested. Mike chuckled nervously.

"Gerbil Jamboree?" I suggested.

Red busted out laughing. "That was it, yeah, Gerbil Jamboree."

"Right, uh, you're talking about Bunny Bloodlust though, right?" Mike confirmed. Red nodded, amused. "Well, we haven't rehearsed or done a gig or anything in over a month."

"Has it been that long? Shit," Red said. "A lot's been going on." Xe gestured around at the drones whizzing overhead, tent city, cops, etc.

"It has. But I was wondering if y'all wanted to practice some-time soon?"

"How?" I asked. "I mean, our practice space is like fifty people's bedrooms now."

"Yeah, it's weird to play with so many people around," Red said, kicking at the tar roof.

"So many people?" Mike asked, exasperated. "Do you want to be rock stars or what?"

"A show is different," Gestas said. "People choose to come to that. But it just seems rude for us to practice where a thousand people are living."

"The drum circle people don't seem to care about that," Mike said, scowling in the direction of the never-ending heartbeat.

"Exactly, and everyone else cannot fucking stand them," Red said.

"So, let's practice at my place," Mike offered. "Gestas can Skype in or something."

"No Gestas cannot fucking Skype in!" Red cried.

"Then you agree—we have to practice here?" Mike said. "That or we're not really in a band, are we?"

Red and Gestas looked at each other. A few months ago, before we got that damn eviction notice, the band was everything to us. Red was a barback; Gestas was watching his twenties devoured by AHICA, forced to do data entry for pennies an hour. I had teaching—but at a shit school with a bitch principal. It was just a paycheck. Bunny Bloodlust was the dream. But lately, amid the nonstop party-party-protest of the Village, we'd all but forgotten it.

"Yeah, okay," Red said finally. "Sunday, like around eleven. Shayna's got a big protest planned that day, so the place'll be a bit emptier. I suppose the folks sleeping in the living room won't mind getting kicked out for a few hours."

The prospect of playing together that weekend transformed Red. Xe was writing lyrics and songs at night again. Scribbling in xir notebook or picking out melodies. Xe drank less, spending all evening with xir guitar instead of a bottle.

On Sunday, a dozen friends watched us practice in Red and Gestas's living room. It felt like old times. Red showed us two new songs xe'd written, and they had killer melodies. The first time Red played us "(The people say) Fuck TxDOT!" I had this feeling like xe couldn't possibly have written it—because it was such a perfect pop-protest anthem that surely it came from the 1960s, though the lyrics were urgent and modern. I was nervous about playing "Brine in the Bulldozer," but later, Red pointed out that since we were known for being an anarchist post-punk band, it would've been more suspicious for us *not* to sing about it.

It felt wonderful and correct to be playing music again. When I shifted the bridge of "Brine" into a minor key, transforming the song into an aching, haunting, grunge-y ballad, Red looked at me like I was pure magic. That's still one of my favorite moments of my whole life, ever.

At that first practice, we attracted a few onlookers from the tent city outside, and some of them live streamed us on social media. Things blew up for us after that. Our SoundCloud page exploded with listens. Our Twitter account grew to 30K followers in a few nights. A local producer asked if he could record "Brine in the Bulldozer" pro bono. A few weeks later, we had to lock the door to Gestas's apartment when we practiced, to keep from being overrun by fans. Even Shayna liked our new tracks and invited us to play at some of the protest actions that were staged on the property.

The attention was flattering, overwhelming, a bit terrifying. Sometimes other teachers at school would comment that they'd seen a picture of me with my band on the news, or in some video their kid had shown them, and I'd feel like I was standing naked there in the copy room.

Those heady days, as the summer's brutal heat finally loosened its grip on the city, our victory over TxDOT seemed assured. Our star as a band was rising. Angel was coming home from war soon, and everything was going to be alright.

39

We threw a Halloween-y party-protest in mid-October, and the kitchen team was expecting a bigger crowd than ever. I was in charge of cooking up vats of vegan mac and cheese. The "kitchen" was now located outside, in an industrial tent big enough for a wedding.

Despite our best efforts, the line was moving slowly. Hundreds of unhoused people had joined the Village by this point. Damian, I'd learned eventually, was one of them, even though he had the skills to run a kitchen that fed thousands. In fact, a good number of the kitchen crew had been living on the streets before joining the Village. And the few dozen kids who lived at the Village were all the children of unhoused families. The vast majority of unhoused folks were no different than any other villager.

But there were a few people in the Village with untreated mental illness or addictions that made them difficult. Even scary. There were folks who ranted to thin air with incredible anger. A few, high out of their minds, had attacked other protestors just for looking in their direction. Every night now, Shayna pleaded with folks at the People's Musters about not leaving drug paraphernalia lying around. The Clinic tent ran a needle exchange and kept plenty of Narcan on hand. But in an echo of NIMBY city politics, some villagers at the People's Musters complained that the needle exchange had only made the drug problems worse. Lately, Fox News's segments often started with a shot of a discarded needle in the gutter along Calcott, or an addict passed out back near the edge of the cane.

That night, something about everyone being in costumes seemed to rile everyone up. A couple of the rowdier Villagers started scream-ing about the wait and shoving costumed party-goers out of the line. Damian went over to try to calm them down, and one of them swung at him, gave him a black eye. A bunch of folks, Red included, swarmed the guy and dragged him to the edge of the tent city, shov-ing him towards the night. They told him he wasn't welcome back. He pulled out a knife and waved it overhead, screaming that he was going to kill us all in our sleep. Red and some others chased him down the road, but it cast a weird vibe over the whole evening.

When my shift was finally over, I ate my plate on the front porch with Red and Gestas and some other friends. None of us had bothered with costumes, but it was fun to look at everyone else's. Shayna had encouraged folks to dress up as the real mon-sters of our world—so there were folks wearing suits emblazoned with the logos of oil and gas corps and weapons manufacturers. One guy had made a costume out of cardboard boxes and vacuum tubes, in the spitting image of the Valiant refinery behind the Lab. Blackened Poly-Fil smoke rose up from its smokestacks.

We were just goofing about nothing, making each other laugh, when this bright-eyed, bushy-tailed blond boy with a clipboard walked up and asked if we'd already made a plan to vote. He was wearing a "Donnelly 2020" T-shirt.

"Yes, we're good," I said quickly, hoping he'd hurry away.

Too late. "Why should I vote?" Gestas asked dangerously.

The boy launched into this slick, incredibly condescending speech about the importance of engaging in democracy. With each platitude, Gestas looked more and more eager to eat the young man alive.

"We've had thirty years of Democrats in power—ever since '92, yeah?" Gestas replied. "And what've they done? They've locked up more Black people than Republicans ever did, starting with the 1994 Crime Bill. Since 2002, mass incarceration has exploded under the supposed 'reform' of AHICA. Democrats started using these fucking things"—Gestas gestured to the drones buzzing loudly overhead—"ostensibly to reduce police violence by mechanizing it—only let me tell you, teargassing people with a drone is still fucking violent. Breaking their legs with drone dogs is fucking violent. So now we're all living in this carceral, surveillance-state dystopia, all thanks to Democrats."

I'd seen this play out before, with me, with Angel. Predictably, the organizer said, "I don't agree with everything the Democrats have done—but don't you think it would've been worse under Republicans? What about the 'War on Climate Change'? Republicans didn't even start acknowledging climate change existed until the 2010s!"

Gestas shrugged. "Maybe we're better off than we would've been under Republican rule. Who knows? Twenty years ago, the presidential election came down to a single state. In 2000, if Florida hadn't gone to Gore, then George W. Bush would've become president. Did you know that?"

"I mean, I was a baby," the organizer muttered.

"Sure, me too," Gestas said. "But okay, there's these people who call themselves 'Butterfly Prophets'—kind of a fun internet rabbit hole to go down—and they find these turning points in history, when the world turned on a few votes, or a single judge's decision, and they write, like, fan fiction, about what would've happened if things had gone the other way."

"Okay . . ." Blondie said, looking confused about where this was going.

"So sure," Gestas conceded. "Their predictions for where the climate would be in 2020 if Gore hadn't won are terrifying. It's highly unlikely that a President Bush would've declared 'War on Climate' like Gore did. They even point to this failed terrorist plot from 2001. No one remembers it anymore, but these Butterfly Prophets predict that if Bush had won, and that attack on the World Trade Center had succeeded, Bush might've used that as a pretense to take us into a different kind of war—a shooting war—over oil in the Middle East."

"You're proving my point," said the organizer. "That sounds like a much shittier timeline."

"Sure. If Bush had won, we'd probably have kept on accelerating fossil fuel use. We wouldn't have built maglevs and hyperways and the solar farm network. We'd probably be further along the road to hell planet. Instead, Gore created the Bureau of Carbon Reclamation, and the US Government has done everything in its power to stave off climate change—or so the media would have us believe." Gestas flicked his hand dismissively.

"But for all the BCR has done, we're still putting more carbon into the atmosphere than we're taking out. More than fifty percent of our energy still comes from burning fossil fuels. I suppose fifty is better than eighty or a hundred percent, but it's not good enough."

Gestas leaned forward, staring down the organizer as he picked up speed. "Nearly every ecosystem on earth is in decline, habitats are shrinking, forests are falling to loggers and wildfires. The ocean is filling with plastic, warming and acidifying. Under a liberal democracy doing its 'utmost'"—he traced air quotes—"to prevent climate change, we've bought ourselves a decade or two at most."

"That's . . . better, though, right?" said the organizer, extending the clipboard hopefully.

Gestas ignored it, resting his elbows on the step behind him. "If Bush had been elected, maybe things would be worse—more wildfires and drought, worse hurricane seasons, millions of climate refugees worldwide. Maybe even a zoomorphic pandemic!"

"Zoo-oh-morphic Pandemic," Red repeated, a little stoned. "That's a good song title."

"Things aren't that bad yet," Gestas went on. "But they're getting there. And unless we can transform society—massively, fundamentally, on every conceivable level, and soon—we're still headed for that nightmare world."

"So how do we do that?" I asked. "Transform society?"

"Now that's the big question," Gestas said. "What we're doing here—the Free People's Village—this is part of it, I think. I don't have all the answers. But we sure as shit aren't going to save the planet just by voting for fucking Democrats."

Blondie was looking paler than ever, like he might be sick. "But—but Horneck! Horneck is definitely worse than Donnelly, right? At least vote to keep the Republicans out of power."

"There's no way that asshole's going to win," Red said, glaring at the counter-protestors across the street. There were more of them today, maybe two dozen. And last night a few of them had gotten in a brawl with some tankies. The cops had only arrested our people.

"Horneck's polling at forty-eight percent," the organizer said.

"I don't believe it." Red chewed on a cuticle. "Those polls are bogus. People aren't *that* racist. Horneck straight up blames Black people and immigrants for climate change. He wants to make it a felony to have a gas stove in your house. The guy's an eco-fascist!"

"See . . . where you said, 'people aren't *that* racist,'" Gestas began, "that's where you're wrong. Never underestimate the racism of the United States of America. I think there's a very good chance Horneck could win. I think Horneck has been a long time coming."

Blondie finally lost his cool. "Then why won't you vote for Donnelly?!"

"Because fuck the Democrats too! And I don't know—I probably fucking will, okay?" Gestas shouted back. "Because harm reduction, and because this neoliberal two-party system doesn't give us any decent choice. Maybe I will, maybe I won't, but not because your punk ass with a clipboard told me to."

"People like you are going to hand Horneck the election," the organizer said, shaking his head in disappointment.

"People . . . like me?" Gestas repeated softly. Everyone collectively held a breath. "What do you mean by that? Do you mean *Black* people?"

"No." Blondie started shaking his head furiously.

"Trans people?"

"I didn't—"

"AHICA inmates?" Gestas stood up and flexed his chest. I could tell he was joking around, but Blondie started backing away. "COMMUNISTS?" Gestas roared.

"Get the fuck out of here, neolib," Red called, and xe chucked a piece of cornbread at the organizer's feet. He yelped and jumped back. Gestas, Lorenzo, and Nimo all busted out laughing, then copied Red, chucking their own leftover cornbread at the organizer.

"Yeah, neolib, fuck off!" Lorenzo cried.

Blondie jogged backwards. "It'll be your fault when Horneck gets elected!" he shouted, and then he was lost in the crowd.

"Oh it's *my* fault," Gestas grumbled, turning back to his food. "Not any of the Democrats in power who do nothing but lock up Black people, and sign oil-drilling permits, and suck oligarch dick. No, me and my little leftist punk friends are to blame that they sold out the world."

In almost a whisper, I asked, "But you . . . you are gonna vote for Donnelly, right?"

"YES I'M FUCKING VOTING FOR DONNELLY!" Gestas roared, and then he picked up his take-plate and went inside, slamming the door behind him.

"You too?" I asked, pointing at Red.

Xe shrugged, maddeningly.

"You too?!"

Red made a cringey face. "I would've . . . if I'd remembered to get registered to vote?"

"Jesus Christ," I said, my head falling into my hands. With just a few weeks to go before the election, that was the first time I seriously considered the possibility that Richard Horneck might become the next president of the United States of America.

40

Something terrible happened in the Free People's Village that night, to a girl who'd taken a bus down from Oklahoma City. A girl whose name was never released by the media. Because she was a minor.

We had a "Safety and Restorative Justice" working group to deal with these sorts of things, but she went to the cops instead. A lot of Villagers blamed her for that, but I understood it. The SRJ was toothless. When people brought issues to them (no rapes before this, but sexual harassment, racial slurs, theft) the victims were made to endure long restorative roundtables with the people who'd violated their boundaries. Sometimes violators had been kicked out or suspended from the Village, but there was no mechanism to enforce those sentences. The violators invariably crept back in a few days, resuming their offensive behavior. Some of the leaders of the SRJ were even friends with the harassers, who'd been accused of creepy behavior by multiple women.

So I get why she didn't go to the SRJ, although I can't imagine the cops were any better. They never caught whoever raped her, but they sure as hell used her. The chief of police gave a press conference the morning after Halloween, painting the entire Village as a den of crime and drugs and sin, enticing poor runaway kids to corruption. All the media outlets ran hit pieces on us that day—not just Fox News. It was like a switch had been flipped, and suddenly any pretense of sympathetic coverage was gone. I got a feeling that the mainstream media had been waiting for this moment, salivating for something tragic to happen, so they could pounce and tear the movement to shreds.

And the thing is, all the hit pieces the media ran the next few days—it was all true. It just wasn't the whole story. Yeah, we were running out of food in the kitchen line each night. Yeah, the heroin-addicted population was getting increasingly rowdy and there'd been a few folks narrowly saved from overdoses. Yeah, the residents of the neighborhood around us were getting fed up with the constant noise, particularly the drum circles. And yeah, the leadership of most of the working groups had been taken over by white boys from Brooklyn, who'd somehow percolated to the top with the reverse osmosis of the extremely privileged.

The origins of the movement—Save the Eighth, even the hyper-way expansion itself—they were never mentioned by the media anymore. After all, there were sixty cities in the US now with their own Free People's Villages, and dozens more abroad. Plenty united us—opposition to the Amazonian War, the greenwashing bullshit of the BCR, the way Black and brown communities were bearing the brunt of the "War on Climate Change," mass incarceration, police violence, accelerating climate change—all of it tying back to the beating heart of the world's suffering: racial capitalism.

But those TV reporters, they just *could not* figure out what us kids were upset about. The liberal stations painted us as a party, not a protest, of leaderless, drug-addicted, mostly white and privileged, spoiled whiners who'd rather complain about the government than get jobs. The right-wing stations brought on talking heads who called us traitors in the climate war, saying we should be thrown in jail or shot.

So October 11th was a bad day. The mood around the Village was strained. Peter was decrying the media coverage as baseless slander, defending the Village as if we had no sins. "I guarantee—whoever did this to that girl was one of those Nazi-fuck counter-protestors. I told you they've been infiltrating our camp. There's no way it was one of our people."

Something in me snapped at that, and I told him to shut up, because he didn't know what he was talking about. Lorenzo whistled and held his hands up, saying, "Whoa, whoa."

Vida glared at both of them. "Maybe watch what you say today, because pretty much anyone who isn't a cis dude is feeling triggered."

Nimo looked at her meaningfully and rubbed her back.

I had to go somewhere to be alone. My ears were ringing and my heart was pounding and I felt a panic attack coming on. I had never been raped—I was one of the few women I knew who could say that—so why did I feel triggered?

I pushed my way through the crowds in the Lab, feeling like the walls were closing in on me. Finally I got to Red's room and locked the door behind me.

Red was lying on the bed, staring up at the ceiling, plucking at xir acoustic guitar.

I burst into sobs and fell on the bed, my breaths coming faster and faster in spite of myself.

Red rolled over and put a hand on my shoulder. "What? What happened?"

"No, it's—I don't know why—I'm freaking out." My words came out between lungfuls of air rushing in too fast. "Something about that girl's story—"

"Who hurt you? Who do I gotta fight?"

"No, no it's not—" I finally managed to take a deep, slow breath. I rolled onto my back and hit my inhaler. My breath started coming sensibly, but tears wouldn't stop leaking from my eyes. "I don't even know what it is. I mean . . . I don't think I've ever been . . . *assaulted.*" I couldn't bring myself to say the r-word.

"Was it Fish?" xe said. "Did he ever force you? Because I'll fuck-ing kill him."

"No, I don't think so, but . . . actually—" And suddenly I was flooded with a visceral memory of him panting away on top of me, half-drunk. Me, feeling nothing but pain below, desperately bored and sad and hoping he'd finish soon. "I let him. I always *let* him do it. But that was it, you know? Except for in the very beginning—just the first couple weeks, I guess—I never wanted to. I felt like I had to."

Red said nothing. There was a wild look in xir eyes I didn't recognize, as xe stared at the wall, staring a hundred miles or years away, focusing on nothing. I couldn't tell if xe was mad at me—because I'd brought up my sex life with Fish—or if xe was about to make good on xir threat and run off and kill him. Red's eyes were red-rimmed, veins standing out on xir neck. For a sec-ond I thought maybe xe was having some kind of stroke or some-thing, but then I smelled it—the sour, sickly sweet reek of liquor sweats.

"Are you fucking drunk?" I asked. Anger roared up out of nowhere, chasing off the horrible thing I'd been feeling before.

"I've had a few drinks." Red snapped out of the weird emotion and tried to grin charmingly, but xir unfocused eyes spoiled the effect.

"It's not even fucking noon, dude!"

"So? S'my day off." Red shrugged.

"What is wrong with you?"

Red recoiled as if I'd hit xim.

"What's wrong with *me*? Fuck." Red leaned away from me. "You're one to talk."

"What does that mean?" I asked.

Red rolled over and picked up xir guitar. "I'm not the one who has a panic attack every five seconds. Over nothing."

It was the first time Red had ever said something like that—to hurt me, on purpose. It cut like a razor. And I wanted to hurt xim back. "Well, maybe it's better to feel things than to just drown all your emotions like a pathetic drunk."

"Feel what?" Red roared. "You said it yourself, you've never been raped! You didn't even know this girl on the news. So what the fuck are you hyperventilating for? What, because you let Fisher Wellman fuck you when you weren't in the mood? You have to make everything about you, even when this shit has nothing to do with you!"

"Wow. You're an asshole," I said, grabbing my bag off the bed. "A drunk asshole, and I can't believe I'm doing this again."

"You don't know me, Maddie," Red said quietly. "You don't know the first fucking thing about me."

I hung in the doorway. I had every right to storm out, and maybe I should've. No point arguing with a mean drunk, right? And what Red had said to me was horrible. But something held me there. The weird look in Red's eyes when I'd told xim about Fish. And this last thing xe'd said—*You don't know the first fucking thing about me.* Something was lurking there, right below the surface. There'd been a thousand hints over the past year—but I'd written them all off as band drama, or resentment that I was with Fish instead of Red.

I took a steadying breath. "Maybe I don't know you, but I want to. So what is it? What happened between you and Fish?"

Red's hand froze on the guitar strings. Xe had that far-off, pained look again.

I came slowly towards xim, took the guitar gently and slid it to one side. "What happened between you and Fish?" I repeated, sitting on the bed.

Tears stood out in Red's eyes, and I had never seen that before. Red did not cry. Xir eyes darted around the room, unwilling to meet mine.

"I—" xe tried to start saying something, but it was like xe was choking on the words. Tears spilled from xir eyes. Xir mouth clamped shut after a moment, and xe sat up, shaking xir head no.

"Whatever it is, you can tell me."

A convulsion racked xir body. I thought it was a sob and reached for xim, but then Red's mouth opened, and xe let out a powerful stream of vomit, all over my arms, the bed, xir lap.

I just kind of froze there for a second. Red looked up, eyes still streaming, a drip of puke running down xir chin. "Sorry, Mads."

"You gonna go again?" I asked. I was an old hand at caring for puking drunks.

Red shrugged. I sighed.

"Let's get you to the toilet."

Red threw up twice more, then dry heaved into the bowl for a while, hugging the filthy seat. I changed both of us out of our puked-on clothes. I couldn't find a clean washcloth, so I got a T-shirt soapy and washed our skin with that.

When Red was cleaned up, and I'd changed the soiled sheet, I tucked xim back in bed and lay down, despairing that this was my lot again. I wasn't sure if Red had been on the verge of telling me some terrible secret about Fish, or whether the emotion I'd thought I'd seen there was just vomit bubbling to the surface.

But then, just as I was drifting to sleep, Red started to talk.

"It was a few days before I met you. That first week we moved into the Lab." I held my breath, in case the slightest sound might cause Red to stop. "Fish threw a party in his apartment. He was talking about how he was going to be our producer and record us and make Bunny Bloodlust huge, and he kept pouring us shots of this really mellow, aged tequila. We drank the whole bottle, and I guess I fell asleep in his bed? And then I woke up—"

Red sniffed and fell silent. I reached for xim in the dark and scooted closer.

"—I woke up and he was *in* me."

Red started to cry, and I held xim closer. My mind felt blank. I couldn't process it. Fish had raped Red. Fish had raped Red in xir sleep. Before I had even met xim. The whole time—through my whole relationship with Fish, every band practice, every long afternoon hanging out on the couches—all along, every second of it, Red had been silently suffering in the presence of xir rapist. Why? Red, who started bar fights with biker gangs. Fiery, king-of the-world, rock-star Red.

Xir body stilled, and xir breaths came slower.

"I don't get it," I whispered. "Why then—why not tell me? Why'd you put up with him?"

"He was our fucking landlord," Red spat, voice thick with loathing. "After his arrest, Gestas had gone back to living with his mom and stepdad, and they were awful to him. I had to get him out of there. Then Fish comes along and offers us this ridiculously cheap rent. Says he's gonna promote our band and buy us gear. We can play shows here, so Gestas can actually perform. It sounded too good to be true. It was. Because then when what happened . . . happened . . . and I just figured, okay, that was the fine print on our lease. That was the missing rent money. And if I made a big deal about it, we'd get kicked out. Gestas would have to go back to getting beat up by his stepdad. Or worse, go to brick-and-mortar prison. I just—I couldn't." Red broke off, xir voice cracking. "And I'm sorry, Maddie. When you were with him, I wanted to . . . to warn you, but I just—I couldn't—" Red shook with sobs.

"No, it's—" I was about to say, "It's okay," but was it? Should Red have warned me? When I searched my heart, all I found was sorrow for what had happened to Red and fury at Fish. "I just— now *I* want to kill him."

Red snort-sobbed a laugh.

"I won't stop you," Red said, and now I laughed. "But listen, you can't ever tell Gestas. I don't want him to know. He'd blame himself, and—well, *we're* joking about it, but Gestas? He might literally kill Fish, and he doesn't need that added to his rap sheet."

"I won't," I whispered. "Blood oath to Satan."

I intended to keep the promise. But I had no idea what I'd do the next time I saw Fisher Wellman.

41

Over the next few weeks, the vibes at the Free People's Village got very bad. The media was running hit pieces in earnest—finding the most incoherent, high, and creepy Villagers to interview, filming spots of filth and litter before our sanitation crews could get to them.

The Musters were such a mess, I could hardly bear to listen to them anymore. Tempers were running very high. The feminist working group attacked the SRJ for doing nothing to protect folks of marginalized genders. Save the Eighth and the Brown Bloc accused the leadership of most of the working groups of being racist and speaking over Black and brown voices. More and more, people were not respecting the stack and the mic-check system, and Musters dissolved into fractious shouting matches—which the media cameras were all too happy to project around the world.

Bulldozers and excavators arrived, demolishing the houses further down Calcott. That big pile of Fish's junk furniture that we'd pulled out of the Lab on the first day of the occupation had been sitting in the elements, getting rained on and providing spider and snake habitat all this time. Some enterprising Villagers piled it in front of the bulldozers as a makeshift barrier. A pitiful gesture, because anyone could see it would only take seconds for the heavy machinery to gouge through it.

There was no question of sabotaging these diggers either. The police presence was heavier than ever, 24-7, with mounted human officers, dozens of dogs—real and robotic—and so many buzzing mosquito drones that you had to shout to be heard while outdoors.

I had the same feeling I always got right before a hurricane, when the air became real still and the sky turned green, and you knew that this was it—no more time to gather supplies or decide to evacuate. The outer bands would be here soon, and all you could do was hunker down and pray.

Amidst all the chaos and hostility, Red was my safe harbor. Things had changed between us since our fight and xir revelation, but it's hard to explain just what. We didn't talk about what Fish had done. And it's not like Red suddenly opened up and poured out xir life story. But there was more tenderness in our shared looks. I still felt all the hunger and magnetic attraction to xim from before. But there was also a quieter feeling . . . safety, maybe.

That feeling was shattered, for both of us, the next time Fish paid a visit.

It was a few weeks before the election. President Donnelly had made a statement condemning the Free People's Villages nationwide as "dangerous disruptions of civic order." While he sympathized with the original aims of the protest, he was charging mayors with doing whatever was necessary to address the hazardous conditions in the occupations. Everyone was holding their breath, expecting the worst.

After work, Red and I were on the roof with Vida and Lorenzo, having a mellow time after eating some edibles. Down on the porch below, some roadie-looking guy showed up and started setting up a podium with all these official-looking microphones. Then a fleet of luxury SUVs rolled up, and Fish and his lawyer Chad, and a bunch of other golf-course-looking dudes in Brooks Brothers suits spilled out of them.

I looked at Red. Xir hands were balled into fists, knuckles blanched white.

"You okay?" I mouthed.

Red scowled. "I'm going to get a drink."

"Wait—" I called, but Red was already storming off. I felt I should probably follow xim, make sure xe didn't do anything reckless, but Fish was just tapping the mics and adjusting his tie in front of all the media cameras, and I wanted to hear a bit of whatever the fuck he'd come here to say. I had this wild, irrational feeling that he was here to apologize to Red.

But no. It was the same speech he'd been giving for weeks. That he supported the free speech of the Villagers on his property, and the city and state had no grounds to interfere with property-owners' rights. It was as if he'd come just to remind us that the entire Village only existed at his pleasure. As badly as I wanted to hock up a big wad of spit onto his head—yet again, we could not afford to fuck with him.

Feeling a spike of panic about what Red was up to, I rushed downstairs.

A blast from the Marshall stacks greeted me from the Lab. Gestas was already adjusting his drum throne. Red had plugged in and started pounding out some power chords, tapping on the pedals arrayed before xim. A half-empty bottle of J&B sat next to the mic.

"Band practice?" I asked.

Gestas shrugged in an "I guess?" gesture. Red didn't look up. Mike Algebra was at work, so it'd be just the three of us. This was good, I thought—of all the things Red could be doing right now, while Fish held a press conference out front, band practice was probably the healthiest.

Red launched into our new songs, playing breakneck fast and loud enough to drown out Fish's press conference. Most of the new tracks were folkier and poppier than our earlier stuff, but not the way Red was playing them. My fingers ached and my biceps burned just trying to keep up. Gestas was loving it, head thrown back in bliss, whooping in between songs. Red took a long swig of J&B at the end of each song. Lorenzo came downstairs to help with the soundboard, and Vida and Nimo started dancing in a corner as a bunch of other Villagers streamed in from outside. Soon we had an impromptu show going, and the crowd of a few dozen people was loving it, dancing, singing along, or live streaming us from their phones. Lorenzo jabbed his fingers at the sky, his long hair tracing fractals in the air as he headbanged.

We were halfway through "Slaying Cane" when a blur of movement at the back cargo doors caught my eye. Fish had come inside, tie loosened, and was leaning against the wall there, nodding his head along. Fuck.

Red stopped playing abruptly. Gestas took a few more measures to realize we'd dropped out and stilled his drumsticks.

Red tapped the mic three times, and the *pouf pouf pouf* reverberated around the room.

"Fisher. Fisher Wellman," Red said into the mic, in this weird voice, sounding like someone talking over the loudspeaker at Target. "Get. The Fuck. Out."

Heads whipped around, searching. Everyone—even the Villagers who weren't our friends from before—knew Fish's face from all his interviews. Suddenly all eyes were on him, and he grinned and gave this obnoxious fucking half wave. He thought Red was clowning on him in a friendly way. I held my breath.

"Heh-heh-heh," Red fake laughed menacingly into the mic. "I said—"

Red stepped away from our practice area, unslinging xir guitar over xir head. It was a cherry-red Fender Strat, a beautiful fucking guitar, a guitar Fish had bought for xim. Suddenly I knew what was going to happen and started forward, but my foot got caught on some cables. Red raised the guitar by the neck, straight overhead. The crowd yelped and jumped back.

"GET!"

Red brought the guitar smashing down into the cement floor of the Lab. Its side exploded, shards torpedoing into the flinching crowd.

"THE FUCK!"

Xe brought it down again in a full-body swing, strings snapping. I'd managed to get my guitar off me and ran for Red.

"OUT!"

The rest of the body exploded into fragments and Red straightened, holding only the jagged edge of the fingerboard like a sword, pointed right at Fish's heart.

I switched directions, running for Fish instead of Red. I had a horrible premonition Red might actually murder him.

"Fish, listen to xim. Just go," I yelled, pushing through our small crowd.

Lorenzo cackled with delight. He scooped up shards of guitar and chucked them in Fish's direction. "You heard Red. Get the fuck out!"

Fish just stood, mouth hung open, looking between the three of us like his brain could not process how deeply unwelcome he was here.

I reached him first. Red was doing this slow, deadly walk, with the fingerboard still held straight out at heart-level. I shoved Fish towards the cargo doors, and he stumbled back awkwardly.

"What the hell is going on, Maddie?" he yelled at me, backing up. "What the hell did I do to deserve this?"

I kept shoving him until he was out on the back porch and halfway down the loading ramp, where we were out of sight of the Lab.

"You know what you did," I hissed. "To Red. Before you and I even met. Red told me."

"What?" He laughed, uncomprehending. "That we hooked up? What, are you jealous? Did I start a lover's quarrel?"

"No you fucking jackass, you didn't hook up with Red, you raped xim."

Fish gaped like I'd socked him in the gut. I couldn't tell if it was an act, or if he really had no idea that that's what he'd done. His brow furrowed. There was this brief, fleeting instant where I thought I saw something like horror and understanding and remorse flit across his features. But it was just an instant, and then he was furious.

"No . . . no, what the fuck are you talking about? I didn't"—he whispered the next word—"*rape* Red! [Xe] came on to *me*, okay? If [xe] regretted it the next day—"

Only Fish didn't say "xe."

Thankfully, I didn't have to listen to any more of Fish's bullshit excuse, because someone pushed past me, and then a fist shot out and smashed into Fish's face with a beautifully satisfying *thwuck*!

"Those aren't xir fucking pronouns," Lorenzo panted, shaking out his fist.

Fish held his jaw, blood trailing from his mouth. "Wha tha fuck!" he roared, eyes widening at someone behind me. I turned and saw Gestas on the back porch, beside Red, who held the guitar neck limply at xir side, face drained of all color. Shit. How much had they heard? Behind them, a crowd craned their necks to see. For one breath, everyone was frozen in place.

Then Red surged forward, brandishing the guitar neck like a club. Gestas and Nimo grabbed xim. Gestas shouted, "Get out of here, Fish!"

Lorenzo was pushing Fish further down the ramp, and a bunch of the bigger folks from our crowd joined him, forming a huddle around Fish, who was shouting, "I own this place! You can't kick me off my property!"

Two cops appeared around the side of the Lab, moving towards us. Lorenzo clocked them, then jabbed Fish in the chest with a finger. "You better not set foot here again, 'cause if Red doesn't kill you, I fucking will. And that's a promise."

Shit—maybe they'd heard everything.

"You're going to regret this!" Fish yelled, ducking into an idling SUV. It sped off. Lorenzo intercepted the approaching cops before they reached us. "Just a little band drama," he called with an exasperated grin. The cops looked over the scene of all us on the loading dock, then moved on, weaving through the tent city. Gestas had his arms around Red and was squeezing xim tight, despite Red's thrashing, talking quietly in Red's ears. I was afraid to get closer. I was afraid I'd betrayed Red in a really terrible, unforgivable way.

But then xe looked up and met my eyes, and all xir muscles went slack. I came forward, arms out, and Gestas released xim. Red took a step forward and collapsed into me, holding me painfully tight, sobbing into my neck. I held xim back as tight as I could.

"God, this is fucking embarrassing," Red said, stepping back, wiping xir eyes with the back of xir hand. Xe made a pitiful noise like, "Hyeuh!" and half-assedly chucked the broken fingerboard at the spot where Fish had stood. It landed with a *thunk* in the mud beside the loading ramp. Gestas snorted a laugh.

"Shame about the guitar though," Gestas said.

Red barked a laugh. "It sounded great, didn't it? I loved that fucking thing. Oh well."

"We don't need his shit," I said.

"Damn straight," Gestas said, pulling out his cigarettes. "We don't need *him*. And if his help is the only thing keeping this protest afloat, then"—he paused to light the cigarette—"let it all burn. It's about time anyways."

I didn't know quite what he meant. But I understood why Red had never told him what Fish had done. Gestas never would've let Red go through all that trauma, constantly being shadowed by xir rapist, playing in a band with him, living under his roof. No, Gestas would not have let Red do that—not for him. Not for anything.

42

That night a strong cold front moved through, jostling the trees, bringing sheets of frigid rain. The mud soon got saturated, seeping into tents through zippers and seams. A lot of the locals went home to their apartments, while out-of-towners crammed into the Lab, streaking the floors with a thousand muddy footprints. Gestas sat at his table in the corner, where he ran a lending library seeded with his personal collection of leftist books, now swollen with hundreds more donations. He had lots of visitors that night, all eager to find something to take their minds off the chill, and the boredom, and the impending sense of doom that we felt, now that the media and president and mayor had announced their intent to destroy us.

Gestas was the only person who didn't look gloomy. In fact, he seemed downright giddy, because Angel, his unlikely soldier-love, was coming home on leave in a few weeks' time. All of us who knew Angel felt a surge of warmth every time we thought about it. Strong, competent, dad-friend Angel. There was no fight you couldn't win, no project you couldn't tackle with Angel at your side. Red was definitely smiling more than usual, knowing xir brother was coming home, and xe'd been drinking less too. I'd always vaguely wished Angel could be my big brother, and now that I was dating Red, it'd kind of be like that.

I cooked a miserable shift that night. Somewhere in the kitchen tent, there was a live wire touching the mud, and the soggy ground conducted it, electrifying everything metal. So if you touched the stove, or a tent pole, or the stainless-steel counters, you'd get lightly electrocuted. Meanwhile, my feet were soaking in a pair of Converse, I was shivering violently, and my fingertips were so cold I couldn't feel them while I was chopping onions, which seemed like a recipe for disaster.

I was so relieved to come off that shift, I skipped the People's Muster for an indulgently long, hot shower in Red's bathroom.

Red was at work, barbacking. I climbed into bed alone and fell asleep watching streams of the day's protest action on my phone, listening to the rain sheeting off the windowpanes.

How could I have known it was my last night in the Village?

I woke to screams.

Terrible things were happening in the tent city outside. My first thought was that I wasn't wearing a bra—did I have time to put a bra on under the band shirt I was wearing? If I was about to be arrested, I thought, I'd like it to be while wearing a bra. But then I pictured cops busting down the door while I was in the middle of changing, which seemed equally horrific.

As I hesitated for a few long seconds, the sounds of fighting and wailing from outside grew louder, and I could feel a tickle of tear gas in my lungs. A siren was blaring. "You are trespassing on private property. Vacate the premises or face felony trespassing charges." Fuck. I could *not* get charged with a felony—I would automatically lose my teaching license. Surely though, they just meant the people outside, right? Red was a tenant here, and I was xir guest—they wouldn't arrest *me*. I decided to put on proper clothes and find my inhaler. My hands were shaking violently as I pulled on jeans, praying I'd have enough time to get them over my bare ass before the cops burst in. I was still hoping maybe the violence wouldn't come inside the brick walls of the Lab.

But even as I thought that, a *Slam! Slam!* started up that shook the walls of the apartment, coming from the general direction of the front door. Taking a preemptive puff from my inhaler, I cast one last look around Red's room. I had this gut feeling I wouldn't see it again, as if floodwaters were rising, and I had seconds to decide what to save. Our acoustic guitars were too big, and likely to get smashed in their soft cases if I tried to carry them out. Finally, I just snatched Red's notebook, the one with the lyrics to all our songs, and shoved it halfway down the back of my jeans, pulling my T-shirt over the top.

The living room was empty, which was weird. I checked Gestas's room, but he wasn't there. Out in the hall, a dozen people were braced against the doors that the cops were trying to smash open from the other side. Shayna and Toussaint were shoulder to shoulder up against the wood that was shuddering with terrible violence. I stood there, frozen, unsure how to help, until someone called my name.

I turned, and Gestas shoved a cardboard box full of books in my hands. I sagged momentarily under the weight.

"Put 'em in my room, okay? And bring me another box—there's some empties near the fridge."

Before I could respond he dashed back towards the Lab, towards his library. He wanted to save the books before the cops got inside.

Grateful to have something useful to do, I hurried to his room and stashed the box behind his bed. Then I found the liquor boxes by the fridge and hurried out to the main Lab area. The cargo bay doors were all locked shut, but they were being jostled from outside. Peter, Nimo, and some others were piling mattresses in front of them for a makeshift barricade. Other folks were just holding each other and crying. I got to work beside Gestas, packing stacks of leftist theory into the cardboard boxes.

Fresh screams from inside the Lab. I spared a glance and saw one of the cargo bay doors thrown open, and in stormed armor-clad, gas-masked, pigs in black, silhouetted against billows of horrible pink gas. I took another hit off my inhaler.

"Keep packing!" Gestas shouted, and I obeyed. It's not that I wasn't afraid. The sickening sounds of beatings and screaming behind me had me so terrified that if I *didn't* have something to do, I would've drowned in fear. Just pissed myself and collapsed into the puddle. Plus, I was telling myself that as soon as I filled the box, I could run back to Gestas's room and hide.

But they reached us in seconds. Gestas was jerked suddenly backwards, and I screamed. He was on the ground by the time I turned my head, with a cop kneeling on his back, zip-tying his wrists together.

"He lives here!" I tried to yell, but my voice came out thin and shaking. "He's a tenant."

Then I caught a lungful of the tear gas, and I was coughing and choking and crying. A line of cops had formed and were shoving a whole bunch of us towards the back cargo doors. Other Villagers were randomly thrown to the ground, kicked, bashed with batons, and arrested. I caught a glimpse of Nimo flinching away, hands over his head, as a cop charged at him with a baton. Even as blurry as my vision was, I could see the pattern. Darker-skinned folks were getting beat up. Us white folks were being pushed towards the exit. My fear was stronger than my sense of injustice, and I let myself be herded out, stepping over the ankles of fellow Villagers, prone, with their wrists and ankles zip-tied. Once I got outside, I could slip away, find some clear air to breathe, avoid the felony charges, and *then* find a way to help those getting arrested.

Through the back doors, I saw the devastation of our once-beautiful Village. Drizzling rain had helped dissipate the worst of the tear gas. Dozens of people were pinned to the earth by locked-on drone dogs, some trying to drag themselves away through the sucking mud. Everything was smashed and trodden and ruined. Thousands of tents, the crocheted art installations, the kitchen— all wreckage now, like a tornado had blown through.

A flash of color beside me caught my eye. A big cop held the lime-green Bacardi box I'd just packed up. He hoisted it and then flung out all the books. They arced through the air, briefly suspended among the rain droplets glittering in the refinery lights, before landing with a *splat!* in the mud below, pages splayed.

Without realizing what I was doing or thinking about the consequences, I yelled, "Why would you do that?" at the cop. Because really—why? It was so unnecessary. There were so many people to arrest and brutalize—why take a moment out just to destroy some books? I'm not proud that *that's* what it took for me to yell in a cop's face. I could've shown my outrage earlier—when they'd grabbed Gestas, when they'd been beating and arresting my friends—that would've been the heroic time to scream at a pig. But it was the books that did it for me. Gestas's books, broken and scattered in the mud.

I didn't know what a charmed life of immense privilege I had lived up to that moment. I had never really known violence. Despite having had drunks for a father, ex-husband, and ex-boyfriend, none of them had been violent towards me. I had never been physically attacked by a grown man before. I hadn't really known the pain, and the powerlessness, and the terror of it.

It happened so fast. The cop grabbed me by the front of my shirt and slammed me to the cement floor of the Lab, and my entire body exploded in pain I couldn't believe. One second I was standing, the next I'd hit the cement so hard I couldn't suck in a breath and thought I never would again. From the stabbing pain in the back of my skull, I was sure it had cracked open, and I was bleeding out. The pig kicked me on my side, and my rib cage felt like it shattered. Then he was kneeling on my back, grabbing my arms. For a horrible moment I thought he was planning to rip them off. I was sobbing into the concrete, just abject mortal terror, choking on tear gas all the while, not sure which of my injuries would kill me first, or if I'd suffocate.

And then he was off me, and I realized he'd just been zip-tying my wrists together. I peered through bleary eyes ahead, and there were dozens of other people lying on the ground like I was. I knew they were all hurt as bad, or worse, than I was. And I cried for all of them—I cried because those fucking pigs had come through and hurt so many people, so quickly, and they'd enjoyed it—you could tell by the way they moved. They were laughing and tossing people's clothes and Gestas's books, and anything they could get their hands on out into the mud, having the time of their damn lives. What had just happened to me was the most traumatic, terrifying, painful experience of my life, and yet it was so damn common—they'd done it to hundreds of us, just that night. They'd done it to thousands more people I'd watched getting beat down by cops on video. Hell, they'd done it to that grandmother Miriam. I'd had no clue how badly it hurt. How it humiliated and terrorized. We'd built this community, painstakingly, over months, with the labor of thousands of idealistic people hoping for a better world—

They'd smashed it to bits in half an hour.

And then I spotted the guy in camo, with the skull balaclava over his face and a "Horneck 2020" patch on his backpack. He wasn't a cop—he was one of those counter-protestors. The cops had brought their buddies along to join in the fun. He was pointing the long barrel of his AR-15 at each of us in turn, probably getting off on seeing our eyes go wide with terror. I wanted to be brave, to spit at him when it was my turn, but when his boots stopped inches from the tip of my nose, I closed my eyes tight and went completely still, Hail Marys running through my head out of old habit, until I heard his steps moving off.

They left us lying there a long time. Maybe ten minutes, maybe an eternity, maybe an hour. At some point I realized I'd pissed myself, and the urine had cooled on my jeans, and I was shivering uncontrollably. My adrenaline started to wear off, which meant every minute or so, a new part of my body would come back online and start telling me how it hurt—like that the zip-ties were digging painfully into the flesh of my wrists, and my fingertips were tingling from lack of circulation. I was sure they'd fall off too. I was still convinced that there was no way I could survive what was happening to me. That surely I was dying of some internal injuries.

I have a hard time remembering a lot of the details after that point, which Dr. Abner said is part of the trauma response. I don't remember how they dragged us up and into the paddy wagons. I don't remember much about that long, awful night at the jail in the holding pen. But I do remember, with vivid clarity, sitting on the bench in the paddy wagon, looking out the back doors at the Free People's Village—all wrecked now, all bedraggled and mud and filth and flotsam. And I remember the refinery lights glowed orange in the drizzly haze, and Vida's big, beautiful mural, "Save the Eighth," in its elephant-sized bubble letters and towering wild-flowers, lit up all brilliant in the floodlights. And then a cop leaned in to close the doors to the van, blocking out the image until it was just a sliver of riotous color. Then—darkness.

III.
THE
REVOLUTION

43

They held us overnight in crowded cells, divided by their assumptions about our genders, where there was only room to sit with our knees to our chins. Sometime midmorning, it was my turn to get booked—and I heard in a sleep-deprived, injured, gutted-out haze that I had been charged with felony trespassing and resisting arrest. My brain had exhausted its entire stock of neurotransmitters, and I was running on fumes. They could've told me I was charged with murdering Martians, and it would've meant as much to me.

After that, I was allowed to make a call from a pay phone—they'd taken our cell phones when they'd patted us down. An old-school, paper phone book was chained to the booth, and I looked up the only lawyer I knew—Chad McMannis. I couldn't believe it, but his office was actually open, and the receptionist actually connected me to him, and he *remembered* me. Remembered me as Fish's ex-girlfriend.

He was furious at Fish. Here he'd been working this case against TxDOT for months, playing up the rights of Fish's tenants, and then, unilaterally, Fish had decided to call the city and sic the cops on the encampment. Chad wanted to know, "What the fuck was he thinking?"

I did not feel up to filling Chad in on what Fish had done to Red, and how we'd confronted him about it, so I just said, "I don't know. He's an asshole."

"Well, given that he has actively sabotaged his own case, my firm has terminated our contract with Fisher Wellman," Chad growled. "I don't give a fuck if he's my brother-in-law. I'm not going to work with a guy like that." It turned out I did have a bit of happy brain chemicals left, because that gave me a flicker of pleasure.

Chad said the charges against me were utter bullshit, and not only would he represent me pro bono, we were going to counter-sue the city for the trauma they'd inflicted. He was very animated, very confident, in a way that made me want to cry with relief. I told him Gestas had been arrested too, and I hadn't seen him since. At that, Chad cursed and said he'd get right on finding out what they'd done with Gestas.

There was a fat bail fund for us, swollen with donations from all the secret suburban socialists who'd pinned their hopes for a better world on our Village. I could afford my own bail though, so I didn't make use of it. Hundreds of us had been taken, and I knew a lot of folks had no job or savings.

As it turned out I didn't have a job either, though, so maybe I should've taken the money. When I got my cell phone back, there was a voicemail from my AP, Nora. I listened to it at the mag-lev station outside the jailhouse, staring at some dried, blackened gum on the platform. She'd been notified through an automated system that I'd been charged with a felony, which meant my teaching license had been indefinitely suspended. Her voice sounded professional, smiling, dripping with disrespect. I was not legally allowed to return to campus until my case was resolved. Unfortunately, she would not be able to hold my position for me until that time. If and when I was absolved of the felony charge, I was welcome to reapply for another available position at Washburn High School.

Just like that, I wasn't a teacher anymore. *Couldn't* be a teacher anymore.

Luckily, I didn't seem to have enough emotional reserves left to care.

I had a bunch of texts and missed calls from Red, who'd been finishing up xir shift when we got attacked. Xe was staying with Slime and Filthy Ed at the warehouse on Canal Street—which was about the last fucking place in the world I wanted to go. I texted to say I needed to get some sleep. I'd call xim when I woke up.

I hadn't been to my apartment in days, and there was a notice stuck under my door, saying I'd missed too many gardening shifts, so my carbon taxes would go up next month. Inside, my apartment smelled stale and unfamiliar. I tossed my keys on the counter next to a stack of my first period's papers on Malcolm X's *By Any Means Necessary*, which I would now never grade. I'd been bracing myself to get fired, but I'd assumed it'd happen over assigning texts like that. Antoine, Princess, Kenya—I'd probably never see them again. I wished I'd been able to say goodbye.

It was so quiet up in my place. The large windows spanning the far wall looked out on the waving prairies and glinting Community towers of Midtown, but you couldn't hear the wind or the grass swishing, or even a neighboring tenant's dog. The only sound, ever, was the deep thrumming of the building's air ducts. I sat on the edge of the bed, hating the apartment's open floor plan, glinting stainless-steel kitchen fixtures, and pristine walls. How I missed chipped paint scrawled with graffiti, vines that pushed through ancient windowpanes, even the cockroaches dead in the tub. A cockroach never had, and never would, make it up the five flights of stairs here to die in my bathtub. This was a dead space, designed only for a single human, living alone.

I fell asleep like that, crying for lack of dead roaches.

44

When I woke up, mid-evening, I headed straight to the Canal warehouse. Vida and Peter were smoking outside, and they gave me the rundown on what had happened to all our friends—who'd been arrested and who'd escaped the raid. Nimo had needed stitches in his scalp, and his sister had picked him up to go stay with her in Galveston. Just about everyone was out on bail already except Gestas, who'd been denied AHICA placement for getting arrested while already serving time. He'd been transferred to a brick-and-mortar prison in Sugar Land, and Peter was setting up a website advocating for his release. Shayna had called for a People's Muster at her house later, and that gave me a flicker of hope—maybe we could retake the Lab like we'd done once before.

All through my horrible ordeal at the jailhouse, I'd fantasized about seeing Red again, running into xir arms, and sobbing there. But when I walked into the echoing warehouse, xe was sitting on some gross couches with Slime and Filthy Ed, and I didn't want them to see me break down like that. So I just walked over casually and sat next to Red, who flung an arm over my shoulders and kissed my hair.

"You okay?"

I nodded, afraid if I said anything I'd burst into tears.

The Canal warehouse looked a lot like how the Lab had in the early days—lots of empty space, grimy surfaces, a scattering of curb-scrounged furniture. But the vibes were off. Instead of Vida's beautiful, nature-inspired murals on the walls, the graffiti was mostly ugly tags, with a few big murals of topless women, guns, dice, and other shit you might see on a flash sheet at a third-rate tattoo shop. Red was talking to the other guys about the worst old horror movies—the kind of pointless conversation we had a lot back in the day—but these guys weren't funny, didn't clown around. They were white boys, but talked with a stolen blaccent and hand gestures—saying, "Dope, dope," and "Tha's wha' I'm talkin' bout! That flick was the shiznit!" Underneath the familiar smells of stale beer and weed smoke, there was a particularly noxious, chemical odor I didn't recognize. Later, I'd learn it was the lingering smell of burnt meth.

I started walking around out of boredom and found a familiar pile of stuff, heaped together behind a couch. My guitar and amps were there, Gestas's disassembled drum kit, the box of books I'd managed to stash, and another box of a bunch of Red's belongings, jumbled together. I pulled Red's acoustic out of its soft case. Red saw me picking through the stuff and came over.

"I went down there with Lorenzo this morning. Chad McLawyerface worked out some deal with them, where we had an hour to grab our stuff. I couldn't get everything." There was a catch in Red's voice that xe was trying to cover up with anger. "It's like an army base now—they got the National Guard out there and everything."

I looped my arms around xir waist and worked up some courage.

"Why don't you come stay with me? At my Community? At least we'd have privacy."

Red took a step back and raked a hand through xir hair. "That's sweet, Maddie, but, argh—I like you too much to live with you." Xe rested xir forehead against mine. "Trust me, it won't work out. I'm not good with that domesticity thing. Tried it before and—no. But I'll come over whenever you want company, okay?" Red shot me a hungry-looking grin.

I smiled, even though I felt miserable at the rejection. I didn't give a fuck if it hadn't worked out for Red, living with xir cheating ex-girlfriend Natalie. I wanted xim to try it with me. But I was afraid to push too far and seem clingy.

"Sure, okay," I said, hating the quaver in my voice. I cleared my throat. "Anyways, we should get going soon. The People's Muster starts in an hour."

"Yeah, about that." Red whacked a fresh pack of cigarettes against xir palm. "You go ahead."

"You're not coming?" I asked, hurt curdling into anger. Red pulled the cellophane twisty off, and I don't know what was pissing me off more in that moment—Red's apathy, or that xe was killing ximself with smokes, or the single-use plastic still used to wrap them.

"Shayna wants us to try to take back the Lab again, but you didn't see it, Mads. They've got fucking machine guns out there and tanks. *Tanks.* No, I'm not fucking going. And unless you want to get arrested again, you shouldn't either. Besides, I've been to enough goddamn People's Musters to last a lifetime."

"You're just going to give up like that?"

Red shrugged. One of the graffiti guys called xir name from over by the couches. The dudes were all hunched over the coffee table, where rows of white powder were lined up on a mirror.

"You want a bump?" Red asked.

"No," I said, furious.

"Suit yourself." Xe shrugged and turned xir back on me.

Maybe I should've tried harder. Maybe I should've dragged Red outside and lectured xim about the dangers of drugs. Maybe I should've gotten on my knees and sobbed and begged xim to come live with me at my Community. Maybe that would've worked, but I doubt it.

Instead, I met up with Vida and Peter outside, and together we biked over to Shayna's. My mind wasn't on the Lab or the Village.

I was worried about Gestas, and what was happening to a trans guy at that prison out in Sugar Land. I was worried about Red, and thinking that the Canal warehouse was about the worst possible place for an addict like xim.

45

At Shayna's house, I got déjà vu. The scene was just like when we'd retaken the Lab after the last raid. A few hundred people spread across her lawn as she gave another rousing speech—reminding us that there were now over eighty Free People's Villages worldwide. That the raid had been one battle in a war—a global revolution, which we were winning! She also told everyone about how Gestas was still being held in brick-and-mortar prison, and gave everyone time to go to the website Peter had set up and sign the petition for his release. Gestas and Shayna had always been at odds, frequently arguing against each other's tactics at People's Musters, but it didn't surprise me that she would show up for him 100 percent.

She also reminded everyone that a bunch of us had recently been arrested, and we couldn't afford to get arrested again, so we were not to do anything to provoke the cops.

With a wave of her bullhorn, she sent us off marching for the Lab to reclaim it, chanting, "Whose streets? Our streets!" and "We don't want no hyperway—we just wanna save the Eighth!"

But the feeling of déjà vu ended abruptly when we turned onto Calcott Street. Red hadn't been exaggerating. It looked like a war zone.

At the sight of that line of National Guard, wearing army fatigues with huge guns across their chests, my blood pressure skyrocketed. Dozens of mosquitoes were buzzing overhead, drone dogs prowled the sidewalks, and hundreds of cops in riot gear stood all around the Lab, looking just like the one who'd slammed me to concrete. And there were tanks, or vehicles that looked close enough. Big, armored SUVs with huge guns mounted on top were stationed every few hundred feet. Every instinct in my body was screaming at me to flee.

Only focusing on Shayna, her courage in walking right up to that line of soldiers, kept me rooted to the pavement. I kept to the back of the march, though, telling myself at the first sign of trouble, I would bolt. Our crowd, which had felt huge and powerful moments before, looked pitiful in comparison to the army now surrounding the Lab.

We stood there for half an hour, kept a few feet back from the line of soldiers, chanting our slogans to their faces, which alternated between stoic, derisively amused, and seething with loathing. Peter was crouched at the sidelines as usual, live streaming everything. I stood by Vida, trying my best to keep chanting, but my heart was already breaking.

And then someone cried out. I thought maybe the cops were attacking, and I braced to run. A huge excavator machine trundled up slowly to the side of the Lab. Its shoveling arm reared up, and then—to cries of pain from all us who'd once called the Village home—it dug its clawed shovel into the side of the building, smashing through the kitchen window for the upstairs apartment. Its arm raked down the side of the Lab, crumbling the outer wall like a sandcastle before a rising tide.

"I can't watch," Vida whispered, and she threw her arms around me. I held her as she cried, but me—I couldn't look away. I watched every cruel pull of that excavator's shovel. The place I'd met Gestas and Red, where we'd written all our music, played all our shows, spent countless lazy Sunday afternoons goofing and shooting the shit, where I'd fallen in love—really in love—for the first time in my life, where I'd learned to cook, where we'd held the first People's Musters, where I'd been radicalized, where we'd started a revolution—the excavator clawed our home to rubble like it was held together with dust.

Then someone screamed in a different way. A white boy had thrown himself at the line of soldiers and tried to push through, and suddenly everything was chaos and sirens and screams, and I was running away as fast as my legs could carry me.

46

That night, cops descended on the Free People's Villages of New York City, Portland, and Oakland, attacking those occupations with terrible violence. I couldn't bring myself to watch the videos; they were too triggering. By the end of the week, Free People's Villages all over the world were crushed—tents smashed, belongings destroyed, bodies battered, bruised, and gassed. With a speed that neoliberal governments reserve solely for upholding the carceral state, cities all over the country passed anti-encampment ordinances banning the use of tents within city limits, even on private property. Sorry, kids, no backyard campouts.

I kept going to the People's Musters at Shayna's house, even though I badly didn't want to. They were depressing. Each night, fewer people showed up, until we didn't even need to use the front yard anymore, because we could fit inside Shayna's living room. Red wouldn't come. Red never wanted to leave the warehouse on Canal, which was a nonstop party. On Sunday, I managed to drag xim back to my place, but I could tell xe was bored and restless in my quiet apartment. I cooked chili for dinner, which we ate while watching a cheesy sci-fi movie. It should've been this nice, normal date, you know? But after the aliveness and drama and purpose of life at the Village, being alone with xim in my apartment gave me this howling, empty feeling. I started sobbing in the middle of the movie, and Red asked if I wanted to go for a bike ride.

We rode fast, blowing through all the red lights of Midtown until we reached the greenway, then taking the bike path all the way to Hermann Park. Red wanted to climb the fence and break into the zoo, but I absolutely refused. I had to grab xir ankle as xe was scrambling up the fence and beg xim to stop. I did not want to get arrested again. Finally, xe gave up the idea and settled for walking around the lagoon, taking turns sipping on a bottle of J&B. We were drunk and laughing, and I could feel the love between us again. The lights of the hospitals, towering above the live oaks, twinkled like fireflies. By the time we got to the Japanese Garden, I was drunk enough to let xim talk me into hopping that fence, and we made some lovely memories there, on the rocks beside the artificial waterfall.

47

Election Day took me by surprise. I'd voted early, for Donnelly of course, but unemployed, depressed, crashing on a
filthy couch with Red most nights at the Canal street warehouse,
I'd lost track of the days. No one I knew was seriously stressed
about the election. Democrats had held a stranglehold on the
three branches of government for thirty years, ever since Bill Clin-
ton became president. Sure, the polls had been tighter than usual
this election season. But no one I knew, except Gestas, thought
Horneck could really win. He'd run on a platform of bald-faced
racism, blaming Black and brown people outright for the climate
crisis. He wouldn't just put a hyperway through the Eighth Ward,
he wanted to bulldoze all the "inefficient"—historically Black—
neighborhoods in the US. He'd called for an end to AHICA and a
reinvestment in brick-and-mortar prisons. He was a warmonger,
saying the US needed to go beyond the war in Brazil—invading
any country in the Global South that wasn't protecting its climate-
regulating natural resources, never mind that the US was still the
biggest emitter of fossil fuels. At the same time, he wanted to close
all borders to climate migrants—all those folks escaping the chaos
in their countries, which *we'd* spent the last century causing. The
only consistent logic in his platform was cruelty.

Election night, Peter hooked up a projector to his laptop and
pointed it at a patch of white wall near the ceiling of the Canal

Street warehouse. A party was raging, with maybe a hundred people there, using the election as an excuse to get drunker than usual. Indiana and Kentucky were called first—both for Horneck, but that was no surprise. Donnelly got Vermont. The Bible Belt states followed, and the amount of bright red splashed across the wall was unnerving, but of course they always went Republican. After a couple hours, though, I heard Ohio called for Horneck, and a feeling of doom stuck in my throat. Mike Algebra—the only other person who seemed to be paying attention—was chewing his thumbnail.

"Isn't Ohio supposed to be a blue state?" I asked.

"There's still a lot of states to go," Mike said. "But yeah, that's . . . not good."

I sat down next to Mike to watch. What the fuck was happening? All the midwestern states, which were supposed to be solidly blue, were going red or too close to call. The commentators' voices became tight and nervous, as they discussed the narrowing possibilities for Donnelly to win. I was growing furious with everyone else—all of them laughing, joking around, while the country seemed about to tip into full-on fascism.

Eventually, more people caught on and began watching with us. "What's happening?" they whispered. "He's not really going to win, is he?" By midnight, nearly everyone had quieted and was sitting down, watching the anchors in horror. Texas was called for Horneck, of course, and our senator's and governor's races went red too. Everyone booed, though none of us had been alive while a Democrat was in charge of Texas.

One pundit started blaming the Free People's Villages for the tight presidential race—saying the protests had depressed Democratic voter turnout.

"Oh fuck you!" Lorenzo yelled, and he chucked an empty bottle of Lone Star at the wall, where it shattered and left drips down the side of the guy's face.

Finally, it all came down to Pennsylvania. If Donnelly didn't get Pennsylvania, game over—Horneck would be our president. I couldn't see Red in the warehouse, and I desperately needed some human comfort, so I went in search of xim.

The far side of the warehouse had been carved up into apartments even shittier than the ones at the Lab. One of the doors was slightly ajar, and I pushed inside. Red was lying on a couch, eyes glazed, half-smiling at me—drunk as hell, probably. But then I spotted the tourniquet on xir arm, and the syringe on the table next to xim. Filthy Ed sat on the futon across from xim, actively shooting up.

I couldn't seem to inhale, as if all the oxygen had been sucked out of the room. My mind was grasping for some excuse, some reason to reject what was painfully obvious. Was this the first time, or had Red been doing this for a while, behind my back?

"Why you crying, Mads?" Red slurred, as I crossed over to xim.

"Because you're shooting up heroin, you asshole," I sobbed, dropping to the cushions.

Red chuckled. "Iss fine."

"It's not fine. Heroin is bad! It can kill you! Haven't you seen *Trainspotting*? Or—or *Requiem for a Dream*?"

"Chill, man," Filthy Ed said. "Red only did a little bit, and this stuff is real clean."

"Shut the fuck up," I hissed at him, with all the venom I could muster.

"Yeesh, bad vibes," he said, leaning back and closing his eyes.

Red reached up and cupped my cheek, wiping the tears away with xir thumb. "Don't cry, Mads. Everything's gonna be okay." But only someone on very strong drugs could possibly have said that. Because at that moment, I heard Wolf Blitzer's voice booming out, impossibly loud.

"At this time, CNN is prepared to make the call—" He spoke like he couldn't believe what he was reading. "The forty-seventh president of the United States will be Richard Horneck."

48

While everyone else in my world panicked about the new presidential administration, I was consumed by fears for Red. I lit into xim the next day, as soon as xe woke up. I cried, and begged, and lectured about the dangers of heroin use, and how even just xir drinking scared the hell out of me. Couldn't we try to get sober together? Couldn't we get the hell out of that warehouse?

Red swore xe'd never shoot up again. That xe'd just wanted to try it. That xe wanted to try everything in this life at least once.

I said that was a shit philosophy. "You want to try everything once? How about eating shit? How about beating me up? Breaking my heart? Are you going to try those things too?"

Red didn't fight back, just looked down at the ground, the bumps of xir spine sticking out of xir shirt. Had xe always been so frail?

I didn't go out and look for a job. I didn't go back to my Community, and I didn't go to the sad, diminished People's Musters anymore. I was terrified that if I let Red out of my sight for a second, xe was going to shoot up again. I knew I couldn't babysit xim forever, but I had this feeling that if I could just hold out a few more days, until Angel came home on leave, we would figure out a way to save Red together. In my fanny pack, I kept a naloxone inhaler alongside my albuterol one, in case Red ever overdosed.

I called Chad McMannis and told him about Angel coming home—how he was Gestas's boyfriend, and he'd only have leave for two weeks before he went back to Brazil, and was there any way we could get Gestas out by then? I don't know what Chad did to make it happen, but somehow he got Gestas an AHICA review hearing the day before Angel arrived. A couple dozen of us showed up to the courthouse in solidarity.

I was a fragile mess throughout the hearing. The thought of Angel coming home, and not being able to embrace Gestas, after those boys had written each other hundreds of pages of letters all through the occupation—I couldn't stand it. Tears kept springing to my eyes every time Chad or the judge said something, or if I even looked at Gestas, dressed in that horrible orange jumpsuit. Everything had been going so terribly lately, I was braced for the worst.

But to my shock, after a five-minute exchange, the judge granted Gestas release to AHICA. I was surprised to hear the judge read aloud the address where Gestas would be confined—it wasn't the warehouse on Canal. It was Shayna's address. I shot Red a look, and xe shrugged. "He said he didn't want to live in another fucking party warehouse."

"So no more band?"

"Not with him, I guess."

Given what went on at the Canal Street warehouse, I didn't blame him.

49

When Angel arrived the next day, he picked Red up like a baby and swung xim around, and Red's face lit up with a smile I hadn't seen in a long time—not since before the Village was destroyed, maybe not since Angel had left for war.

It felt amazing to be wrapped up in Angel's bear hug again. Surely shoulders that strong could help me carry the weight of my worry for Red.

"How are you even more jacked?" I asked, as he released me from his trunk-like arms.

"I've been working out a lot," he said.

"Oh yeah? They got a gym at the war?" I asked jokingly.

"They do," he said, his smile falling. "And there's not much else to do. Turns out war is mostly boring, actually." His voice sounded tight, and I regretted mentioning it.

We were at Shayna's house, hanging out in the backyard. A dozen Halloween pumpkin-light decorations were sunk into the mud in a half circle around the back of the house—sketching the limit of Gestas's AHICA range. Angel had flown in early that afternoon, and Red, Lorenzo, Vida, Peter, and I had all come over to see him—after giving him and Gestas a few hours alone together, of course.

A heaviness hung in the air. We were all curious, dying to ask about the war, but not sure how. Angel took a long swig off a Lone Star, probably wanting to forget. Suddenly, Red dashed behind him, yelled "Butt Punch!" and socked him in the ass, then took off running. Angel dropped his beer and sprinted after, both of them giggling like twelve-year-olds.

Angel caught up to Red easily at the back of the yard, scooped xim up over his shoulder with one hand, and punched xim in the butt with the other. Red hammered on his back with both fists.

I looked to Gestas who shrugged, laughing. "It's a weird sibling thing, I guess?"

Angel yelled, "Chokeslam!" and lifted Red up with one hand around xir neck and one around xir back, then slammed xim to the earth, though I could tell he did it gently. Red got up and shouted, "Rock Bottom!" then ran at Angel, catching him across the chest with xir arm. Angel didn't even sway, just stood there laughing while Red kicked at his knees, yelling, "Go down, you fucking boulder!"

After that, the vibes were good again. We were all so happy to be together, only talking about meaningless shit, old times, and absurd what-if scenarios. It was one of those perfect, late-fall Houston evenings, the air just a little bit chilly, so we could wear hoodies for once. Lorenzo had the idea to grill us some food and pulled a rusty, old Weber from the spiderwebs on Shayna's back stoop. Angel, Red, and I set off for the store in Lorenzo's van to pick up charcoal and provisions, with me driving because I'd only had one beer. I was nervous behind the wheel, because though I'd gotten my license in college, I'd hardly ever driven since I divorced Colton. And I'd certainly never driven anything as big as that van.

Angel insisted on paying for everything—loading the shopping cart with an obscene amount of red meat—burgers and brats, with cheese to put on top, plus the cost of briquettes. It must've cost a hundred carbon credits, at least.

On the way back to Shayna's, I was braking before a stop sign when I heard the back door slide open. "What the fuck?" I said, twisting around. Red was leaning out the side, puking into the street as I screeched to a halt. "Jesus, you could've said something."

"Didn't wanna be a bother," Red said, sitting up and wiping the puke from xir mouth with the back of xir hand. Xe pulled the door shut.

I was so mad. I'd been watching Red like a hawk, and by my count xe'd only had three beers—which shouldn't've been enough to make xim puke. Had xe been drinking before I got there? Snuck some liquor while I was in the bathroom?

Angel was laughing at Red, and I shot him kind of a dirty look without meaning to. He held my gaze and gave me a questioning look back. But I didn't know how to bring it up there, out loud, in front of Red. So I just kept driving.

Back at Shayna's, Lorenzo got the coals going. When the meat hit the grill, Shayna came out to join us.

"I thought I'd give y'all some privacy, since I don't really know Angel, but that smells way too good to resist," she said. "Y'all have extra?"

"You weren't staying in there on my account?" Angel looked horrified. "You're putting up Gestas—that makes us family in my book. And hell, you started the Free People's Village! Ach, I can't tell you how mad I am that I missed it."

"It was something . . ." Shayna said, frowning down at her beer.

"These last few months, I dreamed about getting to see it," Angel said wistfully. "Then a week before I show up, it gets smashed."

"I think the end was inevitable after whatever jackass brined those bulldozers. They were never going to let us stick around long after that," Shayna said.

I tried not to squirm, but Gestas cut in. "Nah, nah—they were never going to let you stick around, period. If anything, the bulldozer incident raised our profile to the international level— bought us way more media attention, which bought us *more* time standing in the way of their precious hyperway."

"You know, if you didn't have that chip in your arm I'd think *you* did it, Gestas," Shayna said, squinting at him dangerously.

He shrugged in a cartoonish, "Who, me?" kind of way.

Shayna smiled wryly. "Anyways, they may have taken the Lab, but they haven't destroyed the Village. Tomorrow we'll get to work on what's next," she said.

"Here, here!" Angel cried. "Viva the Village!"

Everyone laughed and clinked beers. Lorenzo handed Shayna a brat in a toasted bun.

Red stared at her and went, "Huh."

"Wha—?" Shayna asked, mid-bite.

"Nothing, I just figured you were vegan. Never saw you eat meat before."

Shayna swallowed. "Look, if someone else puts up the carbon credits, I don't care what I'm eating. Especially if Lorenzo's cooking it."

Everybody laughed at that, and Shayna stayed outside hanging out with us, and it was the first time I'd ever really seen her relax. At the Free People's Village, she had always seemed exhausted and stressed, always running a meeting or fixing something broken or solving some conflict. Now she was just . . . eating a brat and drinking a beer, joking around. I'd always felt she was so much more grown-up than my friends, but really, she was just a few years older than the rest of us.

Red went to the bathroom and stayed gone a long time. When I went looking, I found xim inside, asleep on a couch, snoring-drunk.

"Gestas is worried about Red," Angel said, coming up behind me. "He says xe's getting blackout drunk every night. He told xim not to live with those gutter punks on Canal."

I opened my mouth to tell Angel about catching Red doing heroin—but then I couldn't get the words out. Angel was only home for a few weeks, and then he'd go back to war. Maybe I didn't want to burden him with it. Maybe saying it aloud would've made it too real, when part of me hoped I'd just had a bad dream, that terrible election night. Maybe I actually believed that Red was telling the truth, and shooting up was a one-time thing that would never happen again.

All I said was, "Gestas is right. I hate that warehouse. And I'm worried about Red too."

"I wish—" Angel broke off and shook his head, like there were so many things he wished for that it seemed pointless to mention any of them.

Later it got too cold to be outside, and Lorenzo, Vida, and Peter went back to the Canal Street warehouse. I thought I should go too—give Gestas and Angel some privacy—but I couldn't rouse Red, so Shayna offered me her other couch to crash on. The five of us ended up hanging out in Shayna's living room. Gestas and Angel took the other couch. Shayna sat cross-legged on the floor, and I lifted Red's head into my lap, so I'd have a place to sit.

We were talking about some bullshit or other, and Angel mentioned how shitty the food was down in Brazil. There was another long, awkward pause. I was opening my mouth to change the subject, but Shayna turned to Angel and asked, "So what do you do down there?"

Angel cleared his throat. "I'm in MI," he said. "Military Intelligence."

"It's not as bad as it sounds," Gestas said. "He's got a desk job. Just stuff with computers." His voice faltered even as he spoke the words. Angel's golden skin had gone a sickly greenish white. "It's just a desk job, right?" Gestas repeated.

Angel pressed his lips together and looked down at Gestas's legs, draped across his lap. He made a noise like he was about to say something, but then shook his head. Gestas slid his legs off Angel's lap and sat on his knees. Him and Shayna were both still staring at Angel like hawks. I looked away, feeling like I was eavesdropping on something deeply personal. I busied myself with running my fingers through Red's hair.

"But what do you actually do?" Shayna repeated.

When Angel looked up again, his eyes were red. He opened his mouth to speak, and strands of spit spanned the cavern of his mouth. He looked like the words were choking him, like someone should rush up and do the Heimlich maneuver to get them out.

Gestas put a hand on his knee. "Tell us," he said.

"I—I can't," Angel managed.

"Why? To protect US Army secrets? Fuck that. I swear I won't post it on Twitter, okay?" Gestas said. "You don't have to go into detail, just—"

"No, it's not that." Angel shook his head. He swallowed hard, and his voice came out shaky and thin. "If I tell you, that'll be it. You won't—no one would, but especially not you. You won't want anything to do with me."

"Maybe these high-and-mighty fuckers won't, but I will," came a growl from my lap. Red cracked an eye open.

"I know where you've been, dude," Gestas said, leaning his body away from Angel. "Fighting an imperial war that is deeply fucking evil. I've felt conflicted about even, like, I don't know—whatever this is between us. But it seemed like, based on your values—you just didn't understand! You'd consumed so much propaganda!" He sat back further, cranking up speed. "At first it was like an experiment. Could I reverse the brainwashing of the military industrial complex? And then you told me you had this desk job, and—fuck, I've been so naïve, haven't I?" Gestas pulled back his hair. "Fuck, you lied to me?"

Angel just nodded, looking like he was going to puke in his lap.

"He went to war, Gestas, and you're worried the worst thing he's done is lie to you?" Shayna said. "What is it you can't say, Angel? Have you killed people?"

309

I gasped. I couldn't believe she'd asked the horrible question aloud, after the rest of us had spent all night carefully pretending it wasn't pressing on our minds.

Angel's eyes, red-rimmed again, darted around the room, seeing threats everywhere. Finally, they landed on Red's gaze and held firm. I froze my hand in xir hair, like this moment was made of rice paper, and if I breathed, I would disturb it. Tears slid freely down Angel's jaw as he spoke. At first the words came torturously slowly, each one lodging like a brick in his throat.

"Not—not directly. Not by my hand or my gun. But we have these satellites, that can see, like, a fucking bug on a leaf from space. Only with the jungle canopy, that's not always helpful, so my job is—we take over their phones, their radio frequencies, socials—anything electronic they use to communicate. And we trick them. *I* trick them into going places where—where other soldiers are waiting, or drones, or bombs . . . ," he trailed off, and when he spoke again, his voice came gasping between tears. "And I see it. I'm not there, but on the satellites, I see it. So . . . yeah. Yeah, I've killed people."

With the last three words, his whole body shook with shuddering sobs, head in his hands. Gestas and Shayna looked like they were frozen, just staring at him in horror. I wanted to go to him, because here was a man who I loved, who looked totally broken, who was in the worst pain of his life. But at the same time, here was a man who had killed—invaded another country and killed, or gotten people killed who were just trying to defend their homes. And was that why Gestas and Shayna would extend him no comfort? Was it wrong to do so?

Red slid off the couch onto the floor, reeled with dizziness, stumbled the few steps to the other couch, and draped xirself over Angel's shoulders. Angel clawed for his twin's shoulders like a drowning man, and they clung to each other like that for a long time, Red saying, "I got you. I got you."

After Angel kind of got it together, they cautiously broke apart, and Red collapsed to the carpet in front of Angel. Gestas was sitting with his knees tucked under him on the far corner of the couch, chewing on his thumbnail like it was to blame for the riot that must've been raging in his mind. He was in love with a soldier—what had he expected?

"I'm so sorry, Angel," I whispered, past the lump in my throat.

"No." He shook his head. "No, don't you say sorry to me. I—look, they pump us full of lies. They tell us we're saving the rain forest, saving the world. They make these people out to be monsters who want to burn trees for a quick buck. They plaster the news we get with all the casualties and IEDs and executions, but fuck, man. They're just like . . . poor people. Farmers and shit, trying to feed their families, with these sad little homemade bombs and stolen guns. Or they're the Native folks who just live *in* the forest. They don't—they're not trying to destroy it! They're the ones trying to protect it! And I never would've known that except Gestas sent me all this shit to read, that honestly—and it's pretty dangerous for me to even look at that stuff down there. But I did. And now I know it. I knew it, and I . . . I did my job anyways. So no, don't—please don't ever fucking say sorry to me." I had never heard a person sound as broken as he did. And suddenly I was thinking of all the statistics about skyrocketing suicides in the military, and I was terribly afraid for him.

"What I meant is—" I felt really out of my depth but tried to put it in words. "Like here I am . . . And I'm a citizen of the US. I pay taxes that are funding the war. Like . . . and I didn't grow up poor like you and Red. I went to a good school, went to college. I never even considered enlisting—not for a second. And so I don't know exactly what I'm trying to say, but—"

"You're recognizing your complicity in the US war machine," Shayna offered. I nodded. "And the white privilege and economic privilege that's kept you from ever having to consider getting your hands bloodied by the violence that's the foundation of our society."

"Yeah, that," I repeated, grateful. "Like I could not pay my taxes, but then I'd go to jail. So . . . honestly? I'm not gonna fucking do that. And no one expects me to. So I don't feel like I'm really in any position to judge Angel? Anyone who isn't like . . . already in jail for protesting the war—we're all complicit, you know? So I am sorry. I'm sorry he's been over there doing this violence that the rest of us don't have to know about or even think about."

"But you did know about it—and you were with us at the Free People's Village, protesting the greenwashing of carbon, and the war, and the whole capitalist death machine," Gestas said. He was still eyeing Angel with a mix of hurt, suspicion, and disgust.

I shook my head. "I might've gotten swept up in that, but only because it happened at our band house. Like if that hyperway hadn't cut through the Lab, honestly, I probably wouldn't have showed up to a single protest. So who am I to judge anyone?"

"Even if you didn't. Even for people who never protest at all, there's a difference. There has to be a-a meaningful difference," Gestas said, tugging on his beard, eyes wide and manic like he'd been doing coke. "I mean you didn't know—but does ignorance protect us from the moral ramifications? But surely the choice to-to hack the phone, jam the signal, send the drone—whatever it is you're doing there, Angel. That choice—but then, Maddie never is faced with that choice. I'm never faced with that choice. But we have been—we've been out protesting, as I said, the capitalist death machine. Suppose we hadn't been? Is the complacent, oblivious, suburban soccer mom carbon-offsetting her McMansion's AC bill really less culpable for the violence in the Amazon than the soldier with blood on his hands?"

"Yes," Angel moaned. His face was in his hands. "Fucking trust me."

"Just don't go back, dude," Red said from where xe was lying on the floor.

Angel huffed an attempt at a laugh. "Right."

"I'm serious." Red peeled ximself up to a seat. "What're they gonna do? They won't shoot you, right? If you don't go back, what do they do?"

"It depends. First, I'd get arrested."

"Who hasn't been?" Shayna asked.

"You could say you're a conscientious objector," Gestas said slowly. "That's a thing."

"That's a powerful form of protest," Shayna said.

"I think even if you just say that—they don't have to grant it," Angel said. "They could find me guilty of being AWOL or 'missing movement.' I could go to jail for my entire service commitment, or longer," he said.

"Maybe you'll get AHICA," Gestas said, with an ironic half smile.

"I doubt it. They'd want to make an example of me. And even then—it'd probably be a dishonorable discharge. I'd have a hard time getting work the rest of my life."

"Depends on the kind of work. I promise you, at the Lone Star Beer Hole they do not care," Red said. "You could come barback with me. Hell, brains you got, you could study up and be a fancy-schmancy full-blown bartender!"

"He shouldn't have to go to jail and ruin his career—" I began.

"No, he shouldn't," Gestas cut me off and turned to Angel. "But either way, the next three years, until your commitment is up, you won't be free. You'll be trapped here, in AHICA or even a brick-and-mortar jail, or you'll be trapped on some post in Brazil, committing terrible acts of violence."

Angel looked around at us with his wide, red eyes and started giggling. It was weirdly high-pitched coming from his huge, mus-cled frame. "Y'all are crazy. What? Just don't go back?"

"Just don't fucking go, man!" Red shouted, flinging xir arms out.

"The Free People's Village doesn't recognize the authority or legitimacy of the US Government," Shayna said. "And as far as I'm concerned, this house is the Free People's Village. I, for one, will not extradite you."

Angel stood up and started pacing. "What if I didn't? Just didn't go? Fuck, FUCK! What if I *didn't*?"

"Hey Angel," Shayna said, and he didn't hear her at first. "Hey—hey Angel!"

He stopped and stared down at her.

"You know what you were talking about—hacking into radios and cell phones and shit?" Shayna grinned wickedly. "Can you do that . . . here?"

I've spent a lot of time running the what-ifs on that evening. What if I'd told Angel about Red shooting up? What if I'd managed to stop that conversation in its tracks, and Angel had gone back to war like a good little soldier, and we'd never hatched the plan that followed? I have been down those labyrinthine rabbit holes—and learned that they only lead to pain.

Dr. Abner at the inpatient clinic taught me that letting go of regret is particularly hard, because it means finally letting go of the notion that the past can be changed. As long as we cling to regret, we haven't truly accepted what has happened.

As long as we cling to regret, we don't have to fully grieve what we've lost.

50

The next two weeks, we all moved with purpose again. The leadership of a bunch of evicted Free People's Villages had agreed on a global day of action. It was public knowledge that on December 1, we would reclaim a site for encampment. Where that camp would be, however, was a closely held secret. Only folks who'd been with the movement from the beginning, who Shayna and Gestas trusted completely, were allowed to be part of those conversations.

Shayna and Gestas were working in lockstep now. He needed her ability to mobilize masses of people, and she acknowledged that to reestablish an occupation, we'd need to use some of his more unconventional tactics.

I wasn't in those leadership meetings, but I felt honored enough—just knowing a bit about what the other teams would be up to the night of December 1. Originally, I'd wanted to be on Red's team, but xe vetoed it right away. "Mads, I love you, but you chickened out once before, and let's be real, you're probably going to do it again." Then xe kissed me on the forehead. "Besides, Shayna has a better job for a white girl as cute as you."

That was the first time Red had told me xe loved me.

Red was ximself again. Xe stayed up long into the night, drinking coffee—not booze—to keep alert through planning meetings in Shayna's bedroom. I'd be locked out, doing grunt work in the living room, making posters or crocheting with the fiber artists. Red would slip out of the head-honcho meetings to go to the bathroom

315

or refill xir coffee, and xe'd always shoot me a seductive grin or give me a kiss in the hall, hips pushing me up against the wall.

I only got jealous when Slime and Filthy Ed were invited into those top-secret meetings in Shayna's bedroom—because they were the only white people involved in the highest level of planning. I cornered Gestas about it once, asking him why the hell those junkies were being trusted with the fate of the movement. He reminded me that "those junkies" had proven themselves braver and more trustworthy than me when it came to the go-karts. "They're willing to do some extremely dangerous and . . . just plain ol' nasty work that needs doing."

"I don't trust them. What is it? I'll do it!" I said.

He barked a laugh. "The thought of that!" he said, and walked away, shaking his head with an amused smile.

I may not have known all the details, but I knew we were going to put everything on the line December 1. The part of my mind that had read too many young adult novels believed that surely we would prevail against the evil, prison-military-industrial-fossil-fuel-world-eating machine. The cynic at the back of my head never really got convinced, but for once, she wasn't putting up too much of a fuss. The future was a rapidly approaching cliff that I chose not to think about.

So I wasn't worried, yet, about getting a job to pay next month's rent. In retrospect, it doesn't make sense that I was so calm. Chalk it up to groupthink. The vibes were so good, those days printing flyers at Shayna's, or riding around town, posting "Whose City? Our City! 12/1" stickers to streetlights and stop signs. Even though we were now planning some extremely illegal shit, it felt just like when we threw shows at the Lab. The fun of it all tricked the abject coward in me into shutting up, for once, and I was able to enjoy our beautiful, shared dream—that the young and brave could remake the world into something beautiful. That we only had to join together to speak freedom into existence.

51

I awoke in a cold sweat the morning of the first, after a nightmare of being slammed to concrete by faceless police. I was wrapped in Red's arms, crammed in the crack of xir filthy couch at the Canal Street warehouse. I got up to make coffee, hoping the hot drink would settle my nerves, but it just made me feel jittery.

We biked over to Shayna's midmorning. The sun was halfway up the sky, glinting off the dew still clinging to the tall grasses that lined the bike path. Everything looked crystalline, fragile, and I felt incredibly in-the-moment, wondering if this would be my last bike ride with Red for a while, or ever. Even if we succeeded tonight, there was a good chance that many of our friends would wind up arrested, injured, or worse. I didn't know how violent the cops would get, and I was even more scared of counter-protestors— unhinged Horneck voters with assault rifles and twitchy fingers. Red had promised they had a plan for dealing with the paramilitary goons, but not knowing what it was, I didn't find that very reassuring.

There were already fifty people at Shayna's, including all the working group leaders from our Village days. Over the next hour, a hundred more folks showed up, and then the house was standing-room only, and the yard was filling as well. As our numbers grew, so too did the barely restrained panic attack fluttering around my chest. I found Angel posted up in a quiet corner, sitting on the floor with his laptop. His presence—just the sheer mass of him—always made me feel calm, so I sat down with him.

"Going over code for tonight?" I asked. "Not like I know exactly what you'll be doing."

He shook his head. "It's a letter."

"For Gestas?" I asked, confused.

"To my commanding officer," Angel said. "It's a conscientious objector statement."

"Damn. You're really doing it," I said, and the dread in my gut grew heavier.

Gestas came over and dropped down beside Angel. He skimmed over whatever was on the screen, nodding. "Comma here." He pointed. When he got to the end, he said, "It's good."

"Yeah?" Angel asked, beaming as he looked up into Gestas's face.

"You're a good writer for someone with muscles that big. I liked the critical analysis of the profit motive behind the war and that bit about 'a flimsy moral pretense for the greatest theft of freshwater in global history.'"

Angel ceremoniously lifted a finger and brought it down on the keyboard. "Sent."

Gestas's eyes lit up, and he pressed his lips to Angel's in a long, soft kiss. "My turn," he said.

I didn't know what he meant, but it seemed like an intimate moment, so I got up and moved off. A half hour later, a crowd gathered on Shayna's back stoop, and I peered over their heads to see what was going on. Angel was heating a switchblade with a lighter, and Gestas was rubbing an alcohol wipe over his shoulder muscle, right at the spot where a green light glowed beneath his skin.

My teacher brain took over. "No, no, absolutely not," I said, pushing to the front of the crowd. "Gestas, what are you going to do?" My voice came out squeaky and panicked.

"What does it look like?"

"Dude, you just got out of brick-and-mortar. If you do this, you're going right back."

"He knows what he's doing," said a voice in my ear. Red looped an arm around my waist and pulled me back gently.

But I wasn't going to sit back and watch my friend throw his life away. The panic attack I'd been barely holding at bay was pounding at the door now. I looked something up quickly on my phone. "Five years, Gestas. That's the minimum for tampering with or removing an AHICA chip. Five years of your life—it's not worth it!"

"Dammit, Maddie, do you fucking mind?" Gestas said, nodding at Peter, who was squatting at his feet with a phone.

"Everything is worth it," Angel said, with this sad smile and thousand-yard stare. I couldn't say anything to that. He'd been to war and knew the shape of the world and the true nature of violence in a way I couldn't begin to grasp. If Angel said this was worth it, who was I to contradict him?

"Okay we're streaming," Peter said.

Gestas took a long drink of J&B, and moments later, the light inside his arm flashed red, detecting the alcohol in his bloodstream.

"Tell everyone why you're doing this," Peter said.

"I've been in AHICA since I was eighteen. Four years, my whole adult life. I've spent them sitting on back stoops, trapped in my house, watching my friends come and go, leaving me behind. And the state—this evil, fucking, white-supremacist enslavement machine—I'm forced to work for them, for pennies, while they pocket the profits of my labor. And sure, it's white-collar work. Data entry. And sure, it's not a cell—it's a house where I get to live with my friends." He glared down at the chip in his arm. "But that's the mindfuck, right? Because freedom is always right there, just outside the door. All I have to do is take a *step.* So they've made me my own jailer, you know? No walls, no guards—only my fear keeps me inside. They stick this fucking sensor in my arm, and then they have total control." Gestas leveled his eyes at the camera, jaw set. "I'm not going to jail myself anymore. If they want my freedom, they're going to have to try a lot fucking harder to take it away from me."

The crowd of onlookers roared and cheered. I peered at Peter's phone—30K watching the live stream.

"You ready?" Angel mouthed.

Gestas nodded, bracing his elbow on his thigh.

Angel pinched the skin around the glowing red light, and I could see the lump beneath. A cry escaped my throat as Angel made the cut. Blood streamed down Gestas's arm. It took just a few moments. Then Gestas took the tiny chip from Angel's outstretched palm, stared at it, and started to laugh. The crowd cheered. Gestas jumped up onto the railing of Shayna's back porch and hooked his heel into the gutter, hoisting himself onto the roof. He scrambled up the slope to the apex and punched his clenched fist in the air. The crowd went wild.

Old Jim from the *Chronicle* snapped the iconic image of that moment—you've seen the one. Gestas wears all black. His arm is streaked with blood, the gaping wound still unbandaged. His eyes reflect the setting sun, and his smile is huge, giddy, and free.

A million people would watch Peter's video by the next day, and over a hundred AHICA inmates would dig their chips out of their arms to join our movement.

A few thousand people had amassed at Shayna's house, but there were larger crowds meeting at other parks around the city. A month out from the destruction of the Lab, we'd had a chance to take a breath and mourn what was lost. Now we were eager for another big action. And tens of thousands of new faces—folks who'd never come to the Village—had showed up, maybe realizing that this was their last chance to be a part of history. The vagueness of all our promotion had successfully created an air of mystery. "Whose City? Our City!" stickers and graffiti had become omnipresent sights, seemingly overnight. But we'd kept the details vague, so people felt very cool to be "in the know," to get one of the digital invites to a staging meet-up. The next morning, journalists would claim widely varying numbers, anywhere from a thousand to a hundred thousand—but the most credible historians now estimate that somewhere around fifty thousand people marched with us that night.

Shayna climbed up beside Gestas with her bullhorn and addressed the crowd, which had spilled into yards up and down the block. "The violent police state has invaded our neighborhood, attacked us in our sleep, and destroyed our homes, for the sake of an oil pipeline and a hyperway out to wealthy, white suburbs. They've done all this in the name of the 'War on Climate Change,' but call it what it is. The only war this country has ever fought— has always fought—is the war on Black and Indigenous people! It's the same damn war they're fighting in Brazil. Well, if it's war they want, it's war they'll get!" Shayna screamed, and I had never seen her like this, all her spillways opened, unleashing pure righteousness and rage as tears streamed down her face. "The Free People's Village is no longer a protest. That time has passed. This— this is a revolution!" The crowd hollered and whooped. Shayna and Gestas clasped fists and embraced, silhouetted by the fiery sunset. My heart pounded wildly. I was more terrified than ever of what the night had in store. Gestas and Angel had put everything on the line—like either they'd see the birth of a new world or die trying. But I couldn't kid myself into thinking I was as brave as them.

I looked for Angel and saw him through the door, inside, sitting on Shayna's couch, staring at his computer, alongside a bunch of folks from the technology working group. The only one I knew by name was Mizhir, the guy who'd coded CarbonSwap for Fish.

"Whose Streets?" Shayna and Gestas roared from the roof.

"OUR STREETS!" the crowd cried in answer.

Three cop drones that had been hovering above the house faltered, hung in the air a moment as their rotors slowed, then careened wildly, crashing to the earth. Where they landed, people screamed and dashed out of the way in panic.

Inside, Angel grinned at his laptop.

Shayna pointed at the drones now shattered on the street. "You see? They can't stand up to the power of our voices. Now I'll ask you again: Whose City?"

"OUR CITY!" roared the crowd.

"Let's take it back." And with a wave of her bullhorn, she urged us to march.

Lorenzo broke off with a few dozen people from the kitchen working group, heading south. A phalanx of bikers moved off to the north. Meanwhile, the vast bulk of the crowd allowed Shayna to shove her way to the front and lead them west. I was supposed to be up there beside her, but first I turned to Red.

Xe was pulling a black balaclava over xir face, and I held it for a moment before it came down over xir lips. I kissed xim for a long time, not wanting the moment to end, trying to crystallize every instant in my memory, because I was terrified it'd be our last.

"I'll be alright, Mads," Red whispered, breaking away first.

"Please be safe," I said.

"You know I can't promise that, right?" Xe wiped a tear off my cheek. "I'll see you at our new digs!" And with one last kiss on my forehead, xe pulled the balaclava down, obscuring all but xir eyes, and hoisted a baseball bat over one shoulder. Then xe turned and joined a large group of black-clad folks with bats and heavy backpacks, and they hurried through the crowd, hopping onto pop-up bikes and veering down a side street. When they disappeared around a corner, I started making my way to the front of the march.

52

Like the vast majority of the tens of thousands who marched that night, I had no clue where we were headed. Toussaint had filed a "protest plan" with the city, showing that three different groups would march through Downtown, then head back to the Eighth Ward, ending at the construction site that used to be the Lab. I knew that was not our ultimate destination. I knew that Red's group, and a dozen other "riot teams" would sow chaos around Downtown, to spread the cops thin. I knew Angel and his team of hackers had crashed the operating system of the police drones, and they'd be sending false movement information to the cops' radios. And I knew that each of the three marches would split up, deviating from the official plan, and take circuitous routes known only to the leaders in order to meet up as one massive army at our final destination—wherever that was.

I walked alongside Shayna at the front of our march, shouting, "No Justice, No Peace!" grateful for the call-and-response. It's hard to think or worry while you're screaming. Mike Algebra was at the front of the crowd too, and a bunch of kids from the Socialist Democrats. Shayna had asked us to be here on purpose—she wanted white folks up front and at the edges of the march, using the privilege afforded our bodies to protect the Black and brown folks in our midst.

I hadn't prayed in a very long time, certainly not since my divorce, but that night the old habit kicked in. *Remember, O most gracious Virgin Mary*—not that I believe in you anymore, sorry about that—*that never was it known that anyone who fled to thy protection, implored thy help, or sought thine intercession was left unaided*—please keep them safe. Please, let us get wherever we're going. Let the people win, just this once—*Inspired by this confidence, I fly unto thee, O Virgin of virgins, my mother*—fuck, if you were real, if there was any fucking justice to be had in this life, I wouldn't even have to ask, would I?—*despise not my petitions, but in thy mercy hear and answer me*—and please keep Red from punching a cop—*Amen*. I went on like that, in a loop, the neurons in my mind firing over familiar grooves, sending mental energy floating up to the cosmos.

Naturally, all I saw and heard that night was what happened on the streets in front of me. But since then, I've heard so many stories, watched every scrap of video I could find, and read all the memoirs, so that now, when I remember that night, it's as if I was spread all over the city, a being with a hundred eyes, running alongside Red, galloping with Gestas, tensely watching lines of code with Angel, and, of course, at the end of it all, standing before the reflecting pool in my own two shoes, staring up at City Hall.

In the videos, you can tell how much glee Red felt that night. In one, xe pauses mid-run to swing xir bat at a malfunctioning cop dog that's limping in circles. Xir bat cracks against its hull, sending it flying down the alleyway, and xe lets out this booming laugh I'd know anywhere. Later, the pigs would show me that clip over and over, asking me to identify the perpetrator, threatening me, offering to drop my felony case if I could just tell them who it was. I had to bite down on my bottom lip until it bled to keep from laughing.

The riot teams caused mayhem alright. Just ahead of some of the marchers, they'd smash luxury store windows, inviting in streams of looters. They tipped over a half-dozen police cars and set fire to four of them. Some of the teams set up traps for the cops. They scattered homemade caltrops—just bent nails shoved through strips of old tires, all down a side street. Then a false radio call sent a motorcycle unit through there, shredding the bikes' tires. Gestas's crew strung wire across a particularly narrow alley. Then they taunted some pigs on horseback into chasing after them. The cops got caught by the wire around chest or neck height and were pulled from their saddles. Some of them were dragged for a while, one ankle stuck in a stirrup, as their mounts panicked.

Some of the riot team stole the mounts, and I have sworn in a court of law that I do not know the identity of any of them. But, let's just say, my favorite video is of a Black, balaclava'd cowboy with a bandage peeking out under the sleeve of his T-shirt, vaulting up onto a horse and taking off through the streets. You can tell the dude in the video has never ridden a horse before. He's bouncing up and down wildly, grasping for the reins, but then he pulls back on them, the horse slows to a trot, and he finds his rhythm, pulling the horse to the left and right experimentally before disappearing around a corner. The mounted riders appear in the background of lots of videos from that night, taunting cops on foot, leading them away from the marchers. When shit got heavy, and the pigs brought in their tanks and tear-gas canisters, whoever was riding those horses climbed down and let them go, slapping their rumps until they took off, eventually finding their way to the prairieways, where they were recaptured the next day, grazing on the grass along the bayous.

As we marched, I scanned every side street and rooftop for the flash of camouflage or the barrel of a long gun, bracing to run into violent counter-protestors. What I didn't know was that Slime and Filthy Ed had spent months—long before we'd gotten evicted from the Lab—infiltrating local hate groups on Facebook with false identities, attending KKK meetings in disguise, and becoming trusted, local white supremacists so they could stay one step ahead of Horneck-loving counter-protestors. They were playing double agents, pretending to be spying on the Village *for* the white supremacists. Gestas was right—it was dangerous and nasty work, because to gain the trust of leading local racists, Slime and Filthy Ed had needed to fully act the part, probably throwing around slurs and heiling Hitler. I still hate them for being the people who enabled Red's addiction, but I have to admit, that without their role on December 1st, that night might've turned far more deadly.

See, Slime and Filthy Ed had convinced their hate-militia buddies that the protests Downtown were all a cover for our real target—the Mall. Twenty miles away from Downtown. They said that at midnight, we were going to regroup at the Galleria and mass loot all the luxury stores. This narrative played into the white supremacists' assumptions about the true nature of Villagers—as lazy, criminal freeloaders. Slime and Filthy Ed had provided detailed maps and fabricated plans showing where we were going to meet up and approach the Galleria. They'd suggested the counter-protestors take up sniper positions on the rooftop of a nearby office building, where they could monitor our approach.

So on December 1st, Slime and Filthy Ed had met them at that five-story office building—dressed up in soldier cosplay and carrying rifles of their own. They'd picked the lock on the stairwell for the racists, held the door open wide as all those dudes hoping to kill a protestor barreled inside. And then, rather than following them in, Slime and Filthy Ed shut and padlocked the doors from the outside.

They'd chosen this particular office building because you needed a key card to exit the stairwell on any of the floors above the first. The thick cement walls blocked cell phone reception completely. Those white supremacists spent the entire weekend locked in the stairwell, rationing the meager supply of water and food they'd brought with them. When terrified custodians discovered the trapped fascists on Monday morning, they were all severely dehydrated and rushed to the hospital.

Filthy Ed and Slime shaved their facial hair and got new haircuts after that. I couldn't believe they didn't leave the city. One time I asked—weren't they terrified that they'd run into one of their old racist buddies and get killed? But they were confident that their identities hadn't been traced. Most of those paramilitary dudes lived out in the suburbs or the country anyways, only coming into the city for the chance to kill protestors. Slime did shake his head bitterly though, saying he felt guilty that those guys had probably taken their anger at him and Ed out on their families.

So I didn't know it then, but thanks to Slime and Filthy Ed, I didn't see a single counter-protestor on the march to our final destination—the site of a new occupation, the place that was supposed to be the birthplace of our revolution, that art deco fortress: City Hall. Shayna and Gestas reckoned that if we could take City Hall that night, we'd be able to hold it against the cops. But once inside, we'd be under siege. We'd need food and water to sustain the occupiers—at least for a few days. Beyond that, each organizer had differing plans. Peter was excited to use the Council Chamber's live broadcasting equipment to share our message with everyone in Houston. Shayna wanted to access all the city politicians' files, computers, financial records—and find dirt. She wanted leverage to blackmail city leaders into actually working for the people. Toussaint hoped organizers in the dozens of other cities holding actions that night would seize similarly powerful buildings and coordinate a national plan for returning power to the people. And Gestas was hoping that City Hall would be only the first symbol of the police state to fall. From there, he envisioned us staging takeovers of police precincts and jails. He foresaw not a hundred, but hundreds of thousands of AHICA inmates slicing out their chips and joining him in an armed revolution.

First, though, we'd need to feed and water the occupation. Luckily, provisions to feed an army of businesspeople were stored in the restaurants twenty feet below the streets, in the Downtown Tunnels. Houston was so hot most of the year that businesspeople preferred to take their lunches in the network of air-conditioned, subterranean mini-malls beneath the skyscrapers. There were dozens of restaurants down there, and Lorenzo, Damian, and fifty others handpicked by Gestas and Shayna were going to steal their food, wheel it to City Hall, and infiltrate the building from below.

There are no videos of what went down in the Tunnels, but I've heard firsthand accounts. Only a single security guard stood at the entrance they used, and when he saw fifty balaclava wearers with baseball bats approaching, he ran. They flew down the stalled escalators into the Tunnels.

One of the people on Lorenzo's crew was this girl named Kayleigh—a redheaded sous chef, tattooed up to her chin, who worked at a steakhouse down in the Tunnels. Kayleigh and Lorenzo had planned a route to City Hall that would pass a whole bunch of restaurants. On the night we marched, Kayleigh led them to a supply closet filled with carts for moving around supplies underground, and they stole ten. Whoever wasn't pushing the carts hitched a ride on them, flying down the darkened linoleum Tunnels. In front of each food court area, one of the carts would park, and the folks riding would spill out, load the cart with pallets of water and bags of rice and beans—all the stock in the restaurant—then take off again towards City Hall.

They ran across a few more security guards, who they tried to chase down before the guards could call for help, but one got a message out before they could take his radio off him. When they rounded the last corner to the elevators beneath City Hall, they found a line of cops wearing gas masks waiting for them.

Twenty feet above their heads, I had just reached the reflecting pool.

53

I never learned if we got ratted out over the course of the night, or if the cops had managed to piece together our plan themselves. It's clear that when our action started, they didn't know what to expect. They'd stationed a few hundred cops at our "planned" destination—the site of the torn-down Lab. The cyberattack on their drones' operating system had taken them by surprise, and they were reeling from the loss of their robotic eyes and ears around the city. In the back rooms of police stations, cops scrambled to dig out handheld gas canisters and flash grenades they hadn't used in years.

The chaos sparked by the riot teams also worked beautifully, deftly drawing the cops away from the route of the main marches, which made it easy for us to simply push aside the unmanned barricades that were supposed to keep us on our "official" route.

About a half hour in, my nose picked up the first whiffs of gas, and then we started to hear the sounds of flash grenades and screaming from streets to our right and left. I hit my inhaler preemptively and pressed forward, losing myself in the call-and-response, trying not to worry whether the screams ringing out across the night came from someone I knew.

Six groups of marchers were supposed to converge on City Hall simultaneously. The finance working group led the crowd that came down off McKinney and Smith. A block to our north, a march led by Toussaint met a critical mass of bikes who'd left from Discovery Green. More marchers came from the north on Bagby—but to the south, Bagby was empty.

I scanned the converging crowds of thousands to figure out who was missing. It must've been the group Nimo and Vida had marched with—mostly made up of the GCIA and Palestinian organizers—because I didn't spot any keffiyehs or Palestinian flags.

The crowd was pressing me forward, towards the lawn in front of City Hall, and the reflecting pool, and the hundreds of cops stationed there. It was an important part of the plan that we be able to completely surround the building, to cut off the streets, so the pigs couldn't send reinforcements. I watched the dark, empty entrance off the square to Bagby Street with growing dread.

Then, a cheer went up. Someone carrying a flag of black, red, green, and white came jogging around the corner, and then thousands of people hurried through the skyscrapers flanking Bagby Street, many of them wearing black-and-white keffiyehs or carrying Palestinian flags. The young people among them were whooping, jumping up and down as they ran, and I wondered what had made them so hyped. Next came a line of men from the GCIA, drumming a fast-paced infectious beat, followed by Nimo and Vida, carrying a banner stretched between them: "Land Back! From Houston to Palestine!"

Later I'd see the videos of the incident that made them late and had them charging into the square with such infectious energy. The police had targeted that group of marchers the most fiercely—because of Islamophobia or anti-Indigeneity, or just randomly, I don't know. A double line of cops in riot gear had blocked their group between Bell and Clay Streets. The cops had attacked with clubs, pulling out a half-dozen men at random from the front of the march to arrest—Juan Pablo from the GCIA and a number of Palestinian students. They'd ordered the march to disperse, but instead, the marchers had pressed forward in total solidarity, chanting, "Let them go! Let them go!" until the cops were surrounded, pressed up against the front doors to a financial building. In the videos of the incident, Vida and Nimo are at the front of the crowd, pumping their fists in the air in time to the chant. After ten solid minutes of shouting, the frightened, kettled cops release the kidnapped men. There's a YouTube video of that moment where you can see Nimo and Juan Pablo embracing fiercely, which always chokes me up.

The de-arrest they accomplished had worked exactly the way Shayna hoped things would go at City Hall: if you surround police, they lose their nerve and back down. Now that our last group had arrived, we had the cops surrounded.

But there was a fuck ton of them. In just the last twenty minutes before we arrived, every cop in the city had been ordered to pull back to City Hall. And they'd brought their armored tanks, and blinding lights, and guns, and riot gear, and gas masks. They had erected orange barricades on either side of the reflecting pool, stretching in a perimeter all the way around the building to the back. I started to panic, remembering the feeling of getting slammed to the concrete, the crack of my skull, how I'd thought I was dying, the humiliation and suffering of waiting all night, shivering in a jail cell with a hundred people in urine-soaked clothes.

I wanted to turn and run but couldn't, because a wall of ten thousand people pressed forward, and I was carried along. I wound up standing at the edge of the reflecting pool beneath the tower. The cops hadn't thought to put a barricade *in* the water, so there was a clear expanse stretching between me and a spread-out line of cops stationed at the doors to City Hall. I looked to my left and right, and, true to Shayna's plan, it was all white folks standing in the front. We were the least likely to experience excessive violence at the hands of the police. It would be harder for the media to criminalize us in the minds of their viewers.

That's what Shayna had told me the day before, when she and Gestas invited me into her bedroom. "What are you, five foot four?" she'd asked.

"Five five," I had clarified.

"A very nonthreatening height," Shayna had said. She herself was about five eleven. "And so pretty, no tattoos."

"Shame you're not a blonde," Gestas said from where he was lying on Shayna's bed. "Ooh, could you dye your hair before tomorrow?"

I gaped at them. Shayna laughed, "No, no, bleached blond is no good. Brown is better—girl next door, right?"

"Why am I not bleaching my hair?" I'd asked.

"Because according to white supremacist pigs, you have, like, the least shootable face of anyone I know," Shayna said. "Not that you're going to get shot!"

"That's the whole point," Gestas said. "We just want you to be at the front of the march. Just stand at the front and be a buffer between some of our more melanated Villagers and the cops."

"And there may come a moment," Shayna said, "when there's a kind of—like a standoff, right? And—and someone needs to take a step forward. I can't think of anyone who, like, physically, would be less threatening to cops than you."

My ears were ringing then, and I wanted to cry, but I couldn't—I wouldn't—do the white-woman-tears thing to the two of them. I cleared my throat. "I still have nightmares, uh . . . about getting arrested. That cop slammed me down, you know . . . he didn't think I looked too cute or whatever not to hurt."

Shayna braced her elbows on her knees so we could see each other eye to eye. "Look I'm not saying it's not risky. And I can't promise you won't get arrested again, or even hurt. I can't promise any of that. But trust me, there are going to be comrades out there doing way more dangerous, illegal shit than what we're asking of you." Behind her, Gestas nodded knowingly. "And hey—you've been with the Village since the very beginning—since before! I remember you from that Save the Eighth meeting at the Baptist church. You actually care about this movement. And this is your chance to do something big."

When Shayna had said that, I'd felt like a total fraud. Let's be real, I had never really cared about the Eighth Ward. I had gone to that first meeting out of pure selfishness—because I loved partying at the Lab, and I didn't want to lose my band house. And if I hadn't been sleeping with Red, I never would've spent nearly so much time at the Village. Every shift I'd worked in the kitchen, I'd only done because I liked hanging out with Lorenzo. I agreed with Gestas and Shayna when they gave passionate speeches about the connections between oil and hyperways and white supremacy, the car manufacturers and the carbon offsetters and the war in Brazil, but I couldn't explain it all myself. I'd never managed to finish *Black Marxism*, the last book Gestas had loaned me. I got about fifty pages in, but it was so damn academic, I couldn't get myself to read any more. All along, I'd just been chasing a good time, not standing up for my principles.

But of course I didn't say any of that. And then Shayna said, "Lord, I just remembered how during that first meeting, we were naming off ancestors." She turned to Gestas. "And Maddie's ass said, 'Assata Shakur.'" Gestas burst out laughing. "For a second I was like, hold up, what happened to Sister Shakur? Why'd no one tell me?"

"I was confused about the prompt," I mumbled, face burning.

"She actually told me about that," Gestas said, grinning at me. They were teasing me, sure, but I knew they both genuinely cared about me by that point. I deeply did not want to disappoint their faith in me, though I was sure it was misplaced.

"Believe me, at that meeting I did not expect I'd someday be asking you to head up a protest march, but here we are." Shayna spread her hands wide. "I'm just saying, if there comes a moment when you can take a step for the movement? Take it."

Ever since that conversation, I'd been running over what she'd said in my mind. Wondering what she'd meant by "take a step." Did she mean I should punch a cop? Or get myself arrested?

But then I found myself standing in front of City Hall, with only the reflecting pool between me and our destination. And an angry voice was booming out over a painfully loud speaker—unlawful assembly, past curfew, disperse or you will be arrested." And these blindingly bright lights were shining down on us from the tops of dozens of armored trucks, and long lines of pigs in riot gear and gas masks with guns stood between us and the building. But surrounding them were tens of thousands of us. We had overwhelming numbers.

And I thought about one of the last lessons I'd taught my first-period students, before my teaching license was revoked. We were going to examine poetry and essays about the fall of the Berlin Wall. But first I had to teach them the whole history of that moment.

Antoine and D'Unte had at least heard of the Berlin Wall, saying, "Wasn't that when democracy beat communism?" So then I had to teach them about how authoritarianism versus democracy were *political* systems, while communism versus capitalism were *economic* systems. And by the end of that, most of them had realized they actually were communist—-they just didn't like the whole authoritarianism bit. Finally, we watched a bunch of videos of the night the wall fell. Princess and Naiya were goofing on all the 80s outfits and hair. The room fell silent as the crowds of marching people approached the wall.

"You have to understand," I said, "that this wall—it was this incredible symbol of power and control that had stood for nearly thirty years. People your age had never known a world without it. And people who approached the wall from the eastern side got shot."

"Fuck, Miss, are you about to show us snuff?"

I shook my head, hoping that Rishad only knew about snuff films as a concept, not from experience.

"That's the incredible thing about this moment, right?" I went on. "It easily could've ended in terrible violence, all because of a miscommunication between the government and the military. It all came down to one commanding officer on duty. He saw the overwhelming numbers of the people, and when they stepped forward, he did not give the order to fire."

My students watched in silence as, on the projector screen, a few brave souls stepped forward into no-man's-land, followed by a massive crowd that streamed past the armed, befuddled guards. I was watching my students' faces, lit blue by the glow of the screen. They looked younger, watching that video. They'd gone real still, mouths slightly agape, eyes filled with a rare kind of hope— confirmation that sometimes, even just once in a generation, the monstrous bullies of the world can be defeated, and the people will triumph.

I was remembering them, there at the reflecting pool. I was remembering Shayna telling me to "take a step." I was thinking about Red, god-knows-where in the city, possibly already arrested or beaten or worse. I was thinking about Gestas, standing on Shayna's roof with blood streaming down his arm. I was thinking about Shayna laughing at me, about that time I'd said "Assata Shakur."

I was staring at the six inches of water in the reflecting pool, and trying to psych myself up. *It's just a step. Just a step down into the water. Your shoes will get wet, no big deal.* I did not want to do it. I did not want to be there, facing off against this army of cops. I wanted to be home, in my quietly humming apartment, binge-watching cartoons. But there were tens of thousands of people at my back, and I couldn't exactly turn around and say, "Excuse me, I'd rather not." The quickest way to get this fucking night over with was to step forward, and whatever happened, would happen. And I hoped to God the cops would choose peace.

I really hate the video someone streamed of that moment, because it's so misleading. It was all over the news and got millions of views on social media. To this day, when I meet new people, sometimes they bring it up and thank me. I tell them, "Don't," which makes them act weird and disappointed.

First of all, I know what I was thinking at the time, and it wasn't courage that propelled me to take that step into the pool, but white guilt, and shame, and exhaustion, and more than anything, the delusional, magical thinking that I was going to be like those people who toppled the Berlin Wall.

And the other reason it's misleading is because all you see is me taking that first step, and then whoever was shooting the video pans away, up the line of protestors, towards where Mike Algebra and a group of dudes had started pulling down the barricades, and then there's a *boom!* and screams, and smoke and running, and gunshots, and you never see what I did after that first step—

My foot splashed down in the water, and as soon as it did, ten other people jumped in and charged ahead of me, sloshing towards City Hall. But I froze, because I saw the cops level their guns at us.

They fired rubber rounds, but I didn't know that then. And you couldn't tell, because they sounded like gunshots, and when someone got hit, they dropped. After I saw a guy in front of me go down, my mind became a screaming white blank, just pure animal instinct, and I turned and ran. People were falling around me, and I was shoving and clawing my way back through the panicking crowd. There was gas everywhere. I hit my inhaler as I ran and pulled my T-shirt up over my face, and I was crying and choking and running and running and there were horrible *booms* and *cracks* and screams behind me. I was certain a bullet would tear through the skin of my back any instant.

And then I was clear. The crowd had thinned to mere hundreds, running in the same direction as me, down Walker. The screams and sirens sounded muffled, far behind. I pulled myself into a doorway to cry and cough until my breathing steadied. And when I finally realized that I wasn't going to suffocate to death, that I hadn't been shot, that I wasn't going to be arrested, I got up and started walking towards the Canal warehouse, which was the closest place I knew to find shelter.

54

Months later, when I was in inpatient treatment, Dr. Abner told me that shame is not rational. Like regret, shame can be a coping mechanism, a way of convincing ourselves that we matter, that our actions could've changed these highly complex events that were set in motion by zillions of chain reactions stretching back to the dawn of time.

Shame is also the most uncomfortable feeling for our psyche to handle. People will destroy relationships, blow up their lives, do terrible violence to avoid feeling shame for even an instant. Because shame is a bottomless pit, and once you trip over that edge, you might never stop falling.

I was so deep down the well that I almost refused to see her, when Shayna came to visit me at the clinic. We hadn't really talked since City Hall, and I had a feeling she'd come to scream at me, blame chickenshits like me for the death of the Free People's Movement. If I'd just kept wading forward in that reflecting pool, if enough of us had pressed our bodies forward, consequences be damned, instead of turning to run, we would've overwhelmed the police in minutes. We would've taken City Hall, and this worst-possible timeline would never have come to pass.

Ultimately, though, I decided the shame of not even being able to face her might actually, physically, kill me. So I met her, in the "visiting garden," a couple benches which would someday be shaded by the live oak saplings planted around them. The sun blared down on our heads. The lawns of the clinic, which must've once looked like a golf course, had been converted to prairie, without much care for biodiversity. Fields of black-eyed Susans stretched clear to the highway, an oppressive riot of yellow and black.

I couldn't look Shayna in the eyes at first, bracing myself for an onslaught of abuse.

She asked me how I was.

Not sure how to answer, I shrugged. There was an interminable pause.

She asked if I needed anything? Wanted anything? I just shook my head.

She asked if I wanted to know about the others' cases? I nodded yes.

She started with the good news first: people who'd beaten their court cases since I'd been in treatment—Lorenzo, Mike Algebra, and Peter. She saved the news about Gestas and Angel for last.

The night we marched, the riot teams all doubled back as we converged on City Hall. Gestas headed back to Shayna's to collect Angel, and they got on his motorcycle and headed for Mexico. They drove through the night, making it all the way to Brownsville before getting stopped at a border checkpoint. The ICE pigs searched Gestas and Angel for drugs, finding nothing. But while one agent was patting down Gestas, he'd noticed the bandage beneath Gestas's sleeve, where he'd cut out the AHICA chip. They both got arrested, and soon the cops had connected them to the protests in Houston.

Angel had been turned over to the military for court-martial. He was suspected to be behind the virtual attacks on the cop drones, and faced a laundry list of crimes, including treason. Gestas had been transferred to a brick-and-mortar jail to await trial for his part in the riots.

I'd known all this before entering treatment. Shayna didn't have much news, just updates from their lawyers, and the viral social media campaign to free them. Chad thought that the evidence against Gestas was mostly hearsay and inadmissible. Still, he was urging Gestas to plead guilty and take a deal—five more years added to his AHICA sentence. Because if a jury rendered a guilty verdict for all his other charges, he could face up to forty-five years in brick-and-mortar prison. Gestas still hadn't decided what to do.

Angel's case was a national media circus. Try as they did to demonize him, a lot of people found it hopeful and downright hilarious, watching those videos of cop drones spiraling to the earth and glitching-out drone dogs. It helped that Angel was a beautiful, charismatic soldier. The Right was painting him as a traitorous coward, but he'd become a darling of the Left, and there were huge protests outside each of his hearings to set him free.

That was nice to hear. Whether all the attention would sway the US Army, though, seemed unlikely. Angel's lawyers had argued that he should be tried in a civilian court, not a military tribunal, because he'd emailed his commanding officer on the night of the protest with his intent to resign his commission as a conscientious objector. The military hadn't gone for it.

"I'm so sorry," I said, starting to cry, even though I hated to cry in front of Shayna. White women's tears and all that. So I said, "I'm so sorry," for the tears, and then I just kept repeating it. "I'm sorry. I'm sorry."

"Why?" Shayna asked, matter-of-fact.

I looked up into her face for the first time that visit. She looked good, better rested than I'd ever seen her, skin clear, like she'd been drinking plenty of water. Her hair was done in fresh box braids. "Why are you saying sorry?"

"Because—" I stammered for a bit. "Because I ran! At City Hall. As soon as they started shooting, I turned and ran."

"That's . . . understandable? Everyone started running?"

"But you'd told me—you said that you wanted me to 'take a step,' and then it turns out they were just rubber bullets."

"Just rubber bullets? Those can kill. Hell, they blinded that kid from U of H. And we didn't know—none of us knew what they were shooting."

"But you got arrested! Again! Most of our people did, and I—I got away."

Shayna laughed in an exasperated way, staring off at the fields of flowers.

"Did you shoot at me, Maddie?"

"No."

"Did you fire tear gas at me? Did you arrest me?"

"No."

"Did you try to knock down my house with a bulldozer?"

I shook my head.

"Then stop apologizing, dammit! Hell, this isn't about you! You don't need to carry the actions of the entire fucking white-supremacist, capitalist police state on your shoulders."

I started really sobbing then, because I had never expected Shayna to tell me such comforting lies. I knew in her heart she blamed me and loathed me, but she was being kind because of my condition, and I didn't deserve it.

"Oh Jesus," Shayna said. She flicked some braids from one side of her head to the other. "Listen, what would you say to anyone else who marched with us on City Hall that night? All those tens of thousands of people who didn't get arrested? Do you blame them too?"

I sniffled, trying to get myself under control. "No, I mean, I'm grateful they showed up at all. But that's different. That's them."

"What about back at the Village—all the folks who showed up for an action or two, but then had to go home to their kids or their jobs, so they didn't camp out. Do you blame them for the raid on the Village?"

341

"No."

"The cops are the ones who chose violence that night, alright? Not you. You gotta stop putting all this on yourself. It's not like if you'd gotten arrested, Angel and Gestas wouldn't have been— okay? You're not responsible for what happened to them. And you're not responsible for what happened to *xim* either," Shayna added, in a softer voice.

I was a mess after that. When I finally got my breathing under control, Shayna went on.

"Look, you can't think this way. If I thought like you are—hell, I'm the one that planned the damn mission. The whole thing was my idea! And you think you're to blame? I mean if that's true, then I'm really on the hook for all this, huh?"

"No, no," I moaned. "That's—of course you're not—"

"All of us, we made our own choices that night. All of us who marched, we chose liberation. Gestas, and Gestas alone, chose to dig that chip out of his arm. Angel chose to tell the army to fuck off and do what he allegedly did. You chose to step into the reflecting pool. And then each of those pigs chose to shoot rubber bullets at peaceful protestors. You, Maddie, are not in charge of how things turned out. Hell, it's even debatable if you're entirely in charge of yourself. When those gunshots fired, that was a fight-or-flight response. I hit the ground, instead of running like you did, and that's why I got picked up. Well, that and I'm Black."

I nodded along, wiping eyes that wouldn't stop leaking. I was trying to take what she said to heart, though part of my brain was still fighting against it, still fighting to make me responsible for all that had happened.

"And Red—xe made xir decisions too. You're not responsible for that either. You know that, right?"

I nodded again, biting down hard on my bottom lip. Not trusting myself to speak. My heart was cracking open again.

"Hell, I know I'm supposed to go easy on people in your situation but . . . I mean, can I just point out—it's a bit white-savior-y isn't it? To blame yourself for everything that happened? Like, the movement did not come down to you. You are not, and could never have been, our savior. You're just . . . Maddie Ryan."

I snorted a laugh, and it was so unexpected. Nothing had made me laugh in months. Shayna grinned. "Wow, I did not expect that calling you a white savior would be the thing to cheer you up."

I genuinely chuckled at that. "It's like what Dr. Abner says—that my shame is a way of thinking the past could've been changed. It's like—it's so I don't accept what happened, really."

"Dr. Abner sounds smart," Shayna said.

"She marched with us that night," I said. "All the other doctors here think I'm mental for even living at the Village in the first place. But she gets it."

There was a long silence, and I didn't want Shayna to leave. "Thank you . . . for coming. You're the only person who's visited, besides my folks. And they're no help. You made me feel a lot better. Oh, fuck—" I cut off, burying my face in my hands.

"What?"

"It just occurred to me that—well, you're Black, and I'm white, and you're here, like, making me feel better? And it's just like—you shouldn't have to do this emotional labor—for me."

"It'd be fucked up if you were some random stranger on the internet, demanding that I make you feel better. But hell, Maddie, you're my friend! Of course I want to make you feel better. I don't want you to fucking kill yourself!"

I was shocked. I had no clue Shayna thought of me as a friend. Suddenly, I realized I'd known her for the better part of a year now. We'd lived through the Village together. I'd crashed on her couch a half a dozen times. Some part of me had always assumed Shayna must have a "real life" apart from the movement, real friends who she hung out with and watched movies with. But when would that have been? In all her free time outside work, she lived and breathed for the Eighth Ward. She didn't date, though I'd caught hints that she'd once had something with Toussaint—now ancient history. Her comrades in Save the Eighth were her friends, and over the course of this year, we'd become her friends too. That's why she'd invited Gestas to stay with her. All that bickering over leftist theory and tactics? That was friendship to Shayna.

And was it any different for me? Shayna was the only friend who'd come to visit me in the clinic. Vida and Nimo had face-timed me once, but that was it. Lorenzo had sent a box of cookies in the mail. Maybe they didn't even know they could visit. I hadn't asked them to. But Shayna had figured it out on her own, must've called the front office, learned when visiting hours were. Mike Algebra, and all the hundred other friends I had in bands— none of them had so much as texted after my suicide attempt. Maybe comrades were tighter than bandmates, at least when shit got rough.

"It's an honor to be counted among your friends, Shayna," I said. "I think of you as a friend too."

Shayna laughed a little, and I realized how formal I'd sounded.

"How much longer you in here?"

"Two weeks. That's all my folks can afford, so," I shrugged.

"You going to be okay?" she asked. "You got a place to stay?"

"My parents' house," I said. "Until I figure something out."

"Well, Gestas's room is still open, until we get him out of brick-and-mortar, at least. You're welcome to it. I could use some rent money for the mortgage."

After she left that night, I tried to picture myself living at Shayna's house, sleeping in the sunroom where Gestas and Angel had stayed for those impossibly hopeful, long-lost weeks before City Hall. Shame roared that I did not deserve to stay in that space. I fought back, reminding myself that Shayna had invited me. She needed help with the mortgage, and I could find work and give her that help. I was her friend.

For the first time, the thought of going back to real life after treatment felt almost bearable.

55

DECEMBER 2020

I know you want to know what happened to Red. It's just so hard to write it.

Red didn't get arrested the night we marched on City Hall. Xe got away when the riot teams bolted and headed back to Shayna's. Xe was there to say goodbye to Angel and Gestas, before they took off on Angel's motorcycle for the border.

Xe met me at the Canal Street warehouse after that, and we crashed on one of the couches, sleeping in each other's arms. I wanted us to go back to my apartment that night, but we were so tired, and it was a long bike ride, and the trains had stopped running hours before.

Around five a.m., cops stormed the place while everyone was still sleeping. They took us all to the police station and held us for hours while they interrogated us in turn. They thought Red might be one of the people in the video someone had live streamed of the riot teams—the one where xe—or whoever—smashes the drone dog with a baseball bat.

I said I didn't know what any other kids from the warehouse had been up to, as I'd been in the middle of the protestors the whole time, peacefully marching. I got let go. Red got charged with malicious destruction of property and inciting a riot. I had to use what was left of my meager savings to get xim out on bail and pay a retainer for a lawyer for xim. After City Hall, Chad was done taking on our cases pro bono.

I needed a job, immediately, or I was going to get evicted. I couldn't do anything working with schools, since my felony case was still pending.

I wound up getting hired by this place called Patio Warehouse as a "content writer." I had to take an hour's worth of connecting trains to get to Sugar Land, where I was shown to a bank of desks in an office space carved out of a warehouse, all white drywall and drop-tile ceilings and liminal nightmarish void. "Honest Dave," the mustachioed founder of Patio Warehouse, explained I was to spend eight hours every day creating fake blogs, purportedly written by "patio furniture and accessory enthusiasts." I was to then fill these blogs with glowing reviews of patio products, linking each one to Patio Warehouse's online shop.

This was a job that could've easily been done from my home, but when I asked if that was a possibility, Dave looked genuinely appalled and asked, "Then how will you learn to exemplify Patio Warehouse culture?"

Patio Warehouse culture, I'd come to learn, meant enjoying the smell of burnt popcorn and Folger's in the lunchroom, sweating through my work clothes by nine a.m. because the warehouse thermostat was set to eighty-two degrees, and enduring my deskmate Rhonda's unhinged rants about something-something-China controlling the weather, or how "the Jews" were hoarding everyone's carbon credits to fund Amazonian militants.

About five hours into my first day writing Patio-related content, I had my first suicidal thought. I was working on "The Ten Best Fire Pits for Cozy Backyard Bonfires," and all of a sudden my brain just went, "Maybe it'd be nicer to be dead." The thought just popped into my head like that. I wasn't feeling despair, wasn't crying, wasn't having a panic attack. Just kinda wanted to be dead.

The matter-of-factness of the feeling scared me. I banished the thought and decided to start writing all my sentences in haiku structure, five then seven then five syllables, with some kind of punctuation between each.

Listen, s'more lovers:
get that perfect golden toast,
right in your backyard!

That kept my mind busy for another hour, but then it happened again. "What if you have to do this for the rest of your life? Wouldn't it be better to just . . . not?" So then I started working in iambic pentameter. *A pop-up grill is great for smaller yards!* That got me through the end of the first day.

I texted Red on the way home, asking if xe would come over to my place. I was exhausted and wanted to sleep in a real bed. Plus, I had to wake up at six the next morning to get to work on time, and the Canal warehouse was usually a party until at least three a.m. I couldn't live like that anymore, not with a nine-to-five. What I wanted, more than anything in the world, was to order a pizza and make fun of Honest Dave and Rhonda with Red, maybe watch some pointless reality show and go to bed early in xir arms.

But Red was just starting xir shift at the bar, and xe couldn't come over. For the first time, I did the math, and realized that with our opposing schedules, we'd only be able to hang out Tuesday night through Wednesday afternoon, and then Saturday until four, and Sunday mornings. That scared the hell out of me. I was scared that our love would fall apart with so little time together. I was scared that I couldn't survive without seeing Red and touching xim every day. And I was terrified of what Red would do all those nights at the warehouse, if I wasn't around to keep an eye on xim.

All that night and the next day at work, my mind ran over what I'd say to Red, the next time I got to see xim again. I would lay my heart bare. I would tell xim I loved xim. And also how I was terrified by xir drinking and that time I'd caught xim shooting heroin. I'd explain that I wanted us to be together, to get through this dark time—what with the fall of the Free People's Village, and Gestas and Angel in jail, and that fascist Horneck taking office. My brain kept going over the words, imagining it play out like a Hallmark Channel movie.

But things didn't go how I'd planned. When I opened the door to my apartment, Red swooped in, kissing me hungrily, picking me up like a rag doll, and carrying me to the bed. We were starved for each other, and it was an hour or so before we rolled apart. My brain never worked too good after, so I was scrambling to figure out how to bring it all up—my big plan. My heartfelt confessions.

Red had grabbed the stuffed fox that had been my childhood fluffy and was making it walk around the bed, going "Doo, doo-doo, doo-doo." Xe made the fox start twerking, then breakdancing.

"I need to talk to you about something," I said. Red made the fox put its hand under its chin in an eerily realistic "I'm listening" pose. "No, I'm serious. We really need to talk."

"Shit, it's like that. Okay, well can we order pizza first? I'm starving."

We didn't have enough carbon credits between us for the dairy tax, so we had to settle for a cashew-cheez and soy-sausage pizza. Once the order was in, I set down my phone and tried again. "So, what I wanted to say—can you not be on your phone for a sec?"

Red dropped the phone, flipped over onto xir stomach, and put xir chin in xir hands, staring at me with wide-open eyes. "You have my full attention."

I had planned to start with "I love you," but with Red doing that jokey pose, I couldn't bring myself to do it. The mood didn't seem right. I wanted Red to be serious for once, before I said it, so I started in with logistics. With the difficulties of our schedule, and how little we'd get to see each other unless one of us got a different job.

"So quit," Red said.

"Me quit? I'm the one who has a lease to pay!"

"So? Move in with me at the warehouse. Then you won't."

"Half of a filthy couch in a dirty warehouse where no one ever sleeps is not a home!"

Red shrugged. "It is to me."

"What if you got another job, a nine-to-five, so we'd have the same hours?"

Red picked at the bedspread. "I like barbacking. I like working at the Beer Hole. Everyone's chill there. Now what? I'm supposed to get a new job because you've been working for Patio Warehouse for two whole days? Why don't you come work with me?"

"Because I can make way more money at Patio Warehouse!"

"Oh, so it's like that," Red said. "So because your job is white collar, mine doesn't matter?"

"No, it's not—"

"You want me to become some corporate stooge like you?"

"First of all, ouch," I said, trying to keep the anger out of my voice. "Second of all, getting a daytime job doesn't mean being some corporate sellout. Look at Vida—she works at a print shop. Rick from Okonomiyaki Riot works at a tattoo parlor."

"Hey, Lorenzo works at the Valiant Refinery, and he makes good money. Maybe I could get a job through him, huh? Buy some coveralls? Just sell my soul to an oil company?"

"You're being impossible."

"You're the one telling me to quit my job of two years so my schedule matches up with the job you've had for two days!"

"This isn't how I wanted this to go," I said, frustrated that we were spiraling into an argument. "I just—I need you, okay? I need to see you more than a few hours a week!"

"I don't see why that means I should quit my job that I like," Red grumbled.

"Because it's not a real job!" I shouted. Red recoiled, looking shocked. I instantly felt ashamed.

"And what's a real job? Writing fake blogs about patio furniture?"

"I just—I don't want you to have to live in that awful fucking warehouse anymore."

"What is this, shame-all-my-life-choices hour?"

Everything was going horribly wrong, and I couldn't figure out how to get back on track. "Look, I just—I want us to be together," I pleaded. "And if you got a daytime job, and moved in here, then we would be together. Like a normal couple."

"Normal?" Red said. "Have you seen me?" Xe swept a hand down xir body, the whole beautiful length of it—scars, tattoos, piercings, and all. Xe was only wearing a pair of tight boxer-briefs. "Why are you with me if you want to be a normal couple? Why are you trying to turn me normal? Doesn't everything about me scream that I am very fucking uninterested in normal?"

"I didn't mean I want *you* to be normal—"

"No, but I'm supposed to get a nine-to-five and move in with you and go to bed at nine-thirty and not drink too much?"

"Would that be so terrible?" I yelled. I didn't understand how everything I was trying to say was coming out so twisted. "Would it be so terrible to just—live with me?"

"First you want me to change my job, and change where I live, and then—what, when I'm under your roof, you'll start harping on how much I drink all the time, won't you? And I'll have to quit smoking 'cause of your asthma. And then you'll think I spend too much time on music and not enough taking you on dates. And I won't do the dishes enough, so you'll institute a fucking chore chart that you'll stick up on the fridge with a shitty little magnet. You'll start to micromanage every fucking inch of my life, how I dress, how I spend money, what I eat and drink and do with my time, all trying to turn me into a respectable little boyfriend you can bring home to your momma, so maybe she'll think you're the church-going kind of gay, but I promise you, that's never going to work with me."

"I don't know who the fuck did all that to you, but that's really unfair, Red." I shook my head. "You're making me out to be some trans-hating normie? Fuck, I just spent the last six months working for the Free People's Village. I got a felony arrest. I got fired from my teaching job, lost my certification. Am I still not edgy enough for you? Do I still not have enough street cred or something?"

"Exactly!" Red said, jumping off the bed and splaying out xir hands. "What are you doing? You're this righteous commie babe, but now you want to work for Patio Warehouse, and for us to move in together—in fucking *Midtown*? How is this place not death to you?"

"You wanna know what's death? Heroin is death, okay? People OD on that shit." I grabbed my fanny pack off my nightstand, pulled out the naloxone inhaler, and chucked it on the bed in front of xim. "You could at least carry this shit like I asked!"

"I told you, I'm not doing that stuff—" Red started, but I cut xim off.

"I'm trying to get health care, pay my rent, pay my lawyer—that's survival. I don't want to work for Patio-fucking-Warehouse, okay? But I have to, if nothing else, just to keep me in albuterol! Life can't just be parties and protests all the time. I'm exhausted. They won. They fucking won. So maybe we just get normie jobs, and watch TV at night, and cuddle, and grow the fuck up. Because the only other option I can see is us winding up dead, or in jail."

Red was staring out the window, lips set in a thin line, xir jaw muscle working furiously. Maybe I shouldn't have said what I did at the end there—bringing Angel and Gestas into the room. I think Red carried a ton of shame that they were both behind bars while xe was out on bail, just facing misdemeanor charges.

"Grow the fuck up," xe repeated in a soft voice, turning over the words, so I could hear how cruel they sounded. "I know myself, Maddie. I could try what you want me to. I could try my very hardest, but it won't work. I can't be that person. So if you need that, we should probably just break up."

"Don't say that," I said, breaking into a sob. All my anger and frustration dissolved, and I felt only panic. If xe walked out the door to my apartment, it would be like all the light in the world had winked out.

Xe came back over and sat on the bed, petting my hair. "Why not? You're so cute, Maddie. You'll get yourself a normie boyfriend in a second. Or a girlfriend, if you're into that. They'll work normal hours and watch TV with you. Just forget about me."

"I can't!" I sobbed.

"Why not?" Red said, picking up the fox again and twisting its head to the side, like a curious dog.

"Because, you asshole, I'm in love with you."

56

We didn't break up. I kept going to my job at Patio Warehouse, and xe kept barbacking and living on Canal Street. And for the one night and two afternoons per week that our schedules lined up, we had desperate, furious sex at my place, and then talked about music or scene gossip or anything other than what really mattered. Mike Algebra texted us sometimes about finding a time to get together and rehearse, but it felt sacrilegious to play without Gestas, so we left his texts on read.

We took off work to go to Gestas's arraignment, and we went to each other's pretrial hearings. Shayna and Peter were leading the social media campaign to free Angel, and I shared everything they posted. Shayna held a couple call-a-thons for Angel, inviting folks over to make calls to various politicians and military officials. I went, but Red couldn't get the time off work. Xe said xe'd make the calls in xir free time. I don't know if xe ever did or not.

I never went to the Canal warehouse anymore, until one afternoon, Vida texted to say she missed me. She and Peter were moving out of the warehouse the following week. And she was worried about Red.

This was maybe six weeks after our fight. Red's trial was coming up in another two weeks, and I was sick at heart about it, because xir lawyer was urging xim to plead guilty and take a plea deal of 180 days in AHICA. That meant 180 days trapped at the Canal

Street warehouse, because Red had said, "Don't even bother," the time I brought up xim living out xir AHICA sentence with me.

So I went over to the warehouse after work one day, when Red wouldn't be expecting me, and I found xim in one of the back apartments, gone fucking cosmic from snorting oxycodone.

I just got furious. I was so mad I wasn't thinking straight. And Red was too high to stop me when I went over to xir little curtained-off couch, and rifled through xir boxes and suitcases, where all xir filthy laundry was jumbled up with books and guitars, and in a drawer in a side table, I found two used syringes and a tourniquet.

Red swore they weren't xirs. But I knew xe was lying about that. And I also knew, for the first time, that all those jokes Red made about wanting to die young—they weren't really jokes.

I said, "I can't watch you destroy yourself."

And Red said, "So go."

"Are you trying to get yourself killed?"

Red shrugged and said, "Maybe."

I started crying and said, "But I love you."

And Red held me and promised, promised, promised that xe'd never shoot up again. Said all that was over. "Don't cry, Maddie." But xe was still really high, and I wondered if xe would remember any of it in the morning.

Then it was the day before Red's court trial, and I got a call midmorning from Vida. I was at Patio Warehouse, and when I saw her name pop up on my phone, at that hour, on a weekday, my gut turned to ice. I went out to the parking lot to take the call, already shaking. We were having a freak January heat wave, so it was humid and eighty degrees out, and I started sweating in my polyester blouse.

Patio Warehouse was actually a complex of three warehouses, all of which opened onto a massive asphalt lot filled with box trucks emblazoned with the Patio Warehouse logo. I walked past them, past the dumpsters, out to the edge of the lot, where it ran down into a drainage ditch filled with illegally dumped tires. Across the way stretched a few hundred yards of prairie, before some kind of massive chemical refinery reared out of the grass, all jumbled pipes and storage tanks and stacks belching steam.

I sat there at the edge of the drainage ditch and called Vida back. Her voice shook as she told me the news, and she burst into tears by the end of it. But I felt nothing yet, just a howling in my ears, like the outer bands of a hurricane.

I ended the call and sat there, staring at those tires down in the ditch, waiting for the world to end now that Red wasn't alive in it.

But minutes kept crawling by. A cricket landed on a tall blade of grass, then jumped away. My brain refused to wrap around it. I'd known people who'd died—a pair of grandparents, some distant acquaintances, but not anyone woven into the fabric of my life like this. I figured I must be in shock, since the light seemed very crystallized, and my ears were ringing, and I felt a little feverish. But my heart felt nothing—in fact, it felt like there was nothing there but that howling wind. Very calmly, I texted Honest Dave that I'd gotten food poisoning and needed to head home.

I got my things from inside, rode my bike to the maglev station, sat on the train. All the while the howling inside grew louder. I didn't look at anyone's face, because I had this weird thought that if I made eye contact with anyone, I would explode. I didn't read or scroll my phone on the train, I just stared at the grime on the floor, as if those bits of hardened gum and crumbs were anchors in a storm.

And then I was walking in the door to my apartment. I dropped my things on the ground because placing them somewhere felt pointless. I trudged to my bed and saw the little stuffed fox lying there. That was when I fell apart.

57

'd never known that grief could be so physical, that just the knowledge of someone missing from the world could make every muscle in your body ache, and even your blood hurt, like you were sick with the flu. I'd wake up in the morning from tormented dreams of being lost in drop-tile-ceiling labyrinths, where I'd searched endlessly for something I'd lost, something terribly important, though I couldn't remember what it was.

I kept telling myself that I would feel better with time, but months passed, and if anything, I was getting worse. Food tasted like ash. TV shows were all trite and pointless. Being with friends only reminded me of Red's absence. The night after Red died, Vida and Peter had hosted an impromptu memorial at the Canal warehouse. Hundreds of people showed, all of them pathetically not-Red, all of them shadows, casting me weird half-pitying, half-jealous looks because I was the one Red had loved. I couldn't stop fantasizing about burning the place down. My brain sought out dusty corners, lined with stacks of books. Dump some liquor, touch a lighter, and the whole place would go up. The fantasy was so strong I couldn't listen to the words coming out of the mouths of my friends, their sad little memories about a time Red had paid them five seconds of attention.

Weirdly, the only conversation that didn't annoy the hell out of me was the one I had with Nimo. His hair had finally gotten long enough to pull back into a stubby braid. "I'm so sorry for your loss, Maddie," he said, resting a hand on my forearm. "Even though it's no secret that Red and I weren't the closest."

"You weren't?" I asked, genuinely confused. I'd never really paid attention to the interactions between the two of them.

"Well, no. To be honest"—Nimo cringed—"I always kind of thought xe was an asshole."

Something bubbled up in me—something I expected to be a surge of righteous anger. But it was laughter that burst out of my mouth. A hysterical, high-pitched giggle. Heads whipped around to look at us.

"Xe was an asshole," I whispered. "Such an asshole move—to OD like that." I was still laughing, but my eyes were leaking real tears. "But xe was my asshole, you know? The best asshole—"

"Oh honey, I'm so sorry," Nimo said. "I shouldn't have said that. I'm a messy bitch."

I snorted one more laugh. "It's alright," I said, wiping my eyes with the sleeve of my flannel. "Red was hard to love." I stuck by Nimo's side from then on. Why did it feel good to be around the one person who'd never been swept away by Red's charm?

Then, around midnight, Filthy Ed had the nerve to show his face. I wanted to scream at him. I wanted to ask him how many times he'd done heroin with Red, and had he given Red xir first hit, and had he been there the day xe died? I wanted to beat his face concave with a wine bottle.

Instead, I just left early.

I didn't even take the next day off work, because I was terrified of what would happen to me if I didn't go in, if I didn't have that chunk of hours when I could disassociate and think only about water-resistant, fade-proof porch-swing cushions in antique damask with hidden zippers. Soon, the suicidal thoughts became a constant barrage. I would look at a letter opener and imagine tearing open my flesh. On the maglev platform, I'd fantasize about throwing myself in front of an arriving train.

These thoughts had started before Red had even died. Even then, I'd been grieving—we'd both been grieving. Even before the

Village, we'd lost our carefree lives at the Lab, when it was all parties and shows and band rehearsal, skateboarding inside and drawing on the walls and staying up all night laughing at 80s music videos. It had been a beautiful year, the year we'd fallen in love, and we'd never taken the time to mourn it when the occupation started. And then the Village—the rhythm of those days, cooking and serving and long afternoons of heated discourse, everyone coming together for People's Musters, the incessant heartbeat of the drum circle, escaping to the roof with friends, looking out over the sea of tents, always someone painting or playing music, always a protest to go to, because we were busy changing the world. The beauty of that life had been destroyed by chemical weapons and bulldozers and violence. And even worse was the loss of something more intangible. Even Red, who'd always acted so cynical, so bored by Gestas and Shayna's philosophical debates—even Red, for all xir jadedness, hadn't been immune to hope. All of us who'd marched that night to City Hall had nurtured that flame—hope that the world could really be changed. That the people, united, could never be defeated.

That flame was now decisively snuffed out.

Maybe if Red and I had taken the time to really grieve for all that, to sit with it—

But there I go again. I know better than to go down these rabbit holes. What happened, happened.

I never found out exactly what drugs or mix of them killed Red—xir family never shared the toxicology report. They also did not invite any of us—any of Red's real friends—to the small, religious funeral they held. We only found out about the ceremony weeks later, from Angel.

Once, Red and I had talked about what we wanted done with our bodies after we were dead. Red had said, "Just throw me in the woods, where any animal that wants can come get a meal." I'd pointed out that dumping bodies in the woods was illegal, for health reasons, but Red asked who among us hadn't done crimes? This had been shortly after my arrest, so I'd laughed and promised I'd try to find a forest to throw xir body in when xe died.

But legally, I was nothing to Red, so the hospital had turned xir body over to xir parents, who hadn't spoken to Red in years. Who buried Red, probably dressed in gendered clothes xe would've loathed, on polyester cushions, inside a horrible steel coffin that will prevent the molecules of xir body from returning to the soil and rejoining the circle of life for hundreds of years. I can't stand it, when I think about xir corpse, trapped in that awful, sterile box, like a giant piece of litter in the ground. Xe would've hated it. I've fantasized many times about sneaking into the cemetery at night, digging xim up, and stealing xir corpse to chuck in the swamp down at Brazos Bend. But that's something Red would do, not me. If you haven't figured out by now that I'm a coward, I don't know what to tell you.

The thing that freaked me out most in those months after Red's death—more even than the unwanted thoughts of violence and suicide—was that I couldn't listen to music anymore. All my life, I'd always had tunes playing in the background. Now, I had to rush out of a store where music was playing. The first few bars of any song conjured up the memory of where I'd been with Red the last time I'd heard that track. A flash of xir grin. The skin crinkling around xir eyes. The way xe played guitar lying upside down on the couch with xir feet hanging off the back and head hanging off the seat cushion. Popping an ollie by the kitchen. Ashing xir cigarette with a flick of xir thumb. Sometimes I'd get hit with xir smell— bourbon and Parliaments and sweat. Or I'd remember xir hands on my body, and I'd come undone.

I tried music I was certain we'd never listened to together. Deep-cut orchestral works, new country, obscure international bands. But then it would be like Red was still alive in the room with me, telling me exactly what xe thought of each song. I knew which bass lines xe'd think were sick and which drum patterns annoyed xim. Any sound waves arranged in rhythmic and harmonic patterns only amplified my pain. I played podcasts on the train now, though I couldn't pay attention to the narrators.

I never touched my guitar.

The various orgs and nonprofits that had made up the Free People's Village started doing their own things after City Hall, and for a few months I tried to keep up with them all. I signed petitions, attended meetings, donated the last of each month's paycheck to mutual aid funds. For each petition I signed, I got added to email lists for a dozen more. Meetings were like all the blah-blah-blah of a People's Muster, without any of the fun of life at the Village. I tried to keep up with reading groups. I tried to make it out to each planned direct action, but usually no more than a dozen people showed.

As soon as he'd taken office, President Horneck had signed a flurry of executive orders to suppress protests—making overnight encampments, blocking traffic, and "interfering with police activity" federal crimes. People were scared to come to any kind of protest anymore. The ones I went to were sad little affairs—Shayna with her bullhorn, and a dozen of us with signs, getting flicked off by business dudes in passing cars. Soon my inbox overflowed with URGENT! ACTION REQUESTS! and every evening was spent at some meeting or protest that felt like an enormous waste of time.

So one day I just stopped. Deleted the heartfelt emails unread. Didn't respond to digital meet-up requests. Silenced notifications on my phone. I felt like I should feel guilty about it, but I didn't really. There wasn't much room in my heart for anything but grief. I told myself I was just a piece of shit, like Red had once said. Only Red had said it in a much nicer way than the voice in my head did: "Lying on the couch again, watching TV, you privileged, lazy bitch? What the fuck is wrong with you? Oh, is it too *hard*? Is it too terribly taxing to sign a goddamn petition once in a while? You need to watch cartoons instead of standing up to injustice? Human garbage. You make me sick."

And then it was three months since Red died. Every day, I still woke up in a flood of pain and remembering, although the ache was a bit lessened. My body didn't feel as terrible, physically. My court case had been resolved—the felony trespassing charges didn't stick, as Chad had predicted. He deterred me from countersuing the city, though, because none of the courts had been settling in protestors' favor. You'd think the end of my legal journey would've come as a relief, but without any court dates on the horizon, time stretched forward like the endless, gray hallways in the featureless corporate labyrinths of my recurring nightmares.

One afternoon, Honest Dave took me and Rhonda and the IT folks out to lunch at Potbelly. We were waiting for our sandwiches when a couple guys in suits came in. At first my eyes skimmed over them, just three business bros out to lunch. But then I recognized one.

It was Fish. He'd lost some weight, gotten a taper fade, and was wearing a very expensive suit. He looked at me, all the color drained from his face, and then an instant later he looked away, laughing at a joke from one of the other business boys.

My mind played out scenes of all sorts of violence I could do to him with the plastic forks and plate-glass windows at my disposal. But of course I did nothing. Shaking with rage, I Googled his name, desperate to find some clue that his life had become as miserable of a slog as mine was. I found the slick website for his new company: Urban Life Real Estate.

Find your dream home in the heart of the city!

We buy homes—any condition! Call us today!

I looked at the properties they had listed for sale. All of them were in the Eighth or Fifth or Third Ward—the city's predominantly

Black neighborhoods. All of them were tract houses or old brick homes, repainted in trendy, dark gray and cream trim, with solar-tile roofs. All showed slick interiors with open floor plans, new, eco-friendly appliances, and shiny bamboo floors.

All the promotional images decorating the banners featured blond-haired, white families playing with their kids in expertly permacultured yards.

Fish had gone full-on gentrifier mogul, just as his dad had predicted.

I watched him scoot his tray through the order line. I watched him joke with his business friends. I searched for some sign of remorse or shame over what he'd done to Red, or how he'd turned his back on everything he'd once claimed to believe in. But if my staring made him uncomfortable, he didn't show it. He looked utterly self-satisfied and rich. Our orders came up, and Dave went to get them, and then we were leaving and getting in Dave's all-electric SUV.

That night, when I went home, I got out this bottle of Tylenol #3 that I'd been prescribed a few years back for a dental crown. There were maybe twenty pills left in there, and I washed them all down with a glass of wine.

About five minutes after that, I started feeling really good, but part of my brain was still sober enough to panic. The last thing I remember was calling Vida to tell her what I'd done.

58

How do you go on living when the best and bravest people you've ever known are locked away in dungeons—or gone? How do you walk under the blue sky in relative freedom and live with yourself?

Dr. Abner's answer was that you live because you still can, and because you're not responsible, and because there is goodness and sweetness in life that should be enjoyed.

Honestly, I never bought into all that.

Shayna's answer, when I moved in with her, put a little more traction under my feet. She never said it in so many words, but the message was clear:

You go on because your comrades need you, and we don't leave anyone behind.

The hyperway was under construction. In my room—the narrow, walled-in porch at the front of Shayna's house—I woke every morning to the distant rumble of the destruction, half a mile away.

I did not go back to work at Patio Warehouse. Now that my felony charges had been cleared, I could've gone back to teaching full time, but I didn't have the heart for it. I wound up getting a job at a tutoring center, where I got to work with kids, but my schedule was way more low-key.

The battle against the hyperway had been lost, so Save the Eighth pivoted towards helping those of our allies who'd been incarcerated. Our members were exhausted though—disheartened, displaced—some of them didn't even live in the neighborhood anymore, because they'd lost the fight to keep their houses. Attendance at our weekly virtual check-ins dwindled to five or six people, max.

Our most urgent need was money. When the Village's popularity had faded, the offers of pro bono legal services had dried up. We needed to raise massive sums for Gestas, Angel, Lorenzo, and dozens of other Villagers who were facing steep legal challenges. But donations were no longer pouring in. We planned an elaborate fundraising effort—a zine of art commemorating the Village. The planning took weeks of effort, but only a dozen people attended the launch, and we barely raised a three-figure sum from sales of the zine.

I would've given up—then, and a hundred other times—if I hadn't been living with Shayna. Every day when we both got home from work, we'd chat a bit about our days, figure out what we were going to do about dinner, and then, as if by some unspoken agreement, we got to work.

Not like we never rested. But before we'd go to our separate rooms and chill, or watch a movie together, or do laundry, we'd do one thing for our comrades who were locked away. Maybe it was just sending an email, or scheduling a Save the Eighth meeting, or creating yet another Instagram post about Gestas's plight, asking for funds. But most weekdays, between about five-thirty and six, we'd open our laptops, sit on the couch, and do *something*. And for a long time—like, that whole first year—it felt like all those little somethings were adding up to nothing.

Finally, Lorenzo got out of brick-and-mortar—released to AHICA with two years left in his sentence. He moved in with Kayleigh, who'd guided their heist down in the Tunnels, but who'd avoided incarceration thanks to a mistrial. I'm not sure our efforts had much to do with his release—we'd only been able to contribute a few thousand dollars to his legal fees. Still, it felt like our first win.

At the party Kayleigh threw for his return, Lorenzo and Kayleigh wound up making out in the backyard, and everybody looking on cheered. Vida wasn't drinking that night, and she confided in me that she was pregnant—Peter's kid, for sure. Nimo was over the moon and insisted the baby would call him tío. All these changes felt exciting and terrifyingly permanent. I wound up sobbing when I got back to my small, stuffy room that night. Because I'd never get to see Red teasing Lorenzo good-naturedly about his new girlfriend. Red would never hold Vida's baby in xir arms, or even know they existed. So any big news, no matter how joyful, would now always be tinged with grief. Change reminded me that time kept relentlessly, irretrievably passing—a growing gulf between the present moment and when Red was still with me in the world.

That night marked a turning point for Save the Eighth for another reason. Peter had spent most of the party talking Shayna's ear off about this new video-sharing app, Jointly, that was blowing up with teens. Our Twitter and Instagram accounts had gone dead lately, with posts rarely getting more than a hundred likes, despite our having tens of thousands of followers. We didn't know whether we were victims of shadow banning, or if folks had just lost interest in the cause. So Peter came over a few times to help us make some Jointly posts for the anniversary of City Hall. One of them blew up, got over a million views, and we suddenly had tens of thousands of new followers.

The zeitgeist had shifted again. News of atrocities in Brazil—human and ecological—had reached the press, and the war was increasingly unpopular. Energy prices had skyrocketed, thanks to rising oil costs, and Democrats were starting to turn against "Horneck's War" (never mind that it was Donnelly who had launched the fucking invasion). During the heyday of the Free People's Village, our staunch, antiwar stance had been a liability among moderates, who supported the bipartisan war effort. Now, as we approached the two-year anniversary of the Free People's Village, the public's memories of us grew more sympathetic.

We started getting a lot of traction with Jointly posts about Angel—the courageous soldier, locked up for being a conscientious objector against this moral horror of a war. But Angel had been sentenced to a minimum of twenty-five years in the military prison at Fort Leavenworth for using US military-intelligence hacking protocols to take down the police drones. There wasn't a whole lot we could do for him besides tell his story, circulate petitions for his release, and try to pressure some future presidential administration into pardoning him.

We had more hope of securing Gestas's freedom, as he was being tried in a civilian criminal court. My sense of despair or optimism for life in general was often tied up in whatever was going on with Gestas. His trial took almost that entire first year, and we weren't sure how to help besides fundraising and trying to spread awareness and gain media attention. He was given a fifteen-year sentence for the many AHICA violations he'd committed the night of City Hall, with ten years' minimum time in a brick-and-mortar prison, before possibility of release to AHICA.

He was moved to a prison up in Bridgeport. He was housed with the men, which was his preference. But knowing he was locked away there—would be behind those walls until well into his thirties—knowing the types of violence a trans guy might experience in prison—it ate me up inside. It was a good thing I was living with Shayna, who reminded me to do a little work every day. That's all we could do. If I hadn't had that, I might've ended up back in inpatient treatment—or worse.

But Gestas wasn't despairing. Gestas didn't give up. Gestas was organizing.

Wardens do their damnedest to keep news of the outside world from penetrating the walls of their prisons, but Gestas's story had gotten inside. Everyone in the country, even inmates, had seen that picture of him standing on Shayna's roof, blood streaming down his arm where he'd dug out his AHICA chip. Everyone knew—although the prosecutor wasn't able to get the charge to stick—that he was the Black cowboy who'd stolen a police horse the night we'd marched on City Hall. Some of his fellow inmates at Bridgeport had wound up there because they'd seen his streaming video and dug out their own AHICA chips that night. In prison, he found himself an instant celebrity, who already had devoted followers.

He used that influence the same way he had with me and everyone at the Free People's Village—he radicalized folks. While he was at Bridgeport Correctional, we only got the story in bits and pieces—whenever he could get a phone call or some mail through. He started up a reading group which eventually orga-nized a hunger strike, demanding minimum wage for their com-pulsory labor. After twenty days, the participating prisoners were hospitalized and force-fed, and Gestas was put in solitary confine-ment. We had grown our large Jointly following by that point, and we mobilized our people to flood the warden's and state reps' voicemails in protest. But our efforts weren't nearly as effective as those of his fellow inmates, who organized a work stoppage until Gestas was released from solitary. For ten days, over a hundred inmates refused to do any slave labor. On the eleventh day, the COs responded with violence, and a riot broke out.

It was starting to feel like the work we were doing might matter—that our tens of thousands of Jointly followers were wak-ing up to the evils of the war and of modern-day slavery via the "criminal justice system." We were connecting with abolitionist orgs all across the United States, and they wanted to spotlight Ges-tas and the inmates' struggle in Bridgeport.

But the state of Texas and the warden of Bridgeport Correc-tional had had enough of Gestas, and he was transferred to New Jersey, thousands of miles away, to a women's prison. We were heartbroken. We wouldn't be able to drive up to see him every few months any longer. Maybe, once a year, we could get out there. And from everything we'd heard, harassment and sexual assault from COs at women's prisons could be even worse than those at men's prisons. Plus, the constant misgendering would be humiliating for Gestas. It felt like all our struggling to help him had backfired. The only thing that got me through that awful time was that Vida had just had her baby.

I went and stayed with her for a week, doing all the cooking and cleaning, so she and Peter could focus on learning to parent. And I babysat as often as they'd let me after that, figuring Maya might be the closest I ever came to having a kid, or even a niece or nephew, of my own. Whenever I held that warm little glow worm, sleeping in my arms, I didn't question whether I deserved to be alive or free—I was right where I belonged, doing the best possible work.

By the time Maya started sitting up on her own, it had become clear that Gestas's transfer had backfired on the prison administrators who'd thought the move would shut him up. If anything, they'd lit a fire under his story. The ACLU and major LGBTQ+ orgs ran features on Gestas, targeting the civil rights violations of throwing him in SHU or forcing him into a women's prison. On Valentine's Day, we ran a Jointly video highlighting the love story between Angel and Gestas—a Romeo-and-Juliet tale of star-crossed lovers, opposed to war and slavery and all forms of oppression, separated by the US military-prison-industrial complex. Maybe it was tacky to leverage their love like that, for likes. But the video blew up with multimillions of views, and Gestas and Angel became household names among leftists and chronically online teens. Gestas organized a prison-wide labor strike this time, somehow orchestrating across both the men's and women's wards.

Even in my wildest, most optimistic dreams, I didn't expect what happened next. The judge in Gestas's state-level appeal trial released him to AHICA seven years early, but only if he resided outside the state of Texas. The judge reasoned that Gestas's influence was just too disruptive—both to the Lone Star State, and to the inmate populations of brick-and-mortar prisons. An ex-Villager from New York City took him in—a Brooklyn communist, who'd been the de facto leader of our financial working group.

Me, Shayna, and Nimo were planning a trip to visit Gestas around Christmastime. Luckily, the news story broke before we'd bought our plane tickets. Gestas's bloody AHICA tracker had been discovered by police on the kitchen table of the apartment he was supposed to be sharing with finance guy. Presumably, the two of them had fled the country. News outlets ran clips of our old Jointly posts to tell the story of the runaway Villagers.

I grilled Shayna about what was going on, assuming she'd orchestrated his escape or had some knowledge of it, but she seemed as clueless as I was. FBI agents came to the door of Shayna's house to question us, but old habits die hard. She refused to let them in without a warrant. We were eventually subpoenaed, months later, but by then, the whole country knew where Gestas was, and what had happened, so we didn't have much to worry about.

But for those first few weeks after his disappearance, it felt like we were holding our breath, wondering if he'd made it overseas, or if something terrible might've happened to him, or if he'd get caught on his way to wherever he was going.

One night, I was brushing my teeth when my cell dinged with an incoming text from an unknown number. Then I was screaming and running towards Shayna's bedroom to show her my phone. In the picture, the two figures in the foreground are silhouetted by the sunset over the ocean, so their faces are a little hard to make out. But the bearded man in the sarong is clearly Gestas, his arm thrown around the shoulder of a Black woman in her seventies with graying braids.

"Holy fuck, it's Assata Shakur!" Shayna screamed when I showed her. "He's in Cuba!" She cried, and we hugged each other, because we were much too far away to hug Gestas, who'd made it to one of the only places in the world where the long arms of the United States' prison-industrial complex couldn't reach him.

"Look at those happy communists." Shayna sighed, sounding like years' worth of worries were sloughing off her back.

"Anarchist," I corrected. "He's—"

Shayna rolled her eyes like it was all the same to her.

We tried texting back, but my phone said the text was undeliverable. When we checked the news, the story had already broken—how Gestas had resurfaced in Cuba and been granted asylum there.

A few weeks later, he called me, and we were able to talk for about eight minutes before his phone card ran out. I told him I missed him and loved him and gave him the latest on our friends and baby Maya. But then I had to ask.

"When you met Assata, did you tell her—"

"—about the time you named her during the ancestor invocation at an all-Black Save the Eighth meeting in a Baptist church?" He chuckled. "It might've come up. Hey, new claim to fame, Maddie—you made Assata Shakur laugh!"

"I'll put it on my tombstone," I said.

He cleared his throat, fell quiet, and I wished I hadn't said that. I don't know if he was thinking about my suicide attempt, or Red, but either way, Death had joined the call and there was no getting rid of him. These days, Death is always lurking at the edge of any conversation.

59

It's been four years since Red overdosed, and I'm still here.

Lorenzo finished his AHICA sentence, got his journeyman's license, and quit working at the refineries. He's doing electrical in people's homes now, with his own name emblazoned on the side of his van. He's so happy to be working for himself. He throws big parties at the house he and Kayleigh own together, where I hide out in the kitchen with him, helping him cook like old times. I've gotten to know Kayleigh, who I never met in the Village days. She's a little older than us, smart, funny. She and Nimo have gotten close, since they're both going to San Jac for social worker degrees.

Vida and Peter don't usually make it out to those parties, because their hands are full with Maya and her new baby sister, Itzel. Vida makes sure the babies have an endless supply of finger-paints to smear all over the walls of their cute bungalow down by Hobby Airport. I hang out with them once in a while, loving the cozy bubble of their family—until Maya starts up a tantrum, and the baby starts screaming. Whenever I leave, I always feel equal parts relieved that I don't have kids to care for and jealous that I have no family of my own.

Though that's not exactly true. I'm speaking to my parents again. Ever since I started dating Colton, all those years ago, they hadn't said they loved me, or done anything to demonstrate that was the case. But I suppose coughing up seventy grand of their retirement savings so I could go through inpatient psychiatric treatment

372

makes up for that. I spend holidays with them now. Mom calls and asks if I'm eating enough. It's nice to hear her voice, but communicating with them is often difficult. They voted for Horneck.

I have a dog! When Shayna and her partner got serious about a year ago, I moved out on my own. Right away, my mental health plummeted, and my internal voice got cruel and violent again. I adopted Tony because I was afraid to be alone with myself all the time. He's a handsome, thirty-pound terrier mix, black with a white starburst on his chest. I picked him out at the shelter because he looked like he was smiling at me, and the information card said he loved cuddles. He's a sweetheart in the apartment, but a handful on the leash, barking and taking off after every cat and squirrel. We're working on it. It's good for me to have a reason to take lots of walks. I don't know if I'd have made it this far without Tony.

I still don't play guitar.

I tried once. Mike Algebra invited me over to jam, and about ten minutes in, working on a new song he'd written, I started sobbing from missing Red and Gestas. Mike came over and put his big arm around me. I still don't know if he really was trying to comfort me, or if he was putting the moves on me. It felt like the latter, though, when he started rubbing my back. I bolted out of there, and I haven't seen him since.

I've been saving up money, though, to visit Gestas in Cuba. When I go, I think I'll bring my guitar. I might be able to play music again with him, because he loved Red as much as I did.

As much as I still do.

I've tried going on dates, but I get haunted on them. Red will suddenly show up in my brain, clowning on my date's affectations.

"A pocket square? You've got to be kidding."

"Did she seriously just kiss your hand? Oh, milady!"

"That's the longest, most boring story I've ever heard, and I'm pretty sure he only told it to let you know he has a friend who owns a boat."

The dates end up being weirdly fun. I never want to go out with anyone a second time, but their differentness from Red—it summons xim, in a way.

More and more, my brain simply rejects the fact that Red is dead. Instead of time making it more difficult to remember xim, it's like the more time passes, the more I carry Red's essential essence around with me. Freed from the crush of memories, I can imagine how Red would respond to whatever's going on now. And it's not painful anymore. It's nice to be with xim again, even if xe's just a figment of my imagination.

If I was still a Catholic, I'd think Red was my guardian angel.

If I was still at the clinic, I think they'd drug me.

If I was a Buddhist, I think they'd get it. Dr. Abner suggested I read this book by a Buddhist monk, Thích Nhất Hạnh, as part of my recovery. She thought that maybe I was still grieving the loss of my spiritual life and thought Buddhism might fill that void.

I wouldn't call myself a Buddhist, because I don't do all the meditation and stuff, but I like their concept of no birth, no death. It's this idea that the self is just a false concept, so we're never really born and never really die. Everything's always changing, and death is just another transformation. When someone we love dies, we can still visit them in the sunset and the trees and shit like that. I'm not explaining it great, but that's how it is. I'll see a pretty sunset, and suddenly Red is right there with me, twining xir fingers through mine. I don't believe that Red is gone, just—transformed. Not in a supernatural way—but all xir choices, every word xe ever said to me, every time xe ever touched me—all xir energy and vibrations are still ricocheting around inside me, setting off chain reactions down a zillion quantum pathways, echoing out in the world, influencing the universe forever.

And that's what I think about the Free People's Village too.

The night they took the Lab, that night at City Hall—I thought the cops had won. I thought they'd killed the movement. But how can a handful of pigs kill the dreams of fifty thousand? How can gas and rubber bullets dispel a generation's rage at the dying of our world? An excavator can tear down a building, but it can't tear down our desire for revolution.

Don't get me wrong, the world seems darker than ever.

Horneck instituted mandatory brick-and-mortar sentences for minor carbon crimes, stripped voting rights from carbon violators, and closed the southern border to climate refugees. Congress just passed a budget gutting social programs and increasing military spending by trillions. The armed forces will use it to buy all-new equipment, meaning they'll donate their lightly used tanks and drones and guns to local police departments for the subjugation of the citizenry. The Republican Party is co-opting the "War on Climate Change" to hoard ever-more power and wealth and further entrench white supremacy. Global carbon emissions have held steady since 2010, but they're not declining, so the world is still barreling towards climate collapse.

And we're still at war in the Amazon, even though it's now deeply unpopular with most people. Corporations, though—the only "people" who seem to matter to politicians—are still in favor. So the shooting continues, even though the carbon spent fighting for control of the jungle far outweighs what the Amazon could sequester, even in a year without wildfires.

And Angel remains in the military prison at Fort Leavenworth.

When the state locks people away, it's horribly easy to forget about them. Sometimes I'll go a whole day or two without thinking about Angel. Then something small will remind me of him—a hand-addressed envelope, someone ordering a shot of Fireball at a bar—and I get a gut punch of guilt and feelings of worthlessness. But what good are those feelings? Shayna would tell me to channel them into "the work." So I write a post, attend a meeting, recirculate the petition. Horneck won reelection, so there's precious little hope for a presidential pardon for another four years at least. Still, we're working with a bunch of different anti-war groups, planning a massive demonstration in DC for the fall. We keep at the work, because the work is good, and we couldn't live with ourselves otherwise.

Sometimes, when I see headlines about Horneck's latest cruel executive order, I get those "What if I just weren't alive?" thoughts popping in my head again. That's when I text Shayna, and see what she's up to. She got a new job, getting paid to organize these days, as part of a Black-led get-out-the-vote nonprofit.

Since Gestas's escape, Save the Eighth has focused on mutual aid efforts. Right now, we're raising funds for a community garden near the new hyperway. I take notes at our virtual meetings, which are still usually only attended by a half-dozen people. Then I send out calendar invites for the next meeting. It is a small, simple job I can do, one that hopefully sends net-positive vibrations out in the world.

At one of those meetings, one of the other organizers, in a moment of total transparency, said she felt like all our efforts were hopeless. If the city had squashed our movement when tens of thousands marched on City Hall, what difference could six people on a video call make?

Shayna said, "You know big protests like that—those are just the mushrooms, right?"

The folks on the call chuckled in confusion.

"No hear me out. So a fungus is not just the mushroom that pops up out of the ground, okay? That's just the 'fruiting body.' The real fungus is the network of mycelium under the ground."

"Damn, Shayna, you're going all biologist on us!" someone commented.

"Mycologist," Shayna corrected. "Anyways, just listen. This mutual aid work we're doing here—that's the mycelium, the roots of the fungus that spread underground, forming a network through the forest that can spread for miles, unseen, strengthening and feeding the whole organism. Then when conditions are right—the right amount of rain, sun, press exposure, public out-rage, whatever—" Shayna made an exploding gesture with her hand. "All of a sudden, little mushrooms pop up all over the forest. All of a sudden, you've got mass protests springing up across the country. And the thing about mushrooms—"

"Lord, will she ever drop it?" Miriam groaned, but she was loving the metaphor.

"—the thing about mushrooms is, they shoot out spores. Millions of 'em, spreading their fungal secrets everywhere the wind blows. And just like that, each time we have a protest, we're sending out millions of spores that take root in people's minds."

Some of the folks on the call snapped to show their appreciation.

"Now, once a spore lands in fertile soil, it takes a while to start growing. It's got to build up its own network of mycelium."

"She just keeps going," Toussaint said in awe.

"That's right. So protest movements always spread the spores for the *next* protest movement. Like mushrooms, they're only meant to last a short while. Hell, the Free People's Village was a sturdy little mushroom—we were out there for months! And since then, all the zillions of spores we sent into the world? They've been growing. Trust. Now we just got to wait for the next time conditions are right—and be ready. In the meantime, we grow our net-work—we spread our mycelium, we strengthen our community."

I think about that metaphor a lot, any time the world seems too bureaucratically cruel to bear. I thought about it just this afternoon, as we stepped off the curb and into the street.

Shayna had forwarded me the flyer for the protest. She couldn't make it because of work, but wanted us to represent in solidarity with the organizers—the Coalition of Young Palestinians, the same folks who'd de-arrested their friends and arrived late to City Hall.

President Horneck had just approved another billion dollars of military aid for Israel. Meanwhile, the Israeli army was demolish-ing two-hundred-year-old Palestinian houses under the pretense of replacing them with more "carbon-efficient construction" (which would be sold only to Israeli settlers, of course). Videos of Palestinian people being dragged from their homes had gone viral, paired with captions explaining how the Israeli military emitted exponentially more carbon than these poor folks' ancestral homes.

Honestly, I really didn't feel like going to the protest. I'd just gotten off work—eight long hours of geometry and comma rules at the tutoring center. Plus, the protest was at the Galleria, and cops are particularly aggressive near those luxury stores. The roads are all wide highways, and even in the heyday of the Free People's Village, we never managed to take them. There are no large areas to congregate, so protests wind up being sad, little affairs, our numbers split between sidewalks divided by six lanes of traffic. Our only audience there are the rich shoppers in their cars, who just want to merge onto the hyperway, and who are more likely to flip us off than honk in solidarity.

But shame, still my constant companion—the shame that I'm never doing enough, showing up enough, fighting hard enough for a better world—shame was what kicked my ass off the couch and down to the maglev station.

I'm so glad I went.

The crowd was much larger than I expected. All the actions I've been to since City Hall haven't numbered more than a hundred people, but here, suddenly, were thousands. I recognized a bunch of familiar faces from the Free People's Village. Toussaint also came from Save the Eighth. Nimo and Vida were there, with a line of drummers from the Gulf Coast Indigenous Alliance of Houston/Galveston—now twenty members strong. Nimo looked so handsome, with long hair fluttering down to his mid-back, beaded headband, and a tunic embellished with porcupine quills. Vida wore one of her embroidered ceremonial dresses—white linen, decorated with hand-stitched spirals and zig-zags that morphed into snack-cake logos, video-game characters, and song lyrics. At her "Reconstituted Roots" exhibit last month at a fancy Midtown gallery, I'd read a little placard explaining that these pieces, loosely inspired by various Indigenous ceremonial garments, were "irrevocably infused with the psychic detritus of a 2000s childhood in a colonial state, a physical manifestation of the impossible yearning to fully decolonize." The showcase had won some prestigious national award, and the whole GCIA Houston chapter had turned out to support her at the launch. One Apache art critic, though, had called the showcase "not only appropriative, but puerile," which Vida told me made her lose sleep for an entire week. I thought she looked stunning in that gown, carrying a corner of the GCIA banner, but what do I know?.

The Abortion Funders, Jews Against Apartheid, and the Brown Bloc were there too. The RevComs showed up with their Bob Avakian brochures—and I had a weird urge to hug those cult-y grandmas. I recognized some of the young Palestinian organizers who'd once camped at the Free People's Village. Seeing them again made me glad I'd come, to support their movement in turn.

But, thrillingly, I did not recognize most of the people crowding the sidewalks. A new crop of college kids—who would've been in middle school when Bunny Bloodlust still performed at the Lab—carried posters that said things like "End War from Gaza to Rio!" And there were so many families—dads proudly waving Palestinian flags, moms wearing keffiyehs wrapped around their hair, kids in strollers, clumps of teenagers, and grandparents leaning on canes, all raising their voices in chants that were familiar— "No Justice? No Peace!"—and new to me—"From the river to the sea; Palestine will be free!" An entire community had turned out against injustice, not just the city's usual malcontents, and they were full of righteous passion and fresh energy.

I positioned myself towards the back of the sidewalk, letting the Palestinian protestors stand in front of me, and found myself next to two familiar faces. It was my old student, Kenya, and her girlfriend Cely. Kenya, now taller than me by two inches, threw her arms wide for a hug, and my cheeks burned with gratitude. She and Cely were both students at University of Houston Downtown. She caught me up on how everyone else from first period was doing, opening her Instagram app to show me pictures. Jazmin and Jaylen were the only two others who'd gone on to college—both of them at U of H. Naiya and Princess were posing in a bar together with a tray of shots. They're liquor influencers now, getting paid to order and push a certain brand of tequila at crowded nightclubs. LaMarcus and D'Unte both work at the refineries—LaMarcus just put a down payment on a house. Shanelle and Rishad have a two-year-old, and she's pregnant with their second child.

"And the other boys?" I asked, my face warm from smiling so hard at pictures of my former students' baby.

Kenya's face fell. "Not so good. Antoine's in brick-and-mortar lockup for carbon theft. Owen and Trey dropped out later that year you got fired, and they started dealing. Trey's still around, but Owen got shot in a drive-by. He died."

I nodded, unsure what to say, struck by fresh grief.

A young Palestinian organizer with long, black hair got up on a friend's shoulders just then and brought a megaphone to her lips. She gave a speech about what was happening in Palestine, but I had a hard time listening. I was trying to conjure up a memory of Owen's face—that quiet football player who'd sat at the back of my class. I felt dizzied by a sudden sweeping understanding of our collective grief—kids ripped from their homes in Palestine, kids shot in the streets of Gaza and Houston and Rio, the greed, the oil, and guns—it was the same struggle everywhere.

The Palestinian organizer led the crowd in a round of "Whose streets? Our streets!" and then we started to move. She didn't lead us up the sidewalk though, but out—towards the busy intersection. In the moment between red lights, while all the cars were momentarily braked, electric batteries humming, she stepped down into the roadway. A crime—jaywalking. But as soon as the soles of her shoes hit that asphalt, she transformed the protest into an act of rebellion.

A crowd of Palestinian families flooded behind her onto Westheimer Road—spreading across all six lanes, winding between cars, marching with heads held high, pushing strollers before them. Kenya and Cely proudly stepped out after them, hand-in-hand, and I followed after. We took the streets of the Galleria back—from the police and from the cars—and we held them all afternoon.

For hours we marched around Houston's central monument to capitalism. The Galleria was where oil execs, rich off plundering the Gulf and the Permian Basin, spent their obscene, hoarded wealth. We chanted and sang against injustice and empire, needless extraction and reckless destruction, infrastructure in service of white supremacy, and in defense of the Indigenous, poor, and vulnerable worldwide. We were all comrades, laying siege to that bastion of greed and world-wrecking consumption—the fucking *Mall.*

I purposefully walked down the yellow lines dividing the asphalt, where usually only rich people's tires dared to tread. The GCIA's drumming provided a heartbeat to the march. Someone had a bubble machine in their backpack, filling the sky with globular rainbows. Others played music from portable speakers. I couldn't understand the lyrics since they were in Arabic, but the songs sounded beautiful.

A few cop drones hovered at the edges of our march, but they never opened their awful mouths. Maybe the cops showed restraint because of all the families and little kids in the crowd. Maybe it's because this was a rich, white neighborhood, and wealthy shoppers might inhale some tear gas along with us rabble. I don't know, but I was glad they kept their distance.

A teenager climbed up a streetlight and started waving the Palestinian flag. They were tall and lean and just the right height, with a fall of black hair, and I had to do a double take. They weren't Red. But they looked similar enough to conjure Red, and then xe was marching alongside me. Red in my heart, in my lungs, screaming chants—Red in the sonic vibrations we sent to the sky in our best attempt to change the world.

Red wasn't the only ghost marching that day. The Village was there too, alongside every protest that had come before it. Stonewall and Selma and Wounded Knee, labor uprisings, and slave revolts, and Indigenous resistance, fruiting bodies that had launched spores that would radically alter the shape of things to come.

We would not save the world at this protest today. We would not stop an Israeli bulldozer from toppling a home, would not stop the crushing march of empire, would not stop a billion dollars for bombs from flowing to Israel, then flowing right back, to US corporations like KBR and Lockheed Martin, who built those bombs right down the street, here in Houston.

When it comes to defeating capitalism, I'm not so naïve as to think we can win.

Not how you think. Not decisively, for all time. All our protests, all our organizing, they can't defeat the tanks and gas and guns and greed machines—at least not forever, not right now. So what I think, these days, is you have to accept that there's no winning, and learn to live for the joy of the struggle.

And for maybe.

Maybe someday.

The sun set pink and gold, as five thousand people surrounded our hostage—that skyscraper of a mall—blocking traffic, claiming the streets. This city, this state, this country is not free, but for those few shining hours, in that torus of space-time, those of us marching—we were free. And four years ago, for a few glorious months, we carved out a free world from an old, brick warehouse. Every day that the Village stood was a battle we won against empire.

At dusk, the march around the Galleria broke up. Folks rushed to their parked cars or the maglev station, eager to get their kids home for bath time. But some part of each of us marched on, are marching still. The spores we sent out are taking root in the minds of everyone who got stuck in the traffic we blocked that day, and everyone who saw the videos streamed to social media, and especially in all of us who marched.

I was one of the last to leave, and I arrived home, feeling lighter than I had in years. Tony greeted me with a jump on my chest, crying for a walk. And so, even though my feet were sore from hours of marching, we headed back out.

Ever since City Hall, living through each day has required a conscious choice.

I intend to stick around.

Maybe 99.99% of our lives will be spent stuck trudging down the narrow sidewalks afforded to us by capitalism. Roads have taken away our land, our right to roam and play. Artificial scarcity forces us to work ourselves sick at shitty, soul-crushing jobs or we risk death from starvation, homelessness, or medical neglect. Environmental destruction has severed us from our nurturing nonhuman relatives. Colonization has erased our ancestors and histories. Step out of line, raise your voice against the state, make a mistake, and you'll be crushed with swift and brutal violence.

But once in a while, for a brief bubble in time, enough of us get together to defy the ruling classes. To step out in the street and carve our own path. And even if I get to experience that for less than 0.01% of my time on this earth, I'll take it.

I have tasted a free world a few times now, and I crave another bite. I will go to work and walk my dog. I will bide my time, waiting for the conditions to be just right, waiting for the sun and rain and rage and suffering to accumulate just so. I want to be there when the new world tries to give birth to itself again. I want to be there when the injustice grows so thick that people find courage in themselves they never knew existed.

I want to be there, one of the first out in the streets, the next time the people erupt.

ACKNOWLEDGMENTS

Thank you to all the people who worked hard on this book or inspired it with their activism, friendship, or mere brilliant existence.

To Aster—thank you for lending Maddie aspects of your arrest story, for beta reading all my books so far, and for generally being my hero. Thank you to Maxine Kaplan for reading this book when it was a wee larvae and for helping me navigate all the publishing drama. Thank you as well to readers C.H. Zazueta, E.L. Diamond and Karen Heenan for your feedback on the manuscript!

Thank you to our sensitivity reader, Chiara Lillie Beaumont—Your activism in revitalizing the Karankawa nation and organizing with Indigenous Peoples of the Coastal Bend is a powerful and vital force in this region. I was so honored to receive your feedback on the Indigenous representation in this book.

To my editor, Irene Vázquez—thank you for requesting this book based on a tweet. Thank you for being the best editor I could ask for. Thank you for your passion for this story, collaborative approach, and always challenging me to do better by these characters. Thank you for understanding the tragic-beautiful condition of being a young activist in Houston, Texas. I will forever be grateful that I got to work on this book with you!

Thanks to my copy editor Anamika Bhatnagar, for navigating dozens of time jumps, pointing out that three weeks cannot pass in three days, and teaching me how to spell 'fuchsia.' Thank you to proofreader Johanie Martinez-Cools.

Thank you to the book's designer, Jonathan Yamakami for your guidance and making the book look stunning.

Ganzeer, since the first time I saw your art, I've dreamed of having a cover illustrated by you—let alone a case and endpapers and poster art too! Working with you wound up surpassing my wildest expectations. Thank you for your passion, your creative ideas, and for turning the physical object of this book into such a beautiful, punk rock, work of art.

Thank you to everyone else at Levine Querido who helped bring this book into the world: Arthur A. Levine, Antonio Gonzalez Cerna, Nick Thomas, Madelyn McZeal, Arely Guzmán, and Kerry Taylor.

To Rebecca Podos, my agent, thank you for jumping in on this project mid-deal when I was a newly-agentless author. I can't wait to see what we do together in the future!

Thank you to the team at Bloomsbury for use of the quote from Freire's *Pedagogy of the Oppressed*. To Ehigbor Okosun, Nicky Drayden, and Desiree Evans—thank you for late-night zoom hangs and group texts when publishing gets overwhelming. Thank you for all the K-Drama recs, and necessary conversations, and for being genre-busting SFF authors who inspire the crap out of me. I am all of y'alls biggest fan, and I feel ridiculously lucky to be your friend.

To my husband Ike—thank you for all those paper love letters you wrote me once upon a time, for giving me permission to write Angel's story, and for being the most supportive spouse and best co-parent I could ask for. None of my writing is possible without you.

To Lane and Ramona, my brilliant, beautiful girls, thank you for being your wonderful selves, filling my days with joy, and challenging me to appreciate the world anew.

Dad, you taught me to write and (maybe unintentionally) to be a hell-raising activist. You think my politics are a bit too radical these days—but *you* were the one who got arrested a bunch of times for protesting civil rights, got beat up by cops, and met my mother in a nuclear disarmament march. I'm still playing catch-up to your organizing bona fides. Thank you for always being my biggest fan and the best dad I could ask for.

I also want to thank a few locations in space-time: to the S.S. Yahweh circa 2005ish and the 1816 Calumet house, from 2008–2010. Thank you to the people who created those hubs of limitless creativity and community. Thank you to all the people (who weren't creeps or assholes) who hung out there and loved each other and made art and music and threw the best fucking parties in the history of the universe.

And finally, I want to thank everyone fighting for a better world in this blighted bayou of a city, in this political hellscape of a state. I couldn't possibly list them all, but here are a few in particular:

Thank you to María-Elisa Heg, who invited me to paint tombstones for Occupy Houston's Haunted House of Industrial Accidents many moons ago, and who continues to be a pillar of community-building here, alongside all the Zine Fest Houston organizers. Thank you to my dear friends and abortion fund heroes: Sahra Harvin, Aster Dyer, and Hannah Thalenberg. Thank you also to our entire Houston Jewish Voice for Peace chapter, and the Students for Justice in Palestine and Palestinian Youth Movement organizers who continually push the boundaries of what seems possible for direct action in Houston. To all the DSA comrades who mucked out homes after Hurricane Harvey and to Shelly Baker and Say Her Name TX for organizing food drives after Winter Storm Uri. Y'all truly demonstrate the meaning of mutual aid amid climate change! Thanks also to Allyn West of One Breath Partnership, who brought me into the petrochemical watchdog world, and to the Environmental Integrity Project and Air Alliance Houston for holding polluters to account. Thanks to those orgs in particular that inspired Save the Eighth by fighting for Houston's historic Black neighborhoods: Coalition for Environment, Equity, and Resilience, Stop TxDot I-45, and Black Lives Matter: Houston. Finally, an enormous thank you to the Indigenous Peoples of the Coastal Bend whose activism I tried to honor in this book through the fictional GCIA.

Abolish police, end fossil fuels, and land back!

ABOUT THE AUTHOR

Sim Kern is the USA Today bestselling author of *The Free People's Village*, an Indie Next pick. Their debut horror novella, *Depart, Depart!*, was selected for the Honor List for the 2020 Otherwise Award, and their short story collection, *Real Sugar is Hard to Find*, was hailed in a starred review by Publishers Weekly as, "a searing, urgent, but still achingly tender work that will wow any reader of speculative fiction." As a journalist, they report on petrochemical polluters and drag space billionaires. Sim spent ten years teaching English to middle and high schoolers in Houston, Texas, before shifting to writing full-time. Find them all over the internet, but especially on tiktok at @simkern.